THE KNIGHT AND KNAVE OF SWORDS

FRITZ LEIBER

ACE BOOKS, NEW YORK

''The Curse of the Smalls and the Stars'' originally appeared in *Heroic Visions*, copyright © 1983 by Jessica Amanda Salmonson.

''The Mer She'' originally appeared in *Heroes and Horrors*, copyright © 1978 by Stuart Schiff.

''Sea Magic,'' copyright © 1977 by Fritz Leiber.

Portions of ''The Mouser Goes Below'' appeared in *Terry's Universe*, copyright © 1988 by Carol Carr, and in *Whispers*, copyright © 1987 by Fritz Leiber.

This Ace book contains the complete text of the original
edition. It has been completely reset in a typeface
designed for easy reading and was printed from new film.

THE KNIGHT AND KNAVE OF SWORDS

An Ace Book/published by arrangement with
William Morrow and Company, Inc.

PRINTING HISTORY
William Morrow and Company, Inc. edition published 1988
Ace edition/February 1990

ISBN: 0-441-45125-X

Ace Books are published by The Berkley Publishing Group,
200 Madison Avenue, New York, New York 10016.
The name ''ACE'' and the ''A'' logo are trademarks
belonging to Charter Communications, Inc.

PRINTED IN THE UNITED STATES OF AMERICA

10 9 8 7 6 5 4 3 2 1

CONTENTS

ACKNOWLEDGMENTS

To my friends who helped me editorially with this book, my thanks. They are James A. Minor, Miriam Rodstein, Anne Ross, Pamela Troy, David A. Wilson, and particularly Margo Skinner.

THE KNIGHT AND KNAVE of SWORDS

I

Sea Magic

1

On the world of Nehwon and the land of Simorgya, six days fast sailing south from Rime Isle, two handsome silvery personages conversed intimately yet tensely in a dimly and irregularly lit hall of pillars open overhead to the darkness. Very strange was that illumination—greenish and yellowish by turns, it seemed to come chiefly from grotesquely shaped rugs patching the Stygian floor and lapping the pillars' bases and also from slowly moving globes and sinuosities that floated about at head height and wove amongst the pillars, softly dimming and brightening like lethargic and plague-stricken giant fireflies.

Mordroog said sharply, "Caught you that thrill, sister? —faint and far north away, yet unmistakably *ours*."

Ississi replied eagerly, "The same, brother, as we felt two days agone—*our* mystic gold dipped deep in the sea for a space, then out again."

"The same indeed, sister, though this time with a certain ambiguity as to the out—whether that or otherwise gone," Mordroog assented.

"Yet the now-confirmed clue is certain and bears only one interpretation: our chiefest treasures, that were our most main guards, raped away long ages agone—and now at long last we know the culprits, those villainous pirates of Rime Isle!" breathed Ississi.

"Long, long ages agone, before ever Simorgya sank (and the fortunate island kingdom became the dark infernal realm)—and their vanishment the hastener or very agent of that sinking. But now we have the remedy—and who knows when our treasure's back what long sunken things may rise in spouting wrath to consternate the world? Your attention, sister!" snapped Mordroog.

The abysmal scene darkened, then brightened as he dipped his hand into the pouch at his waist and brought it out again holding something big as a girl's fist. The floating globes and sinuosities moved inward inquisitively, jogging and jostling each other. Their flaring glows rebounded through the murk from a lacy yet massy small gold globe showing between his thin clawed silver fingers—its twelve thick edges like those of a hexahedron embedded in the surface of a sphere and curving conformably to that structure. He proffered it to her. The golden light gave the semblance of life to their hawklike features.

"Sister," he breathed, "it is now your task, and geas laid upon you, to proceed to Rime Isle and regain our treasure, taking vengeance or not as opportunity affords and prudence counsels—whilst I maintain here, unifying the forces and regathering the scattered allies against your return. You will need this last cryptic treasure for your protection and as a hound to scent out its brothers in the world above."

Now for the first time Ississi seemed to hesitate and her eagerness to abate.

"The way is long, brother, and we are weak with waiting," she protested, wailing. "What was once a week's fast sailing will be for me three black moons of torturesome dark treading, press I on ever so hard. We have become the sea's slaves, brother, and carry always the sea's weight. And I have grown to abhor the daylight.''

''We have also the sea's strength,'' he reminded her commandingly, ''and though we are weak as ghosts on land, preferring darkness and the deep, we also know the old ways of gaining power and facing even the sun. It is your task, sister. The geas is upon you. Salt is heavy but blood is sweet. Go, go, go!''

Wherewith she snatched the goldy ghost-globe from his grip, plunged it into her pouch, and turning with a sudden flirt made off, the living lamps scattering to make a dark northward route for her.

With the last ''Go,'' a small bubble formed at the corner of Mordroog's thin, snarling, silvery lips, detached itself from them, and slowly grew in size as it mounted from these dark deeps up toward the water's distant surface.

2

Three months after the events aforenarrated, Fafhrd was at archery practice on the heath north of Salthaven City on Rime Isle's southeastern coast—one more self-imposed, self-devised, and self-taught lesson of many in learning the mechanics of life for one lacking a left hand, lost to Odin during the repulse of the Widder Sea-Mingols from the Isle's western shores. He had firmly affixed a tapering, thin, finger-long iron rod (much like a sword blade's tang) to the midst of his bow and wedged it into the corresponding deep hole in the wooden wrist heading the close-fitting leather stall, half the length of his forearm and dotted with holes for ventilation, that covered his newly-healed stump—with the result that his left arm terminated in a serviceably if somewhat unadjustably clutched bow.

Here near town the heath was grass mingled with ankle-high heather, here and there dotted with small clumps of gorse, in and out of which the occasional pair of plump lemmings played fearlessly, and man-high gray standing stones. These last had perhaps once been of religious significance to the now atheistical Rime Islers—who were atheists not in the sense that they did not believe in gods (that would have been very difficult for any dweller in the world of Nehwon) but that they did not socialize with any such gods or harken in any way to their commands, threats, and cajolings. They (the standing stones) stood about like so many mute gray grizzle bears.

Except for a few compact white clouds a-hang over the isle, the late afternoon sky was clear, windless, and surprisingly balmy for this late in autumn, in fact on the very edge of winter and its icy, snow-laden winds.

The girl accompanied Fafhrd in his practicing. The silver-blond thirteen-year-old now trudged about with him collecting arrows—half of them transfixing his target, which was a huge ball. To keep his bow out of the way Fafhrd carried it as if over his shoulder, maimed left arm closely bent upward.

"They ought to have an arrow that would shoot around corners," Gale said apropos of hunting behind a standing stone. "That way you'd get your enemy if he hid behind a house or a tree trunk."

"It's an idea," Fafhrd admitted.

"Maybe if the arrow had a little curve in it—" she speculated.

"No, then it would just tumble," he told her. "The virtue of an arrow lies in its perfect straightness, its—"

"You don't have to tell me that," she interrupted impatiently. "I keep hearing all about that, over and over, from Aunt Afreyt and cousin Cif when they lecture me about the Golden Arrow of Truth and the Golden Circles of Unity and all those." The girl was referring to the closely guarded gold ikons that had been from time immemorial the atheist-holy relics of the Rime Isle fisherfolk.

That made Fafhrd think of the Golden Cube of Square-Dealing, forever lost when the Mouser had hurled it to quell the vast whirlpool which had vanquished the Mingol fleet and threatened to sink his own in the great sea battle. Did it lie now in mucky black sea bottom near the Beach of Bleached

Bones or had it indeed vanished entire from Nehwon-world with the errant gods, Odin and Loki?

And that in turn made him wonder and worry a little about the Gray Mouser, who had sailed away a month ago in *Seahawk* on a trading expedition to No-Ombrulsk with half his thieves and *Flotsam*'s Mingol crew and Fafhrd's own chief lieutenant Skor. The little man (Captain Mouser, now) had planned on getting back to Rime Isle before the winter blizzards.

Gale interrupted his musings. "Did Aunt Afreyt tell you, Captain Fafhrd, about cousin Cif seeing a ghost or something last night in the council hall treasury, which only she has a key to?" The girl was holding up the big target bag clutched against her so that he could pull out the arrows and return them over shoulder to their quiver.

"I don't think so," he temporized. Actually, he hadn't seen Afreyt today, or Cif either for that matter. For the past few nights he hadn't been sleeping at Afreyt's but with his men and the Mouser's at the dormitory they rented from Groniger, Salthaven's harbor master and chief councilman, the better to supervise the mischievous thieves in the Mouser's absence—or at least that was an explanation on which he and Afreyt could safely agree. "What did the ghost look like?"

"It looked very mysterious," Gale told him, her pale blue eyes widening above the bag which hid the lower part of her face. "Sort of silvery and dark, and it vanished when Cif went closer. She called Groniger, who was around, but they couldn't find anything. She told Afreyt it looked like a princess-lady or a big thin fish."

"How could something look like a woman and a fish?" Fafhrd asked with a short laugh, tugging out the last arrow.

"Well, there are mermaids, aren't there?" she retorted triumphantly, letting the bag fall.

"Yes," Fafhrd admitted, "though I don't expect Groniger would agree with us. Say," he went on, his face losing for a bit its faintly drawn, worried look, "put the target bag behind that rock. I've thought of a way to shoot around corners."

"Oh, good!" She rolled the target bag close against the back of one of the ursine, large gray stones and they walked off a couple of hundred yards. Fafhrd turned. The air was very still. A distant small cloud hid the low sun, though the sky was otherwise very blue and bright. He swiftly drew an arrow and laid it against the short wooden thumb he'd affixed to the bow near its center just above its tang. He took a couple of shuffling steps while his frowning eyes measured the distance between him and the rock. Then he leaned suddenly back and discharged the arrow high into the air. It went up, up, then came swiftly down—close behind the rock, it looked.

"That's not around a corner," Gale protested. "Anybody can do that. I meant sideways."

"You didn't say so," he told her. "Corners can be up or down or sideways right or left. What's the difference?"

"Up-corners you can drop things around."

"Yes indeed you can!" he agreed and in a sudden frenzy of exercise that left him breathing hard sent the rest of the arrows winging successively after the first. All of them seemed to land close behind the standing stone—all except the last, which they heard clash faintly against rock—but when they'd walked up to where they could see, they found that all but the last arrow had missed. The feathered shafts stood upright, their points plunged into the soft earth, in an oddly regular little row that didn't quite reach the target-bag—all but the last, which had gone through an edge of the bag at an angle and hung there, tangled by its three goosefeather vanes.

"See, you missed," Gale said, "all but the one that glanced off the rock."

"Yes. Well, that's enough shooting for me," he decided, and while she pulled up the arrows and carefully teased loose the last, he loosened the bow's tang from its wood socket, using the back of his knife blade as a pry, then unstrung the bow and hung it across his back by its loose string around his chest, then fitted a wrought-iron hook into the wrist-socket, wedging it tight by driving the head of the hook against the stone. He winced as he did that last, for his stump was still tender and the dozen last shots he'd made had tried it.

3

As they walked toward the low, mostly red-roofed homes of Salthaven, the setting sun on their backs, Fafhrd studied the gray standing stones and asked Gale, "What do you know about the old gods Rime Isle had?—before the Rime men got atheism."

"They were a pretty wild, lawless lot, Aunt Afreyt says—sort of like Captain Mouser's men before they became soldiers, or your berserks before you tamed them down." She went on with growing enthusiasm, "They certainly didn't believe in any Golden Arrow of Truth, or Golden Ruler of Prudence, or Little Gold Cup of Measured Hospitality—mighty liars, whores, murderers, and pirates, I guess, all of them."

Fafhrd nodded. "Maybe Cif's ghost was one of them," he said.

A tall, slender woman came toward them from a violet-toned house. When Afreyt neared them she called to Gale, "So that's where you were. Your mother was wondering." She looked at Fafhrd. "How did the archery go?"

"Captain Fafhrd hit the target almost every time," Gale answered for him. "He even hit it shooting around corners! And I didn't help him a bit fitting his bow or anything."

Afreyt nodded.

Fafhrd shrugged.

"I told Fafhrd about Cif's ghost," Gale went on. "He thought it might be one of the old Rime goddesses—Rin the Moon-runner, one of those. Or the witch queen Skeldir."

Afreyt's narrow blond eyebrows arched. "You go along now, your mother wants you."

"Can I keep the target for you?" the girl asked Fafhrd.

He nodded, lifted his left elbow, and the big ball dropped down. Gale rolled it off ahead of her. The target-bag was smoky red with dye from the snowberry root, and the last rays of the sun setting behind them gave it an angry glare.

Afreyt and Fafhrd each had the thought that Gale was rolling away the sun.

When she was gone he turned to Afreyt, asking, "What's this nonsense about Cif meeting a ghost?"

"You're getting skeptical as an Isler," she told him unsmiling. "Is something that robs a councilman of his wits and half his strength nonsense?"

"The ghost did that?" he asked as they began to walk slowly toward town.

She nodded. "When Gwaan pushed into the dark treasury past Cif, he was clutched and struck senseless for an hour's space—and has since not left his bed." Her long lips quirked. "Or else he stumbled in the churning shadows and struck his head 'gainst the wall—there's that possibility too, since he has lost his memory for the event."

"Tell me about it more circumstantially," Fafhrd requested.

"The council session had lasted well after dark, for the waning gibbous moon had just risen," she began. "Cif and I being in attendance as treasurer and scribe. Zwaaken and Gwaan called on Cif for an inventory of the ikons of the virtues—ever since the loss of the Gold Cube of Square-Dealing (though in a good cause) they've fretted about them. Cif accordingly unlocked the door to the treasury and then hesitated on the threshold. Moonlight striking in through the small barred window (she told me later) left most of the treasure chamber still in the dark, and there was something unfamiliar about the arrangement of the things she saw that sounded a warning to us. Also, there was a faint noxious marshy scent—"

"What does that window look on?" Fafhrd asked.

"The sea. Gwaan pushed past her impatiently (and *most* discourteously), and then she swears there was a faint blue smoke like muted lightning and in that trice she seemed to see a silent skinny figure of silver fog embrace Gwaan hungrily. She got the impression, she said, of a weak ghost seeking to draw strength from the living. Gwaan gave a choking cry and pitched to the floor. When torches were brought in (at Cif's behest) the chamber was otherwise empty, but the Gold Arrow of Truth had fallen from its shelf and lay beneath the window, the other ikons had been moved slightly from their places, as if they'd been feebly groped, while on the floor were narrow patches, like footprints, of stenchful black bottom muck.''

''And that was all?'' Fafhrd asked as the pause lengthened. When she'd mentioned the thin silvery fog figure, he'd been reminded of someone or something he'd seen lately, but then in his mind a black curtain fell on that particular recollection-flash.

Afreyt nodded. ''All that matters, I guess. Gwaan came to after an hour, but remembered nothing, and they've put him to bed, where he stays. Cif and Groniger have set special watch on all the Rimic gold tonight.''

Suddenly Fafhrd felt bored with the whole business of Cif's ghost. His mind didn't want to move in that direction. ''Those councilmen of yours, all they ever worry about is gold—they're misers all!'' he burst out at Afreyt.

''That's true enough,'' she agreed with him—which annoyed Fafhrd for some reason. ''They still criticize Cif for giving the Cube to the Mouser along with the other moneys in her charge, and talk still of impeaching her and confiscating her farm—and maybe mine.''

''Ah, the ingrates! And Groniger's one of the worst—he's already dunning me for last week's rent on the men's dormitory, barely two days overdue.''

Afreyt nodded. ''He also complains your berserks caused a disturbance last week at the Sea Wrack tavern.''

''Oh he does, does he?'' Fafhrd commented, quieting down.

''How are the Mouser's men behaving?'' she asked.

''Pshawri keeps 'em in line well enough,'' he told her. ''Not that they don't need my supervision while the Gray One's away.''

''*Seahawk* will have returned before the gales, I'm sure of that,'' she said quietly.

''Yes,'' Fafhrd said.

They had come opposite her house and now she went inside with a smiled farewell. She did not invite him to dinner, which was somehow annoying, although he would have refused; and although she had glanced once or twice toward his stump, she had not asked how it fared—which was tactful, but also somehow annoying.

Yet the irritation was momentary, for her mention of the Sea Wrack had started his mind off in a new direction which fully occupied it as he walked a little more rapidly. The past few days he had been feeling out of sorts with almost everyone around him, weary of his left-hand problems, and perversely lonely for Lankhmar with its wizards and criminous folks, its smokes (so different from this bracing northern sea air) and sleazy grandeurs. The night before last he'd wandered into the Sea Wrack, Salthaven's chief tavern since the Salt Herring had burned, and discovered a certain comfort in observing the passing scene there while sipping a pint or two of black ale.

Although called the Wrack and Ruin by its habitués (he'd learned as he was leaving), it had seemed a quiet and restful place. Certainly no disturbances, least of all by his berserks (that had been last week, he reminded himself—if it had really ever happened), and he had found pleasure in watching the slow-moving servers and listening to the yarning fishers and sailors, two low-voiced whores (a wonder in itself), and a sprinkling of eccentrics and puzzlers, such as a fat man sunk in mute misery, a skinny gray-beard who peppered his ale, and a very slender silent woman in bone-gray touched with silver who sat alone at a back table and had the most tranquil (and not unhandsome) face imaginable. At first he'd thought her another whore, but no one had approached her table, none (save himself) had seemed to take any notice of her, and she hadn't even been drinking, so far as he could recall.

Last night he'd returned and found much the same crowd (and the same pleasant relief from his own boredom), and tonight he found himself looking forward to visiting the place again—after he'd been to the harbor and scanned south and east away for *Seahawk*.

4

At that moment Rill came around the next corner and hailed him cheerily, waving a hand that showed a red scar across the palm—memento of an injury that had created a bond between herself and Fafhrd. The dark haired whore-turned-fisherwoman was neatly and soberly clad—a sign that she was not at the moment engaged in either of her trades.

They chatted together, at ease with each other. She told him about today's catch of cod and asked after the Mouser (when now expected) and his and Fafhrd's men and how Fafhrd's stump was holding up (she was the one person he could talk to about that) and about his general health and how he was sleeping.

"If badly," she said, "Mother Grum has useful herbs—or I might be of help."

As she said that last, she chuckled, gave him an inquiring sidewise smile, and tugged his hook with her scarred forefinger, permanently crooked by the same deep burn that had left a red track across her palm. Fafhrd smiled back gratefully, shaking his head.

At that moment Pshawri came up with Skullick behind him to report on the day's work and other doings, and after a moment Rill went off. Some of Fafhrd's men had found employment on the new building going up where the Salt Herring had stood, a couple had worked on *Flotsam,* while the remainder had been cod-fishing with those men of the Mouser's who were not on *Seahawk.*

Pshawri made his report in a jaunty yet detailed and dutiful manner that reminded Fafhrd of the Mouser (he'd picked up some of his captain's mannerisms), which both irritated and amused Fafhrd. For that matter all the Mouser's thieves, being wiry and at least as short as he, reminded Fafhrd of his comrade. A pack of Mousers—ridiculous!

He stopped Pshawri's report with a "Content you, you've done well. You too, Skullick. But see that your mates stay out of the Wrack and Ruin. Here, take these.'' He gave the young berserk his bow and quiver. "No, I'll be supping out. Leave me, now.''

And so he continued on alone toward the Sea Wrack and the docks under the bright twilight, called here the violet hour. After a bit he realized with faint surprise and a shade of self-contempt why he was hurrying and why he had avoided Afreyt's bed and turned down Rill's comradely invitation—he was looking forward to another evening of watching and spinning dreams about the silent slender woman in bone-white and silver at the Wrack and Ruin, the woman with the so distant eyes and tranquil, not unhandsome face. Lord, what romantical fools men were, to overpass the known and good in order to strain and stretch after the mysterious merely unknown. Were dreams simply better than reality? Had fancy always more style? But even as he philosophized fleetingly of dreams, he was wending ever deeper into this violet-tinged one.

5

Familiar voices raised in vehemence pulled him partially out of it. Down the side lane he was crossing he saw Cif and Groniger talking excitedly together. He would have stolen onward unseen, returning entirely to his waking dream, but they spotted him.

"Captain Fafhrd, have you heard the ill news?" the grizzle-haired harbor master called as he approached with long strides. "The treasury's been looted of its gold-things, and Zwaaken who was guarding them struck dead!"

The small russet-clad woman with golden glints in her dark brown hair who came hurrying along with him amplified, "It happened no longer ago than sunset. We were close by in the council hall, ready to share the guard duty after dark (you've heard of last night's apparition?) when there came a cry from the vault and a blue flash from the cracks around the door. Zwaaken's face was frozen in a grimace and his clothes smoked . . . all the ikons were gone.''

It was strange, but Fafhrd barely took in what Cif was saying. Instead he was thinking of how even *she* was beginning to remind him of the Mouser and to behave like the Gray One. They said that people long in love began to resemble each other. Could that apply so soon?

"Yes, now it's not just the Gold Cube of Square-Dealing we lack," Groniger put in. "All, all gone."

His bringing in that roused Fafhrd again a little and nettled him. Altogether, in fact, he strangely found himself more irritated than interested or concerned by the news, though of course he would have liked to help Cif, who was the Mouser's darling.

"I've heard of your ghost," he told her. "All the rest is news. Is there any particular way in which I can help you now?"

They looked at him rather strangely. He realized his remark had been a somewhat cold one, so although he was most eager to get by himself again, he added, "You can call on my men for help if you need it in your search for the thieves. They're at their dormitory."

"On which you owe me rent," Groniger put in automatically.

Fafhrd graciously ignored that. "Well," he said, "I wish you good luck in your hunt. Gold is valuable stuff." And with a little bow he turned and continued on his way. When he'd gone some distance he heard their voices again, but could no longer make out what they were saying—which meant their words happily weren't for him.

He reached the harbor while the violet light was still bright across the sky and realized with a throb of pleasure that that was one reason he had been in such a hurry and impatient of all else. The few folk about moved or stood quietly, unmindful of his coming. The air was still. He crossed to the dock's verge and scanned searchingly south and southeast to where violet sky met unruffled gray sea in a long horizon line, with never a cloud or smudge of haze between.

No sign of a sail or hint of a hull, not one. Mouser and
Seahawk remained somewhere in the seaworld beyond.

But there was still time for sign or hint to appear before
light failed. His dreamy gaze wandered to things closer. East
rose the smooth salt cliffs, gray in the twilight. Between them
and the low headland to the west, the harbor was empty. Off
in that direction, to the right, *Flotsam* was moored close in,
while to the left, nearer, was a light wooden pier that would
be taken up when the winter gales arrived and to which a few
ship's boats and other small harbor craft were moored. Among
these was *Flotsam*'s small sailing dory, in which Fafhrd was
in the habit of going out alone—more training in making do
with a hook for a left hand—and also a narrow, mastless,
shallow craft, little more than a shaped plank, that was new to
him.

6

The violet light was draining away from the sky now and he
once more scanned the southern and southeastern horizon and
the long expanse of water between—a magical emptiness that
drew him powerfully. Still no sign. He turned away regret-
fully and there, coming across the dock so as to arrive at its
verge a score of feet from him, where the pier extended into
the harbor, was his silent, tranquil-faced lady of the Sea
Wrack. She might have been an apparition for all the notice
the few dock-folk took of her; she almost brushed a sailor as
she passed him by and he never moved. Behind her faint
voices called to her from the town (what were they concerned
about—a hunt for something? Fafhrd had forgotten) and the
shadows came down from the north, driving out the last violet
tones from the heavens. The silent woman had a pouch at her
hip that clinked once faintly while her pale hands drew round
her a silver-glinting bone-white robe that also shadowed her

face. And then as she passed closest to him, she turned her head so that her black-edged green eyes looked straight into his, and she put her hand into her bosom and drew forth a short gold arrow which she showed him and then slipped into her pouch, which clinked again, and then she smiled at him for three heartbeats a smile that was at once familiar and strange, aloof and alluring, and then turned her head forward and went out onto the pier.

7

And Fafhrd followed her, not knowing behind his forehead, or really caring, whether her gaze or smile had cast an actual enchantment upon him, but only that this was the direction in which he wanted to go, away from the toils and puzzlements and responsibilities and boredoms of Salthaven and toward the vasty south and the Mouser and Lankhmar—*her* way and whatever mysteries she stood for. Another part of his mind, a part linked chiefly with his feet and hands (though one of them was only a hook), wanted also to follow her on account of the golden arrow, though he could no longer remember why that was important.

As he stepped down onto the wooden pier, she reached its end and stepped onto the new narrow craft he'd noticed, and then without casting off or any other preparatory action, she lifted wide her arms as she faced the prow and the pale gray twilight, her back to him, so that her robe spread out to either side, and it bellied forward as if with an unseen wind, and she and her slight craft moved away toward the harbor mouth across the unruffled waters.

And then he felt on his right cheek a steady breeze blowing silently from the west, and he boarded the sailing dory and cast off and let down the centerboard and ran up the small sail and made it fast and then, taking its sheet in his right hand

and controlling the tiller with his hook, sailed out noiselessly after her. He wondered a little (but not very much) why no one called after them or even appeared to watch them, their craft moving as if by magic and hers so strangely and with such a strange sail.

8

Exactly how long they glided on in this fashion he did not know or care, but the gray sky darkened to black night and stars came out around her hooded head, and the gibbous moon rose, dimming the stars a little, and was for a while before them and then behind (their craft must have turned in a very wide circle and headed north, it seemed), so that the moon's deathly white light no longer dazzled his eyes but was reflected softly from his dory's wind-rounded sail and made the Sea Wrack woman's bone-white silvery robes stand out ahead on her shining craft as they ever bellied forward to either side of her. Very steady was the silent wind that did that, and under its urging his craft gained upon hers so that at the last they almost seemed to touch. He wished that she would turn her head so that he could see more of her, yet at the same time he wanted them to go sailing on enchantedly forever.

And then it seemed to him that the sea itself had tilted imperceptibly upward so that their noiselessly locked craft were mounting together toward the moon-dimmed stars. And at that point she turned around and moved slowly toward him and he likewise rose and moved effortlessly toward her, without any effect whatsoever on the dreamlike motion of their two craft as they mounted ever onward and upward. And she smiled the wondrous smile again at him and looked at him with love, and beyond her hooded head great weaving streamers of soft red and green and pale blue luminescence mounted toward the zenith (he knew them to be the northern lights) as though she stood at the altar of a great cathedral with all its stained-glass windows shedding a glory upon her. Glancing fleetingly to either side, he saw without great surprise or fear that their two craft were indeed mounting toward the stars on a great tongue of dark solid water that rose with precipice to either side, like a vast wall, from the moonlit sea far below. But all he had thought for was her proudly smiling face and daring, dancing gaze, enshrined by the aurora, that summed up for him all the allure of mystery and adventure.

She dipped then into the pouch at her waist and brought up the gold arrow and proffered it to him, holding it by either end in her dainty slim-fingered hands, and the moonlight showed him her small pearly teeth as she smiled.

Then he noted that his hook, which seemed to have a will of its own, had reached out and encircled the short shaft of the arrow between her hands and was tugging at it, while his right hand, which appeared to be operating with like independence of his bewitched mind, had shot forward, grasped the bulging pouch by its neck, and ripped it from her waist.

At that, her loving gaze grew fiercely desirous and her smile widened and grew wild and she tugged sharply back on the arrow so that it bent acutely at its midst, and the blue component of the aurora flaring behind her seemed to enter into her body and flash in her gaze and glow along her arms and hands, and the golden arrow glowed brighter still, a blue aura all around it, and Fafhrd's hook glowed equally, and there was a dazzling shower of blue sparks where hook and shaft met. Glad was Fafhrd then for the wooden wrist between his stump and his hook, for his every hair rose on end and he felt a prickling, tickling strangeness all over his skin.

But still his hook dragged blindly at the arrow, and now it came away with it, sharply bent but no longer blue-glowing. He snatched it off the hook with forefinger and thumb of his right hand, which still clutched the bag. And then as he backed away into his dory, he saw her loving countenance lengthening into a snout, her green eyes bulging and moving apart, swimming sidewise across her face, her pale skin turning to silvery scales, while her sweet mouth widened and gaped to show row upon row of razorlike triangular teeth.

She darted at him, he thrust out his left arm to fend her off, her jaws met with a great snap, while those dreadful teeth closed on his hook with a wrench and a clash.

9

And then all was tumult and swirling confusion, there was a clangor and a roaring in his ears, the solid water gave way and he and his craft plunged down, down, down, gut-wrenchingly, to the sea's surface and without check or hindrance as far again below it—until he and his dory were suddenly floating in a great tunnel of air floored, walled, and roofed by water, as far below the sea's surface as the water-wall had risen above it—and extending up to that surface just as the wall had stretched down to it. This incredible tunnel was lit silver by the misshapen moon glaring down it and greenish-yellow by a general phosphorescence in its taut, watery walls, from within which monstrous fish-faces moped and mowed at him and nuzzled the dory's hull. The other craft and the metamorphosing woman were gone.

The weirdness of the scene (together with the horrid transformation of the Sea Wrack woman) had banished his bewitchment and brought all his mind alive. He knelt in the dory's midst, peering about. And now the roaring in his ears increased and a great wind began to blow up the tunnel from the deeps, filling the dory's small sail and driving it along toward the mad moon. As this infernal gale swiftly grew to a hurricane, Fafhrd threw himself flat, anchoring himself by gripping the base of the dory's mast in the bend of his left elbow (for his hook was gone and his right hand had other employment). Silvery-green water flashed by, foam streamed back from the prow. And now a steady thunder began to resound from the deeps behind, adding itself to the tumultuous roaring, and it flashed through his frantic thoughts that such a sound might be caused by the tunnel closing up behind him, further increasing the might of the wind blowing him up this great silvery throat.

Space opened. The dory leaped like a flying fish, skiddingly struck roiled black water, righted itself, and floated flat— while from behind came a final thunderous crack.

It was as if the sea herself had spat them forth, then shut her lips.

10

In shorter space of time than he'd have thought possible without magic, before even his breathing had evened out, the sea calmed and the dory rode lonely and alone on its dark surface. Southward the moon shone. Its rays gleamed on the fracture where his hook had been bitten off. He realized that his right hand still gripped the neck of the bag he'd grabbed from Cif's ghost (or the Sea Wrack woman, or whatever), while still clipped between his thumb and forefinger was a bent gold arrow.

Northward a ghostly aurora was glimmering, fading, dying. And in the same direction the lights of Salthaven gleamed, closer than he'd have guessed. He got out the single oar, set it across the stern, and began to scull homeward against the steady breeze, keeping wary watch on the silent black waters all around the dory.

11

Fafhrd was once more at archery practice on the heath of gray standing stones, companioned by Gale. But today a brisk north wind was singing in the heather and bending the gorse— forerunner more than likely of winter's first gale . . . and still no sign of *Seahawk* and the Mouser.

Fafhrd had slept late this morning and so had many another Rime Isler. It had been past midnight when he'd wearily sculled up to the docks, but the port had been awake with the theft of civic treasures and his own disappearance, and he'd been confronted at once by Cif, Groniger, and Afreyt—Rill too, and Mother Grum, and several others. It turned out that after Fafhrd's vanishment (none had noted his actual depar- ture—an odd thing, that) a rumor had been bruited about (though hotly denied by the ladies) that *he* had made away with the gold ikons. Great was the rejoicing when he revealed that he had got them all safely back (save for the sharp bend in the Arrow of Truth) and an extra one besides—one which, as Fafhrd was quick to point out, might well be the lost Cube of Square-Dealing, its edges systematically deformed to curves. Groniger was inclined to doubt this and much concerned about both deformations, but Fafhrd was philosophic.

He said, "A crooked Arrow of Truth and a rounded-off Cube of Square-Dealing strike me as about right for this world, more in line with accepted human practices."

His account of his adventures on, above, and below the sea, and of the magic Cif's ghost had worked and her horrid last transformation, had produced reactions of wonder and amazement—and some thoughtful frowning. Afreyt had asked some difficult questions about his motives for following the Sea Wrack woman, while Rill had smiled knowingly.

As for the identity of Cif's ghost, only Mother Grum had strong convictions. "That'll be somewhat from sunken

Simorgya,'' she'd said, ''come to repossess their pirated baubles.''

Groniger had disputed that last, claiming the ikons had always been Rime Isle's, and the old witch had shrugged.

Now Gale asked him as they collected arrows, ''And the fish-lady bit your hook off just like that?''

''Yes, indeed,'' he assured her. ''I'm having Mannimark forge me a new one—of bronze. You know, that hook saved me twice—I'm getting to feel quite fond of it—once from the blue essence of lightning bolt coursing through the sea monster's extremities, and once from having another chunk of my left arm bitten off.''

Gale asked, ''What was it that made you suspicious of the fish-lady, so that you followed her?''

''Come on with those arrows, Gale,'' he told her. ''I've thought of a new way to shoot around corners.''

This time he did it by aiming into the wind so that it carried his arrow in a sidewise curve behind the gray standing stone hiding the red bag. Gale said it was almost as much cheating as dropping an arrow in from above, but later they found he'd hit his target.

II

—⟡—

The Mer She

1

The ripening newrisen moon of the world of Nehwon shone yellowly down on the marching swells of the Outer Sea, flecking with gold their low lacy crests and softly gilding the taut triangular sail of the slim galley hurrying northwest. Ahead, the last sunset reds were fading while black night engulfed the craggy coast behind, shrouding its severe outlines.

At *Seahawk*'s stern, beside old Ourph, who had the tiller, stood the Gray Mouser with arms folded across his chest and a satisfied smile linking his cheeks, his short stalwart body swaying as the ship slowly rocked, moving from shallow trough to low crest and to trough again with the steady southwest wind on her loadside beam, her best point of sailing. Occasionally he stole a glance back at the fading lonely lights of No-Ombrulsk, but mainly he looked straight ahead where lay, five nights and days away, Rime Isle and sweet Cif, and poor one-hand Fafhrd and the most of their

men and Fafhrd's Afreyt, whom the Mouser found rather
austere.

Ah, by Mog and by Loki, he thought, what satisfaction
equals that of captain who at last heads home with ship well
ballasted with the get of monstrously clever trading? None!
he'd warrant. Youth's erotic capturings and young manhood's
slayings—yea, even the masterworks and life-scrolls of scholar
and artist—were the merest baubles by compare, callow fe-
vers all.

In his self-enthusiasm the Mouser couldn't resist going
over in his mind each last item of merchant plunder—and also
to assure himself that each was stowed to best advantage and
stoutly secured, in case of storm or other ill-hap.

First, lashed to the sides, in captain's cabin beneath his
feet, were the casks of wine, mostly fortified, and the small
kegs of bitter brandy, Fafhrd's favorite tipple—those assuredly
could not be stored elsewhere or entrusted to another's over-
watching (except perhaps yellow old Ourph's here), he reminded himself as he lifted a small leather flask from his belt
to his lips and took a measured sup of elixir of Ool Hruspan
grape; he had strained his throat bellowing orders for *Seahawk*'s
stowing and swift departure, and its raw membranes wanted
healing before winter air came to try them further.

And amongst the wine in his cabin was also stored, in as
many equally stout, tight barrels, their seams tarred, the
wheaten flour—plebeian stuff to the thoughtless, but all-
important for an isle that could grow no grain except a little
summer barley.

Forward of captain's cabin—and now with his self-enthusiasm
at glow point, the Mouser's mused listing-over turned to
actual tour of inspection, he first speaking word to Ourph and
then moving prow-wards catlike along the moonlit ship—
forward of captain's cabin was chiefest prize, the planks and
beams and mast-worthy rounds of seasoned timber such as
Fafhrd had dreamed of getting at Ool Plerns, south where
trees grew, when his stump was healed and could carry hook,
such same timber won by cunningest bargaining maneuvers at
No-Ombrulsk, where no more trees were than at Rime Isle
(which got most of its gray wood from wrecks and nothing
much bigger than bushes grew) and where they (the 'Brulskers)

would sooner sell their wives than lumber! Yes, rounds and squares and planks of the precious stuff, all lashed down lengthwise to the rowers' benches from poop to forecastle beneath the boom of the great single sail, each layer lashed down separately and canvased and tarred over against the salt spray and wet, with a precious long vellum-thin sheet of beaten copper between layers for further protection and firming, the layers going all the way from one side of *Seahawk* to the other, and all the way up, tied-down timber and thin copper alternating, until the topmost layer was a tightly lashed, canvased deck, its seams tarred, level with the bulwarks—a miracle of stowage. (Of course, this would make rowing difficult if such became needful, but oars were rarely required on voyages such as the remainder of this one promised to be, and there were always some risks that had to be run by even the most prudent sea commander.)

Yes, it was a great timber-bounty that *Seahawk* was bearing to wood-starved Rime Isle, the Mouser congratulated himself as he moved slowly forward alongside the humming, moonlit sail, his softly shod feet avoiding the tarred seams of the taut canvas deck, while his nostrils twitched at an odd, faint, goaty-musky scent he caught, but it (the timber) never would have been won except for his knowledge of the great lust of Lord Logben of No-Ombrulsk for rare strange ivories to complete his White Throne. The 'Brulskers would sooner part with their girl-concubines than their timber, true enough, but the lust of Lord Logben for strange ivories was a greater desire than either of those, so that when with low drummings the Kleshite trading scow had put into 'Brulsk's black harbor and the Mouser had been among the first to board her and had spotted the behemoth tusk amongst the Kleshite trading treasures, he had bought it at once in exchange for a double-fist lump of musk-odorous ambergris, common stuff in Rime Isle but more precious than rubies in Klesh, so that they were unable to resist it.

Thereafter the Kleshites had proffered their lesser ivories in vain to Lord Logben's major-domo, wailing for the mast-long giant snow serpent's white furred skin, that was *their* dearest desire, procured by Lord Logben's hunters in the frigid mountains known as the Bones of the Old Ones, and in vain had

Lord Logben offered the Mouser its weight in electrum for
the tusk. Only when the Kleshites had added their pleas to the
Mouser's demands that the 'Brulskers sell him timber, offer-
ing for the unique snow serpent skin not only their lesser
ivories but half their spices, and the Mouser had threatened to
sink the tusk in the bottomless bay rather than sell it for less
than wood, had the 'Brulskers been forced by their Lord to
yield up a quarter shipload of seasoned straight timber, as
grudgingly as the Mouser had seemed to part with the tusk—
whereafter all the trading (even in timber) had gone more
easily.

Ah, that had been most cunningly done, a masterstroke! the
Mouser assured himself soberly.

As these most pleasant recollections were sorting themselves to best advantage within the Mouser's wide, many-
shelved skull, his noiseless feet had carried him to the thick
foot of the mast, where the false deck made by the timber
cargo ended. Three yards farther on began the decking of the
forecastle, beneath which the rest of the cargo was stowed
and secured: ingots of bronze and little chests of dyes and
spices and a larger chest of silken fabrics and linens for Cif
and Afreyt—that was to show his crew he trusted them with
all things except mind-fuddling, duty-betraying wine—but
mostly the forward cargo was tawny grain and white and
purple beans and sun-dried fruit, all bagged in wool against
the sea-damp: food for the hungry Isle. There was your real
thinking man's treasure, he told himself, beside which gold
and twinkling jewels were merest trinkets, or the pointy
breasts of young love or words of poets or the pointed stars
themselves that astrologers cherished and that made men
drunk with distance and expanse.

In the three yards between false deck and true, their upper
bodies in the shadow of the latter and their feet in a great
patch of moonlight, on which his own body cast its supervi-
sory shadow, his crew slept soundly while the sea cradle-
rocked 'em: four wiry Mingols, three of his short, nimble
sailor-thieves with their lieutenant Mikkidu, and Fafhrd's tall
lieutenant Skor, borrowed for this voyage. Aye, they slept
soundly enough! he told himself with relish (he could clearly
distinguish the bird-twittering snores of ever-apprehensive

Mikkidu and the lion-growling ones of Skor), for he had kept
tight rein on them all the time in No-Ombrulsk and then
deliberately worked them mercilessly loading and lashing the
timber at the end, so that they'd fallen asleep in their tracks
after the ship had sailed and they had supped (just as he'd
cruelly disciplined himself and permitted himself no freedom
all time in port, no slightest recreation, even such as was
desirable for hygienic reasons), for he knew well the appetites
of sailors and the dubious, debilitating attractions of 'Brulsk's
dark alleys—why, the whores had paraded daily before *Seahawk*
to distract his crew. He remembered in particular one hardly-
more-than-child among them, an insolent skinny girl in tat-
tered tunic faded silver-gray, same shade as her precociously
silver hair, who had moved a little apart from the other
whores and had seemed to be forever flaunting herself and
peering up at *Seahawk* wistfully yet somehow tauntingly,
with great dark waifish eyes of deepest green.

Yes, by fiery Loki and by eight-limbed Mog, he told
himself, in the discharge of his captain's duties he'd disciplined himself most rigorously of all, expending every last
ounce of strength, wisdom, cunning (and voice!) and asking
no reward at all except for the knowledge of responsibilities
manfully shouldered—that, and gifts for his friends. Suddenly
the Mouser felt nigh to bursting with his virtues and somehow
a shade sorry about it, especially the "no reward at all" bit,
which now seemed manifestly unfair.

Keeping careful watch upon his wearied-out men, and with
his ears attuned to catch any cessation of, or the slightest
variation in their snorings, he lifted his leathern pottle to his
lips and let a generous, slow, healthful swallow soothe his
raw throat.

As he thrust the lightened pottle back into his belt, securely
hooking it there, his gaze fastened on one item of cargo
stored forward that seemed to have strayed from its appointed
place—either his concentrated watching or else some faint
unidentified sound had called it to his attention. (At the same
instant he got another whiff of the musky, goaty, strangely
attractive sea odor. Ambergris?) It was the chest of silks and
thick ribbons and linens and other costly fabrics intended
chiefly for his gift to Cif. It was standing out a little way from

the ship's side, almost entirely in the moonlight, as if its
lashings had loosened, and now as he studied it more closely
he saw that it wasn't lashed at all and that its top was wedged
open a finger's breadth by a twist of pale orange fabric
protruding near a hinge.

What monstrous indiscipline did this signify?

He dropped noiselessly down and approached the chest, his
nostrils wrinkling. Was unsold ambergris cached inside it?
Then, carefully keeping his shadow off it, he gripped the top
and silently threw it wide open on its hinges.

The topmost silk was a thick lustrous copper-colored one
chosen to match the glints in Cif's dark hair.

Upon this rich bedding, like kitten stolen in to nap on
fresh-laundered linens, reposed, with arms and legs somewhat
drawn in but mostly on her back, and with one long-fingered
hand twisting down through her tousled silvery hair so as to
shadow further her lidded eyes—reposed that self-same wharf-
waif he'd but now been recalling. The picture of innocence,
but the odor (he knew it now) all sex. Her slender chest rose
and fell gently and slowly with her sleeping inhalations, her
small breasts and rather larger nipples outdenting the flimsy
fabric of her ragged tunic, while her narrow lips smiled
faintly. Her hair was somewhat the same shade as that of
silver-blond, thirteen-year-old Gale back on Rime Isle, who'd
been one of Odin's maidens. And she was, apparently, not a
great deal older.

Why, this was worse than monstrous, the Mouser told
himself as he wordlessly stared. That one or two or more of
all of his crew should conspire to smuggle this girl aboard for
his or their hot pleasure, tempting her with silver or feeing
her pimp or owner (or else kidnapping her, though that was
most unlikely in view of her unbound state) was bad enough,
but that they should presume to do this not only without their
captain's knowledge but also in complete disregard of the fact
that *he* enjoyed no such erotic solacing, but rather worked
himself to the bone on their behalf and *Seahawk*'s, solicitous
only of their health and welfare and the success of the voyage—
why, this was not only wantonest indiscipline but also rankest
ingratitude!

At this dark point of disillusionment with his fellow man,

the Mouser's one satisfaction was his knowledge that his crew
slept deeply from exhaustion he'd inflicted on them. The
chorus of their unaltering snores was music to his ears, for it
told him that although they'd managed to smuggle the girl
aboard successfully, not one of them had yet enjoyed her (at
least since the loading and business of getting under way was
done). No, they'd been smote senseless by fatigue, and would
not now wake for a hurricane. And that thought in turn
pointed out to him the way to their most appropriate and
condign punishment.

Smiling widely, he reached his left hand toward the sleeping girl, and, where it made a small peak in her worn
silver-faded tunic, delicately yet somewhat sharply tweaked
her right nipple. As she came shuddering awake with a suck
of indrawn breath, her eyes opening and her parted lips
forming an exclamation, he swooped his face toward hers,
frowning most sternly and laying his finger across his now
disapprovingly set lips, enjoining silence.

She shrank away, staring at him in wonder and dread and
keeping obediently still. He drew back a little in turn, noting
the twin reflections of the misshapen moon in her wide dark
eyes and how strangely the lustrous coppery silk on which she
cowered contrasted with her hair tangled upon it, fine and
silver pale as a ghost's.

From around them the chorus of snores continued un-
changed as the crew slept on.

From beside her slender naked feet the Mouser plucked up
a black roll of thick silken ribbon, and unsheathing his dirk
Cat's Claw, proceeded to cut three hanks from it, staring
broodingly at the shrinking girl all the while. Then he motioned to her and crossed his wrists to indicate what was
wanted of her.

Her chest lifting in a silent sigh, and shrugging her shoulders a little, she crossed her slender wrists in front of her. He
shook his head and pointed behind her.

Again divining his command, she crossed them there, turning upon her side a little to do so.

He bound her wrists together crosswise and tightly, then
bound her elbows together also, noting that they met without
undue strain upon her slender shoulders. He used the third

hank to tie her legs together firmly just above the knees. Ah, discipline! he thought—good for one and all, but in particular the young!

In the end she lay supine upon her bound arms, gazing up at him. He noted that there seemed to be more curiosity and speculation in that gaze than dread and that the twin reflections of the gibbous moon did not waver with any eye-blinking or -watering.

How very pleasant this all was, he mused: his crew asleep, his ship driving home full-laden, the slim girl docile to his binding of her, he meting out justice as silently and secretly as does a god. The taste of undiluted power was so satisfying to him that it did not trouble him that the girl's silken-smooth flesh glowed a little more silvery pale than even moonlight would easily account for.

Without any warning or change in his own brooding expression, he flicked inside the protruding twist of fabric and closed the lid of the chest upon her.

Let the confident minx worry a bit, he thought, as to whether I intend to suffocate her or perchance cast the chest overboard, she being in it. Such incidents were common enough, he told himself, at least in myth and story.

Tiny wavelets gently slapped *Seahawk*'s side, the moonlit sail hummed as softly, and the crew snored on.

The Mouser wakened the two brawniest Mingols by twisting a big toe of each and silently indicated that they should take up the chest without disturbing their comrades and bear it back to his cabin. He did not want to risk waking the crew with sound of words. Also, using gestures spared his strained throat.

If the Mingols were privy to the secret of the girl, their blank expressions did not show it, although he watched them narrowly. Nor did old Ourph betray any surprise. As they came nigh him, the ancient Mingol's gaze slipped over them and roved serenely ahead and his gnarled hands rested lightly on the tiller, as though the shifting about of the chest were a matter of no consequence whatever.

The Mouser directed the younger Mingols in their setting of the chest between the lashed cases that narrowed the cabin and beneath the brass lamp that swung on a short chain from the low ceiling. Laying finger to compressed lips, he signed them to keep strict silence about the chest's midnight remove. Then he dismissed them with a curt wave. He rummaged about, found a small brass cup, filled it from a tiny keg of Fafhrd's bitter brandy, drank off half, and opened the chest.

The smuggled girl gazed up at him with a composure he told himself was creditable. She had courage, yes. He noted that she took three deep breaths, though, as if the chest had indeed been a bit stuffy. The silver glow of her pale skin and hair pleased him. He motioned her to sit up, and when she did so, set the cup against her lips, tilting it as she drank the other half. He unsheathed his dirk, inserted it carefully between her knees, and drawing it upward, cut the ribbon confining them. He turned, moved away aft, and settled himself on a low stool that stood before Fafhrd's wide bunk. Then with crooked forefinger he summoned her to him.

When she stood close before him, chin high, slender shoulders thrown back by virtue of the ribbons binding her arms, he eyed her significantly and formed the words, ''What is your name?''

''Ississi,'' she responded in a lisping whisper that was like the ghosts of wavelets kissing the hull. She smiled.

2

On deck, Ourph had directed one of the younger Mingols to take the tiller, the other to heat him gahveh. He sheltered from the wind behind the false deck of the timber cargo, looking toward the cabin and shaking his head wonderingly. The rest of the crew snored in the forecastle's shadow. While on Rime Isle in her low-ceilinged yellow bedroom Cif woke with the thought that the Gray Mouser was in peril. As she tried to recollect her nightmare, moonlight creeping along the

wall reminded her of the mer-ghost which had murdered
Zwaaken and lured off Fafhrd from sister Afreyt for a space,
and she wondered how Mouser would react to such a dangerous challenge.

3

Bright and early the next morning the Mouser threw on a
short gray robe, belted it, and rapped sharply on the cabin's
ceiling. Speaking in a somewhat hoarse whisper, he told the
impassive Mingol thus summoned that he desired the instant
presence of Master Mikkidu. He had cast a disguising drape
across the transported chest that stood between the crowding
casks that narrowed farther the none-too-wide cabin, and now
sat behind it on the stool, as though it were a captain's flat
desk. Behind him on the crosswise bunk that occupied the
cabin's end Ississi reposed and either slept or shut-eyed waked,
he knew not which, blanket-covered except for her streaming
silver hair and unconfined save for the thick black ribbon
tying one ankle securely to the bunk's foot beneath the blanket.

(*I'm no egregious fool,* he told himself, to *think that one
night's love brings loyalty.*)

He nursed his throat with a cuplet of bitter brandy, gargled
and slowly swallowed.

(*And yet she'd make a good maid for Cif, I do believe,
when I have done with disciplining her. Or perchance I'll
pass her on to poor-maimed and isle-locked Fafhrd.*)

He impatiently finger-drummed the shrouded chest, wondering what could be keeping Mikkidu. A guilty conscience?
Very likely!

Save for a glimmer of pale dawn filtering through the
curtained hatchway and the two narrow side ports glazed with
mica, which the lashed casks further obscured, the oil-
replenished swaying lamp still provided the only light.

4

There was a flurry of running footsteps coming closer, and then Mikkidu simultaneously rapped at the hatchway and thrust tousle-pated head and distracted eyes between the curtains. The Mouser beckoned him in, saying in a soft, brandy-smoothed voice, "Ah, Master Mikkidu, I'm glad your duties, which no doubt must be pressing, at last permit you to visit me, because I do believe I ordered that you come at once."

"Oh, Captain, sir," the latter replied rapidly, "there's a chest missing from the stowage forward. I saw that it was gone as soon as Trenchi wakened me and gave me your command. I only paused to rouse my mates and question them before I hurried here."

(Ah-ha, the Mouser thought, *he knows about Ississi, I'm sure of it, he's much too agitated, he had a hand in smuggling her aboard. But he doesn't know what's happened to her now—suspects everything and everyone, no doubt—and seeks to clear himself with me of all suspicion by reporting to me the missing chest, the wretch!)*

"A chest? Which chest?" the Mouser meanwhile asked blandly. "What did it contain? Spices? Spicy things?"

"Fabrics for Lady Cif, I do believe," Mikkidu answered.

"Just fabrics for the Lady Cif and nothing else?" the Mouser inquired, eyeing him keenly. "Weren't there some other things? Something of *yours,* perhaps?"

"No, sir, nothing of mine," Mikkidu denied quickly.

"Are you sure of that?" the Mouser pressed. "Sometimes one will tuck something of one's own inside another's chest—for safekeeping, as it were, or perchance to smuggle it across a border."

"Nothing of mine at all," Mikkidu maintained. "Perhaps there were some fabrics also for the other lady . . . and, well, just fabrics, sir and—oh, yes—some rolls of ribbon."

"Nothing but fabrics and ribbon?" the Mouser went on,

prodding him. "No fabrics made into garments, eh?—such as a short silvery tunic of some lacy stuff, for instance?"

Mikkidu shook his head, his eyebrows rising.

"Well, well," the Mouser said smoothly, "what's happened to this chest, do you suppose? It must be still on the ship—unless someone has dropped it overboard. Or was it perhaps stolen back in 'Brulsk?"

"I'm sure it was safe aboard when we sailed," Mikkidu asserted. Then he frowned. "I *think* it was, that is." His brow cleared. "Its lashings lay beside it, loose on the deck!"

"Well, I'm glad you found something of it," the Mouser said. "Where on the ship do you suppose it can be? Think, man, where can it be?" For emphasis, he pounded the muffled chest he sat at.

Mikkidu shook his head helplessly. His gaze wandered about, past the Mouser.

(*Oh-ho*, the latter thought, *does he begin to get a glimmering at last of what has happened to his smuggled girl? Whose plaything she is now? This might become rather amusing.*)

He recalled his lieutenant's attention by asking, "What were your men able to tell you about the runaway chest?"

"Nothing, sir. They were as puzzled as I am. I'm sure they know nothing. I *think*."

"Hmn. What did the Mingols have to say about it?"

"They're on watch, sir. Besides, they answer only to Ourph—or yourself, of course, sir."

(*You can trust a Mingol,* the Mouser thought, *at least where it's a matter of keeping silent.*)

"What about Skor, then?" he asked. "Did Captain Fafhrd's man know anything about the chest's vanishment?"

Mikkidu's expression became a shade sulky. "Lieutenant Skor is not under my command," he said. "Besides that, he sleeps very soundly."

There was a thuddingly loud double knock at the hatchway.

"Come in," the Mouser called testily, "and next time don't try to pound the ship to pieces."

Fafhrd's chief lieutenant thrust bent head with receding reddish hair through the curtains and followed after. He had to bend both back and knees to keep from bumping his naked pate on the beams. (*So Fafhrd too would have had to go about stooping when occupying his own cabin*, the Mouser thought. *Ah, the discomforts of size.)*

Skor eyed the Mouser coolly and took note of Mikkidu's presence. He had trimmed his russet beard, which gave it a patchy appearance. Save for his broken nose, he rather resembled a Fafhrd five years younger.

"Well?" the Mouser said peremptorily.

"Your pardon, Captain Mouser," the other replied, "but you asked me to keep particular watch on the stowage of cargo, since I was the only one who had done any long voyaging on *Seahawk* before this faring, and knew her behavior in different weathers. So I believe that I should report to you that there is a chest of fabrics—you know the one, I think—missing from the fore steer-side storage. Its lashings lie all about, both those which roped it shut and those which tied it securely in place."

(Ah-ha, the Mouser thought, *he's guilty too and seeks to cover it by making swift report, however late. Never trust a bland expression. The lascivious villain!)*

With his lips he said, "Ah yes, the missing chest—we were just speaking of it. When do you suppose it became so?—I mean missing. In 'Brulsk?"

Skor shook his head. "I saw to its lashing myself—and noted it still tied fast to the side as my eyes closed in sleep a league outside that port. I'm sure it's still on *Seahawk*."

(He admits it, the effrontrous rogue! the Mouser thought. I wonder he doesn't accuse Mikkidu of stealing it. Perhaps there's a little honor left 'mongst thieves and berserks.)

Meanwhile the Mouser said, "Unless it has been dropped overboard—that is a distinct possibility, do you not think? Or mayhap we were boarded last night by soundless and invisible pirates while you both snored, who raped the chest away and nothing else. Or perchance a crafty and shipwise octopus, desirous of going richly clad and with arms skillful at tying and untying knots—"

He broke off when he noted that both tall Skor and short Mikkidu were peering wide-eyed beyond him. He turned on his stool. A little more of Ississi showed above the blanket—to wit, a small patch of pale forehead and one large green silver-lashed eye peering unwinking through her long silvery hair.

He turned back very deliberately and, after a sharp "Well?" to get their attention, asked in his blandest voice, "Whatever are you looking at so engrossedly?"

"Uh—nothing at all," Mikkidu stammered, while Skor only shifted gaze to look at the Mouser steadily.

"Nothing at all?" the Mouser questioned. "You don't perhaps see the chest somewhere in this cabin? Or perceive some clue to its present disposition?"

Mikkidu shook his head, while after a moment Skor shrugged, eyeing the Mouser strangely.

"Well, gentlemen," the Mouser said cheerily, "that sums it up. The chest must be aboard this ship, as you both say. So hunt for it! Scour *Seahawk* high and low—a chest that large can't be hid in a seaman's bag. And use your eyes, both of you!" He thumped the shrouded box once more for good measure. "And now—dismiss!"

(They both know all about it, I'll be bound. The deceiving dogs! the Mouser thought. *And yet . . . I am not altogether satisfied of that.)*

5

When they were gone (after several hesitant, uncertain backward glances), the Mouser stepped back to the bunk and, planting his hands to either side of the girl, stared down at her green eye, supporting himself on stiff arms. She rocked her head up and down a little and to either side, and so worked her entire face free of the blanket and her eyes of the silken hair veiling them and stared up at him expectantly.

He put on an inquiring look and flirted his head toward the hatchway through which the men had departed, then directed the same look more particularly at her. It was strange, he mused, how he avoided speaking to her whenever he could except with pointings and gestured commands. Perhaps it was that the essence of power lay in getting your wishes gratified without ever having to speak them out, to put another through all his paces in utter silence, so that no god might overhear and know. Yes, that was part of it at least.

He formed with his lips and barely breathed the question, "How did you *really* come aboard *Seahawk*?"

Her eyes widened and after a while her peach-down lips began to move, but he had to turn his head and lower it until they moistly and silkily brushed his best ear as they enunciated, before he could clearly hear what she was saying—in the same Low Lankhmarese as he and Mikkidu and Skor had spoken, but with a delicious lisping accent that was all little hisses and gasps and warblings. He recalled how her scent had seemed all sex in the chest, but now infinitely flowery, dainty, and innocent.

"I was a princess and lived with the prince Mordroog, my brother, in a far country where it was always spring," she began. "There a watery influence filtered all harshness from the sun's beams, so that he shone no more bright than the silvery moon, and winter's rages and summer's droughts were tamed, and the roaring winds moderated to eternal balmy breezes, and even fire was cool—in that far country."

Every whore tells the same tale, the Mouser thought. *They were all princesses before they took to the trade.* Yet he listened on.

"We had golden treasure beyond all dreaming," she continued, "unicorns that flew and kittens that flowed were my pets, and we were served by nimble companies of silent servitors and guarded by soft-voiced monsters—great Slasher and vasty All-Gripper, and Deep Rusher, who was greatest of all.

"But then came ill times. One night while our guardians slept, our treasure was stolen away and our realm became lonely, farther off and more secret still. My brother and I went searching for our treasure and for allies, and in that search I was raped away by bold scoundrels and taken to vile, vile 'Brulsk, where I came to know all the evil there is under the hateful sun."

This too is a familiar part of each harlot's story, the Mouser told himself, *the raping away, the loss of innocence, instruction in every vice.* Yet he went on listening to her ticklesome whispering.

"But I knew that one day *that one* would come who would be king over me and carry me back to my realm and dwell with me in power and silvery glory, our treasures being restored. And then *you* came."

Ah, now the personal appeal, the Mouser thought. *Very familiar indeed. Still, let's hear her out. I like her tongue in my ear. It's like being a flower and having a bee suck your nectar.*

"I went to your ship each day and stared at you. I could do naught else at all, however I tried. And you would never look at me for long, and yet I knew that our paths lay together. I knew you were a masterful man and that you'd visit upon me rigors and inflictions besides which those I'd suffered in dreadful 'Brulsk would be nothing, and yet I could not turn aside for an instant, or take my eyes away from you and your dark ship. And when it was clear you would not notice me, or act upon your true feelings, or any of your men provide a means for me to follow you, I stole aboard unseen while they were all stowing and lashing and you were commanding them."

(Lies, lies, all lies, the Mouser thought—and continued to listen.)

"I managed to conceal myself by moving about amongst the cargo. But when at last you'd sailed from harbor and your men slept, I grew cold, the deck was hard, I suffered keenly. And yet I dared not seek your cabin yet, or otherwise disclose myself, for fear you would put back to 'Brulsk to put me off. So I gradually freed of its lashings a chest of fabrics I'd marked, working and working like a mouse or shrew—the knots were hard, but my fingers are clever and nimble, and strong whenever the need is—until I could creep inside and slumber warm and soft. And then you came for me, and here I am."

The Mouser turned his head and looked down into her large green eyes, across which golden gleams moved rhythmically with the lamp's measured swinging. Then he briefly pressed a finger across her soft lips and drew down the blanket until her ribbon-fettered ankle was revealed and he admired her beautiful small body. It was well, he told himself, for a man to have always a beautiful young woman close by him—like a beautiful cat, yes, a young cat, independent but with kitten ways still. It was well when such a one talked, speaking lies much as any cat would (*'Twas crystal clear she must have had help getting aboard—Skor and Mikkidu both, likely enough*), but best not to talk to her too much, and wisest to keep her well bound. You could trust folk when they were secured—indeed, trussed!—and not otherwise, no, not at all. And that was the essence of power—binding all others, binding all else! Keeping his eyes hypnotically upon hers, he reached across her for the loose hanks of black ribbon. It would be well to fetter her three other limbs to foot and head of bunk, not tightly, yet not so loosely that she could reach either wrist with other hand or with her pearly teeth—so he could take a turn on deck, confident that she'd be here when he returned.

6

On Rime Isle Cif, strolling alone across the heath beyond Salthaven, plucked from the slender pouch at her girdle a small male figure of sewn cloth stuffed with lint. He was tall as her hand was long and his waist was constricted by a plain gold ring which would have fitted one of her fingers—and that was a measure of the figure's other dimensions. He was dressed in a gray tunic and gray, gray-hooded cloak. She regarded his featureless linen face and for a space she meditated the mystery of woven cloth—one set of threads or lines tying or at least restraining another such set, with a uniquely protective pervious surface the result. Then some odd hint of expression in the faintly brown, blank linen face suggested to

her that the Gray Mouser might be in need of more golden
protection than the ring afforded, and thrusting the doll feet-
first back into her pouch, she strode back toward Salthaven,
the council hall, and the recently ghost-raped treasury. The
north wind coming unevenly rippled the heather.

7

His throat burning from the last swallow of bitter brandy he'd
taken, the Mouser slipped through the hatchway curtains and
stole silently on deck. His purpose was to check on his crew
(surprise 'em if need be!) and see if they were all properly
occupied with sailorly duties (tied to their tasks, as it were!),
including the fool's search for the missing chest he'd sent
them on in partial punishment for smuggling Ississi aboard.
(She was secure below, the minx, he'd seen to that!)

The wind had freshened a little and *Seahawk* leaned to
steerside a bit farther as she dashed ahead, lead-weighted keel
balancing the straining sail. The Mingol steersman leaned on
the tiller while his mate and old Ourph scanned with sailorly
prudence the southwest for signs of approaching squalls. At
this rate they might reach Rime Isle in three more days
instead of four. The Mouser felt uneasy at that, rather than
pleased. He looked over the steerside apprehensively, but the
rushing white water was still safely below the oarholes, each
of which had a belaying pin laid across it, around which the
ropes lashing down the middle tier of the midship cargo had
been passed. This reminder of the security of the ship unaccountably did not please him either.

Where was the rest of the crew? he asked himself. A-search
forward below for the missing chest? Or otherwise busy? Or
merely skulking? He'd see for himself! But as he strode
forward across the taut canvas sheathing the timber treasure,

the reason for his sudden depression struck him, and his steps slowed.

He did not like the thought of soon arrival or of the great gifts he was bringing (in fact, *Seahawk*'s cargo had now become hateful to him) because all that represented ties binding him and his future to Cif and crippled Fafhrd and haughty Afreyt too and all his men and every last inhabitant of Rime Isle. Endless responsibility—that was what he was sailing back to. Responsibility as husband (or some equivalent) of Cif, old friend to Fafhrd (who was already tied to Afreyt, no longer comrade), captain (and guardian!) of his men, father to all. Provider and protector!—and first thing you knew they, or at least one of them, would be protecting *him*, confining and constraining him for his own good in tyranny of love or fellowship.

Oh, he'd be a hero for an hour or two, praised for his sumptuous get. But next day? Go out and do it again! Or (worse yet) stay at home and do it. And so on, *ad infinitum*. Such a future ill sorted with the sense of power he'd had since last night's sailing and which the girl-whore Ississi had strangely fed. Himself bound instead of binding others, and adventuring on to bind the universe mayhap and put it through its paces, enslave the very gods. Not free to adventure, discover, and to play with life, tame it by all-piercing knowledge and by shrewd commands and put it through its paces, search out each dizzy height and darksome depth. The Mouser *bound*? No, no, no, no!

As his feelings marched with that great repeated negation, his inching footsteps had carried him forward almost to the mast, and through the sail's augmented hum and the wind's and the water's racket against the hull, he became aware of two voices contending vehemently in strident whispers.

He instantly and silently dropped on his belly and crawled on very cautiously until the top half of his face overlooked the gap between timber cargo and forecastle.

His three sailor-thieves and the two other Mingols sprawled higgledy piggledy, lazily napping, while immediately below him Skor and Mikkidu argued in what might be called loud undertones. He could have reached down and patted their heads—or rapped them with fisted knuckles.

"There you go bringing in the chest again," Mikkidu was whispering hotly, utterly absorbed in the point he was making. "There *is* no longer any chest on *Seahawk*! We've searched every place on the ship and not found it, so it has to have been cast overboard—that's the only explanation!—but only after (most like) the rich fabrics it contained were taken out and hid deviously in any number of ways and places. And there I must, with all respect, suspect old Ourph. He was awake while we slept, you can't trust Mingols (or get a word out of them, for that matter), he's got merchant's blood and can't resist snatching any rich thing, he's also got the cunning of age, and—"

Mikkidu perforce paused to draw breath and Skor, who seemed to have been patiently waiting for just that, cut in with, "Searched every place *except* the Captain's cabin. And we searched that pretty well with our eyes. So the chest has to be the draped oblong thing he sat behind and even thumped on. It was exactly the right size and shape—"

"That was the Captain's desk," Mikkidu asserted in outraged tones.

"There *was* no desk," Skor rejoined, "when Captain Fafhrd occupied the cabin, or on our voyage down. Stick to the facts, little man. Next you'll be denying again he had a girl with him."

"There was no girl!" Mikkidu exploded, using up at once all the breath he'd managed to draw, for Skor was able to continue without raising his voice, "There was indeed a girl, as any fool could see who was not oversunk in doggish loyalty—a dainty delicate piece just the right size for him with long, long silvery hair and a great green eye casting out lustful gleams—"

"That wasn't a girl's long hair you saw, you great lewd oaf," Mikkidu cut in, his lungs replenished at last. "That was a large dried frond of fine silvery seaweed with a shining, sea-rounded green pebble caught up in it—such a curio as many a captain's cabin accumulates—and your woman-starved fancy transformed it to a wench, you lickerish idiot—

"Or else," he recommended rapidly, cutting in on himself, as it were, "it was a lacy silver dress with a silver-set green gem at its neck—the Captain questioned me closely about just such a dress when he was quizzing me about the chest before you came.''

My, my, the Mouser thought, *I never dreamed Mikkidu had such a quick fancy or would spring to my defense so loyally. But it does now appear, I must admit, that I have falsely suspected these two men and that Ississi somehow did board* Seahawk *solo. Unless one of the others—no, that's unlikely. Truth from a whore—there's a puzzler for you.*

Skor said triumphantly, ''But if it was the dress you saw on's bunk and the dress had been in the chest, doesn't that prove the chest too was in the cabin? Yes, it may well have been a filmy silver dress we saw, now that I think of it, which the girl slipped teasingly and lasciviously out of before leaping between the sheets, or else your Captain Mouser ripped it off her (it looked torn), for he's as hot and lusty as a mink and ever boasting of his dirksmanship—I've heard Captain Fafhrd say so again and again, or at least imply it.''

What infamy was this now? the Mouser asked himself, suddenly indignant, glaring down at Skor's balding head from his vantage point. *It was his own place to chide Fafhrd for his womanizing, not hear himself so chidden for the same fault (and boastfulness to boot) by this bogus Fafhrd, this insolent, lofty, jumped-up underling.* He involuntarily whipped up his fist to smite.

''Yes, boastful, devious, a martinet, and mean,'' Skor continued while Mikkidu spluttered. ''What think you of a captain who drives his crew hard in port, holds back· their pay, puritanically forbids shore leave, denies 'em all discharge of their natural urges—and then brings a girl aboard for his own use and flaunts her in their faces? and *then* plays games with them about her, sends them on idiot's hunt. *Petty*—that's what I've heard Captain Fafhrd call it—or at least show he thought so by his looks.''

The Mouser, furious, could barely restrain himself from striking out. *Defend me, Mikkidu,* he inwardly implored. *Oh the monstrousness of it—to invoke Fafhrd. Had Fafhrd really—*

''Do you really think so?'' he heard Mikkidu say, only a little doubtfully. ''You really think he's got a girl in there? Well, if that's the case I must admit he is a very devil!''

The cry of pure rage that traitorous utterance drew from the sprung-up Mouser made the two lieutenants throw back their heads and stare, and brought the nappers fully awake and almost to their feet.

He opened his mouth to utter rebuke that would skin them alive—and then paused, wondering just what form that rebuke could take. After all, there *was* a naked girl in his cabin with her legs tied wide—in fact, spread-eagled. His glance lit on the lashings of the chest of fabrics still lying loose on the deck.

"Clear up that strewage!" he roared, pointing it out. "Use it to tie down doubly those grain sacks there." He pointed again. "And while you're at it—" (he took a deep breath) "double lash the entire cargo! I am not satisfied that it won't shift if hurricane strikes." He directed that last remark chiefly at the two lieutenants, who peered puzzledly at the blue sky as they moved to organize the work.

"Yes, double lash it all down tight as eelskin," he averred, beginning to pace back and forth as he warmed to his task. "Pass the timber's extra ropings around belaying pins set *inside* the oarholes and then draw them tight across the deck. See that those wool sacks of grain and fruit are lashed really tight—imagine you're corsetting a fat woman, put your foot in her back and really pull those laces. For I'm not convinced those bags would stay in place if we had green water aboard and dragging at them. And when all that is done, bring a gang aft to further firm the casks and barrels in my cabin, marry them indissolubly to *Seahawk*'s deck and sides. Remember, all of you," he finished as he danced off aft, "if you tie things up carefully enough—your purse, your produce, or your enemies, and eke your lights of love—nothing can ever surprise you, or escape from you, or harm you!"

8

Cif untied the massive silver key from the neck of her soft leather tunic, where it had hung warm inside, unlocked the heavy oaken door of the treasury, opened it cautiously and suspiciously, inspected the room from the threshold—she'd been uneasy about the place ever since the sea-ghost's depredations. Then she went in and relocked the door behind her. A small window with thumb-thick bars of bronze illumined not too well the wooden room. On a shelf reposed two ingots of pale silver, three short stacks of silver coins, and a single golden stack, still shorter. The walls of the room crowded in on a low circular table, in the gray surface of which a pentacle had been darkly burnt. She named over to herself the five golden objects standing at the points: the Arrow of Truth, kinked from Fafhrd's tugging of it from the demoness; the Rule of Prudence, a short rod circled by ridges; the Cup of Measured Hospitality, hardly larger than a thimble; the Circles of Unity, so linked that if any one were taken away, the other two fell apart; and the strange skeletal globe that Fafhrd had recovered with the rest and suggested might be the Cube of Square-Dealing smoothly deformed (something she rather doubted). She took the Mouser doll from her pouch and laid it in their midst, at pentalpha's center. She sighed with relief, sat down on one of the three stools there were, and gazed pensively at the doll's blank face.

9

As the Mouser approved the last cask's double lashings and
then dismissed as curtly his still-baffled lieutenants and their
weary work gang—fairly drove 'em from his cabin!—he felt
a surge of power inside, as if he'd just stepped or been
otherwise carried over an invisible boundary into a realm
where each last object was plainly labeled "Mine Alone!"

Ah, that had been sport of the best, he told himself—
closely supervising the gang's toil while standing all the while
in their midst atop the draped chest he'd had them hunting all
day long, and while the girl Ississi lay naked and securely
spread-eagled beneath the blanket spread across his bunk—
and they all somehow conscious of her delectable presence
yet never quite daring to refer to it. Power sport indeed!

In a transport of self-satisfaction he whipped the drape
from the chest, threw back its top, and admired the expanse
of coppery silk so revealed and the bolts of black ribbon.
Now *there* was a bed fit for a princess's nuptials, he told
himself as he filled and downed a brass cup of brandy, a
couch somewhat small, but sufficient and soft all the way
down to the bottom.

His mind and his feet both dancing with all manner of
imaginings and impulses, he moved to the bunk and whirled
off its coverings and—

The bunk's coarse gray single sheeting was covered by a
veritable black snow-sprinkle of ribbon scraps and shreds. Of
Ississi there was no sign.

After a long moment's searching of it with his astounded
eyes, he fairly dove across the bunk and fumbled frantically
all the way around the thin mattress's edges and under them,
searching for the razor-keen knife or scissors that had done
this or (who knew?) some sharp-toothed, ribbon-shredding
small animal secretly attendant on the girl whore and obedient
to her command.

A trilling sigh of blissful contentment made him switch
convulsively around. In the midst of the new-opened chest,
got there by sleights he could scarce dream of, Ississi sat
cross-legged facing him. Her arms were lifted while her

nimble hands were swiftly braiding her long straight silvery hair, an action which showed off her slender waist and dainty small breasts to best advantage, while her green eyes flashed and her lips smiled at him, ''Am I not exceedingly clever? Surpassingly clever and wholly delightful?''

The Mouser frowned at her terribly, then sent the same expression roving to either side, as if spying for a route by which she could have got unseen from bunk to chest past the double-lashed and closely abutting casks—and mayhap for her confederates, animal, human, or demonic. Next he got off the bunk and, approaching her, edged his way around the chest and back, eyeing her up and down as though searching for concealed weapons, even so little as a sharpened fingernail, and turning his own body so that his frown was always fixed on her and he never lost sight of her for an instant, until he faced her once more.

His nostrils flared with his deep breathing, while the lamp's yellow beams and shadows swayed measuredly across his dark angry presence and her moon-pale skin.

She continued to braid her hair and to smile and to warble and trill, and after a short while her trillings and warblings became a sort of rough song of recitation, one shot with seeming improvisations, as though she were translating it into Low Lankhmarese from another language:

''Oh, the golden gifts of my land are six, And round you now they're straitly fixed. The Golden Shaft of Death and Desire, The Rod of Command whose smart's like fire, The Cup of Close Confinement and Minding, The Circles of Fate whose ways are winding. The Cubical Prison of god and of elf, The Many-Barred Globe of Simorgya and Self. Deep, oh deep is my far country, Where gold will carry us, me and thee.''

The Mouser shook his finger before her face in dark challenge and dire warning. Then he slashed lengths of ribbed black silk ribbon from a roll, twisting and tugging it to test its strength, continuing to eye her all the while, and he bound her legs together as they were, slender ankle to calf, just below the knee, and slender calf to ankle. Then he held out his hand for hers imperiously. She rapidly finished plaiting her hair, whipped the braid round her head and tucked it in, so that it became a sort of silvery coronet. Then with a sigh and a

turning away of her somewhat narrow face, she held out her
wrists to him close together, the palms of her hands upward.

He seized them contemptuously and drew them behind her
and bound them there, as he had on the previous night, and
her elbows too, drawing her shoulders backward. And then he
tipped her over forward so that her face was buried in the
coppery silk intended for Cif (how long ago?) and led a
double ribbon from her bound wrists down her spine to her
crosswise-bound lower legs, and drew it tight as he could, so
that her back was perforce arched and her face lifted free of
the silk.

But despite his mounting excitement, the thought nagged
him that there had been something in her warbled ditty
which he had not liked. Ah yes, the mention of Simorgya.
What place had that sunken kingdom in a whore's never-
never lands? And all her earlier babble of moist and watery
influences in the imagined land where she queened, or rather
princessed it— There, she was at it again!

"Come, Brother Mordroog, to royally escort us," she
warbled over the orangy silk, seemingly unmindful of her
acute discomforts. "Come with our guardians, Deep Rusher
your horse—your behemoth, rather, and you in his castle.
Come also with Slasher and vasty All-Gripper, to shatter our
prison and ferry us home. And send all your spirits coursing
before you, so our minds are engulfed—"

The shadows steadied unnaturally as the lamp's swing
shortened quiveringly, then stopped.

On the deck immediately above their heads there was consternation. The wind had unaccountably faded and the sea
grown oily calm. The tiller in Skor's grip was lifeless, the
sheet that Mikkidu fingered slack. The sky did not appear to
be overcast, yet there was a shadowed, spectral quality to the
sunlight, as though an unpredicted eclipse or other ominous
event impended. Then without warning the dark sea mounded
up boiling scarce a spear's cast off steerside—and subsided
again without any diminishment in the feeling of foreboding.
The spreading wave jogged *Seahawk*. The two lieutenants and
Ourph stared about wonderingly and then at each other. None
of them marked the trail of bubbles leading from the place of
the mounding toward the becalmed sailing galley.

10

In the treasury Cif had the sudden feeling that the Mouser stood in need of more protection. The doll looked lonely there at pentagram's center. Perhaps he was too far from the ikons. She gathered the ikons together and after a moment's hesitation thrust the doll, doubled up, into the barred globe. Then she poked the ruler and the crooked arrow in along with him, transfixing the globe (more gold close to him!), almost as an afterthought clapped the tiny cup like a helmet on the protruding doll's head, and set all down on the linked rings. Then she seated herself again, staring doubtfully at what she had done.

11

In the cabin the Gray Mouser rolled the bound Ississi over on her back and regarded the silvery girl opened up for his enjoyment. The blood pounded in his head and he felt an increasing pressure there, as if his brain had grown too large for his skull. The motionless cabin grew spectral, there was a sense of thronging presences, and then it was as if part of him only remained there while another part whirled away into a realm where he was a giant coursing through rushing darkness, uncertain of his humanity, while the pressure inside his skull grew and grew.

But the part of him in the cabin still was capable of sensation, though hardly of action, and this one watched helpless and aghast, through air that seemed to thicken and become more like water, the silvery, smiling, trussed-up

Ississi writhe and writhe yet again while her skin grew more
silvery still—scaly silvery—and her elfin face narrowed and
her green eyes swam apart, while from her head and back
and shoulders, and along the backs of her legs and her
hands and arms, razor-sharp spines erected themselves in
crests and, as she writhed once more again mightily, cut
through all the black ribbons at once so they floated in shreds
about her. Then through the curtained hatchway there swam a
face like her own new one, and she came up from the coppery
silk in a great forward undulation and reached the palms of
her back-crested hands out toward the Mouser's cheeks lovingly on arms that seemed to grow longer and longer, saying
in a strange deep voice that seemed to bubble from her, "In
moments this prison will be broken, Deep Rusher will smash
it, and we will be free."

At those words the other part of the Mouser realized that
the darkness through which he was now coursing upward was
the deep sea, that he was engulfed in the whale-body and great-
foreheaded brain of Deep Rusher, her monster, that it was the
tiny hull of *Seahawk* far above him that his massive forehead
was aimed at, and that he could no more evade that collision
than his other self in the cabin could avoid the arms of Ississi.

12

In the treasury Cif could not bear the woeful expression with
which the blank linen face of the doll appeared to gaze out at
her from under the jammed-down golden helmet, nor the
sudden thought that the sea demoness had recently fondled all
that gold hemming in the doll. She grabbed it up with its
prison, withdrew it from the barred globe and snatched off its
helmet, and while the ikons chinked down on the table she
clutched the stuffed cloth to her bosom and bent her lips to it
and cherished and kissed it, breathing it words of endearment.

13

In the cabin the Mouser was able to dodge aside from those questing silvery spined hands, which went past him, while in the dark realm his giant self was able to veer aside from *Seahawk*'s hull at the last moment and burst out of the darkness, so that his two selves were one again and both back in the cabin—which now lurched as though *Seahawk* were capsizing.

On deck all gaped, flinching, as a black shape thicker than *Seahawk* burst resoundingly from the dark water beside them, so close the ship's hull shook and they might have reached out and touched the monster. The shape erected itself like a windowless tower built all of streaming black boot leather, down which sheets of water cascaded. It shot up higher and higher, dragging their gazes skyward, then it narrowed and with a sweep of its great flukes left the water altogether, and for a long moment they watched the dark dripping underbelly of black leviathan pass over *Seahawk,* vast as a storm cloud, lacking lightning perhaps but not thunder, as he breached entire from the ocean. But then they were all snatching for handholds as *Seahawk* lurched down violently sideways, as though trying to shake them from her back. At least there was no shortage of lashings to grab onto as she slid with the collapsing waters into the great chasm left by leviathan. There came the numbing shock of that same beast smiting the sea beyond them as he returned to his element. Then salt ocean closed over them as they sank down, down, and down.

Afterward the Mouser could never determine how much of what next happened in the cabin transpired underwater and how much in a great bubble of air constrained by that other element so that it became more akin to it. (No question, he was wholly underwater toward the end.) There was a somewhat slow or, rather, measured dreamlike quality to all subsequent movements there—his, the transformed Ississi's, and

the creature he took to be her brother—as if they were made
against great pressures. It had elements both of a savage
struggle—a fierce, life-and-death fight—and of a ceremonial
dance with beasts. Certainly his position during it was always
in the center, beside or a little above the open chest of
fabrics, and certainly the transformed Ississi and her brother
circled him like sharks and darted in alternately to attack,
their narrow jaws gaping to show razorlike teeth and closing
like great scissors snipping. And always there was that sense
of steadily increasing pressure, though not now within his
skull particularly, but over his entire body and centering, if
anywhere, upon his lungs.

It began, of course, with his evading of Ississi's initial
loving and murderous lunge at him, and his moving past her
to the chest she had just quitted. Then, as she turned back to
assault him a second time (all jaws now, arms merged into
her silver-scaled sides and her crested legs merged, but eyes
still great and green), and as he, in turn, turned to oppose her,
he was inspired to grab up with both hands from the chest the
topmost fabric and, letting it unfold sequentially and spread
as he did so, whirl it between him and her in a great lustrous,
baffling coppery sheet, or pale rosy-orange cloud. And she
was indeed distracted from her main purpose by this timely
interposition, although her silvery jaws came through it more
than once, shredding and shearing and altogether making
sorry work of Cif's intended cloak or dress of state or treasurer's robes, or whatever.

Then, as the Mouser completed his whirling turn, he found
himself confronting the in-rushing silver-crested Mordroog,
and to hold *him* off snatched up and whirlingly interposed the
next rich silken fabric in the chest, which happened to be a
violet one, his reluctant gift for Afreyt, so now it became a
great pale purple cloud-wall soon slashed to lavender streaks
and streamers, through which Mordroog's silver and jaw-
snapping visage showed like a monstrous moon.

This maneuver brought the Mouser back in turn to face
Ississi, who was closing in again through coppery shreds, and
this attack was in turn thwarted by the extensive billowing-out
of a sheet of bold scarlet silk, which he had meant to present
to the capable whore-turned-fisherwoman Hilsa, but now was

as effectively reduced to scraps and tatters as any incarna-
dined sunset is by conquering night.

And so it went, each charming or at least clever fabric gift
in turn sacrificed—brassy yellow satin for Hilsa's comrade
Rill, a rich brown worked with gold for Fafhrd, lovely sea-
green and salmon pink sheets (also for Cif), a sky blue one
(still another for Afreyt—to appease Fafhrd), a royal purple
one for Pshawri (in honor of his first lieutenancy), and even
one for Groniger (soberest black)—but each sheet successively defeating a dire attack by silvery sea demon or demoness, until the cabin had been filled with a most expensive sort
of confetti and the bottom of the chest had been reached.

But by then, mercifully, the demonic attacks had begun to
lessen in speed and fury, grow weaker and weaker, until they
were but surly and almost aimless switchings-about (even
floppings-about, like those of fish dying), while (most
mercifully—almost miraculously) the dreadful suffocating pressure, instead of increasing or even holding steady, had started
to fall off, to lessen, and now was continuing to do so, more
and more swiftly.

What had happened was that when *Seahawk* had slid into
the hole left by leviathan, the lead in her keel (which made
her seaworthy) had tended to drag her down still farther,
abetted by the mass of her great cargo, especially the bronze
ingots and copper sheetings in it. But on the other hand, the
greater part of her cargo by far consisted of items that were
lighter than water—the long stack of dry, well seasoned
timber, the tight barrels of flour, and the woollen sacks of
grain, all of these additionally having considerable amounts
of air trapped in them (the timber by virtue of the tarred
canvas sheathing it, the grain because of the greasy raw wool
of the sacks, so they acted as so many floats). So long as
these items were above the water they tended to press the ship
more deeply into it, but once they were underwater, their
effect was to drag *Seahawk* upward, toward the surface.

Now under ordinary conditions of stowage—safe, adequate
stowage, even—all these items might well have broken loose
and floated up to the surface individually, the timber stack
emerging like a great disintegrating raft, the sacks bobbing up
like so many balloons, while *Seahawk* continued on down to

watery grave carrying along with it those trapped below decks
and any desperately clinging seamen too shocked and terror-
frozen to loosen their panic-grips.

But the imaginative planning and finicky overseeing the
Mouser had given the stowage of the cargo at 'Brulsk, so that
Fafhrd or Cif or (Mog forbid!) Skor should never have cause
to criticize him, and also in line with his determination, now
he had taken up merchanting, to be the cleverest and most
foresighted merchant of them all, taken in conjunction with
the mildly sadistic fury with which he had driven the men at
their stowage work, insured that the wedgings and lashings-
down of this cargo were something exceptional. And then
when, earlier today and seemingly on an insane whim, he had
insisted that all those more-than-adequate lashings be doubled,
and then driven the men to that work with even greater fury,
he had unknowingly guaranteed *Seahawk*'s survival.

To be sure, the lashings were strained, they creaked and
boomed underwater (they were lifting a whole sailing galley),
but not a single one of them parted, not a single air-swollen
sack escaped before *Seahawk* reached the surface.

14

And so it was that the Mouser was able to swim through the
hatchway and see untained blue sky again and blessedly fill
his lungs with their proper element and weakly congratulate
Mikkidu and a Mingol paddling and gasping beside him on
their most fortunate escape. True, *Seahawk* was water-filled
and awash, but she floated upright, her tall mast and bedrag-
gled sail were intact, the sea was calm and windless still, and
(as was soon determined) her entire crew had survived, so the
Mouser knew there was no insurmountable obstacle in the
way of their clearing her of water first by bailing, then by
pumping (the oarholes could be plugged, if need be), and

continuing their voyage. And if in the course of that clearing, a few fish, even a couple of big ones, should flop overside after a desultory snap or two (best be wary of all fish!) and then dive deep into *their* proper element and return to their own rightful kingdom—why, that was all in the Nehwonian nature of things.

15

A fortnight later, being a week after *Seahawk*'s safe arrival in Salthaven, Fafhrd and Afreyt rented the Sea Wrack and gave Captain Mouser and his crew a party, which Cif and the Mouser had to help pay for from the profits of the latter's trading voyage. To it were invited numerous Isler friends. It coincided with the year's first blizzard, for the winter gales had held off and been providentially late coming. No matter, the salty tavern was snug and the food and drink all that could be asked for—with perhaps one exception.

"There was a faint taste of wool fat in the fruit soup," Hilsa observed. "Nothing particularly unpleasant, but noticeable."

"That'll have been from the grease in the sacking," Mikkidu enlightened her, "which kept the salt sea out of 'em, so they buoyed us up powerfully when we sank. Captain Mouser thinks of everything."

"Just the same," Skor reminded him sotto voce, "it turned out he did have a girl in the cabin all the while—and that damned chest of fabrics too! You can't deny he's a great liar whenever he chooses."

"Ah, but the girl turned out to be a sea demon, and he needed the fabrics to defend himself from her, and that makes all the difference," Mikkidu rejoined loyally.

"I never saw her as aught but a ghostly and silver-crested sea demon," old Ourph put in. "The first night out from

No-Ombrulsk I saw her rise from the cabin through the deck and stand at the taffrail, invoking and communing with sea monsters.''

"Why didn't you report that to the Mouser?'' Fafhrd asked, gesturing toward the venerable Mingol with his new bronze hook.

"One never speaks of a ghost in its presence," the latter explained, "or while there is chance of its reappearance. It only gives it strength. As always, silence is silver.''

"Yes, and speech is golden," Fafhrd maintained.

Rill boldly asked the Mouser across the table, "But just how did you deal with the sea demoness while she was in her girl-guise? I gather you kept her tied up a lot, or tried to?''

"Yes," Cif put in from beside him. "You were even planning at one point to train her to be a maid for me, weren't you?'' She smiled curiously. "Just think, I lost that as well as those lovely materials.''

"I attempted a number of things that were rather beyond my powers," the Gray One admitted manfully, the edges of his ears turning red. "Actually, I was lucky to escape with my life.'' He turned toward Cif. "Which I couldn't have done if you hadn't snatched me from the tainted gold in the nick of time.''

"Never mind, it was I put you amongst the tainted gold in the first place," she told him, laying her hand on his on the table, "but now it's been hopefully purified.'' (She had directed that ceremony of exorcism of the ikons herself, with the assistance of Mother Grum, to free them of all baleful Simorgyan influence got from their handling by the demoness. The old witch was somewhat dubious of the complete efficacy of the ceremony.)

Later Skor described leviathan arching over *Seahawk*. Afreyt nodded appreciatively, saying, "I was once in a dory when a whale breached close alongside. It is not a sight to be forgotten.''

"Nor is it when viewed from the other side of the gunnel," the Mouser observed reflectively. Then he winced. "Mog, what a head thump that would have been!''

III

---·✦·---

The Curse of the Smalls
and the Stars

1

Late one nippy afternoon of early Rime Isle spring, Fafhrd
and the Gray Mouser slumped pleasantly in a small booth in
Salthaven's Sea Wrack Tavern. Although they'd been on the
Isle for only a year, and patronizing this tavern for an eight-
month, the booth was recognized as *theirs* when either was in
the place. Both men had been mildly fatigued, the former
from supervising bottom repairs to *Seahawk* at the new moon's
low tide—and then squeezing in a late round of archery
practice, the latter from bossing the carpentering of their new
warehouse-and-barracks—and doing some inventorying besides. But their second tankards of bitter ale had about taken
care of that, and their thoughts were beginning to float free.

Around them they heard the livening talk of other recuperating laborers. At the bar they could see three of their lieuten-

ants grousing together—Fafhrd-tall Skor, and the somewhat
reformed small thieves Pshawri and Mikkidu. Behind it the
keeper lit two thick wicks as the light dimmed as the sun set
outside.

Frowning as he pared a thumbnail with razor-keen Cat's
Claw, the Mouser said, "I am minded of how scarce seven-
teen moons gone we sat just so in Silver Eel Tavern in
Lankhmar, deeming Rime Isle a legend. Yet here we are."

"Lankhmar," Fafhrd mused, drawing a wet circle with the
firmly socketed iron hook that had become his left hand after
the day's bow bending, "I've heard somewhere of such a
city, I do believe. 'Tis strange how oftentimes our thoughts
do chime together, as if we were sundered halves of some
past being, but whether hero or demon, wastrel or philoso-
pher, harder to say."

"Demon, I'd say," the Mouser answered instantly, "a
demon warrior. We've guessed at him before. Remember?
We decided he always growled in battle. Perhaps a were-bear."

After a small chuckle at that, Fafhrd went on, "But then
(that night twelve moons gone and five in Lankhmar) we'd
had twelve tankards each of bitter instead of two, I ween,
yes, and lacing them too with brandy, you can bet—hardly to
be accounted best judges twixt phantasm and the veritable.
Yes, and didn't two heroines from this fabled isle next moment stride into the Eel, as real as boots?"

Almost as if the Northerner hadn't answered, the small,
gray-smocked, gray stockinged man continued in the same
thoughtful reminiscent tones as he'd first used, "And you,
liquored to the gills—agreed on that!—were ranting dolefully
about how you dearly wanted work, land, office, sons, other
responsibilities, and e'en a wife!"

"Yes, and didn't I get one?" Fafhrd demanded. "You too,
you equally then-drunken destiny-ungrateful lout!" His eyes
grew thoughtful also. He added, "Though perhaps comrade
or co-mate were the better word—or even those plus partner."

"Much better all three," the Mouser agreed shortly. "As
for those other goods your drunken heart was set upon—no
disagreement there!—we've got enough of those to stuff a
hog!—except, of course, far as I know, for sons. Unless,

that is, you count our men as our grown-up unweaned babes, which sometimes I'm inclined to.''

Fafhrd, who'd been leaning his head out of the booth to look toward the darkening doorway during the latter part of the Mouser's plaints, now stood up, saying, "Speaking of them, shall we join the ladies? Cif and Afreyt's booth 'pears to be larger than ours.''

"To be sure. What else?'' the Mouser replied, rising springily. Then, in a lower voice, "Tell me, did the two of them just now come in? Or did we blunder blindly by them when we entered, sightless of all save thirst quench?''

Fafhrd shrugged, displaying his palm. "Who knows? Who cares?''

"*They* might,'' the other answered.

2

Many Lankhmar leagues east and south, and so in darkest moonless night, the archmagus Ningauble conferred with the sorceress Sheelba at the edge of the Great Salt Marsh. The seven luminous eyes of the former wove many greenish patterns within his gaping hood as he leaned his quaking bulk perilously downward from the howdah on the broad back of the forward-kneeling elephant which had borne him from his desert cave, across the Sinking Land through all adverse influences, to this appointed spot. While the latter's eyeless face strained upward likewise as she stood tall in the doorway of her small hut, which had traveled from the Marsh's noxious center to the same dismal verge on its three long rickety (but now rigid) chicken legs. The two wizards strove mightily to outshout (outbellow or outscreech) the nameless cosmic din (inaudible to human ears) which had hitherto hindered and foiled all their earlier efforts to communicate over greater distances. And now, at last, they strove successfully!

Ningauble wheezed, "I have discovered by certain infallible signs that the present tumult in realms magical, botching my spells, is due to the vanishment from Lankhmar of my servitor and sometimes student, Fafhrd the barbarian. All magics dim without his credulous and kindly audience, while high quests fail lacking his romantical and custard-headed idealisms."

Sheelba shot back through the murk, "While I have ascertained that my illspells suffer equally because the Mouser's gone with him, my protégé and surly errand boy. They will not work without the juice of his brooding and overbearing malignity. He must be summoned from that ridiculous rimplace of Rime Isle, and Fafhrd with him!"

"But how to do that when our spells won't carry? What servitor to trust with such a mission to go and fetch 'em? I know of a young demoness might undertake it, but she's in thrall to Khahkht, wizard of power in that frosty area—and he's inimical to both of us. Or should the two of us search out in noisy spirit realm to be our messenger that putative warlike ascendant of theirs and whilom forebear known as the Growler? A dismal task! Where'er I look I see naught but uncertainties and obstacles—"

"I shall send word of their whereabouts to Mog the spider god, the Gray One's tutelary deity!—this din won't hinder prayers," Sheelba interrupted in a harsh, clipped voice. The presence of the vacillating and loquacious over-sighted wizard, who saw seven sides to every question, always roused her to her best efforts. "Send you like advisors to Fafhrd's gods, stone-age brute Kos and the fastidious cripple Issek. Soon as they know where their lapsed worshippers are, they'll put such curses and damnations on them as shall bring them back squealing to us to have those taken off."

"Now why didn't I think of that?" Ningauble protested, who was indeed sometimes called the Gossiper of the Gods. "To work! To work!"

3

In paradisiacal Godsland, which lies at the antipodes of Neh-won's death pole and Shadowland, in the southernmost reach of that world's southernmost continent, distanced and guarded from the tumultuous northern lands by the Great eastward-rushing Equatorial Current (where some say swim the stars), sub-equatorial deserts, and the Rampart Mountains, the gods Kos, Issek, and Mog sat somewhat apart from the mass of more couth and civilized Nehwonian deities, who objected to Kos' lice, fleas, and crabs, and a little to Issek's effeminacy—though Mog had contacts among these, as he sarcastically called 'em, "higher beings."

Sunk in divine somnolent broodings, not to say almost death-like trances, for prayers, petitions, and even blasphemous name-takings had been scanty of late, the three mismatched godlings reacted at once and enthusiastically to the instantaneously-transmitted wizard missives.

"Those two ungodly swording rogues!" Mog hissed softly, his long thin lips stretched slantwise in a half spider grin. "The very thing! Here's work for all of us, my heavenly peers. A chance to curse again and to bedevil."

"A glad inspiro that, indeed, indeed!' Issek chimed, waving his limp-wristed hands excitedly. "*I* should have thought of that!—our chiefest lapsed worshippers, hidden away in frosty and forgotten far Rime Isle, farther away than Shadowland itself, *almost* beyond our hearing and our might. Such infant cunning! Oh, but we'll make them pay!"

"The ingrate dogs!" Kos grated through his thick and populous black beard. "Not only casting us off, their natural heavenly fathers and rightful da's, but forsaking *all* decent Nehwonian deities and running with atheist men and gone a-whoring after stranger gods beyond the pale! Yes, by my lights and spleen, we'll make 'em suffer! Where's my spiked mace?"

(On occasion Mog and Issek had been known to have to hold Kos down to keep him from rushing ill-advised out of Godsland to seek to visit personal dooms upon his more disobedient and farther-strayed worshippers.)

"What say we set their women against them, as we did last time?" Issek urged twitteringly. "Women have power over men almost as great as gods do."

Mog shook his humanoid cephalothorax. "Our boys are too coarse-tasted. Did we estrange from them Afreyt and Cif, they'd doubtless fall back on amorous arrangements with the Salthaven harlots Rill and Hilsa—and so on and so on." Now that his attention had been called to Rime Isle, he had easy knowledge of all overt things there—a divine prerogative. "No, not the women this time, I ween."

"A pox on all such subtleties!" Kos roared. "I want tortures for 'em! Let's visit on 'em the strangling cough, the prick-rot, and the Bloody Melts!"

"Nor can we risk wiping them out entirely," Mog answered swiftly. "We haven't worshippers to spare for that, you fire-eater, as you well know. Thrift, thrift! Moreover, as you should also know, a threat is always more dreadful than its execution. I propose we subject them to some of the moods and preoccupations of old age and of old age's bosom comrade, inseparable though invisible-seeming—Death himself! Or is that too mild a fear and torment, thinkest thou?"

"I'll say not," Kos agreed, suddenly sober. "I know that it scares *me*. What if the gods should die? A hellish thought."

"That infant bugaboo!" Issek told him peevishly. Then turning to Mog with quickening interest, "So, if I read you right, old Arach, let's narrow your silky Mouser's interests in and in from the adventure-beckoning horizon to the things closest around him: the bed table, the dinner board, the privy, and the kitchen sink. Not the far-leaping highway, but the gutter. Not the ocean, but the puddle. Not the grand view outside, but the bleared windowpane. Not the thunder-blast, but the knuckle crack—or ear-pop."

Mog narrowed his eight eyes happily. "And for your Fafhrd, I would suggest a different old-age curse, to drive a wedge between them so they can't understand or help each other that we put a geas upon him to count the stars. His interests in all else will fade and fail; he'll have mind only for those tiny lights in the sky.''

"So that, with his head in the clouds," Issek pictured, catching on quick, "he'll stumble and bruise himself again and again, and miss all opportunities of earthly delights.''

"Yes, and make him memorize their names and all their patterns!" Kos put in. "There's busy-work for an eternity. I never could abide the things myself. There's such a senseless mess of stars, like flies or fleas. An insult to the gods to say that we created them!"

"And then, when those two have sufficiently humbled themselves to us and done suitable penance," Issek purred, "we will consider taking off or ameliorating their curses.''

"I say, leave 'em on always," Kos argued. "No leniency. Eternal damnation!—that's the stuff!"

"That question can be decided when it arises," Mog opined. "Come, gentlemen, to work! We've some damnations to devise in detail and deliver.''

4

Back at the Sea Wrack Tavern, Fafhrd and the Gray Mouser had, despite the latter's apprehensions, been invited to join with and buy a round of bitter ale for their lady-friends Afreyt and Cif, leading and sometimes office-holding citizens of Rime Isle, spinster-matriarchs of otherwise scionless dwindling old families in that strange republic, and Fafhrd's and the Mouser's partners and co-adventurers of a good year's standing in questing, business, and (this last more recently) bed. The questing part had consisted of the almost bloodless routing from the Isle of an invading naval force of maniacal Sea-Mingols, with the help of twelve tall berserks and twelve small warrior-thieves the two heroes had brought with them, and the dubious assistance of the two universes-wandering hobo gods Odin and Loki, and (minor quest) a small expedition to recover certain civic treasures of the Isle, a set of gold artifacts called the Ikons of Reason. And they had been *hired* to do these things by Cif and Afreyt, so business had been mixed with questing in their relationship from the very start. Other business had been a merchant venture of the Mouser (Captain Mouser for this purpose) in Fafhrd's galley *Seahawk* with a mixed crew of berserks and thieves, and goods supplied by the ladies, to the oft frozen port of No-Ombrulsk on Nehwon mainland—that and various odd jobs done by their men and by the women and girls employed by and owing fealty to Cif and Afreyt.

As for the bed part, both couples, though not yet middle-aged, at least in looks, were veterans of amorous goings-on, wary and courteous in all such doings, entering upon any new relationships, including these, with a minimum of commitment and a maximum of reservations. Ever since the tragic deaths of their first loves, Fafhrd's and the Mouser's erotic solacing had mostly come from a very odd lot of hard-bitten if beauteous slave-girls, vagabond hoydens, and demonic princesses, folk easily come by if at all and even more easily lost, accidents rather than goals of their weird adventurings; both sensed that anything with the Rime Isle ladies would have to be a little more serious at least. While Afreyt's and Cif's love-adventures had been equally transient, either with unromantic and hard-headed Rime Islanders, who are atheistical realists even in youth, or with sea-wanderers, of one sort or another, come like the rain—or thunder-squall—and as swiftly gone.

All this being considered, things did seem to be working out quite well for the two couples in the bed area.

And, truth to tell, this was a greater satisfaction and relief to the Mouser and Fafhrd than either would admit even to himself. For each was indeed beginning to find extended questing a mite tiring, especially ones like this last which, rather than being one of their usual lone-wolf forays, involved the recruitment and command of other men and the taking on of larger and divided responsibilities. It was natural for them, after such exertions, to feel that a little rest and quiet enjoyment was now owed them, a little surcease from the batterings of fate and chance and new desire. And, truth to tell, the ladies Cif and Afreyt were on the verge of admitting in their secretest hearts something of the same feelings.

So all four of them found it pleasant during this particular Rime Isle twilight to take a little bitter ale together and chat of this day's doings and tomorrow's plans and reminisce about their turning of the Mingols and ask each other gentle questions about the times before they'd all four met—and each flirt privily and cautiously with the notion that each now had two or three persons on whom they might always rely fully, rather than one like-sexed comrade only.

During the course of this gossiping Fafhrd mentioned again his and the Mouser's fantasy that they were halves—or perhaps lesser fractions, fragments only—of some noted or notorious past being, explaining why their thoughts so often chimed together.

"That's odd," Cif interjected, "for Afreyt and I have had like notion and for like reason: that she and I were spirit-halves of the great Rimish witch-queen Skeldir, who held off the Simorgyans again and again in ancient times when that island boasted an empire and was above the waves instead of under them. What was your hero's name—or mighty rogue's? —if that likes you better."

"I know not, lady, perhaps he lived in times too primitive for names, when man and beast were closer. He was identified by his battle growling—a leonine cough deep in the throat whene'er he entered an encounter."

"Another like point!" Cif noted. "Queen Skeldir announced her presence by a short dry laugh—her invariable utterance when facing dangers, especially those of a sort to astound and confound the bravest."

"Gusorio's my name for our beastish forebear," the Mouser threw in. "I know not what Fafhrd thinks. Great Gusorio. Gusorio the Growler."

"Now he begins to sound like an animal," Afreyt broke in. "Tell me, have you ever been granted vision or dream of this Gusorio, or heard perhaps in darkest night his battle growl?"

But the Mouser was studying the dinted table top. He bent his head as his gaze traveled across it.

"No, milady," Fafhrd answered for his abstracted comrade. "At least not I. It's something we heard of a witch or fortune-teller, figment, not fact. Have you ever heard Queen Skeldir's short dry laugh, or had sight of that fabled warrior sorceress?"

"Neither I nor Cif," Afreyt admitted, "though she is in the Isle's history parchments."

But even as she answered him, Fafhrd's questioning gaze strayed past her. She looked behind and saw the Sea Wrack's open doorway and the gathering night.

Cif stood up. "So it's agreed we dine at Afreyt's in a half hour's time?"

The two men nodded somewhat abstractedly. Fafhrd leaned his head to the right as he continued to stare past Afreyt, who with a smile obligingly shifted hers in the opposite direction.

The Mouser leaned back and bent his head a little more as his gaze trailed down from the tabletop to its leg.

Fafhrd observed, "Astarion sets soon after the sun these nights. There's little time to observe her."

"God forbid I should stand in the evening star's way," Afreyt murmured humorously as she too arose. "Come, cousin."

The Mouser left off watching the cockroach as it reached the floor. It had limped interestingly, lacking a mid leg. He and Fafhrd drank off their bitters, then slowly followed their ladies out and down the narrow street, the one's eyes thoughtfully delving in the gutter, as if there might be treasure there, the other's roving the sky as the stars winked on, naming those he knew and numbering, by altitude and direction, those he didn't.

5

Their work well launched, Sheelba retired to Marsh center and Ningauble toward his cavern, the understorm abating, a good omen. While the three gods smiled, invigorated by their cursing. The slum corner of Heaven they occupied now seemed less chilly to Issek and less sweatily enervating to Kos, while Mog's devious mind spider stepped down more pleasant channels.

Yes, the seed was well planted, and left to germinate in silence, might have developed as intended, but some gods, and some sorcerers too, cannot resist boasting and gossiping, and so by way of talkative priests and midwives and vagabonds, word of what was intended came to the ears of the mighty, including two who considered themselves well rid of Fafhrd and the Mouser and did not want them back in Lankhmar at all. And the mighty are great worriers and spend much time preventing anything that troubles their peace of mind.

And so it was that Pulgh Arthonax, penurious and perverse overlord of Lankhmar, who hated heroes of all description—but especially fair-complected big ones like Fafhrd—and Hamomel, thrifty and ruthless grand master of the Thieves Guild there, who detested the Mouser generally as a freelance competitor and particularly as one who had lured twelve promising apprentices away from the Guild to be his henchmen—these two took counsel together and commissioned the Assassins Order, an elite within the Slayers' Brotherhood, to dispatch the Twain in Rime Isle before they should point toe toward Lankhmar. And because Arth-Pulgh and Hamomel were both most miserly magnates and insatiably greedy withal, they beat down the Order's price as far as they could and made it a condition of the commission that three fourths of any portable booty found on or near the doomed Twain be returned to them as their lawful share.

So the Order drew up death warrants, chose by lot two of

its currently unoccupied fellows, and in solemn secret ceremony attended only by the Master and the Recorder, divested
these of their identities and rechristened them the Death of
Fafhrd and the Death of the Gray Mouser, by which names
only they should henceforth be known to each other and
within the profession until the death warrants were served and
their commissions fulfilled.

6

Next day repairs to *Seahawk* continued, the low tide repeating, Witches Moon being only one day old. During a late
morning break Fafhrd moved apart from his men a little and
scanned the high bright sky toward north and east, his gaze
ranging. Skor ventured to follow him across the wet sand and
copy his peerings. He saw nothing in the gray-blue heavens,
but experience had taught him his captain had exceptionally
keen eyesight.

"Sea eagles?" he asked softly.

Fafhrd looked at him thoughtfully, then smiled, shaking his
head, and confided, "I was imagining which stars would be
there, were it now night."

Skor's forehead wrinkled puzzledly. "Stars by day?"

Fafhrd nodded. "Yes. Where think *you* the stars are by
day?"

"Gone," Skor answered, his forehead clearing. "They go
away at dawn and return at evening. Their lights are
extinguished—like winter campfires! for surely it must be
cold where the stars are, higher than mountaintops. Until the
sun comes out to warm up things, of course."

Fafhrd shook his head. "The stars march west across the
sky each night in the same formations which we recognize
year after year, dozen years after dozen, and I would guess
gross after gross. They do not skitter for the horizon when

day breaks or seek out lairs and earth holes, but go on
marching with the sun's glare hiding their lights—under cover
of day, one might express it.''

"Stars shining by day?" Skor questioned, doing a fair job
of hiding his surprise and bafflement. Then he caught Fafhrd's
drift, or thought he did, and a certain wonder appeared in his
eyes. He knew his captain was a good general who made a
fetish of keeping track of the enemy's position especially in
terrain affording concealment, as forest on land or fog at sea.
So by his very nature his captain had applied the same rule to
the stars and studied 'em as closely as he'd traced the movements of the Mingol scouts fleeing across Rime Isle.

Though it was strange thinking of the stars as enemies. His
captain was a deep one! Perhaps he did have foes among the
stars. Skor had heard rumor that he'd bedded a queen of the
air.

7

That night as the Gray Mouser and Cif leisurely prepared for
bed in her low-eaved house tinted a sooty red on the north-
western edge of Salthaven City, and whilst that lady busied
herself at her mirrored dressing table, the Mouser himself
sitting on bed's edge set his pouch upon a low bedside table
and withdrew from it a curious lot of commonplace objects—
curious in part because they were so commonplace—and
arranged them in a line on the table's dark surface.

Cif, made curious by the slow regularity of his movements
she saw reflected cloudily in the sheets of silver she faced,
took up a small flat black box and came over and sat herself
beside him.

The objects included a toothed small wooden wheel as big
almost as a Sarheenmar dollar with two of the teeth missing,
a finch's feather, three lookalike gray round pebbles, a scrap

of blue wool cloth stiff with dirt, a bent wrought-iron nail, a hazelnut, and a dinted small black round that might have been a Lankhmar *tik* or Eastern halfpenny.

Cif ran her eye along them, then looked at him questioningly.

He said, "Coming here from the barracks at first eve, a strange mood seized me. Low in the sunset glow the new moon's faintest and daintiest silver crescent had just materialized like the ghost of a young girl—and just in the direction of this house, at that, as though to signal your presence here—but somehow I had eyes only for the gutter and the pathside. Which is where I found those. And a remarkable lot they are for a small northern seaport. You'd think Ilthmar at least . . ." He shook his head.

"But why collect 'em?" she queried. *Like an old ragpicker,* she thought.

He shrugged. "I don't know. I think I thought I might find a use for them," he added doubtfully.

She said, "They do look like oddments that might be involved in casting a spell."

He shrugged again, but added, "They're not all what they seem. *That,* for instance—" He pointed at one of three gray spherelets. "—is not a pebble like the other two, but a lead slingshot, perhaps one of my own."

Struck by his thrusting finger, *that* rolled off the table and hit the terrazzo floor with a little dull yet clinky thud, as if to prove his observation.

As he recovered it, he paused with his eyes close to the floor to study first the crushed black marble of the terrazzo flecked with dark red and gold, and second Cif's near foot, which he then drew up onto his lap and studied still more minutely.

"A strangely symmetric pentapod coral outcrop from sea's bottom," he observed, and planted a slow kiss upon the base of her big toe, insinuated the tip of his tongue between it and the next.

"There's an eel nosed around in my reef," she murmured.

Laying his cheek upon her ankle, he sighted up her leg. She was wearing a singlet of fine brown linen that tied between her legs. He said, "Your hair has exactly the same tints as are in the flooring."

She said, "You think I didn't select the marble for crushing with that in mind? Or add in the gold flakes? Here's a present of sorts for you." And she pushed the small flat black box down her leg toward him from her groin to her knee.

He sat up to inspect it, though keeping her foot in his lap.

On the black fabric lining it, there lay like a delicate mist cloud the slender translucent bladder of a fish.

Cif said, "I am minded to experience your love fully tonight. Yet not as fully, mind you, as to wish that we fashion a daughter together."

The Mouser said, "I've seen the like of this made of thinnest leather well oiled."

She said, "Not as effectual, I believe."

He said, "To be sure, here, it would be something from a fish, this being Rime Isle. Tell me, did harbor master Groniger fashion this, as thrifty with the Isle's sperm as with its coins?" Then he nodded.

He reached over and drew her other foot up on his lap also. After saluting it similarly, he rested the side of his face on both her ankles and sighted up the narrow trough between her legs. "I am minded," he said dreamily but with a little growl in his voice, "to embark on another slow and intensely watchful journey, mindful of every step, such as that by which I arrived at this house this eve."

She nodded, wondering idly if the growl were Gusorio's, but it seemed too faint for that.

8

In the bow of a laden grainship sailing north from Lankhmar across the Inner Sea to the land of the Eight Cities, the Death of Fafhrd, who was tall and lank, dire as a steel scarecrow, said to his fellow passenger, "This incarnation likes me and likes me not.'Tis a balmy journey now but it'll be long and

by all accounts cold as witchcunt at the end, albeit summer.
Arth-Pulgh's a mean employer, and unlucky. Hand me a
medlar from the sack."

The Death of the Gray Mouser, lithe as a weasel and
forever smiling, replied, "No meaner nor no curster than
Hamomel. Working for whom, however, is the pits. I've not
yet shaken down to this persona, know not its likings. Reach
your own apples."

9

A week later, the evening being unseasonably balmy and
Witches Moon at first quarter near the top of the sky, a
hemispherical silver goblet brimful of stars and scattering
them dimmed by moonwine all over the sky as it descended
toward the lips of the west, drawn down by the same goddess
who had lifted it, Afreyt and Fafhrd after supping alone at her
violet tinted pale house on Salthaven's northern edge were
minded to wander across the great meadow in the direction of
Elvenhold, a northward slanting slim rock spire two bowshots
high, chimneyed and narrowly terraced, that thrust from the
rolling fields almost a league away to the west.

"See how her tilt," Fafhrd observed of that slender
mountainlet, "directs her at the dark boss of the Targe—"
(naming the northernmost constellation in the Lankhmar heavens) "—as if she were granite arrow aimed at skytop by the
gods of the underworld."

"Tonight the earth is full of the heat of these gods' forges,
pressing summer scents from spring flowers and grasses.
Let's rest awhile," Afreyt answered, and truly although it
was not yet May Eve, the heavy air was more like Midsummer's. She touched his shoulder and sank to the herby sward.

After a stare around the horizon for any sky wanderer on
verge of rise or set, Fafhrd seated himself by her right side. A

low lurhorn sounded faintly from the town behind them or the sea beyond that.

"Night fishers summoning the finny ones," he hazarded.

"I dreamed last night," she said, "that a beast thing came out of the sea and followed me dripping salt drops as I wandered through a dark wood. I could see its silver scales between the dark boles in the gloom. But I was not afeared, and it in turn seemed to respond to this cue, for the longer it followed me the less it became like a beast and the more like a seaperson, and come not to work a hurt on me but to warn me."

"Of what?" And when she was silent, "Its sex?"

"Why, female—" she answered at once, but then becoming doubtful, "—I think. Had it sex? I wonder why I did not wait for it to catch up, or perhaps turn sudden and walk toward it? I think I felt, did I so, and although I feared it not, it would turn to a beast again, a deep-voiced beast."

"I too dreamed strangely last night, and my dream strangely chimed with yours, or was it by day I dreamed? For I have begun to do that," Fafhrd announced, dropping himself back at full length on the springy sward, the better to observe the seven spiraled stars of the Targe. "I dreamt I was pent in the greatest of castles with a million dark rooms in it, and that I searched for Gusorio (for that old legend between the Mouser and me is sometimes more than a joke) because I'd been solemnly told, perchance in a dream within the dream, that he had a message for me."

She turned and leaned over him, her eyes staring deep into his as she listened. Her palely golden hair fell forward in two sweeping smooth cascades over her shoulders. He readjusted his position slightly so that five of the stars of Targe rose in a semicircle from her forehead (his eyes straying now and again toward her shadowed throat and the silver cord lacing together the sides of her violet bodice) and he continued, "In the twelve times twelve times twelfth room there stood at the far door a figure clad all in silver-scale mail (there's our dreams chiming) but its back was toward me and the longer I looked at it, the taller and skinnier it seemed than Gusorio should be. Nevertheless I cried out to it aloud and in the very instant of my calling knew that I'd made an irreparable mistake and that my voice would work a hideous change in it and to my harm. See, our dreams clink again? But then, as it started to turn, I awoke. Dearest princess, did you know that the Targe crowns you?'' And his right hand moved toward the silver bow drooping below her throat as she bent down to kiss him.

But as he enjoyed those pleasures and their continuations and proliferations while the moon sank, which pleasures were greatly enhanced by their starry background, the far ecstasies complementing the near, he marveled how these nights he seemed to be walking at once toward brightest life and darkest death, while through it all Elvenhold loomed in the low distance.

10

''No question on it, Captain Mouser's changed,'' Pshawri said with certainty, yet also amazedly and apprehensively, to his fellow lieutenant Mikkidu as they tippled together two evenings later in a small booth of the Sea Wrack. ''Here's yet another example if't be needed. You know the care he has for our grub, to see that cookie doesn't poison us. Normally he'll taste a spoon of stew, say what it lacks or not, even order it dumped (that happened once, remember?) and go dancing off. Yet this very afternoon I spied him standing before the roiling soup kettle and staring into it for as long as it takes to stow *Flotsam*'s mainsail and then rig it again, watching it bubble and seethe with greatest interest, the beans and fish flakes bobbing and the turnips and carrots turning over, as though he were reading there auguries and prognostics on the fate of the world!''

Mikkidu nodded. ''Or else he's trotting about bent over like Mother Grum, seeing things even an ant ignores. He had me stooping about after him over a route that could have been the plan of a maze, pointing out in turn a tangle of hair combings, a penny, a pebble, a parchment scrap scribbled with runic, mouse droppings, and a dead cockroach.''

"Did he make you eat it?" asked Pshawri.

Mikkidu shook his head wonderingly. "No chewings . . . and no chewings out either. He only said at the end, when my legs had started to cramp, 'I want you to keep these matters in mind in the future.' "

"And meantime Captain Fafhrd—"

The two semi-rehabilitated thieves looked up. Skor from the next booth had thrust over his balding head, worry-wrinkled, which now loomed above them. "—is so busy keeping watch on the stars by night—and by day too, somehow—that it's a wonder he can navigate Salthaven without breaking his neck. Think you some evil wight has put a spell on both?"

Normally the Mouser's and Fafhrd's men were mutually rivalrous, suspicious, and disparaging of each other. It was a measure of their present concern for their captains that they pooled their knowledge and took frank counsel together.

Pshawri shrugged as hugely as one so small was able. "Who knows? 'Tis such footling matters, and yet . . . ''

"Chill ills abound here," Mikkidu intoned. "Khahkht the Wizard of Ice, Stardock's ghost fliers, sunken Simorgya . . . ''

11

At the same moment Cif and Afreyt, in the former's sauna, chatted together with even greater but more playful freedom. Afreyt confided with mock grandeur, "I'll have you know that Fafhrd compared my niplets to stars."

Cif chortled midst the steam and answered coarsely with mock pride, "The Mouser likened my arse hole to one. *And* to the stem dimple of a pome. And his own intrusive member to a stiletto! Whate'er ails them doesn't show in bed.''

"Or does it?" Afreyt questioned laughingly. "In my case, stars. In yours, fruits and cutlery too.''

12

As the Deaths of Fafhrd and the Mouser jounced on donkeyback at the tail of a small merchant troop to which they'd attached themselves traveling through the forested land of the Eight Cities from Kvarch Nar to Illik Ving, Witches Moon being full, the former observed, "The trouble with these long incarnations as the death of another is that one begins to forget one's own proper persona and best interests, especially if one be a dedicated actor.''

"Not so, necessarily," the other responded. "Rather, it gives one a clear head (What head clearer than Death's?) to observe oneself dispassionately and examine without bias the terms of the contract under which one operates.''

"That's true enough," Fafhrd's Death said, stroking his lean jaw while his donkey stepped along evenly for a change. "Why think you this one talks so much of booty we may find?''

"Why else but that Arth-Pulgh and Hamomel expect there will be treasure on our intendeds or about them? There's a thought to warm the cold nights coming!''

"Yes, and raises a nice question in our order's law, whether we're being hired principally as assassins or robbers.''

"No matter that," Death of the Mouser summed up. "We know at least we must not hit the Twain until they've shown us where their treasure is.''

"Or treasures are, more like," the other amended, "if they distrust each other, as all sane men do.''

13

Coming in opposite directions around a corner behind Salthaven's council hall after a sharp rain shower, the Mouser and Fafhrd bumped into each other because the one was bending down to inspect a new puddle while the other studied the clouds retreating from arrows of sunshine. After grappling together briefly with sharp growls that turned to sudden laughter, Fafhrd was shaken enough from his current preoccupations by this small surprise to note the look of puzzled and wondrous brooding that instantly replaced the sharp friendly grin on the Mouser's face—a look that was undersurfaced by a pervasive sadness.

His heart was touched and he asked, ''Where've you been keeping yourself, comrade? I never seem to see you to talk to these past days.''

'' 'Tis true,'' the Mouser replied with a sharp grimace, ''we do seem to be operating on different *levels,* you and I, in our movings around Salthaven this last moon-wax.''

''Yes, but where are your *feelings* keeping?'' Fafhrd prompted.

Heart-touched in turn and momentarily impelled to seek to share deepest and least definable difficulties, the Mouser drew Fafhrd to the lane side and launched out, ''If you said I were homesick for Lankhmar, I'd call you liar! Our jolly comrades and grand almost-friends there, yes, even those good not to be trusted female troopers in memory revered, and all their perfumed and painted blazonry of ruby (or mayhap emerald?) lips, delectable tits, exquisite genitalia, they draw me not a whit! Not even Sheelba with her deep diggings into my psyche, nor your spicedly garrulous Ning. Nor all the gorgeous palaces, piers, pyramids, and fanes, all that marble and cloud-capped biggery! But oh . . .'' and the underlook of sadness and wonder became keen in his face as he drew Fafhrd closer, dropping his voice, ''. . . the *small things*—those, I tell you honest, *do* make me homesick, aye, yearningly so. The little street braziers, the lovely litter, as though each scrap were sequined and bore hieroglyphs. The hennaed and the diamond-dusted footprints. I knew those things, yet I never looked at them closely enough, savored the *details*. Oh, the thought of going back and counting the cobblestones in the Street of the Gods and fixing forever in my memory the shape of each and tracing the course of the rivulets of rainy trickle between them! I'd want to be rat size again to do it properly, yes even ant size, oh, there is no end to this fascination with the small, the universe written in a pebble!''

And he stared desperately deep into Fafhrd's eyes to ascertain if that one had caught at least some shred of his meaning, but the big man whose questions had stirred him to speak from his inmost being had apparently lost the track himself somewhere, for his long face had gone blank again, blank with a faint touch of melancholia and eyes wandering doubtfully upward.

"Homesick for Lankhmar?" the big man was saying. "Well, I do miss her stars, I must confess, her southern stars we cannot see from here. But oh . . ." And now *his* face and eyes fired for the brief span it took him to say the following words, ". . . the thought of the still more southern stars we've never seen! The untravelled southern continent below the Middle Sea. Godsland and Nehwon's life pole, and over 'em the stars a world of men have died and never seen. Yes, I am homesick for those lands indeed!''

The Mouser saw the flare in him dim and die. The Northerner shook his head. "My mind wanders," he said. "There are a many of good enough stars here. Why carry worries afar? Their sorting is sufficient.''

"Yes, there are good pickings now here along Hurricane Street and Salt, and leave the gods to worry over themselves," the Mouser heard himself say as his gaze dropped to the nearest puddle. He felt *his* flare die—if it had ever been. "Things will shake down, get done, sort themselves out, and feelings too.''

Fafhrd nodded and they went their separate ways.

14

And so time passed on Rime Isle. Witches Moon grew full and waned and gave way to Ghosts Moon, which lived its wraithshort life in turn, and Midsummer Moon was born, sometimes called Murderers Moon because its full runs low and is the latest to rise and earliest to set of all full moons, not high and long like the full moons of winter.

And with the passage of time things did shake down and some of them got done and sorted out after a fashion, meaning mostly that the out of the way became the commonplace with repetition, as it has a way of doing.

Seahawk got fully repaired, even refitted, but Fafhrd's and Afreyt's plan to sail her to Ool Plerns and fell timber there for wood-poor Rime Isle got pushed into the future. No one said, "Next summer," but the thought was there.

And the barracks and warehouse got built, including a fine drainage system and a cesspool of which the Mouser was inordinately proud, but repairs to *Flotsam,* though hardly languishing, went slow, and Cif's and his plan to cruise her east and trade with the Ice Gnomes north of No-Ombrulsk even more visionary.

Mog, Kos, and Issek's peculiar curses continued to shape much of the Twain's behavior (to the coarse-grained amusement of those small-time gods), but not so extremely as to interfere seriously with their ability to boss their men effectively or be sufficiently amusing, gallant, and intelligent with their female co-mates. Most of their men soon catalogued it under the heading "captains' eccentricities," to be griped at or boasted of equally but no further thought of. Skor, Pshawri, and Mikkidu did not accept it quite so easily and continued to worry and wonder now and then and entertain dark suspicions as befitted lieutenants, men who are supposedly learning to be as imaginatively responsible as captains. While on the other hand the Rime Islers, including the crusty and measuredly

friendly Groniger, found it a good thing, indicative that these
wild allies and would-be neighbors, questionable protégés of
those headstrong freewomen Cif and Afreyt, were settling
down nicely into law-abiding and hard-headed island ways.
The Gray Mouser's concern with small material details particularly impressed them, according with their proverb: rock,
wood, and flesh; all else a lie, or, more simply still: Mineral,
Vegetable, Animal.

Afreyt and Cif knew there had been a change in the two
men, all right, and so did our two heroes too, for that matter.
But they were inclined to put it down to the weather or some
deep upheaval of mood as had once turned Fafhrd religious
and the Mouser calculatedly avaricious. Or else—who knows?
—these might be the sort of things that happened to anyone
who settled down. Oddly, neither considered the possibility
of a curse, whether by god or sorcerer or witch. Curses were
violent things that led men to cast themselves off mountaintops or dash their children's brains out against rocks, and
women to castrate their bed partners and set fire to their own
hair if there wasn't a handy volcano to dive into. The trivial-
ity and low intensity of the curses misled them.

When all four were together they talked once or twice of
supernatural influences on human lives, speaking on the whole
more lightly than each felt at heart.

"Why don't you ask augury of Great Gusorio?" Cif suggested. "Since you are shards of him, he should know all
about both of you."

"He's more a joke than a true presence one might address
a prayer to," the Mouser parried, and then riposted, "Why
don't you or Afreyt appeal for enlightenment to that witch, or
warrior-queen of yours, Skeldir, she of the silver-scale mail
and the short dry laugh?"

"We're not on such intimate terms as that with her, though
claiming her as ancestor," Cif answered, looking down diffidently. "I'd hardly know how to go about it."

Yet that dialogue led Afreyt and Fafhrd to recount the
dreams they'd previously shared only with each other. Whereupon all four indulged in inconclusive speculations and guesses.
The Mouser and Fafhrd promptly forgot these, but Cif and
Afreyt stored them away in memory.

And although the curses on the Twain were of low intensity, the divine vituperations worked steadily and consumingly. Ensamples: Fafhrd became much interested in a dim hairy star low in the west that seemed to be slowly growing in brightness and luxuriance of mane and to be moving east against the current, and he made a point observing it early each eve. While it was noticed that the busily peering Captain Mouser had a favorite route for checking things out that led from the Sea Wrack, where he'd have a morning nip, to the low point in the lane outside, to the windy corner behind the council hall where he'd collided with Fafhrd, to his men's barracks, and by way of the dormitory's closet, which he'd open and check for mouseholes, to his own room and shelved closet and to the kitchen and pantry, and so to the cesspool behind them of which he was so proud.

So life went on tranquilly, busily, unenterprisingly in and around Salthaven as spring gave way to Rime Isle's short sharp summer. Their existence was rather like that of industrious lotus eaters, the others taking their cues from the bemused and somewhat absentminded Twain. The only exception to this most regular existence promised to be the day of Midsummer Eve, a traditional Isle holiday, when at the two women's suggestion they planned a feast for all hands (and special Isle friends and associates) in the Great Meadow at Elvenhold's foot, a sort of picnic with dancing and games and athletic competitions.

15

If any could be said to have spent an unpleasant or unsatisfactory time during this period, it was the wizards Sheelba and Ningauble. The cosmic din had quieted down sufficiently for them to be able to communicate pretty well between the one's swamp hut and the other's cave and get some confused

inkling of what Fafhrd and the Mouser and their gods were up
to, but none of that inkling sounded very logical to them or
favorable to their plot. The stupid provincial gods had put
some unintelligible sort of curse on their two pet errand boys,
and it was working after a fashion, but Mouser and Fafhrd
hadn't left Rime Isle, nothing was working out according to
the two wizards' wishes, while a disquieting adverse influence they could not identify was moving northwest across the
Cold Waste north of the Land of the Eight Cities and the
Trollstep Mountains. All very baffling and unsatisfactory.

16

At Illik Ving the Death of the Twain joined a caravan bound
for No-Ombrulsk, changing their mounts for shaggy Mingol
ponies inured to frost, and spent all of Ghosts Moon on that
long traverse. Although early summer, there was sufficient
chill in the Trollsteps and the foothills of the Bones of the Old
Ones and in the plateau of the Cold Waste that lies between
these ranges for them to refer frequently to the seed bags of
brazen apes and the tits of witches, and hug the cookfire
while it lasted, and warm their sleep with dreams of the
treasures their intendeds had laid up.

"I see this Fafhrd as a gold-guarding dragon in a mountain
cave," his Death averred. "I'm into his character fully now,
I feel. And on to it too."

"While I dream the Mouser as a fat gray spider," the other
echoed, "with silver, amber, and leviathan ivory cached in a
score of nooks, crannies, and corners he scuttles between.
Yes, I can play him now. And play with him too. Odd, isn't
it, how like we get to our intendeds at the end?"

Arriving at last at the stone-towered seaport, they took
lodgings at an inn where badges of the Slayers' Brotherhood
were recognized, and they slept for two nights and a day,

recuperating. Then Mouser's Death went for a stroll down by the docks, and when he returned, announced, "I've taken passage for us in an Ool Krut trader. Sails with the tide day after morrow."

"Murderers Moon begins well," his wraith-thin comrade observed from where he still lay abed.

"At first the captain pretended not to know of Rime Isle, called it a legend, but when I showed him the badge and other things, he gave up that shipmasters' conspiracy of keeping Salthaven and western ports beyond a trade secret. By the by, our ship's called the *Good News*."

"An auspicious name," the other, smiling, responded. "Oh Mouser, and oh Fafhrd, dear, your twin brothers are hastening toward you."

17

After the long morning twilight that ended Midsummer Eve's short night, Midsummer Day dawned chill and misty in Salthaven. Nevertheless, there was an early bustling around the kitchen of the barracks, where the Mouser and Fafhrd had taken their repose, and likewise at Afreyt's house, where Cif and their nieces May, Mara, and Gale had stayed overnight.

Soon the fiery sun, shooting his rays from the northeast as he began his longest loop south around the sky, had burnt the milky mist off all Rime Isle and showed her clear from the low roofs of Salthaven to the central hills, with the leaning tower of Elvenhold in the near middle distance and the Great Meadow rising gently toward it.

And soon after that an irregular procession set out from the barracks. It wandered crookedly and leisurely through town to pick up the men's women, chiefly by trade, at least in their spare time, sailorwives, and other island guests. The men took turns dragging a cart piled with hampers of barley cakes,

sweetbreads, cheese, roast mutton and kid, fruit conserves
and other Island delicacies, while at its bottom, packed in
snow, were casks of the Isle's dark bitter ale. A few men
blew woodflutes and strummed small harps.

At the docks Groniger, festive in holiday black, joined
them with the news. "The *Northern Star* out of Ool Plerns
came in last even to No-Ombrulsk. I spoke with her master
and he said the *Good News* out of Ool Krut was at last report
sailing for Rime Isle one or two mornings after him."

At this point Ourph the Mingol begged off from the party,
protesting that the walk to Elvenhold would be too much for
his old bones and a new crick in his left ankle, he'd rest them
in the sun here, and they left him squatting his skinny frame
on the warming stone and peering steadily out to sea past
where *Seahawk, Flotsam, Northern Star,* and other ships rode
at anchor among the Island fishing sloops.

Fafhrd said to Groniger, "I've been here a year and more
and it still wonders me that Salthaven is such a busy port
while the rest of Nehwon goes on thinking Rime Isle a
legend. I know I did for a half lifetime."

"Legends travel on rainbow wings and sport gaudy colors," the harbormaster answered him, "while truth plods on
in sober garb."

"Like yourself?"

"Aye," Groniger grunted happily.

"And 'tis not a legend to the captains, guild masters, and
kings who profit by it," the Mouser put in. "Such do most to
keep legends alive." The little man (though not little at all
among his corps of thieves) was in a merry mood, moving
from group to group and cracking wise and gay to all and
sundry.

Skullick, Skor's sub-lieutenant, struck up a berserk battle
chant and Fafhrd found himself singing an Ilthmar sea chanty
to it. At their next pickup point tankards of ale were passed
out to them. Things grew jollier.

A little ways out into the Great Meadow, where the thor-
oughfare led between fields of early ripening Island barley,
they were joined by the feminine procession from Afreyt's.
These had packed their contribution of toothsome edibles and
tastesome potables in two small red carts drawn by stocky

white bearhounds big as small men but gentle as lambs. And they had been augmented by the sailorwives and fisherwomen Hilsa and Rill, whose gift to the feast was jars of sweet-pickled fish. Also by the witchwoman Mother Grum, as old as Ourph but hobbling along stalwartly, never known to have missed a feast in her life's long history.

They were greeted with cries and new singings, while the three girls ran to play with the children the larger procession had inevitably accumulated on its way through town.

Fafhrd went back for a bit to quizzing Groniger about the ships that called at Salthaven port, flourishing for emphasis the hook that was his left hand. "I've heard it said, and seen some evidence for it too, myself, that some of them hail from ports that are nowhere on Nehwon seas I know of."

"Ah, you're becoming a convert to the legends," the black-clad man told him. Then, mischievously, "Why don't you try casting the ships' horoscopes with all you've learned of stars of late, naked and hairy ones?" He frowned. "Though there was a black cutter with a white line that watered here three days ago whose home port I wish I could be surer of. Her master put me off from going below, and her sails didn't look enough for her hull. He said she hailed from Sayend, but that's a seaport we've had reliable word that the Sea-Mingols burned to ash less than two years agone. He knew of that, he claimed. Said it was much exaggerated. But I couldn't place his accent."

"You see?" Fafhrd told him. "As for horoscopes, I have neither skill or belief in astrology. My sole concern is with the stars themselves and the patterns they make. The hairy star's most interesting! He grows each night. At first I thought him a rover, but he keeps his place. I'll point him out to you come dark."

"Or some other evening when there's less drinking," the other allowed grudgingly. "A wise man is suspicious of his interests other than the most necessary. They breed illusions."

The groupings kept changing as they walked, sang, and danced—and played—their way up through the rustling grass. Cif took advantage of this mixing to seek out Pshawri and Mikkidu. The Mouser's two lieutenants had at first been suspicious of her interest in and influence over their captain—a touch of jealousy, no doubt—but honest dealing and speaking, the evident genuineness of her concern, and some furtherance of Pshawri's suit to an Island woman had won them over, so that the three thought of themselves in a limited way as confederates.

"How's Captain Mouser these days?" she asked them lightly. "Still running his little morning checkup route?"

"He didn't today," Mikkidu told her.

"While yesterday he ran it in the afternoon," Pshawri amplified. "And the day before that he missed."

Mikkidu nodded.

"I don't fret about him o'er much," she smiled at them, "knowing he's under watchful and sympathetic eyes."

And so with mutual buttering up and with singing and dancing the augmented holiday band arrived at the spot just south of Elvenhold that they'd selected for their picnic. A portion of the food was laid out on white-sheeted trestles, the drink was broached, and the competitions and games that comprised an important part of the day's program were begun. These were chiefly trials of strength and skill, not of endurance, and one trial only, so that a reasonable or even somewhat unreasonable amount of eating and drinking didn't tend to interfere with performance too much.

Between the contests were somewhat less impromptu dancings than had been footed earlier: Island stamps and flings, old-fashioned Lankhmar sways, and kicking and bouncing dances copied from the Mingols.

Knife-throwing came early—"so none will be mad drunk as yet, a sensible precaution," Groniger approved.

The target was a yard section of mainland tree trunk almost two yards thick, lugged up the previous day. The distance was fifteen long paces, which meant two revolutions of the knife, the way most contestants threw. The Mouser waited until last and then threw underhand as a sort of handicap, or at least seeming handicap, against himself, and his knife embedded deeply in or near the center, clearly a better shot than any of the earlier successful ones, whose points of impact were marked with red chalk.

A flurry of applause started, but then it was announced that Cif had still to throw; she'd entered at the last possible minute. There was no surprise at a woman entering; that sort of equality was accepted on the Isle.

"You didn't tell me beforehand you were going to," the Mouser said to her.

She shook her head at him, concentrating on her aim. "No, leave his dagger in," she called to the judges. "It won't distract me."

She threw overhand and her knife impacted itself so close to his that there was a *klir* of metal against metal along with the woody *thud*. Groniger measured the distances carefully with his beechwood ruler and proclaimed Cif the winner.

"And the measures on this ruler are copied from those on the golden Rule of Prudence in the Island treasury," he added impressively, but later qualified this by saying, "Actually, my ruler's more accurate than that ikon; doesn't expand with heat and contract with cold as metals do. But some people don't like to keep hearing me say that."

"Do you think her besting the Captain is good for discipline and all?" Mikkidu asked Pshawri in an undertone, his new trust in Cif wavering.

"Yes, I do!" that one whispered back. "Do the Captain good to be shook up a little, what with all this old-man scurrying and worrying and prying and pointing out he's going in for." *There,* he thought, *I've spoken it out to someone at last, and I'm glad I did!*

Cif smiled at the Mouser. "No, I didn't tell you ahead of time," she said sweetly, "but I've been practicing—privately. Would it have made a difference?"

"No," he said slowly, "though I might have had second thoughts about throwing underhand. Are you planning to enter the slinging contest too?"

"No, never a thought of it," she answered. "Whatever made you think I might?"

Later the Mouser won that one, both for distance and accuracy, making the latter cast so powerful that it not only holed the center of the bull's-eye into the padded target box but went through the heavier back of the latter as well. Cif begged for the battered slug as a souvenir, and he presented it to her with elaborate flourishes.

" 'Twould have pierced the cuirass of Mingsward!'' Mikkidu fervently averred.

The archery contests were beginning, and Fafhrd was fitting the iron tang in the middle of his bow into the hardwood heading of the leather stall that covered half his left forearm, when he noted Afreyt approaching. She'd doffed her jacket, for the sun was beating down hotly, and was wearing a short-sleeved violet blouse, blue trousers wide-belted with a gold buckle, and purple-dyed short holiday boots. A violet handkerchief confined a little her pale gold hair. A worn green quiver with one arrow in it hung from her shoulder, and she was carrying a big longbow.

Fafhrd's eyes narrowed a bit at those, recalling Cif and the knife throwing. But "You look like a pirate queen," he greeted her, and then only inquired, "You're entering one of the contests?"

"I don't know," she said with a shrug. "I'll watch along through the first."

"That bow," he said casually, "looks to me to have a very heavy pull, and tall as you are, to be a touch long for you."

"Right on both counts," she agreed, nodding. "It belonged to my father. You'd be truly startled, I think, to see how I managed to draw it as a stripling girl. My father would doubtless have spanked me soundly if he'd ever caught me at it, or rather lived long enough to do that."

Fafhrd lifted his eyebrows inquiringly, but the pirate queen vouchsafed no more. He won the distance shot handily but lost the target shot (through which Afreyt also watched) by a finger's breadth to Skor's other sub-lieutenant, Mannimark.

Then came the high shot, which was something special to Midsummer Day on Rime Isle and generally involved the loss of the contestant's arrow, for the target was a grassy, nearly vertical stretch on the upper half of the south face of Elvenhold. The north face of the slanting rock tower actually overhung the ground a little and was utterly barren, but the south face, though very steep, sloped enough to hold soil to support herbage, rather miraculously. The contest honored the sun, which reached this day his highest point in the heavens, while the contesting arrows, identified by colored rags of thinnest silk attached to their necks, emulated him in their efforts.

Then Afreyt stepped forward, kicked off her purple boots and rolled up her blue trousers above her knees. She plucked her arrow, which bore a violet silk, from her quiver and threw that aside. "Now I'll reveal to you the secret of my girlish technique," she said to Fafhrd.

Quite rapidly she sat down facing the dizzy slope, set the bow to her bare feet, laying the arrow between her big toes and holding it and the string with both hands, rolled back onto her shoulders, straightened her legs smoothly, and loosed her shot.

It was seen to strike the slope near Fafhrd's yellow, skid a few yards higher, and then lie there, a violet taunt.

Afreyt, bending her legs again, removed the bow from her feet, and rolling sharply forward, stood up in the same motion.

"You practiced that," Fafhrd said, hardly accusingly, as he finished screwing the hook back in the stall on his left arm.

She nodded. "Yes, but only for half a lifetime."

"The lady Afreyt's arrow didn't stick in," Skullick pointed out. "Is that fair? A breath of wind might dislodge it."

"Yes, but there is no wind and it somehow got highest," Groniger pointed out to him. "Actually, it's accounted lucky in the high shot if your arrow doesn't embed itself. Those that don't sometimes are blown down. Those that do stay up there are never recovered."

"Doesn't someone go up and collect the arrows?" Skullick asked.

"Scale Elvenhold? Have you wings?"

Skullick eyed the rock tower and shook his head sheepishly. Fafhrd overheard Groniger's remarks and gave the harbormaster an odd look but made no other comment at the time.

Afreyt invited both of them over to the red dogcarts and produced a jug of Ilthmar brandy, and they toasted her and Fafhrd's victories—the Mouser's too, and Cif's, who happened along.

"This'll put feathers in your wings!" Fafhrd told Groniger, who eyed him thoughtfully.

The children were playing with the white bearhounds. Gale had won the girls' archery contest and May the short race.

Some of the younger children were becoming fretful, however, and shadows were lengthening. The games and contests were all over now, and partly as a consequence of that the drinking was heavying up as the last scraps of food were being eaten. Among the whole picnic group there seemed to be a feeling of weariness, but also (for those no longer very young but not yet old) new jollity, as though one party were ending and another beginning. Cif's and Afreyt's eyes were especially bright. Everyone seemed ready to go home, though whether to their own places or the Sea Wrack was a matter of age and temperament. There was a chill breath in the air.

Gazing east and down a little toward Salthaven and the harbor beyond, the Mouser opined that he could already see low mist gathering around the bare masts there, and Groniger confirmed that. But what was the small lone dark figure trudging up-meadow toward them in the face of the last low sunlight?

"Ourph, I'll be bound," said Fafhrd. "What's led him to make the hike after all?"

But it was hard to be sure the big Northerner was right; the figure was still far off. Yet the signal for leaving had been given, things were gathered, the carts repacked, and all set out, most staying near the carts, from which drinks continued to be forthcoming. And perhaps these were responsible for a resumption of the morning's impromptu singing and dancing, though now it was not Fafhrd and the Mouser but others who took the lead in this. The Twain, after a whole day of behaving like old times, were slipping back under the curses they knew not of, the one's eyes forever on the ground, with the effect of old age unsure of its footing, the other's on the sky, indicative of old age's absent-mindedness.

Fafhrd turned out to be right about the up-meadow trudger, but it was few words they got from Ourph as to why he'd made the hike he'd earlier begged off from.

The old Mingol said only to them, and to Groniger, who happed to be by, "The *Good News* is in." Then, eyeing the Twain more particularly, "Tonight stay away from the Sea Wrack."

But he would answer nothing more to their puzzled queries

save "I know what I know and I've told it," and two cups of
brandy did not loosen his Mingol tongue one whit.

The encounter put them behind the main party, but they did
not try to catch up. The sun had set some time back, and now
their feet and legs were lapped by the ground mist that
already covered Salthaven and into which the picnic party
was vanishing, its singing and strumming already sounding
tiny and far off.

"You see," Groniger said to Fafhrd, eyeing the twilit but
yet starless sky while the mist lapped higher around them,
"you won't be able to show me your bearded star tonight in
any case."

Fafhrd nodded vaguely but made no other answer save to
pass the brandy jug as they footed it along: four men walking
deeper and deeper, as it were, into a white silence.

18

Cif and Afreyt, very much caught up in the gayety of the
evening party, and bright-eyed drunk besides, were among
the first to enter the Sea Wrack and encounter arresting
silence of another sort, and almost instantly come under the
strange, hushing spell of the scene there.

Fafhrd and the Mouser sat at their pet table in the low-
walled booth playing backgammon, and the whole tavern
frightenedly watched them while pretending not to. Fear was
in the air.

That was the first impression. Then, almost at once, Cif
and Afreyt saw that Fafhrd couldn't be Fafhrd, he was much
too thin; nor the Mouser the Mouser, much too plump (though
every bit as agile and supple-looking, paradoxically).

Nor were the faces and clothing and accouterments of the
two strangers anything really like the Twain's. It was more
their expressions and mannerisms, postures and general man-

ner, self-confident manner, those and the fact of *being at that
table*. The sublime impression the two of them made was that
they were who they were and that they were in their rightful place.

And the fear that radiated from them with the small sounds
of their gaming: the muted rattle of shaken bone dice in one
or the other's palm-closed leather cup, the muted clatter as
the dice were spilled into one or other of the two low-walled
felt-lined compartments of the backgammon box, the sharp
little clicks of the bone counters as they were shifted by ones
and twos from point to point. The fear that riveted the attention of everyone else in the place no matter how much they
pretended to be understanding the conversations they made,
or tasting the drinks they swallowed, or busying themselves
with little tavern chores. The fear that seized upon and recruited each picnic newcomer. Oh yes, this night something
deadly was coiling here at the Sea Wrack, make no mistake
about it.

So paralyzing was the fear that it cost Cif and Afreyt a
great effort to sidle slowly from the doorway to the bar, their
eyes never leaving that one little table that was for now the
world's hub, until they were as close as they could get to the
Sea Wrack's owner, who with downcast and averted eye was
polishing the same mug over and over.

"Keeper, what gives?" Cif whispered to him softly but
most distinctly. "Nay, sull not up. Speak, I charge you!"

Eagerly that one, as though grateful Cif's whiplash command had given him opportunity to discharge some of the
weight of dread crushing him, whispered them back his tale
in short, almost breathless bursts, though without raising an
eye or ceasing to circle his rag.

"I was alone here when they came in, minutes after the
Good News docked. They spoke no word, but as though the
fat one were the lean one's hunting ferret, they *scented out*
our two captains' table, sat themselves down at it as though
they owned it, then spoke at last to call for drink.

"I took it them, and as they got out their box and dice cups
and set up their game, they plied me with harmless-seeming
and friendly questions mostly about the Twain, as if they
knew them well. Such as: How fared they in Rime Isle?
Enjoyed they good health? Seemed they happy? How often

came they in? Their tastes in drink and food and the fair sex? What other interests had they? What did they like to talk of? As though the two of them were courtiers of some great foreign empire come hither our captains to please and to solicit about some affair of state.

"And yet, you know, so *dire* somehow were the tones in which those innocent questions were asked that I doubt I could have refused them if they'd asked me for the Twain's heart's blood or my own.

"This too: The more questions they asked about the Twain and the more I answered them as best I might, the more they came to look like . . . to resemble our . . . you know what I'm trying to say?"

"Yes, yes!" Afreyt hissed. "Go on."

"In short, I felt I was their slave. So too, I think, have felt all those who came into the Sea Wrack after them, save for old Mingol Ourph, who shortly stayed, somehow then parted.

"At last they sucked me dry, bent to their game, asked for more drink. I sent the girl with that. Since then it's been as you see now."

There was a stir at the doorway through which mist was curling. Four men stood there, for a moment bemused. Then Fafhrd and the Mouser strode toward their table, while old Ourph settled down on his hams, his gaze unwavering, and Groniger almost totteringly sidled toward the bar, like a man surprised at midday by a sleepwalking fit and thoroughly astounded at it.

Fafhrd and the Mouser leaned over and looked down at the table and open backgammon box over which the two strangers were bent, surveying their positions. After a bit Fafhrd said rather loudly, "A good rilk against two silver smerduke on the lean one! His stones are poised to fleet swiftly home."

"You're on!" the Mouser cried back. "You've underestimated the fat one's back game."

Turning his chill blue eyes and flat-nosed skull-like face straight up at Fafhrd with an almost impossible twist of his neck, the skinny one said, "Did the stars tell you to wager at such odds on my success?"

Fafhrd's whole manner changed. "You're interested in the stars?" he asked with an incredulous hopefulness.

"Mightily so," the other answered him, nodding emphatically.

"Then you must come with me," Fafhrd informed him, almost lifting him from his stool with one fell swoop of his good hand and arm that at once assisted and guided, while his hook indicated the mist-filled doorway. "Leave off this footling game. Abandon it. We've much to talk of, you and I." By now he had a brotherly arm—the hooked one, this time—around the thin one's shoulders and was leading him back along the path he'd entered by. "Oh, there are wonders and treasures undreamed amongst the stars, are there not?"

"Treasures?" the other asked coolly, pricking an ear but holding back a little.

"Aye, indeed! There's one in particular under the silvery asterism of the Black Panther that I lust to show you," Fafhrd replied with great enthusiasm, at which the other went more willingly.

All watched astonishedly, but the only one who managed to speak out was Groniger, who asked, "Where are you going, Fafhrd?" in rather outraged tones.

The big man paused for a moment, winked at Groniger, and smiling said, "Flying."

Then with a "Come, comrade astronomer," and another great arm-sweep, he wafted the skinny one with him into the bulging white mist, where both men shortly vanished.

Back at the table the plump stranger said in loud but winning tones, "Gentle sir! Would you care to take over my friend's game, continue it with me?" Then in tones less formal, "And have you noticed that these mug dints on your table together with the platter burn make up the figure of a giant sloth?"

"Oh, so you've already seen that, have you?" the Mouser answered the second question, returning his gaze from the door. Then, to the second, "Why, yes, I will, sir, and double the bet!—it being my die cast. Although your friend did not stay long enough even to arrange a chouette."

"*Your* friend was most insistent," the other replied. "Sir, I take your bet."

Whereupon the Mouser sat down and proceeded to shake a masterly sequence of double fours and double threes so that the skinny man's stones, now his own, fleeted more swiftly to victory than ever Fafhrd had predicted. The Mouser grinned fiendishly, and as they set up the stones for another game, he pointed out to his more thinly smiling adversary in the table-top's dints and stains the figure of a leopard stalking the giant sloth.

All eyes were now back on the table again save those of Afreyt. And of Fafhrd's lieutenant Skor. Those four orbs were still fixed on the mist-bulging doorway through which Fafhrd had vanished with his strangely unlike doublegoer. Since babyhood Afreyt had heard of those doleful nightwalk-ers whose appearance, like the banshee's, generally beto-kened death or near mortal injury to the one whose shape they mocked.

Now while she agonized over what to do, invoking the witch queen Skeldir and lesser of her own and (in her extrem-ity) others' private deities, there was a strange growling in her ears—perhaps her rushing blood. Fafhrd's last word to Groniger kindled in her memory the recollection of an exchange of words between those two earlier today, which in turn gave her a bright inkling of Fafhrd's present destination in the viewless fog. This in turn inspired her to break the grip upon her of fear's and indecision's paralysis. Her first two or three steps were short and effortful ones, but by the time she went through the doorway, she was taking swift giant strides.

Her example broke the dread-duty deadlock in Skor, and the lean, red-haired, balding giant followed her in a rush.

But few in the Sea Wrack except Ourph and perhaps Groniger noted either departure, for all gazes were fixed again on the one small table where now Captain Mouser in person contested with his dread were-brother, battling the Islanders' and his men's fears for them as it were. And whether by smashing attack, tortuous back game, or swift running one like the first, the Mouser kept winning again and again and again.

And still the games went on, as though the series might well outlast the night. The stranger's smile kept thinning. That was all, or almost all.

The only fly in this ointment of unending success was a

nagging doubt, perhaps deriving from a growing languor on the Mouser's part, a lessening of his taunting joy at each new win, that destinies in the larger world would jump with those worked out in the little world of the backgammon box.

19

"We have reached the point in this night's little journey I'm taking you on where we must abandon the horizontal and embrace the vertical," Fafhrd informed his comrade astronomer, clasping him familiarly about the shoulders with left arm, and wagging right forefinger before that cadaver face, while the white mist hugged them both.

The Death of Fafhrd fought down the impulse to squirm away with a hawking growl of disgust close to vomiting. He abominated being touched except by outstandingly beautiful females under circumstances entirely of his own commanding. And now for a full half-hour he had been following his drunken and crazy victim (sometimes much too closely for comfort, but that wasn't his own choosing, Arth forbid) through a blind fog, and mostly trusting the same madman to keep them from breaking their necks in holes and pits and bogs, and putting up with being touched and arm-gripped and back-slapped (often by that doubly disgusting hook that felt so like a weapon), and listening to a farrago of wild talk about long-haired asterisms and bearded stars and barley fields and sheep's grazing ground and hills and masts and trees and the mysterious southern continent until Arth himself couldn't have held it, so that it was only the madman's occasional remention of a treasure or treasures he was leading his Death to that kept the latter tagging along without plunging an exasperated knife into his victim's vitals.

And at least the loathsome cleavings and enwrappings expressive of brotherly affection that he had made himself submit to had allowed him to ascertain in turn that his intended wore no undergarment of chain mail or plate or scale to interfere with the proper course of things when knife time came. So the Death of Fafhrd consoled himself as he broke away from the taller and heavier man under the legitimate and friendly excuse of more closely inspecting the rock wall they now faced at a distance of no more than four or five yards. Farther off the fog would have hid it.

"You say we're to climb this to view your treasure?" He couldn't quite keep his incredulity out of his voice.

"Aye," Fafhrd told him.

"How high?" his Death asked him.

Fafhrd shrugged. "Just high enough to get there. A short distance, truly." He waved an arm a little sideways, as though dispensing with a trifle.

"There's not much light to climb by," his Death said somewhat tentatively.

Fafhrd replied, "What think you makes the mist whitely luminous an hour after sunset? There's enough light to climb by, never fear, and it'll get brighter as we go aloft. You're a climber, aren't you?"

"Oh, yes," the other admitted diffidently, not saying that his experience had been gained chiefly in scaling impregnable towers and cyclopean poisoned walls behind which the wealthier and more powerful assassin's targets tended to hide themselves—difficult climbs, some of them, truly, but rather artificial ones, and all of them done in the line of business.

Touching the rough rock and seeing it inches in front of his somewhat blunted nose, the Death of Fafhrd felt a measurable repugnance to setting foot or serious hand on it. For a moment he was mightily minded to whip out dagger and end it instanter here with the swift upward jerk under the breastbone, or the shrewd thrust from behind at the base of the skull, or the well-known slash under the ear in the angle of the jaw. He'd never have his victim more lulled, that was certain.

Two things prevented him. One, he'd never had the feeling of having an audience so completely under his control as he'd had this afternoon and evening at the Sea Wrack. Or a victim so completely eating out of his hand, so walking to his own destruction, as they said in the trade. It gave him a feeling of being intoxicated while utterly sober, it put him into an "I can do anything, I am God" mood, and he wanted to prolong that wonderful thrill as far as possible.

Two, Fafhrd's talk perpetually returning to treasure, and the way the invitation now to climb some small cliff to view it so fitted with his Cold Waste dreams of Fafhrd as a dragon guarding gold in a mountain cavern—these combined to persuade him that the Fates were taking a hand in tonight's happening, the youngest of them drawing aside veil and baring her ruby lips to him and soon the more private jewelry of her person.

"You don't have to worry about the rock, it's sound enough, just follow in my footsteps and my handholds," Fafhrd said impatiently as he advanced to the cliff's face and mounted it, the hook making harsh metallic clashes.

His Death doffed the short cloak and hood he wore, took a deep breath and, thinking in a small corner of his mind, "Well, at least this madman won't be able to fondle me more while we're climbing—I hope!" went up after him like a giant spider.

It was as well for Fafhrd that his Death (and the Mouser's too) had neglected to make close survey of the landscape and geography of Rime Isle during this afternoon's sail in. (They'd been down in their cabin mostly, getting into their parts.) Otherwise he might have known that he was now climbing Elvenhold.

20

Back in the Sea Wrack the Mouser threw a double six, the only cast that would allow him to bear off his last four stones and leave his opponent's sole remaining man stranded one point from home. He threw up the back of a hand to mask a mighty yawn and over it politely raised an inquiring eyebrow at his adversary.

The Death of the Mouser nodded amiably enough, though his smile had grown very thin-lipped indeed, and said, ''Yes, it's as well we write finished to my strivings. Was it eight games, or seven? No matter. I'll seek my revenge some other time. Fate is your girl tonight, cunt and arse hole, that much is proven.''

A collective sigh of relief from the onlookers ended the general silence. They felt the relaxation of tension as much as the two players, and to most of them it seemed that the Mouser in vanquishing the stranger had also dispersed all the strange fears that had been loose in the tavern earlier and running along their nerves.

''A drink to toast your victory, salve my defeat?'' the Mouser's Death asked smoothly. ''Hot gahveh perhaps? With brandy in't?''

''Nay, sir,'' the Mouser said with a bright smile, collecting together his several small stacks of gold and silver pieces and funneling them into his pouch, ''I must take these bright fellows home and introduce 'em to their cellmates. Coins prosper best in prison, as my friend Groniger tells me. But sir, would you not accompany me on that journey, help me escort 'em? We can drink there.'' A brightness came into his eyes that had nothing whatever in common with a miser's glee. He continued, ''Friend who discerned the tree sloth and saw the black panther, we both know that there are mysterious treasures and matters of interest compared to which these clinking counters are no more than that. I yearn to show you some. You'll be intrigued.''

At the mention of ''treasure,'' his Death pricked up his ears much as his fellow assassin had at Fafhrd's speaking the word. Mouser's would-be nemesis had had his Cold Waste dreams too, his appetites whetted by the privations of long drear journeying, and by the infuriating losses he'd had to put up with tonight as well. And he too had the conviction that the fates must be on his side tonight by now, though for the opposite reason. A man who'd been so incredibly lucky at backgammon was bound to be hit by a great bolt of unluck at whatever feat he next attempted.

''I'll come with you gladly,'' he said softly, rising with the Mouser and moving with him toward the door.

"You'll not collect your dice and stones?" the one queried. "'Tis a most handsome box."

"Let the tavern have it as a memorial of your masterly victory," his Death replied negligently, with a sort of muted grandiloquence. He tossed aside an imaginary blossom.

Ordinarily *that* would have been too much to the Mouser, arousing all his worst suspicions. Only rogues pretended to be *that* carelessly munificent. But the madness with which Mog had cursed him was fully upon him again, and he forgot the matter with a smile and a shrug.

"Trifles all," he agreed.

In fact the manner of the two of them was so lightly casual for the moment, not to say la-di-da, that they might well have gotten out of the Sea Wrack and lost in the fog without anyone noticing except of course for old Ourph, whose head turned slowly to watch the Mouser out the door, shook itself sadly, and then resumed its meditations or cogitations or whatever.

Fortunately there were those in the tavern deeply and intelligently concerned for the Mouser, and not bound by Mingolly fatalisms. Cif had no impulse to rush up to the Mouser upon his win. She'd had too strong a sense of something more than backgammon being at stake tonight, too lingering a conviction of something positively unholy about his were-adversary, and doubtless others in the tavern had shared those feelings. Unlike most of those, however, any relief she felt did not take her attention away from the Mouser for an instant. As he and his unwholesome doublegoer exited the doorway, she hurried to it.

Pshawri and Mikkidu were at her heels.

They saw the two ahead of them as dim blobs, shadows in the white mist, as it were, and followed only swiftly enough to keep them barely in sight. The shadows moved across and down the lane a bit, paused briefly, then went on until they were traveling along back of the building, made of gray timbers from wrecked ships, that was the council hall.

Their pursuers encountered no other fog venturers. The silence was profound, broken only by the occasional *drip-drip* of condensing mist and a few very brief murmurs of conversation from ahead, too soft and fleeting to make out. It was eerie.

At the next corner the shadows paused another while, then turned it.

"He's following his regular morning route," Mikkidu whispered softly.

Cif nodded, but Pshawri gripped Mik's arm in warning, setting a finger to his lips.

But true enough to the second lieutenant's guess, they followed their quarry to the new-built barracks and saw the Mouser bow his doublegoer in. Pshawri and Mikkidu waited a bit, then took off their boots and entered in stocking feet most cautiously.

Cif had another idea. She stole along the side of the building, heading for the kitchen door.

Inside, the Mouser, who had uttered hardly a dozen words since leaving the Sea Wrack, pointed out various items to his guest and watched for his reactions.

Which threw his Death into a state of great puzzlement. His intended victim had spoken some words about a treasure or treasures, then taken him outside and with a mysterious look pointed out to him a low point in a lane. What could that mean? True, sunken ground sometimes indicated something buried there—a murdered body, generally. But who'd bury a treasure in the lane of a dinky northern seaport, or a corpse, for that matter? It didn't make sense.

Next the gray-clad baffler had gone through the same rigmarole at a corner behind a building of strangely weathered, heavy-looking wood. That had for a moment seemed to lead somewhere, for there'd been an opalescent something lodged in one of the big beams, its hue speaking of pearls and treasure. But when he'd stooped to study it, it had turned out to be only a worthless seashell, worked into the gray wood Arth knew how!

And now the riddlesome fellow, holding a lamp he'd lit, was standing in a bunkroom beside a closet he'd just opened. There didn't seem to be much of anything in it.

"Treasure?" the Mouser's Death breathed doubtfully, leaning forward to look more closely.

The Mouser smiled and shook his head. "No. Mice holes," he breathed back.

The other recoiled incredulously. Had the brains of the masterly backgammon player turned to mush? Had something in the fog stolen away his wits? Just what *was* happening here? Maybe he'd best out knife and slay at once, before the situation became too confusing.

But the Mouser, still smiling gleefully, as if in anticipation of wonders to behold, was beckoning with his free hand into a short hall and then a smaller room with two bunks only, while the lamp he held beside his head made shadows crawl around them and slip along the walls.

Facing his Death, he threw open the door of a wider closet, stretched himself to his fullest height and thrust his lamp aloft, as if to say, "Lo!"

The closet contained at least a dozen shallow shelves smoothly surfaced with black cloth, and on them were very neatly arranged somewhere between a thousand and a myriad tiny objects, as if they were so many rare coins and precious gems. As if, yes . . . but as to what these objects really were . . . recall the nine oddments the Mouser had laid out on Cif's bed table three months past . . . imagine them multiplied by ten hundred . . . the booty of three months of ground peering . . . the loot of ninety days of floor delving . . . you'd have a picture of the strange collection the Mouser was displaying to his Death.

And as his Death leaned closer, running his gaze incredulously back and forth along the shelves, the triumphant smile faded from the Mouser's face and was replaced by the same look of desperate wondering he'd had on it when he told Fafhrd of yearning for the small things of Lankhmar.

21

"We've reached our picnic ground," Afreyt told Skor as they strode through the mist. "See how the sward is trampled. Now cast we about for Elvenhold."

" 'Tis done, lady," he replied as she moved off to the left, he to the right, "but why are you so sure Captain Fafhrd went there?"

"Because he told Groniger he was going flying," she called to him. "Earlier Groniger had said that none could climb Elvenhold without wings."

"But the Captain could," Skor, taking her meaning, called back, "for he's scaled Stardock," thinking, though not saying aloud, *But that was before he lost a hand.*

Moments later he sighted vertical solidity and was calling out that he'd found what they were seeking. When Afreyt caught up with him by the rock wall, he added, "I've also found proof that Fafhrd and the stranger did indeed come this way, as you deduced they would."

And he held up to her the hooded cloak of Fafhrd's Death.

22

Fafhrd, followed closely by his Death, climbed out of the fog into a world of bone-white clarity. He faced away from the rock to survey it.

The top of the mist was a flat white floor stretching east and south to the horizon, unbroken by treetop, chimney or spire of Salthaven, or mast top in the harbor beyond. Overhead the night shone with stars somewhat dimmed by the light of the round moon, which seemed to rest on the mist in the southeast.

"The full of Murderers Moon," he remarked oratorically, "the shortest and the lowest running full of the year, and come pat on Midsummer's Day Night. I told you there'd be light enough to climb by."

His Death below him savored the appropriateness of the lunar situation but didn't care much for the light. He'd felt securer climbing in the fog with the height all hid. He was still enjoying himself, but now he wanted to get the killing done as soon as Fafhrd revealed where the cave or other treasure spot was.

Fafhrd faced around to the tower again. Soon they were edging up past the grassy stretch. He noted his white-flagged arrow and left it where it was, but when he came to Afreyt's he reached over precariously, snagged it with his hook, and tucked it in his belt.

"How much farther?" his Death called up.

"Just to the end of the grass," Fafhrd called down. "Then we traverse to the opposite edge of Elvenhold, where there's a shallow cave will give our feet good support as we view the treasure. Ah, but I'm glad you came with me tonight! I only hope the moon doesn't dim it too much."

"How's that?" the other asked, a little puzzled, though considerably enheartened by the mention of a cave.

"Some jewels shine best by their own light alone," Fafhrd replied somewhat cryptically. Clashing into the next hold, his hook struck a shower of white sparks. "Must be flint in the rock hereabouts," he observed. "See, friend, minerals have many ways of making light. On Stardock the Mouser and I found diamonds of so clear a water they revealed their shape only in the dark. And there are beasts that shine, in particular glowwasps, diamondflies, firebeetles, and nightbees. I know, I've been stung by them. While in the jungles of Klesh I have encountered luminous flying spiders. Ah, we arrive at the traverse." And he began to move sideways, taking long steps.

His Death copied him, hastening after. Footholds and hand-holds both seemed surer here, while back at the grass he'd twice almost missed a hold. Beyond Fafhrd he could see what he took to be the dark cave mouth at the end of this face of the rock pylon they'd mounted. Things seemed to be happening more quickly while simultaneously time stretched out for him—sure sign of climax approaching. He wanted no more talk—in particular, lectures on natural history! He loosened his long knife in its scabbard. Soon! Soon!

Fafhrd was preparing to take the step that would put him squarely in front of the shallow depression that looked at first sight like a cave mouth. He was aware that his comrade astronomer was crowding him. At that moment, although the two of them were clearly alone on the face, he heard a short dry laugh, not in the voice of either of them, that nevertheless sounded as if it came from somewhere very close by. And somehow that laugh inspired or stung him into taking, instead of the step he'd planned, a much longer one that took him just past the seeming cave mouth and put his left foot on the end of the ledge, while his right hand reached for a hold beyond the shallow depression so that his whole body would swing out past the end of this face and he would hopefully see the bearded star which was currently his dearest treasure and which until this moment tonight Elvenhold itself had hid from him.

At the same moment his Death struck, who had perfectly anticipated his victim's every movement except the last inspired one. His dagger, instead of burying itself in Fafhrd's back, struck rock in the shallow depression and its blade snapped. Staggered by that and vastly surprised, he fought for balance.

Fafhrd, glancing back, perceived the treacherous attack and rather casually booted his threatener in the thigh with a free foot. By the bone-white light of Murderers Moon, the Death of Fafhrd fell off Elvenhold and, glancingly striking the very steep grassy slope once or twice, was silhouetted momentarily, long limbs writhing, against the floor of white fog before the latter swallowed him up and the scream he'd started. There was a distant *thud* that nevertheless had a satisfying finality to it.

Fafhrd swung out again around the end of the cliff. Yes, his bearded star, though dimmed by the moonlight, was definitely discernable. He enjoyed it. The pleasure was, somewhat remotely, akin to that of watching a beautiful girl undress in almost dark.

"Fafhrd!" Then again, "Fafhrd!"

Skor's shout, by Kos, he told himself. And Afreyt's! He pulled himself back on the ledge and, securely footed there, called, "Ahoy! Ahoy below!"

23

Back at the barracks things were moving fast and very nervously, notably on the part of the Mouser's Death. He almost dirked the vaunting idiot on sheer impulse in overpowering disgust at being shown that incredible mouse's museum of trash as though it were a treasure of some sort. Almost, but then he heard a faint shuffling noise that seemed to originate in the building they were in, and it never did to slay when witnesses might be nigh, were there another course to take.

He watched the Mouser, who looked somewhat disappointed now (had the idiot expected to be praised for his junk display?), shut the closet door and beckon him back into the short hall and through a third door. He followed, listening intently for any repetition of the shuffling noise or other sound. The moving shadows the lamp cast were a little unnerving now; they suggested lurkers, hidden observers. Well, at least the idiot hadn't deposited in his trash closet the gold and silver coins he'd won this night, so presumably there was still hope of seeing their "cell mates" and some real treasure.

Now the Mouser was pointing out, but in a somewhat perfunctory way, the features of what appeared to be a rather well-appointed kitchen: fireplaces, ovens, and so forth. He rapped a couple of large iron kettles, but without any great enthusiasm, sounding their dull, sepulchral tones.

His manner quickened a little, however, and the ghost at least of a gleeful smile returned to his lips as he opened the back door and went out into the mist, signing for his Death to follow him. That one did so, outwardly seeming relaxed, inwardly alert as a drawn knife, poised for any action.

Almost immediately the Mouser stooped, grasped a ring, and heaved up a small circular trapdoor, meanwhile holding his lamp aloft, its beams reflecting whitely from the fog but not helping vision much. The Mouser's Death bent forward to look in.

Thereafter things happened very rapidly indeed. There was a scuffling sound and a thud from the kitchen. (That was Mikkidu tripping himself by stepping on the toe of his own stocking.) The Mouser's Death, his nerves tortured beyond endurance, whipped out his dirk and next fell dead across the cesspool mouth with Cif's dagger in his ear, thrown from where she stood against the wall hardly a dozen feet away.

And somewhere, along with these actions, there were a brief growl and a short dry laugh. But those were things Cif and the Mouser claimed afterward to have heard. At the present moment there was only the Mouser still holding his lamp and peering down at the corpse and saying as Cif and Pshawri and Mikkidu rushed up to him, "Well, he'll never get his revenge for tonight's gaming, that's for certain. Or do ghosts ever play backgammon, I wonder? I've heard of them contesting parties at chess with living mortals, by Mog."

24

Next day at the council hall Groniger presided over a brief but well-attended inquest into the demise of the two passengers on the *Good News*. Badges and other insignia about their persons suggested they were members not only of the Lankhmar Slayers Brotherhood, but also of the even more cosmopolitan

Assassins Order. Under close questioning, the captain of the *Good News* admitted knowing of this circumstance and was fined for not reporting it to the Rime Isle harbormaster immediately on making port. A bit later Groniger found that they were murderous rogues, doubtless hired by foreign parties unknown, and that they had been rightly slain on their first attempts to practice their nefarious trade on Rime Isle.

But afterward he told Cif, "It's as well that you slew him, and with his dagger in his hand. That way, none can say it was a feuding of newcomers to the Isle with foreigners their presence attracted here. And that you, Afreyt, were close witness to the other's death."

"I'll say I was!" that lady averred. "He came down not a yard from us—eh, Skor?—almost braining us. And with his hand death-gripping his broken dagger. Fafhrd, in future you should be more careful of how you dispose of your corpses."

When questioned about the cryptic warning he'd brought the Mouser and Fafhrd, old Ourph vouched, "The moment I heard the name *Good News* I knew it was an ill-omened ship, bearing watching. And when the two strangers came off and went into the Sea Wrack, I perceived them as dressed up, slightly luminous skeletons only, with bony hands and eyeless sockets."

"Did you see their corpses at the inquest so?" Groniger asked him.

"No, then they were but dead meat, such as all living become."

25

In Godsland the three concerned deities, somewhat shocked by the final turn of events and horrified to see how close they'd come to losing their chief remaining worshippers, lifted their curses from them as rapidly as they were able.

Other concerned parties were slower to get the news and to believe it. The Assassins Order posted the two Deaths as "delayed" rather than "missing," but prepared to make what compensation might be unavoidable to Arth-Pulgh and Hamomel. While Sheelba and Ningauble, considerably irked, set about devising new stratagems to procure the return of their favorite errand boys and living touchstones.

26

The instant the gods lifted their curses, the Mouser's and Fafhrd's strange obsessions vanished. It happened while they were together with Afreyt and Cif, the four of them lunching al fresco at Cif's. The only outward sign was that the Twain's eyes widened incredulously as they stared and then smiled at nothing.

"What deliciously outrageous idea has occurred to you two?" Afreyt demanded, while Cif echoed, "You're right! And it has to be something like that. We know you two of yore!"

"Is it that obvious?" the Mouser inquired, while Fafhrd fumbled out, "No, it's nothing like that. It's . . . No, you've all got to hear this. You know that thing about stars I've been having? Well, it's gone!" He lifted his eyes. "By Issek, I can look at the blue sky now without having it covered with the black flyspecks of the stars that would be there now if it were dark!"

"By Mog!" the Mouser exploded. "I had no idea, Fafhrd, that your little madness was so like mine in the tightness of its grip. For I no longer feel the compulsion to try to peer closely at every tiny object within fifty yards of me. It's like being a slave who's set free."

"No more ragpicking, eh?" Cif said. "No more bent-over inspection tours?"

"No, by Mog," the Mouser asserted, then qualified that
with a "Though of course little things can be quite as interesting as big things; in fact, there's a whole tiny world of—"

"Uh-uh, you better watch out," Cif interrupted, holding
up a finger.

"And the stars too are of considerable interest, my unnatural infatuation with 'em aside," Fafhrd said stubbornly.

Afreyt asked, "What do you think it was, though? Do you
think some wizard cast a spell on you? Perchance that Ningauble
you told me of, Fafhrd?"

Cif said, "Yes, or that Sheelba you talk of in your sleep,
Mouser, and tell me isn't an old lover?"

The two men had to admit that those explanations were
distant possibilities.

"Or other mysterious or even otherworldly beings may
have had a hand in it," Afreyt proposed. "We know Queen
Skeldir's involved, bless her, from the warning laughter you
heard. And, for all you make light of him, Gusorio. Cif and I
did hear those growlings."

Cif said, the look in her eyes half wicked, half serious,
"And has it occurred to any of you that, since Skeldir's
warnings went to you two men, that *you* may be transmigra-
tions of her? and we—Skeldir help us!—of Great Gusorio? Or
does that shock you?"

"By no means," Fafhrd answered. "Since transmigration
would be such a wonder, able to send the spirit of woman or
man into animal, or vice versa, a mere change of sex should
not surprise us at all."

27

The backgammon box of the two Deaths was kept at the Sea
Wrack as a curiosity of sorts, but it was noted that few used it
to play with, or got good games when they did.

IV

———— ✦ ————

The Mouser Goes Below

1

It is an old saw in the world of Nehwon that the fate of heroes who seek to retire, or of adventurers who decide to settle down, so cheating their audience of honest admirers—that the fate of such can be far more excruciatingly doleful than that of a Lankhmar princess royal shanghaied as cabin girl aboard an Ilthmar trader embarked on the carkingly long voyage to tropic Klesh or frosty No-Ombrulsk. And let such heroes merely whisper a hint about a "last adventure" and their noisiest partisans and most ardent adherents alike will be demanding that it end at the very least in spectacular death and doom, endured while battling insurmountable odds and enjoying the enmity of the evilest archgods.

So when those two humorous dark-side heroes the Gray Mouser and Fafhrd not only left Lankhmar City (where it's said more than half the action of Nehwon world is) to serve the obscure freewomen Cif and Afreyt of lonely Rime Isle on the northern rim of things, but also protracted their stay there for two years and then three, wiseacres and trusty gossips alike began to say that the Twain were flirting with just such a fate.

True, their polar expedition had seemed to begin well enough, even showily, with reports filtering back of them gathering and training (or taming) small bands of adventurers mad as themselves to serve them, and then word of a great victory where they turned back from the frigid island of philosophic fishermen a two-pronged invasion of suicidal Sea-Mingols, during which they enforced the service of two weird outlander gods outlandishly named Loki and Odin, and also played fast and loose with the five gold Ikons of Reason, which were atheist Rime Isle's chiefest treasure, and otherwise made fools of the Isle's gruff and slow-moving and -speaking dwellers.

But then, especially when they stayed on and on in the chilly north, second reports began to undercut and diminish all these feisty achievements. It was said that their victory had been a trivial psychological one, got by delaying maneuvers—what in a more familiar world would have been called Fabian tactics—and that in the end it never would have been won except for an unexpected unseasonal change in the winds, the simultaneous but fortuitous eruption of Rime Isle's volcanos Hellglow and Darkfire, and the coincidental surging of the Island's notorious Great Maelstrom, which sucked under a few leading galleys in the Mingols' advance squadron and so discouraged the rest.

That (so these second reports went) far from playing tricks on the Islanders, the Mouser and Fafhrd were making friends with them, copying their sober ways, and forcing their henchmen to do likewise—transforming these cutpurses and berserks into law-abiding sailors, fishermen, mechanics, even carpenters who'd built for themselves and their two masters a year-round barracks.

That instead of playing ducks and drakes with the gold Ikons, Fafhrd had actually rescued four of them from a thievish sea-demoness from the sunken empire of Simorgya, whom the Mouser had additionally thwarted in the course of a trading voyage to No-Ombrulsk to get timber and grain for the wood-poor, corn-hungry, sea-girt republic.

Furthermore, that he (the Mouser) had used the fifth Ikon, the Skeleton Cube of Square-Dealing, enwedged with a cinder sacred to the stranger fire-god Loki and containing the essence of that alien god's being, to sling into the center of the Great Maelstrom after it had pulled under the Mingol picket ships and magically still forever its spinning whorls before they scuppered the rickety Rime fleet also. There the cube lay snuggled in sand and slickly slimed at whirlpool-maw's center seventeen fathoms down, a precious heavy handful, kernel for legends and bait for treasure seekers, locking the Maelstrom tight and prisoning a god.

Finally, that in place of swindling and abandoning Cif and Afreyt, as they'd been known to serve some earlier employers and lovers alike, the two disgustingly reformed rascals and rakes were busily courting the two freewomen, clearly with lasting relationships of mutual benefit in view.

These disquieting—nay, shocking—secondary rumors were what caused many to at last give credence to a widely-disbelieved early report: that in the almost bloodless final battle with the Mingols, Fafhrd had somehow lost his left hand, eventually replacing it with a leather socket for his bow, fork, knife—a whole kit of tools. This was seen now as part of the working out of the old Nehwonian saw about the woes that afflict heroes who try to step down from their glorious and entertaining destinies. The luck of Fafhrd and the Gray Mouser had turned at last, it was said, and they were on the road to oblivion.

The ones who believed this—and they were many—were also quick to accept the report that the wizardly mentors of the Twain, Sheelba of the Eyeless Face and Ningauble of the Seven Eyes, had turned against them in disappointment and disgust and moved their no-account gods—spiderish Mog, limp-wristed Issek, and lousy Kos—to inflict upon them the curse of old age, turning them into cranky old men before their time. Likewise the secret news that figures no less illustrious and powerful than the Overlord of Lankhmar and the Grandmaster of its Thieves Guild had sent assassins to Rime Isle to wipe them out. Even when word came drifting southward that the two tarnished heroes had somehow thwarted their assassins at the last moment and wriggled out from under the old-age curse, detractors were quick to point out that this was not to their credit since it could hardly have been managed without a lot of help from Cif, Afreyt, and those two ladies' Moon Goddess.

No, these detractors maintained, Fafhrd and Mouser were on the skids (as good as dead) for disdaining their proper hero-villain roles and seeking a snug harbor for their declining years, and as soon as some proper god (Kos, Mog, and Issek were nobodies!) got the ear of Death in his low castle in the Shadowland and spoke a word into it, they were forever done for.

Now, if these criticisms and dire forecasts had been referred to the two heroes at whom they were directed, Fafhrd might well have replied that he'd come north on a dare and great challenge, and that since then problems and menaces had been coming at him hot and heavy, and as for his hand, he'd lost that saving the necks of his mistress Afreyt and her three girl acolytes of the Moon Goddess and he was trying to make the best of his deficiency, so why the criticism? While the Gray Mouser might well have answered, "What did the fools expect?" *He'd* never worked as hard in his life at being a hero as he had up here in the shivery inclement arctic clime, taking responsibility not only for his twelve witless apprentice hero-thieves under their barely less imbecilic lieutenants Mikkidu and Pshawri *and* for his lady Cif and her dependents as well, but *also* from time to time for Fafhrd's berserks too, and half the dwellers of Rime Isle besides.

Yet despite these protests each of the Twain felt a gloomy shiver stiffen his short hairs now and again, for both knew well how cruelly and unreasonably demanding audiences can be and how unendingly bitter the enmity of gods as the two of them fumbled with their twisted, slowly unraveling destinies in a world that from time to time imitates that of fancy and romance most cunningly, so as to keep its creatures concerned and moving to prevent their sinking into black despair or bored inaction.

2

Pshawri, the Gray Mouser's slender young lieutenant, sat with head bowed and taking slow deep breaths on the aft thwart of the sailing dory *Kringle*, anchored in a dead calm two Lankhmar leagues east of Rime Isle above the dark center of the Great Maelstrom, quiescent now for an unprecedented seventeen moons, though when a-spin, a ridgy, ship-devouring, roaring water monster.

The noonday sun of late summer's Satyrs Moon beat down on his wiry nakedness as he studied the five smooth leadstone boulders, each big as his head, lying firm on the dory's bottom. From a snug thong low around his middle hung a scabbarded and well-greased dirk and a bag of stout fishnet, its mouth marked and held open by a circlet of reed. With each belly-bulging inhalation the thong indented his slim side just above where three grayish moles made an inconspicuous equilateral triangle on his left hip.

Against the gunnel opposite him sprawled his sworn-to-secrecy sailing comrade, Fafhrd's seven-foot second sergeant Skullick. This lean yet comically hulking one left off staring lazily yet doubtfully at Pshawri to turn half on his side and scan down through the near pellucid saltwater at the sea floor seventeen fathoms below. It was mostly pale sand, green-tinged by depth. He could see *Kringle*'s tiny shadow and her anchor line going down almost vertically toward the dark cluster of savage rocks marking the whirlpool's maw, and around that the dim shapes of gnawed wrecks waiting a long, long time now for storms and the whirlpool's own action to break them up and drive their waterlogged timbers ashore on the Beach of Bleached Bones, there to be salvaged by the wood-starved Rimers.

"All clear, as yet," he called softly overshoulder. "Nary a tiger ray nor black hog-nose showing. No fish of size at all.

"Nonetheless," he added, "if you take my reed, you'll try

to spot and snag the gift you intend Captain Mouser on your first dive, before you've roiled the fine sand or roused a man-eater. Foot-steer for the likeliest wreck, scanning carefully ahead for treasure-glints, then swiftly snatch, were the best way. Anything metal'd be a fine memento for him of his scuppering the Sunwise Mingol fleet whilst saving the Rimer ships. Don't set your heart on finding the golden Whirlpool Queller itself—'' His voice grew loving ''—the twelve-edged skeleton cube small as a girl's fist, with the cindery black torch end wedged within it that holds all that's left in Nehwon of the stranger god Loki who maddened us Rimers a year and five moons ago when Maelstrom last time spumed and spun. Small swift profits are surest, as I've more than once heard your captain tell mine when he thinks Fafhrd's dreaming too big.''

Pshawri replied to this glib palaver with never a word or sign, nor did aught else to break his measuredly deep breathing, his surfeit-feast of air. Finally he lifted his face to gaze tranquilly beyond Skullick at the Rime Isle coast, mostly low-lying, except to the north, where the volcano Darkfire faintly fumed and dimmer ice-streaked crags loomed beyond.

His gaze went up and south from the volcano to where five neat shapely clouds had come coursing out of the west like a small fleet of snowy-sailed, high-castled galleons.

Skullick, who'd been copying Pshawri's peerings burst out with, ''I'll swear I've seen those same five clouds before.''

Pshawri used the breath in one of his slow exhalations to say somewhat dreamily, ''You think clouds have beings and souls, like men and ships?''

''Why not?'' responded Skullick. ''I think that all things do bigger than lice. In any case, these five presage a change in weather.''

But Pshawri's gaze had dropped to the Isle's south corner, where the White Crystal Cliffs sheltered the low red and yellow roofs of Salthaven; beyond them, the low hump of Gallows Hill and the lofty leaning rock needle of Elvenhold. His expression hardly changed, yet a shrewd searcher might have seen, added to his tranquillity, the solemnity of one who perhaps looks on cozy shores for the last time.

Without breaking the rhythm of his breathing, he rummaged the small pile of his clothes beside him, found a moleskin belt-pouch, withdrew a somewhat grimy folded sheet with broken seal of green wax with writing in violet ink, unfolded and perused it swiftly—as one who reads not for the first time.

He refolded the sheet, remarking evenly to Skullick, "If, against all likelihood, aught should befall me now, I'd like Captain Mouser to see *this*." He touched the broken seal before returning the item to the moleskin pouch.

Skullick frowned, but then bethought himself and simply nodded.

Hoisting the nearest small leadstone boulder and clasping it to his waist, Pshawri slowly stood up. Skullick rose too, still forbearing to speak.

Then Lieutenant Pshawri, serene-visaged, stepped over *Kringle*'s side with no more fuss than one who goes into the next room.

Before his swift and almost splashless transition from the realm of the winds to that of the cold currents, Skullick remembered to call after him merrily, "Sneeze and choke, burst a blood vessel!"

As the water took them, Pshawri felt the boulder grow lighter, so that his right hand alone was enough to hug it close. Opening his eyes to the rushing fluid, he looped his left arm loosely round the anchor line beside him, directing his descent toward the rock cluster.

He looked down. The bottom seemed still far away. Then as the water tightened its grip on him, he saw the rock cluster slowly open into a five-petaled dark flower with a circle of pale sand at its heart.

The wrecks around came plainer into view so that he could make out the green weed-furred skull of the bow-stallion of the nearest, but disregarding Skullick's advice, Pshawri directed his descent toward the center of the circle of virgin sand, where he discerned *something*, a slightly darker point.

As the water squeezed him tight, then tighter yet, and there began a pulsing in his ears, and he felt the first urge to blow out his breath, he unhooked his arm from the anchor line and coasted down between the huge jagged rocks, let go the stone, and thrusting down both hands before him, seized on the central *something*.

It felt smoothly cubical in form, yet with something grainy and rough-wedged inside its twelve edges. It was surprisingly massy for its size, resisting movement. He rubbed an edge along his thigh. Just before the cloud of loamy sand raised by his feet and the stone's plunge engulfed it, he saw along the rubbed edges a yellowish gleam. He brought it against his waist, found the mouth of the fishnet bag by the feel of the reed circlet, and thrust in his trophy.

At the same time a dry voice seemed to say in his ear, "You shouldn't have done that," and he felt a sharp pang of guilt, as if he'd just committed a theft or rape.

Fighting down a surge of panic, he straightened his body, thrusting his hands high above his head, and with a threshing of his legs and a powerful downward sweep of his palms, drove upward out of the sand cloud, between the savage rocks, and toward the light.

At the same moment Skullick, who'd been following all this as best he might from seventeen fathoms above, saw fully a half-dozen similar sand puffs erupt from the quiescent green-tinged sand plain of wrecks all around and a like number of black hog-nosed sharks, each about as big as *Kringle*'s shadow, streak toward the rock cluster and the tiny swimming figure above it.

Pshawri stroked upward alongside the anchor line, feeling he climbed a cliff, his gaze fixed on *Kringle*'s small spindle shape. Blood pounded in his ears and to hold his breath was pain. Yet as the spindle shape grew larger, he thought to stroke so as to rotate his body for a cautionary scan around and down.

He had not completed a half turn when he saw a black shape driving up toward him head on.

It speaks well for Pshawri's presence of mind that he completed his rotation, making sure there was no nearer attacker to deal with, before facing the hog-nose.

Continuing to coast upward, threshing his legs a little, he drew his dirk. There was yet barely time to thrust his right hand through the loop of the pommel thong before he gripped it.

The scene darkened. He aimed the dirk, his arm bent just a little, at the up-rushing mask which somewhat resembled that of a great black boar.

His shoulder was jolted, his arm wrenched, a *long* black shape was hurtling past, rough hide scraped his hip and side, then he was driving upward again with strong palm-sweeps toward *Kringle*'s hull, very large now though the scene remained strangely darkened.

He felt a blessed surge of relief as he broke surface close alongside and grasped for the gunnel. But in the same instant he felt himself strongly gripped under the shoulders and powerfully heaved upward, his legs flying, and he heard the clash of jaws.

Skullick, his rescuer, saw a red line start out on the mallet snout of the black shark as the beast breached, bit air, then sneezed before falling back—and also the red points that began to fleck his comrade's side as he lowered him to the deck.

Pshawri's spent legs were wobbly yet he managed to stand. He saw that the first of the five fish-shaped clouds hid the sun. It had veered north, as though curious about the Maelstrom and determined to inspect it, and the other four had followed it in line. A strong breeze from the southwest explained this and chilled Pshawri, so he was glad for the large rough towel Skullick tossed his way.

"A goodly tickle you gave him in the nose, my boyo," that one congratulated. "He'll sneeze longer than you bleed where he scraped you, never you fear. But, by Kos, Pshawri, how they all came after you! You'd no sooner raised sand than they were up and streaking in from far and near. Like lean black watchdogs!" He appealed incredulously, "Think you they *felt* your stone-abetted impact through the sand so far? By Kos, they must have!"

"There was more than one?" Pshawri asked, shivering as he spoke for the first time since his dive.

"More? I counted full five blacks at the end, besides two tiger rays. I told you it was more dangerous than you dreamed, and now events have proved me sevenfold right. You're lucky to have got out with your life, lucky you found no treasure to delay you. A few moments more and you'd not have been facing one shark, but three or four!''

Pshawri had been about to display his golden find for his comrade's admiration when Skullick's words not only told him the latter hadn't seen him make it, but also reawakened the strange pang of guilt and foreboding he'd felt below.

While hurrying into his clothes, a process in which he was speeded by the quickening breeze and absence of sun, he managed to switch the slimy cube from the uneasy revealment of the net bag to the revealing concealment of his moleskin belt pouch, while Skullick scanned the sky.

''See how the weather shifts,'' that one called. ''What witch has whistled up this frigid wind? Cold from the south, at any rate southwest—unnatural. Mark how that line of clouds that hides the sun veers widdershins. Lucky you did *not* find the whirlpool-queller, or else we'd have the spinning of that element to deal with. As it is, I fear our presence irks the Maelstrom. Up anchor, cully, hoist sail and away! We'll find your captain's gift another day!''

Pshawri was happy to spring to with a will. Relentless action left less time for feeling strange guilts and thinking crazy thoughts about clouds. And the calm waters, though wind-ruffled, showed no other signs of movement.

3

In jam-packed Godsland, which lies lofty and mountaingirt near Nehwon's south pole, a handsome young god, who had been drawing crowds in the stranger's pavilion by sleeping entranced for seventeen months, woke with an enraged shout that seemed loud enough to reach the Shadowland at Godsland's antipodes, and that momentarily deafened half the divinities and all the demi-divinities in his heavenly audience.

Among the latter were Fafhrd's and the Gray Mouser's

three particular godlings—brutal Kos, spiderish Mog, and the limp-wristed Issek—who had been teased to come witness the feat of supernal hibernation not only out of sheer curiosity, but also from intimations that the handsome young sleeping stranger and his record-breaking trance were somehow involved with their two most illustrious (though often backsliding) worshippers. The three reacted variously to the ear-splitting cry. Issek covered his while Kos dug a little finger into one.

And now it became apparent that Loki's piercing shout had indeed reached the Shadowland, for the slender, seemingly youthful, opalescent-fleshed figure of Death, or its simulacrum, appeared at the foot of the silken bier on which the angry young god crouched, and the two were seen by the deafened divinities to hold converse together, Loki fiercely commanding, Death raising objections, placating, temporizing, though nodding repeatedly and smiling winningly at the same time.

Yet despite the latter's amiable behavior there were shrinkings back among the members of the motley heavenly host, for even in Godsland Death is not a popular figure nor widely trusted.

Fafhrd's and Mouser's three oddly matched godlings, who had earlier wormed their way quite close to the red-draped bier, regained their audition in time to hear Loki's last summary command:

"So be it then, sirrah! So soon as all the essential formalities of your paltry world are satisfied and necessary niggling conditions met—so soon and not one instant later!—I want the impious mortal who consigned me to deep watery oblivion to be sent a like distance underground. It is commanded!"

With a final bow and strange obsequious look, Nehwon's Death (or its simulacrum) said softly, "Harkening in obedience," and vanished.

"I like that!" quick-witted Mog remarked in an indignant ironic undertone to his two cronies. "Out of sheer spite toward the Gray Mouser for his dunking, this vagabond Loki proposes to rob us of one of our chief worshippers."

After a face-saving haughty glare around (for Death's departure had been snubbingly abrupt), Loki slid off the bier to confer in urgent whispers with another stranger god, dignified

but elderly to the point of doddering, who responded with
rather senile-seeming nods and shrugs.

"Yes," Issek replied venomously to Mog. "And now, see,
he's trying to persuade his comrade, old Odin, to demand of
Death a like doom for Fafhrd."

"No, I doubt that," Kos protested. "The dodderer has
already revenged himself on Fafhrd by taking his left hand.
And he's had no indignities visited on him to reawaken his
ire. He's hung on here while his comrade slept because he has
nowhere better to go."

"I'd not count on that," Mog said morosely. "Meanwhile,
what's to do about the clear threat to the Mouser? Protest to
Death this wanton raid by a *foreign* god on our dwindling
congregation?"

"I'd want to think twice before going that far," Issek
responded dubiously. "Appeals to him have been known to
backfire on their makers."

"I don't like dealing with him myself, and that's a fact,"
Kos seconded. "He gives me the cold shivers. Truth to tell, I
don't think you can trust the Powers any further than you can
trust foreign gods!"

"He didn't seem too happy about Loki's arrogance toward
him," Issek put in hopefully. "Perhaps things will work out
well without our meddling." He smiled a somewhat sickish
smile.

Mog frowned but spoke no more.

Back in one of the long corridors of his mist-robed mazy
low castle under the sunless moist gray skies of the Shadowland, Death thought coolly with half his mind (the other half
was busy as always with his eternal work everywhere in
Nehwon) of what a stridently impudent god this young stranger
Loki was and what a pleasure it would be to break the rules,
spit in the face of the other Powers, and carry him off before
his last worshipper died.

But as always good taste and sportsmanship prevailed.

A Power must obey the most whimsical and unreasonable
command of the least god, insofar as it could be reconciled
with conflicting orders from other gods and provided the
proprieties were satisfied—that was one of the things that
kept Necessity working.

And so although the Gray Mouser was a good tool he would have liked to decide when to discard, Death began with half his mind to plan the doom and demise of that one. Let's see, a day and a half would be a reasonable period for preparation, consultations, and warnings. And while he was at it, why not strengthen the Gray One for his coming ordeal? There were no rules against that. It would help him if he were heavier, massier in body and mind. Where get the heaviness? Why, from his comrade Fafhrd, of course, nearest at hand. It would leave Fafhrd light-headed and -bodied for a while, but that couldn't be helped. And then there were the proper and required warnings to think about . . .

While half Death's mind was busy with these matters, he saw his Sister Pain slinking toward him from the corridor's end on bare silent feet, her avid red eyes fixed on his pale slate cool-gray ones. She was slender as he and like complected, except that here and there her opalescence was streaked with blue—and to his great distaste she padded about, as was her wont, in steamy nakedness, rather than decently robed and slippered like himself.

He prepared to stride past her with never a word.

She smiled at him knowingly and said with languorous hisses in her voice, "You've a choice morsel for me, haven't you?"

4

While these ominous Nehwonal and supernal events were transpiring that so concerned them, Fafhrd and the Gray Mouser were relaxedly and unsuspectingly sipping dark brandy by the cool white light, which Rime Islers call bistory, of a leviathan-oil lamp in the root-and-wine cellar of Cif's snug Salthaven abode while that lady and Afreyt were briefly gone to the lunar temple at the arctic port-town's inland outskirts on some business involving the girl acolytes of the Moon Goddess, whose priestesses Cif and Afreyt were, and the girl acolytes their nieces.

Since their slaying of their would-be killers and the lifting of the old-age curse, the two captains had been enjoying to the full their considerable relief, leaving the overseeing of their men to their lieutenants, visiting their barracks but once a day (and taking turns even at that—or even having their lieutenants make report to them, a practice to which they'd sunk once or twice lately), spending most of their time at their ladies' cozier and more comfortable abodes and pleasuring themselves with the sportive activities (including picnicking) which such companionship made possible and to which their recent stints as grumpy and unjoyous old men also inclined them, abetted by the balmy weather of Thunder and Satyrs Moon.

Indeed, today the last had got a bit too much for them. Hence their retreat to the deep, cool, flagstoned cellar, where they were assuaging the melancholy that unbridled self-indulgence is strangely apt to induce in heroes by rehearsing to each other anecdotes of ghosts and horrors.

"Hast ever heard," the tall Northerner intoned, "of those sinuous earth-hued tropical Kleshite ghouls with hands like spades that burrow beneath cemeteries and their environs, silently emerge behind you, then seize you and drag you down before you can gather your wits to oppose it, digging more swiftly than the armadillo? One such, it's said, subterraneously pursued a man whose house lay by a lich-field and took him in his own cellar, which doubtless had a feature much like *that*." And he directed his comrade's attention to an unflagged area, just behind the bench on which they sat, that showed dark sandy loam and was large enough to have taken the passage of a broad-shouldered man.

"Afreyt tells me," he explained, "it's been left that way to let the cellar breathe—a most necessary ventilation in this clime."

The Mouser regarded the gap in the flagging with considerable distaste, arching his brows and wrinkling his nostrils, then recovered his mug from the stout central table before them and took a gut-shivering slug. He shrugged. "Well,

tropic ghouls are unlikely here in polar clime. But now I'm
reminded—hast ever heard tell?—of that Ool Hrusp prince
who so feared his grave, abhorring earth, that he lived his
whole life (what there was of it) in the topmost room of a
lofty tower twice the height of the mightiest trees of the Great
Forest where Ool Hrusp is situated?''

"What happened to him in the end?'' Fafhrd duly inquired.

"Why, although he dwelt secure two thousand leagues
from the edge of the desert southeast of the Inner Sea and
with all that water between to distance him, a monstrously
dense sandstorm born on a typhoon wind sought him out,
turned the green canopy of the forest umber, sifted his stone
eyrie full, and suffocated him.''

From upstairs came a smothered cry.

"My story must have carried,'' the Mouser observed. "The
girls seem to have returned.''

He and Fafhrd looked at each other with widening eyes.

"We promised we'd watch the roast,'' the latter said.

"And when we came down here,'' the other continued,
"we told ourselves we'd go up and check and baste it after a
space.''

Then both together, chiming darkly, "But *you* forgot.''

There was a swift patter of footsteps—more than one pair—
on the cellar stairs. Somehow five slender girls came down
into the cool bistoric glow without tripping or colliding. The
first four wore sandals of white bearhide, near identical knee-
length tunics of fine white linen and yashmacks of the same
material, hiding most of their hair and all of their faces below
their eyes, whose merry flashing nevertheless showed they
were all grinning.

The fifth, who was the slenderest, went barefoot in a
shorter white-belted white tunic of coarser weave and wore a
yashmack of reversed white unshorn lamb's hide and, despite
the weather, gloves of the same material. Her gaze seemed
grave.

All but she tore off their yashmacks together, showing
them to be Afreyt's flaxen-haired nieces May, Mara, and
Gale, and Cif's niece Klute, who was raven-tressed.

But Fafhrd and Mouser knew that already. The two had
risen.

May danced toward them excitedly. "Uncle Fafhrd! We've had an adventure!"

Following at her heels, Mara cut in, "We were almost kidnapped aboard an Ilthmar trader that was a secret slaver!"

"Anything could have happened to us!" Gale exulted, taking her turn. "Imagine! They say Eastern princes will pay fortunes for twelve-year-old blonde virgins!"

"Only, our new friend escaped from the trader and warned Aunts Cif and Afreyt," black-haired Klute topped her triumphantly, looking back toward the fifth girl, who hadn't come forward or unyashmacked. "She'd been kidnapped herself at Tovilyis and been a prisoner on *Weasel* all Satyrs Moon!"

Gale grabbed back the news-telling with, "But she's a novice of Skama just like us. Tovilyis coven. Her mother was a priestess of the moon."

"And she's a princess herself too!" May topped them all. "A really-truly princess of south Lankhmar land!"

"You can tell she's a princess," Mara fairly shrieked, "because she always wears gloves!"

"Don't squeal like a piglet, Mara," May reproved, seeing a surer way to hog attention, and for a longer time. "Girls, we have omitted to introduce our new friend and rescuer." And when that one still hung back, dropping her eyes demurely, May placed herself beside her and gently impelled her forward.

"Uncle Fafhrd," she said gravely, "may I introduce you to my new friend and rescuer of all of us, the princess Fingers of Tovilyis? And, dear Princess, my friend, may I tender your hand to our most honored guest Captain Fafhrd, a great hero of Rime Isle, my Aunt Afreyt's lover, and my own dearest uncle?"

The strangely yashmacked girl dropped her eyes still farther and seemed to shiver slightly all over, yet let her left hand be drawn forward.

Fafhrd took it and, bowing ceremoniously low and looking straight into the hooded and half-averted face, said, "Any friend of May's is a friend of mine, most honored Princess Fingers, while as the rescuer of her and all my other friends here, I owe you eternal gratitude. My sword is yours." And he kissed the lamb's hide for three heartbeats. Her head tipped up a trifle and her eyelashes fluttered.

All the other girls ooh'ed and aah'ed, though there was a hard expression on Klute's face, while the Mouser's gaze grew somewhat sardonic.

May repossessed herself of the gloved hand and swung it toward the Mouser.

"Dear Uncle Mouser," she intoned, her voice speeding up just a little because of the repetition, despite her efforts to vary her speech, "could I introduce you to my new friend and benefactress of all us girls, the princess Fingers of south Lankhmar land? Princess dear, my friend, could I entrust your precious hand to our honored guest Captain Mouser, Klute's Aunt Cif's lover and my own good, beloved, honorary uncle—and hero of Rime Isle second only to Fafhrd?"

The Mouser's eyebrows lifted formidably. "Her left hand? No, you may not," he dismissed May harshly, setting his fists upon his hips and standing as tall as possible, which involved leaning back a little. Then, looking sneeringly down his nose at the scrawny figure cowered before him, he made a fearsome face and barked commandingly, "Manners, child!— for it is a child you are, an ill bred and conceited snit of a girl-child, whatever else you may be."

The other girls gasped in consternation at this turn of talk, while Fafhrd gave his comrade an unfriendly glare, but the one addressed swiftly drew off her gloves and unyashmacked, revealing a piquant face blushing almost the same hue as her close-cropped hair as she tucked the three lambskin items inside her belt.

Lifting her eyes to the Mouser, she said in a low clear voice, "You rebuke me well, sir. I most humbly apologize." She spoke (though with a strange lisping accent) the same Low Lankhmarese the others all had used, which was the common trade language of most of Nehwon. Then she extended up toward him palm down a slender pale right hand.

He took it without gripping, resting it on his spread fingers as he observed it thoughtfully. "Fingers," he said slowly, as though savoring the word. "Now that's an odd name for a princess."

"I am no princess, sir," she responded instantly. "That's

but something I told the priestesses when I came off *Weasel,* to be sure my warning would be listened to.''

The other girls stared at her as though betrayed, but the Gray Mouser only nodded ruminatively, hefting her hand as though appraising it. "That fits better with what I find here," he said, "much as your speech says Ilthmar to my ear and not Tovilyis. Observe," he continued, as if lecturing, "though narrow, this is a strong and efficient working hand, has done much gripping and squeezing, rubbing and slapping, twisting and prodding, tapping and stroking, finger dancing, et cetera." He turned it over, so her palm lay upward, and rubbed that testingly with his thumb in a circle. "And yet despite the work it's done, it's moist and most pleasingly soft. That's from the oil in the lambswool of the gloves. I doubt not that her uncommon yashmack equally benefits her cheeks, lips, and winsome chin, making them all luxuriously smooth." He sighed thoughtfully. Then, "May, approach us! Hold out your hand." The blond girl obeyed wonderingly. He dropped the hand he'd been supporting into it and turned toward Klute, who was grinning wickedly.

"How does my favorite niece?"

The other girls appeared to be hunting furiously for something to say. Fafhrd swung toward the Mouser, Fingers looked tranquil, when all of a sudden Afreyt called briskly from the top of the stairs, "That's enough games in the cellar and skulking in the forecastle! On deck all of you and earn your dinners!"

Klute and the Mouser led the way, gossiping airily, he making much of her, Mara and Gale followed somewhat glumly. Fafhrd deftly caught up May and Fingers where the Mouser had left them standing bemusedly hand in hand and, holding them comfortably in either arm, brought up the rear.

"My co-captain has somewhat crabbed ways," he explained to them lightly. "Would question the credentials of the Queen of Heaven, yet be jealous of a chipmunk that won attention. He treasures an insult above all else."

5

Cif's kitchen was wide and low-ceilinged, ventilated and somewhat cooled by an early evening breeze sweeping through opposite open doors, although the low rays of the setting sun still struck in.

Tall silver-blond Afreyt and lithe green-eyed Cif were still in their long white priestess tunics, though both had unyashmacked. After embracing the Mouser, the latter directed him and Fafhrd as to carrying the two tables and some benches outdoors on the room's shadeside. The girls were gathered about Afreyt, May and Gale eagerly addressing her in low voices while gazing around from time to time over their shoulders.

When the two men returned from their task, they found the two Moon priestesses standing side by side and changed to gayer scoop-necked tunics of yellow-striped violet and green spotted with brown. The girls, apparently already given their directions, set to carrying tablecloths and trays of condiments and dining utensils outside.

Cif said, "I gather you've already been acquainted with our new guest?"

"And told of the signal service she did our nieces and all Rime Isle, for that matter?" Afreyt added.

"We have indeed," Fafhrd affirmed. "And I assume you've already taken measures against the miscreants captaining and crewing *Weasel*?"

"That we have," Afreyt affirmed. "The Council was convened in jig time and swiftly persuaded to deal with the matter Rime Isle fashion—they imposed a considerable fine (on other charges than intended kidnapping: that *Weasel*'s woodwork showed holes suspiciously like those of the boreworm that swiftly infests other craft) and sent the infamous trader packing posthaste."

"We invited Harbormaster Groniger home to dinner with

us," Cif took up, "but he's gone by way of the headland to check that that pestilent *Weasel* has dock-parted as sworn to and is on her way."

"So what's all this, most dear Gray Mouser," Afreyt demanded quietly, "about your badgering the poor child and ignoring she's a novice of the Goddess and even refusing to grip hands with her?"

Straightening himself and folding his arms across his chest and looking her in the eye, even doing the leaning back bit, the Mouser retorted loudly, "Poor child, forsooth! She is no princess, as she swift confessed, nor any kidnapped moon novice from Tovilyis, I'll be sworn. What her game is I do not know, though I could guess at it, but here's the truth: She's nothing but a cabin girl from Ilthmar where the rat is worshipped, the lowest of the low, beneath recognition, a common child ship-whore hired on for the erotic solacing of all aboard, unfit to share your roof, Lady Afreyt, or company with your innocent nieces or with Cif's except to corrupt them. All signs point to it! Her name alone is proof. As Fafhrd here would instantly confirm, were he not lost in romancing, fondly willing to play knight-and-princess games for a child audience whatever the risk. Which is his chief weakness, you may be sure!"

The others tried to hush or answer him, the girls all listened wide-eyed, slowing in their chores, but he doggedly maintained his tirade to its end, whereupon silver-blond Afreyt, her blue eyes flashing lightning, spoke arrow-swift, "One thing's confirmed beyond question, mean-minded man, she is a true novice of the Goddess: she knows the cryptic words and secret signs."

To which Cif swiftly added, "She knows the color. She wears the garment and the yashmack."

"And gloves?" the Mouser inquired blandly. "I never knew you and Afreyt wear gloves of any hue in summertime. Even in winter it is mittens only. The girls the same, goes without saying."

Cif shot back, "We at Rime Isle are but one twig of the sisterhood. Doubtless they have different local customs in Tovilyis."

The Mouser smiled. "Dear lady, you are far too innocent,

and limited in your knowledge by your island life. There's more evil in gloves than you ever dreamed, more uses for a yashmack than a badge of purity or advertisement of a man's possession, or for a mask. Amongst the more knowing Ilthmar cabingirls (and this one is no novice, I'll be bound!) it is the practice to wear such things to keep their hands soft, also their lips and faces, while as for their privities, you may be sure they enjoy the close covering of oily wool, being tweaked shamelessly hairless besides. For, hark you, on Ilthmar ships the cabingirl delights the crewmen by her hands alone, the short knowing dance of her most pliant fingers; there'd be too much risk of damage to her otherwise, and fresh cabingirls do not grow on sea trees, as they say. *That*, by the by, is why her name is proof. The mates and lesser officers have the freedom of her face and teats, all above waist, while what's below is reserved for his eminence the captain alone, besides all else he wants. But he, the wisest aboard, can be trusted to see she doesn't conceive. The arrangement is swift, efficient, and practical—helps maintain discipline and status both.''

By this time the girls were all gathered close around, four of them goggle-eyed, Fingers respectfully attentive.

''But is this true he says?'' Afreyt asked Fafhrd with some indignation. ''Are there such cabingirls and naughty practices?''

''I'd like to lie to spite him for his boorishness,'' the Northerner averred, ''but I must agree there are such practices and cabingirls, and not alone on Ilthmar ships. Mostly their parents sell them to the trade. Some grow up to become hardy sailors themselves, or wed a passenger, though that is rare.''

''All men are beasts,'' Cif said darkly. ''New proofs keep coming in.''

''And women beastesses,'' the Mouser added sotto voce. ''Or animalesses?''

Afreyt shook her head, then looked at Fingers, who did, alas, appear to have been hearing all these enormities with remarkable coolness.

''What say you to all this, child?'' she asked, straight out.

''All Captain Mouser said is mostly true,'' Fingers replied simply, making a little grimace suiting her piquant mien, ''about cabingirls and such, I mean, although I only know what I learned serving aboard *Weasel*. Unwillingly. But on

the first legs of our voyage there was a two-years-older
cabingirl, jumped ship at Ool Plerns, who taught me much.
And my parent did not hire or sell me into the trade. I was
stolen from her—that much is true of 'kidnapped.' But I did
not tell you about these matters, Lady Afreyt and Lady Cif,
when I escaped and brought you my warning, singling out
you two because you wore the color and the yashmack,
because I did not think that they were vital.''

The Mouser butted in complacently with, ''So much for the
story of *Weasel* being a slaver. Her tale is fishy.''

''She never told us *Weasel* was a slaver!'' Afreyt snapped.

''She lost one cabingirl at Ool Plems,'' Cif put in eagerly.
''What more natural than that the brutes should plot to steal
a replacement here?—where are none such for hire, I'll
be bound. All Rime Isle women serving sailors must be
full-grown.''

The Mouser launched in again satisfiedly with, ''But surely,
Lady Afreyt, you and Cif cannot have taken this tale of
multiple slavings and kidnappings very seriously. Else you'd
not now be letting *Weasel* sail free away without thorough
search of every space aboard might harbor prisoners?''

''Again, you're wrong,'' the tall woman told him angrily.
''The two men sent aboard to discover boreworm holes searched
her most thoroughly before they found them!''

''No other girls aboard *Weasel*?'' the Mouser inquired
ingenuously. ''No females at all?'' Both women nodded,
glaring at him. ''So, no evidence at all for kidnap theories,''
he concluded blandly.

''But Cif's suggestion about their lusting afer a second
cabin-girl—or maybe four—'' Afreyt began exasperatedly.

''Your pardon, my dear,'' Fafhrd interrupted without heat
yet commandingly, ''but would it not be best if we do our
guest Fingers the courtesy of listening to her full story without any more interruptions?—especially sly, argumentative
ones!'' And he gave the Mouser a very hard look. ''She tells
it well, speaking concisely.'' He smiled at her.

''That's sensible,'' Afreyt admitted graciously. ''But before we do, since it's oppressive here, let's go outside
where she can speak and we can listen comfortably. We'll

delay serving dinner. It will not spoil. Yes, girls, you may come along,'' she added, seeing their expressions, ''and place yourselves at the same table. Chores can wait, but no chattering.''

6

Outside, Rime Isle's treeless summer verdure stretched out to the sea and to the nearby headland, which was still in sunshine, broken only by a few low juts of rock and fewer grazing sheep, and, like a giant's round shield cast down close by on the turf, the dark bronze flatness of a large moondial that marked a white-witch dwelling and traced the wanderings of Nehwon's moon through the constellations of Nehwon's broad zodiac; the several bright star pairs of the Lovers, the dim stars of the Ghosts, and the skinny long triangle of the Knife, with the bright tipstar red as blood. The ghostly moon herself, on the verge of full, hung low above the watery eastern horizon, from behind which she'd emerged within the quarter hour. The cooling eve breeze rippled around them gently. The house they'd just left hid them from the sun (soon to plunge into the western sea) save where its flat red rays gleamed from the open kitchen door and windows behind them.

The four adults took seat with Fingers in their midst. The four other girls leaned into the four spaces between.

She began, ''I was born at Tovilyis, where my mother was an officer in the Guild of Free Women and a moon priestess besides. I never knew my father. Quite a few Guild children didn't. I became a moon novice there, where truly white gloves are worn, though not of lamb's hide.'' She touched those under her belt. ''The Guild falling into hard times, I journeyed with my mother for a space, settling in Ilthmar, where we worked as weavers, from my dexterity at which occupation and at the flute and small drum and the games cat's cradle and shadow shape, I got the nickname Fingers, which later proved to be most ominous indeed. We got Ilthmar accents. Mother says, fit in! We even paid lip service to the Rat and made sacrifice on his holidays at his dockside temple on the Inner Sea. Beneath the dark low portico of which I was one night sandbagged, as I later deduced, awakening to find myself aboard *Weasel*, choppy gray Inner Sea all around, feeling dizzy and headachy. I was more than naked, being shorn and shaved of all hair save my eyelashes and brows. And I was being instructed by one of her officers and this two-year-older cabingirl called Hothand in the latter's arts, which are by no means always exercised in cabins.

"When I balked at some of their directions and demands, they set boreworms to me."

"Monstrous!" Fafhrd exclaimed. Afreyt frowned at him and flirted an admonitory hand for silence while the Mouser laid a remindful finger across his blandly smiling lips.

Fingers continued, "As you may know, those bristly gray caterpillars, though feeding solely on wood, will flee the light if brought outside their tunnels by wriggling into the nearest crevice or small orifice, whether it be in inert material or living flesh, thereafter writhing deeper and deeper until they starve for lack of dead wood or proper food. My instructress told me they're sometimes used to break in or discipline new whores, young or older, since they mostly do no lasting damage, only excruciate."

"So there *were* boreworms—" the Mouser began, instantly clapping his hand over his mouth.

"So I complied, recalling my mother's rule, Fit in!—and learned another sort of finger-work and other skills besides, until I earned the grudging praise of my young instructress. I did not seek to excel her, since I needed friends and she was my chief watchdog when we were in ports. I did not, for example, copy her signature, which also accounted for her nickname, and which was to blow into her hand before she used it in her work. I walked my fingers upon the bodies of those I serviced, keeping up a glib patter as I approached the target area, about my hand being a lost and ensorcelled princess, conjured tiny, who marveled innocently at all the items she encountered in her little world and the actions that she was moved to perform upon them. The sailors relished that. It fed their fancy.

"So occupied, and under Hothand's hard and watchful eye, I first saw the docks of Lankhmar, forest-girt Kvarch Nar, Ool Hrusp, and other cities on the Inner Sea.

"I also early came to the conclusion that my period of sandbagged unconsciousness had been prolonged with drugs, not for hours but days at least. For as soon as I'd been able to examine myself at leisure, I'd discover that my head hair had grown and my skin paled as much as it had during my fortnight's seclusion before my novice's initiation, while all my body hairs had been tweaked out. But what else had happened during this period, and if I'd been prisoned at one place or carried about before being taken aboard *Weasel*, I could never learn, nor would (or perhaps could) Hothand tell me. There was in my mind only a weltering sea of dark nightmarish impressions I couldn't decipher.

"Hothand became my friend, but not to the point where she invited me to desert with her at Ool Plerns. I think she might have, except she knew that losing both cabingirls would be a sure way to ensure a desperately determined pursuit. In fact, before she left she tied me up most securely (she was expert at that) and gagged me, saying mysteriously, before she kissed me goodbye, 'I am doing this for your own good, little Fingers. It may save you a beating.'

"And indeed I was not beaten, but when *Weasel* next docked, at No-Ombrulsk before our long reach here, I was confined below, tethered to timber by a chain and an iron-studded locked collar to which the captain alone held the key. It had previously chained his pursuit hound until the bitch died on *Weasel*'s last voyage but this.

"I've never felt lonelier than I did on the long wearisome sail that next came. At the worst moments I'd comfort myself by remembering Hothand's last kiss, though hating her madly at the same time. I also determined to escape ship at Rime Isle (which I'd always before thought a fable) no matter how strange and savage its inhabitants." She looked around at them all and her eyes twinkled. "I knew that my first step must be to do all in my power to ensure I was not again chained below. So, no longer having to fear Hothand's resentment, I devoted all my ingenuity and imagination to heightening and prolonging the ecstasies of all I serviced, though not long enough, of course, in the case of crewmen, to offend captain or officers if such were about. And sympathize with them all, goes without saying, in a motherly way, working to increase the area of familiarity and trust among us.

"With the result that when we finally raised Rime Isle and docked in Salthaven, I was allowed on deck for a short look and a breath, though under guard. I soon decided the shorefolk were civil and humane, but I pretended fear and distaste of all I saw, which helped persuade my captors there was little risk of my sneaking off.

"When you, May and Gale, joined those peering at the newly-arrived ship, I soon was hearing indecently lustful whispers from all the *Weasel*'s crew around me."

"Really?"

"Truly?"

She nodded solemnly at the two girls and went on, "I pretended to be angry with them, wanting barbarian girls when they had me, but that night I confessed to the captain how much I would enjoy teaching you with his aid the arts in which Hothand had instructed me and disciplining you when you turned balky, complaining I'd had no one to humiliate since becoming chief cabingirl. He said he'd like to please me but that kidnapping you would be too risky. I kept on wheedling him, however, and he finally told me it would be another matter if I went ashore and lured you to come aboard secretly without telling anyone. I pretended to be terrified of setting foot on savage Rime Isle, but in the end I let him persuade me.

"So that's how I was able to escape from *Weasel* and warn you, dear Lady Afreyt and Lady Cif," Fingers concluded with a doubtful smile.

"You see?" the Mouser broke his enforced silence almost gleefully. "She planned the whole kidnapping herself! Or at least forced the *Weasel*'s captain to sharpen his plans. It's the old saw, 'A devious plot? Some woman wove it!' "

"But she only did it in order to—" Cif began furiously.

Afreyt said simultaneously, "Captain Mouser, with all respect, you are impossible!"

Cif rebegan, "She only employed the tricksy guile you
would yourself in like situation."

"That's pure truth," Fafhrd confirmed. "Guest Fingers,
you are the Princess of Plotters. I never heard a braver tale."
Then, sotto voce to Afreyt, "I declare, Mouser gets more
stubborn-cranky every day. He can't have shaken the old-age
curse. That would explain it."

Mara piped up, "You wouldn't really have enjoyed beating
us, would you, Fingers?"

KLUTE: I bet she would. With a dogwhip! The pursuit
hound's.

GALE: No, she wouldn't, she'd think of something worse,
like putting boreworms up our noses.

MAY: Or in our ears!

KLUTE: Or maybe in our salad.

GALE: Or up our—

AFREYT: Children! That's quite enough. Go and fetch out
our dinners, all of you. Quickly. Fingers, please help them.

They trooped off excitedly, beginning to whisper as they
reached the kitchen.

7

Afreyt said, "And while we're eating our dinners, Mouser, I
hope you won't—"

But he interrupted, "Oh, I know well enough when you're
all against me. I'll be wordless willingly. Let me tell you, it's
hard work being the voice of prudence and good sense when
you're all being noble and generous and riding your liberal
hobby horses recklessly."

Cif smiled with a shrug and one eye toward heaven. "Just

the same, I'd feel better if you'd go a little further than just
being quiet and—''

"Why not?" he demanded hugely with the ghost of a
growl. "Break one, break all. Princess Fingers," he called,
"would your majesty please approach me?"

The girl put down the covered tray of hotcakes she'd just
carried in and turned toward him with eyes lowered respectfully. "Yes sir?"

He said, "My friends here tell me I should take your right
hand." She extended hers. He took it, saying, "Princess, I
admire your courage and cunning, in which latter quality they
tell me you resemble myself. Good guesting and all that!"
and he squeezed. She hid a wince as she smiled up at him. He
held on. "But hear this, royalty: no matter how clever you
are, you're not as clever as I am. And if, through you, any of
these girls, or any of my other friends should come to harm,
remember you will have me to answer to."

She replied, "That's a proviso I'll accept and abide by
most happily, sir," and with a little bow she hurried back to
the kitchen.

"Bring out four more settings," Afreyt called after her. "I
see Groniger coming in company from the headland. Who are
those walk beside him, Fafhrd?"

"Skullick and Pshawri," he told her, scanning the group
moving down toward them out of the last sunset gleam,
"come to make report to us of the day's accomplishments.
And old Ourph—these days the ancient Mingol often suns
his old bones up there where he can scan both the harbor to
the south and the sleepy Maelstrom to the east beyond."

The last sun patch upon the headland darkened and the
misty moon at once seemed to grow brighter above the four
oncomers.

"They hurry on apace," Cif commented. "Old Ourph as
well, who commonly lags behind."

Afreyt assured herself the girl's task was done and extra
places set. "Then fall to, all of you, with the Goddess'
blessing. Else we'll never start feeding."

They had sampled the pickled and spiced and nibbled
garden-fresh radishes and were chomping roast lamb and sweet
mint conserves by the time the four striders drew nigh. Simul-

taneously the cloud ceiling swiftly went lemon pale with reflected light from the setting or set sun, like a soft sustained trumpet peal of welcome. Their faces showed sudden clear in the afterglow, as if they'd all unmasked.

Groniger said laconically, *"Weasel* left harbor. Dappled sky to the north presages a wind to speed her on her way. And there's news of a rather greater interest," he added, glancing down toward bent and wrinkle-visaged Ourph.

When that one didn't speak at once, or anyone immediately ask, "What is it?" Pshawri launched out with, "Before *Weasel* got off, Captain Mouser, I traded deer pelts and a sable for seven pine planks, two slabs of oak, and peppercorn Cook wanted. We harvested the field of ear-corn and white-washed the barn. Gilgy seems healed of his sunstroke."

"The wood was seasoned?" Mouser asked testily. Pshawri nodded. "Then next time say so. I like conciseness, but not at the expense of precision."

Skullick took up. "Skor had us careen *Seahawk,* Captain Fafhrd, it being Satyrs' lowest tide, what with moon's full tomorrow night, and we finished copper-sheathing her steerside. There was a wildfowl hunt. I took *Kringle* fishing. We caught naught."

"Enough," Fafhrd said, waving him silent. "What's this news of import, Ourph?"

Afreyt arose, saying, "It can wait on courtesy. Gentlemen, join us. There are places set."

The three others nodded thanks and moved to the well to rinse up, but the ancient Mingol held his ground, bending on Fafhrd a gaze black as his long-skirted tunic and saying portentously, "Captain, as I did take my watch upon the headland, in midafternoon, the sun being halfway descended to the west, I looked toward the great Maelstrom that for this year and half year, this last six seasons, has been still as mountain lake, unnaturally so, and I saw it 'gin to stir and keep on stirring, slowly, slowly, slowly, as though the sea were thick as witch's brew."

To everyone's surprise, the Mouser cried out a long loud *"What?"* rising to his feet and glaring direly. "What's that you say, you dismal dodderer? You black spider of ill omen! You dried up skeleton!"

"No, Mouser, he speaks true," Groniger reproved him, returning to take his place prepared next to the women. "I saw it with my own eyes! The currents have come right again at last and Rime Isle's whirlpool is spinning sluggishly. With any luck—and help of northern storm that's gathering—she'll spin ashore the rest of the Mingol wrecks for us to salvage, along with other ships have sunken since. Cheer up, friend."

The Mouser glowered at him. "You calculating miser greedy for gray driftwood gain! No, there are things sea-buried there I would not have fished up again. Hark ye, old Ourph! Ere the 'pool 'gan spin, saw ye any ill-doers sniffing about? I smell wizard's work."

"No wizards, Captain Mou, no one at all," the ancient Mingol averred. "Pshawri and Skullick—" He waved toward the two taking places farther down the table. "—took *Kringle* there earlier and anchored for a while. They will confirm my statement."

"What?" Again that low-shrieking, long-drawn-out accusatory word sped from the Mouser's lips as he swung glaring toward the two Ourph had mentioned. "You took out *Kringle*? Meddled in the Maelstrom?"

"What matter?" Skullick retorted boldly. "I told you we went fishing. We anchored for a while. And Pshawri did one dive." Old Ourph nodded. "Nothing at all."

"Fafhrd can deal with you," the Mouser told him dismissingly. Then, focusing on his own man, "What mischief were you up to, Pshawri? What were you diving for? What did you hope to find? Plunging in Maelstrom's midst without my order or permission? *What did you bring up with you from the dive?"*

Flushing darkly, "Captain, you do me wrong," Pshawri replied, looking him straight in the eye. "Skullick can answer for me. He was there."

"He brought up nothing," Skullick said flatly. "And whatever he might have brought up, I'm sure he would have saved to give to you."

"I do not believe you," the Mouser said. "You're insubordinate, both of you. With you, Lieutenant Pshawri, I can deal. For the rest of this moon you are demoted to common seaman. At new moon I will reconsider your case. Until then the matter is closed. I wish to hear no more of it.''

Fafhrd spoke from mouth's corner to Afreyt beside him. "Two temper tantrums in one evening! No question, the old-age curse still grips him."

Afreyt whispered back, "I think he's taking out on Pshawri what's left of his strange anger at the Fingers girl."

PSHAWRI: Captain, you wrong me.

MOUSER: I said, "No more!"

OURPH: Cap Mou, I singled out your lieutenant and Fafhrd's sergeant to bear me witness, not accuse 'em of aught.

GRONIGER: We of Rime Isle abhor wizardry, superstition, and ill-speaking all. Life's bad enough without them.

SKULLICK: There have been some accusations made this eve and ill words spoken—

FAFHRD: An' so let's have no more of them. Pipe down, Sergeant!

During these interchanges the Mouser sat scowling straight ahead and, save for his curt admonition, with lips pressed tightly together.

Afreyt got to her feet, drawing Cif up with her, who sat on her other side. "Gentlemen," she said quietly, "this evening you would all gratify me by following Captain Mouser's wise advice, which as you can see he follows himself, setting us good example, of no more words on this perplexing matter." She looked the table around with a particularly asking eye toward Pshawri.

Cif said, "And after all, it is Full Moon Day Eve."

"So please eat up your dinner," Afreyt went on, smiling, "or I shall think you do not like our cooking."

"And replenish your mugs," Cif added. "In wine's best wisdom."

As they sat down, Fafhrd and Groniger applauded lightly in approval and the girls all clapped imitatively.

Old Ourph croaked, "It's true, silence is silver."

Sitting beside Fingers, May told her, "I've an extra white tunic I can lend you for tomorrow night."

On her other side Gale said, "And I have a spare yashmack. And I believe Klute has—"

"Unless, of course," May interrupted, "you'd want to wear your own things."

"No," Fingers hastened to say, "now I'm on Rime Isle. I want to look like you." She smiled.

Cif whispered to Afreyt, "It's a strange thing. I know the Mouser's behaved like a monster tonight, and yet I can't help feeling that in some way he's *right* about Fingers and Pshawri, that they both lied to us in some way, maybe different ways. She was so cool about it all, almost the way a sleepwalker would talk.

"And Pshawri—he's always trying to impress the Mouser and win his praise, which rubs Mouser the wrong way. But a fortnight back, when the last Lankhmar trader came in—the *Comet,* she was—she carried a letter with a green seal for Pshawri, and since then there's been something new about his clashes with Mouser, something new and heavy."

Afreyt said, "I've sensed a different mood in Pshawri myself. Any idea what was in the letter?"

"Of course not."

"Then tell me this: This strange feeling you have about the Mouser and the other two, does it come from your own thinking and imaginings, or from the Goddess?"

"I wish I were sure," Cif said as the two of them looked out together at the misted and ghastly bare gibbous moon.

AFREYT: Perchance at tomorrow night's ceremony she'll provide an answer.

CIF: We must press her.

8

That night Rime Isle most unaccountably grew wondrous cold and colder still, a blizzardly north wind blowing until the massive driftwood chimes in the leviathan-jaw arch of the Moon Temple clanked together dolefully and all sleepers suffered heavy sense-drugging nightmares, some toilsome and shivery heaving ones. When dawn at last came glimmering through swirls of powder snow, it was revealed that Fafhrd in ill nightcrawler's grip had somehow worked his way, dragging the covers after, up the maze of silver and brazen rods heading Cif's grand guest bed until the back of his head pressed the ceiling and he hung as one crucified asleep, while she below, hugging his ankles, dreamt they wandered a wintry waste embraced until a frigid gust parted them and whirled the Northerner high into the ice-gray sky until he seemed no bigger than a struggling gull, and that a like Morphean bondage had drawn the Gray Mouser, naked save for hauled-with sheet, out of and then under the second-best guest bed whereon he and Cif had gone excitingly to their slumbers, and she dreamed that they endlessly traversed shadowy subterranean corridors, their only light an eerie glow emanating from the Mouser's upper face, as if he wore a narrow glowing mask in which his eyes were horrid pits of darkness, until the Gray One slipped away from her through a trapdoor whereon was writ in phosphorescent Lankhmarese script, "The Underworld."

But all such personal plights and predicaments, ominous nightsights and sleepwalks, were soon almost forgot, became hazy in memory, as the extent of the general calamity was realized and a desperate rush to correct it began.

There were loved ones to be chafed, lost sheep to be succored—aye, and half-frozen shepherds too and other sleepers-out—cold ovens to be cleared of summer stowage and fired, kindling cut and seacoal shoveled, winter clothes dug from the bottoms of chests, strained moorings doubled and trebled of ships tossing at their docks and anchors, hatches battened in roofs and decks, lone dwellers visited.

When there was time for talk and wondering, some guessed that Khahkht the Wizard of Ice was on a rampage, others that the invisible winged Princes of lofty Stardock were out raiding or—alarmist!—that the freezing glacial streams had at last tunneled through Nehwon's crust and dowsed her inner fires. Cif and Afreyt looked to find answers at the full moon ceremony, and when Mother Grum and the Senior Council canceled it on grounds of inclement weather (it being held outdoors), went on with their preparations anyway. Mother Grum raised no objections, believing in freedom of worship, but the Council refused it formal sanction.

So, it was no great wonder that the congregation that gathered before the chimes-arch of the open Moon Temple, with its twelve stone columns marking the year's twelve moons, was such a small one: in the main, exactly those who had dined at Afreyt's the previous evening and been pressed to attend by her and Cif. Those two were there, of course, being ringleaders of the outlaw rite, snug in their winter-priestess garb of white fur-hooded robes, mittens, and wool-lined ramskin boots. The five girls came as obedient novices, though it would have been hard to keep them away from what they considered a prize adventure. They wore like gear, only with shorter capes, so that from time to time their rosy knees showed, and the weird weather made Fingers' lamb's hide yashmack and gloves highly appropriate. Fafhrd and Mouser came as their ladies' lovers, although they'd spent a hard day working, first at Afreyt's, then at their barracks. Both looked a little distant-minded, as though each had begun to remember the nightmares that had accompanied their strange nightcrawlings. Skullick and Pshawri turned up with them. Presumably their captains had reinforced with commands the entreaties of their captains' mistresses, though Pshawri had an oddly intent look, and even the carefree Skullick a concerned one.

Ourph had not been pressed by anyone to attend, in view of his great age, but he was there nevertheless, close-wrapped in dark Mingol furs, with conical black-fur cap and sealskin boots to which small Mingol snowshoes were affixed.

Harbormaster Groniger too, whose atheism might have been expected to keep him away. He said in explanation, "Witchery is always my business. Though arrant superstition, three out of four times it's associated with crime—piracy and mutiny at sea, all manner of ill-workings on land. And don't tell me about you moon priestesses being white witches, not black. I know what I know."

And in the end Mother Grum showed up herself, fur-bundled to the ears and waddling on snowshoes larger than Ourph's. "It's my duty as coven mistress," she grumbled, "to get you out of any scrapes your wild behavior gets you into and to see that in any case no one tries to stop you.'' She glared amiably at Groniger.

With her came Rill the Harlot, also a moon priestess, whose maimed left hand gave her a curious sympathy (unmixed with lechery, or so 'twas thought) with Fafhrd, who'd lost his entirely.

These fifteen, irregularly grouped, stood looking east across the sharp-serrated snow-shedding gables of the small, low, close-set houses of Salthaven, awaiting moonrise. They rapidly shuffled their feet from time to time to warm them. And whenever they did, the massy gray slabs of the sacred wind chime chain-hung from the lofty single-bone leviathan-jaw arch seemed to vibrate faintly yet profoundly in sympathy, or in memory of their earlier hollow clanking when the gale had blown, or perhaps in anticipation of the Goddess' near apparition.

When the low glow of that approach intensified toward a central area above the toothed roofs, the nine females drew somewhat apart from the six males, turning their backs on them and crowding together closely, so that the invocatory words Afreyt whispered might not be overheard by the men, nor the holy objects Cif drew from under her wide cloak and showed around be glimpsed by them.

Then, when a dazzlingly white fingernail clipping of the orb's self, serrated by the teeth of the central-most roof, showed, there was a general sigh of recognition and fulfillment which was echoed inanimately by an intensification of the chimes' real or imagined low vibrations, and the groups broke up and intermingled and joined hands in one long line, the girls leading with May at their head, the rest linked at random, and the whole company began a slow rhythmic circling of the Temple, twice all the way around, then interweaving the carven stone moon pillars—that of the Snow, the Wolf, the Seed, the Witch, the Ghost, the Murderer, the Thunder, the Satyr, the Harvest, the Second Witch, the Frost, and the Lovers—by sixes, by fours, by threes, by two, and individually.

The girls wove their way one after the other, linked hand to hand, gracefully as in a dream. Old Ourph footed it agilely, stamping out the time, while Mother Grum moved briskly for all her fat and with a surprisingly sure rhythm. Rill brought up the rear, swinging a leviathan oil lamp, unlit, from her maimed hand.

As the moonlight slowly strengthened, Fingers marveled somewhat fearfully at the strange Rimish runes and savage scenes carved in the thick moon pillars. Gale squeezed her hand reassuringly and told her in whispered snatches how they represented the adventures of the legendary witch queen Skeldir when she descended into the Underworld to get the help that enabled her to turn back the three dire Simorgyan invasions in the Isle's olden days.

When the seven slow mystic circlings had been completed and the glaringly white orb of Skama (the Goddess' holiest name) fully arisen, so that sky-black hugged her all around, May led the weaving line out across the great meadow to the west, moving forward confidently in the full moonshine. For a short way the shadows of the twelve pillars and the jaw-hung chime accompanied them, then they launched out one by one across the trackless moonlit expanse, the frozen and snow-dusted grass crackling under their feet. May followed a serpentine course, veering now left, now right, that copied their last pillar-weaving, but went straight west, their shadows preceding them.

And then Afreyt called out in vibrant tones the sacred name, "Skama!" and they all began to chant, in time to their dancing advance, the first song to the Goddess:

"Twelve faces has our Lady of the Dark
As she walks nightly cross her starry park:
Snow, Wolf, and Seed Moon, Witches, Ghosts, and Knife,
The Murderer's badge; six more of dark and light:
Thunder, Lust, Harvest, Witches second life;
Then end the year with Frost and Lovers bright;
Queen of the Night and Mistress of the Dark
In your black veils and clinging silver sark."

Their voices fell silent for five beats, Afreyt again called, "Skama!" and they began Her second song, their steps becoming longer and more gliding to suit the changed rhythm:

> *"These be your signets, dread Mistress of Mystery:*
> *Rainbow and bubble, the flame and the star,*
> *Nightbee and glow wasp, volcano, cool bistory,*
> *Things that are hintings of wonders afar;*
> *Comet and hailstone and strange turns of history,*
> *Queen of the Darkness and Lamp of the Night,*
> *Lover of Terror, cruel and sisterly—*
> *Crone, Girl, and Mother, arise in your white!"*

A four-beat pause, once more "Skama!" from Afreyt, and now their dance became a rapid and stamping one, as though they advanced to the pounding of a drum:

> *"Snow Moon, Wolf Moon, Seed Moon, Witch Moon;*
> *Ghost Moon, Knife Moon, Blast Moon, Lust Moon;*
> *Sickle, Witch Two, Frost Moon, Fuck Moon.*
> *Skama beckons, Skeldir goes down*
> *By the lightless narrow stoneway,*
> *Buried Rimish fashion feet first,*
> *Bravely facing poison monsters,*
> *Treading serpents with her bare feet;*
> *Through dry earth and solid rock;*
> *Sinks like ghost into the granite;*
> *Skeldir's courage fails, she falters—*
> *When she spies the moon below her,*
> *In the heart of darkness, light!"*

This time Afreyt let twenty beats go by before giving her invocation, and the hand-linked linear company began a repetition of the three songs while they continued their curving and countercurving westward advance. A little toward the north Elvenhold loomed, a pale stout needle of rock and scrub heather to whose square top the strongest bow could not loft arrow. Two moons ago, on fateful Midsummer Day, all of them save Fingers and Ourph had picnicked there. While toward the south began a series of low rolling hills, at first mere swells in the sea of moonlit grass. And toward these hills May now began to lead their way, an overall southward veering of the dancing line.

By the songs' second repetition islands of gorse and furze

were appearing in the grassy ocean. May led between them toward a somewhat higher hill.

"Our destination?" Fingers asked Gale, softly singing the question into the song they were on.

"Yes," Gale replied in murmured snatches while swaying to the song. "In old times had a gallows. Then 'twas the ghost god Odin's hill when he counseled Aunt Afreyt. I was one of his handmaids."

FINGERS: What did you have to do?

GALE: For one thing, I was his cabingirl, you could say.

FINGERS: You were? You said he was a ghost. Was he solid enough for such things?

GALE: Enough. He wanted all sorts of touching, both do and be done by.

FINGERS: Gods are just like men. Your aunt let you?

GALE: It was very important information she was getting from him. Helped save Rime Isle. Also, I braided nooses for him. He made us wear them around our necks.

FINGERS: That sounds scary. Dangerous.

GALE: It was. That's how Uncle Fafhrd lost his left hand. He was wearing them all around his left wrist in that battle I told you about. When Odin and the gallows vanished up into the sky, the nooses all tightened to nothing and shot up after—and Uncle Fafhrd's hand with them.

FINGERS: Really scary. If you'd kept them round your necks—

GALE: Yes. Later, when Aunt Cif and Mother Grum purified the hill and cut down the bower where May and Mara and I had loved up the old god, they changed its name from Gallows to Goddess' Hill, and we've been holding the summer full-moon rites on it.

MARA: Whatever are you two whispering about? I can see Aunt Afreyt frowning at you.

They instantly took up the song, which by now was another.

"The little demons!" Afreyt whispered to Fafhrd in a not particularly angry voice.

He turned back toward her and nodded, though even less concerned than she, just as he'd sometimes been chanting tonight and sometimes not, as the mood took him.

The chill air was very still and fantastically clear. It occurred to Fafhrd that he had never in his life seen the full moon shine so bright, not even from Stardock. At that instant, as though some hidden cord of weakness deep in his vitals had been shrewdly plucked, he felt a spasm of unmanning faintness flurry through him, a feeling of insubstantiality, as if the world were about to fade away from him, or he from the world. It was all he could do to stand upright and not shake.

As the weird qualm receded somewhat, he looked along the curving line of brightly lit moonlit faces to learn if it were something others had felt. Halfway up the hill the five girls moved on slowly in line, chanting raptly. Fingers, nearest of them but for Gale, looked toward him, but tranquilly, as though she'd simply sensed his gaze upon her. Next closest after the girls, Pshawri, dutifully chanting, or at least moving his lips. Finally, not five feet away, the Mouser, making not even pretense of chanting, seemingly lost in a brown study, but very much at ease, hood thrown back to bare his close-cropped head to the frosty air, while Fafhrd's covered his ears.

Looking on his other side he saw, in orderly succession and absorbed in the ceremony: Afreyt, Groniger, Skullick, old Ourph the Mingol, Cif, fat Mother Grum the Witch, and Rill the Harlot.

And then Fafhrd looked at Cif again (she must have started) and saw that she was now staring past him, her pale face of a sudden contorted with an expression of incredulous horror.

He whipped around and saw, on his side, one face fewer than there'd been before. While he'd been looking in the other direction, the Mouser had gone away somewhere and his fingers dropped away unfelt from the hook that was the Northerner's left hand.

And then he noticed that Pshawri, with an expression on his face not unlike that of Cif's, was staring at the Northerner's knees as if the Gray Mouser's young lieutenant were stupefiedly witnessing some horrifying miracle. Fafhrd looked down and saw that the Mouser had indeed dropped away! Straight down feet first into the frozen earth so he was buried upright to his waist and was no taller than a dwarf. Impossible! But there it was.

Just then, as if some subterranean being gripping the Mouser's ankles had given another mighty yank, Fafhrd's comrade swiftly sank another half yard so he was buried to the chin like a Mingol traitor whom vengeful mates will leisurely dispatch by bowling rocks at his head and leaden-weighted skulls, though only after his concubines have been allowed (or forced) to kiss him one time each full on the lips.

And then the Mouser looked up at Fafhrd with moonlit eyes widening, as if in full realization of his horrid plight, and gasped in piteous appeal, "Help me!" And his tall comrade could only quake and stare.

Fafhrd heard from behind the sound of onrunning footsteps, boots ringing on frozen earth. And for a moment it seemed to him that he could see the moonlit ground through the Mouser's head, as if the little man were becoming attenuated, insubstantial. Or was that only his strange qualm returning? His own swimming eyes?

And then, as if those subterranean hands were giving another tug, the Mouser began to move downward once again rapidly.

From behind him Cif cast herself full length on the frozen ground, her outstretched hands snatching at the disappearing head.

Fafhrd regained his power of movement and swiftly scanned around in case the Mouser's ghost were floating off in some other direction. The air seemed full of movement, but nothing substantial when he looked closely.

With three exceptions everyone was staring at Cif or else hurrying toward her, who was now scrabbling through the scant frozen grass, as though frenziedly hunting for a jewel she'd dropped there. Afreyt and Groniger were looking off intently toward Elvenhold. The tall woman pointed at something and the deliberate man nodded in agreement.

While Fingers was staring straight at Fafhrd in cool accusal, as if asking, "Why didn't you save your friend?"

9

From the Gray Mouser's point of view, what had happened was this:

He'd been staring toward the moon, quite unmindful of the cold and the ceremony, lost in puzzlement as to how he could at once feel so heavy—as though wearied to death and barely able to stay erect, victim of some heatless fever—and yet at the same time so listless-light and insubstantial, as if he were thinning out to become a ghost whom the slightest breeze might blow away. The two feelings didn't agree at all, yet both were there.

Without warning, he experienced a spasm of strange faintness, like Fafhrd's but more intense, so that he blacked out completely. It was as if the ground had been taken out from under his feet. When he came to his senses again, he was looking up at his northern comrade, who had never before seemed quite so tall.

He must have simply keeled over, he told himself, and fallen flat. But when he tried to get up, he found he could move neither hand nor foot, bend waist or knee. Was he paralyzed? Everywhere below his neck something gripped him closely, and when he moved his fingers and thumbs against each other (both hands being imprisoned down by his sides so he couldn't spread fingers or make fist), that *something* felt suspiciously grainy, like raw earth.

In the most horrifying reorientation he'd ever experienced in the course of an eventful life, flat-on-my-back became buried-to-my-neck. Oh dismal! And so incredible that he couldn't really say whether it was the world, or he, that had moved to effect the dreadful exchange.

Something terribly swift in his mind scanned almost instantaneously the pressures all over his body. Were they slightly greater around his ankles? As if he wore gyves, as if something or *someone* gripped both his legs—such as the quick-

sand nixies Sheelba had warned him against in the Great Salt
Marsh. Oh Mog, no!

His gaze traveled up Fafhrd, who seemed tall as a pine,
and he gasped out his agonized plea—*and the great lout
would only goggle and grimace at him, mop and mow in the
moonlight, not only withholding help, but also seeming utterly unmindful of the priceless privilege he enjoyed of standing free atop the ground rather than being immured in it!*

Beyond Fafhrd he saw Cif running straight at him. If she
kept on, she'd boot his face, the mad maenad! He instinct-
ively tried to duck aside and only succeeded in wrenching his
neck. And then he felt the grip on his ankles tighten and cold
earth mount his chin, as his whole being was drawn downward. He clapped his lips tightly together to keep dirt out,
drew one swift breath, then tried to narrow his nostrils,
finally closed tight his eyes as his engulfment continued. Last
thing he saw was the moon. As the gray glow of it transmit-
ted through his eyelids vanished upward, he felt his pate
scratched and his topknot sharply tweaked. Then even that
was gone and there remained only a grainy coldness sliding
up his cheeks. Strangely, then, it seemed to grow a little
warmer and—a very little—looser, so he could puff some of
the air trapped in his mouth out into his cheeks. The texture
of the stuff scraping his cheeks changed from earth to wool to
earth again. He realized his cowl had been dragged upward
from around his neck and left buried above him. And then the
rough sliding seemed to stop. One other thing he had to
admit: the feeling of heaviness that had so long dogged him
was completely gone. However closely confined, he seemed
now rather to be floating.

The swift something in his mind produced for his consider-
ation a list of the beings who might hate him enough to wish
him such a horrid doom and also conceivably have the magical power to effect it on him. The wizards Quarmal of
Quarmall, Khakht the Ice Wizard, Great Oomforafor, Hisvin
the Rat King, his own mentor Sheelba turned against him,
dear diabolic Hisvet, the gods Loki and Mog. It went on and on.

One thing stood out: any world in which a man could be
twitched into his grave by the legerdemain of some mad
principality or power was *monstrously* unfair!

10

Aboveground, Cif rose to her knees, from where she'd been crouched, breaking her fingernails scrabbling at the frosty ground, and stretched her arms around the girls, who had been crowding in close and all trying to touch her, more for their own comfort and reassurance than for hers. She tried to touch them all in turn and draw them to her, hushing their clamors, though as much for her own comfort as for theirs. They felt cold.

Dumbstruck, Fafhrd turned back to ask Afreyt exactly what she'd seen when Mouser had seemed to sink into the ground impossibly. To his confusion he saw that she and Groniger were already a dozen yards away, hurrying toward Elvenhold, while Rill was sprinting after them at an angle from where she'd been at the end of the ritual line, the unlit lamp still streaming out behind her.

With a slow, puzzled headshake he turned forward again and saw, beyond the huddled backs of Cif and the girls, Pshawri convulsed in an agony, his features grimaced, his eyes squeezed half shut, his taut body rocking forward and back, and literally tearing his hair. By Kos, did the knave think it was mourning time already?

Then the tortured eyes of the Mouser's young lieutenant fixed upon Cif. They widened, his body ceased to rock, he left off tearing his hair and he threw out both arms to her in mute appeal.

She responded immediately, pushing fully to her feet to go to him. But at that moment Fafhrd found his voice.

"Don't move a step!" he called commandingly in carefully enunciated battle tones. "Stay where you are exactly—or we will lose the spot where Mouser disappeared into the ground."

And he moved toward her deliberately, his sound right hand working to free his doubled-headed hand ax from the case where it hung at his side, its short helve pendant.

"The spot where we must dig," he amplified, going to his knees close behind her.

She turned around, and seeing him bringing out his ax and thinking he meant to chop into the ground with it, cried in alarm, "Oh, don't do that, you might hurt *him*."

He shook his head reassuringly, and grasping the ax at the juncture of its head and helve, scraped with it strongly inward toward his knees, feeling with his hook through the earth he uncovered. He scraped three like swaths behind the first, baring a space about as big as a trapdoor, and then repeated the process, going an inch deeper.

Meanwhile Pshawri was approaching Cif, fumbling his pouch and babbling, "Sweet Lady, I am responsible for this dire mishap to my captain. I alone am guilty. Here, let me show you. . . ."

Without ceasing his work, Fafhrd called sharply, "Forget that, Pshawri, and come here. I have an errand for you."

But when that one did not seem to hear his words, only continuing to stare desperately at Cif and now groping at her arms to draw her attention, Fafhrd signed to her to draw the madman aside and hear his mouthings, meanwhile commanding, "You, Skullick, then! Come here!"

When his young sergeant swiftly obeyed, though not without an uneasy glance toward Pshawri, Fafhrd instructed him tersely, while keeping on with his scrapings, "Skullick, run like the wind back to the barracks. Find Skor and Mikkidu. Bid them haste here with one or two men apiece bringing heavy work gloves, scoops, shovels, pails, lanterns, and ropes. Don't try to explain anything—here, take my ring. Then do you choose a man each of the Mouser's men and mine—and a Mingol—and come on after with planks and the instruments needful for shoring a shaft, more rope, pulleys, food, fuel, water, a keg of brandy, blankets, the medicine case. Come as soon as these can be gathered. Use the dogcarts. Mannimark to remain in command at the barracks. Any questions? No? Then go!"

Skullick went. Instantly Rill took his place.

"Fafhrd," she said urgently, "Afreyt and Groniger bid me tell you that whatever you believe we saw, or think we saw, deceived perhaps by a phantom, the Mouser, at the end, raced with preternatural speed toward Elvenhold and then took cover. They go to hunt him. They urge you join them, after sending for lanterns, the dogs Racer and Gripper, and an unwashed piece of the Mouser's intimate clothing.''

Fafhrd left off scraping out the square hole, which was five or six inches deep, to look around questioningly at those who had been listening.

"Captain, he sank into the ground where you are digging," said Ourph the Mingol. "I saw."

"It's true," growled Mother Grum, "though he grew somewhat insubstantial at the end."

Cif broke away from the importunate Pshawri to aver with great certitude, "He went down there. I touched his pate and top hair before he sank away."

Pshawri followed behind her, crying, "Here, Lady, I've found it. Here is the proof I lied to the Captain when I told him yesternight I brought up nothing from my Maelstrom dive."

It was a skeleton cube of smooth metal big as an infant's fist with something dark wedged inside. The metal looked like silver in the moonlight, but Cif knew that without question it was gold—the Rimish ikon that the Mouser had slung into the Great Maelstrom's center to quieten it after the wrecking of the Sea-Mingol armada.

"My taking of this from the whirlpool's maw," madeyed Pshawri proclaimed, "though meant to please him, has been the means of my captain's doom. As he himself feared might hap. Gods, was ever man so cruelly self-deceived?"

"Why did you lie to him, then?" Fafhrd asked. "And why did you so desire to possess it?"

"I may not tell you," Pshawri said miserably. "That is a private matter between myself and the Captain. Gods, what's to do? What is to do?"

"We keep on digging here," Fafhrd decided, suiting action to word. "Rill, tell Afreyt and Groniger of my decision."

"First let me make your work here easier," that one said, bringing the leviathan lantern from behind her and planting it on the ground next the square hole Fafhrd was diggin, then snapping the fingers of her right hand thrice.

"Burn without heat," she said simultaneously.

The simple magic worked.

Leviathan light white as new-fallen snow, pure bistory, sprang into being and illumined the surroundings like a piece of the full moon brought down to earth, so that every dirt grain inside the new-digged square seemed individually visible.

Fafhrd thanked her duly and Rill made off briskly toward Elvenhold.

Fafhrd turned back and said, ''Pshawri, sit across the hole from me and feel through the new dirt uncovered by each of my ax scrapes. Two hands work faster than a hook. Gale! You—and Fingers here—come and kneel beside me and clear off to either side the earth my ax scrapes up. Now I'm through the frozen turf, I can take deeper swaths. Pshawri, while you are feeling for the Mouser's head, tell us, coolly and clearly, all that your conscience will allow about your Maelstrom dive.''

''You think he may yet survive?'' Cif asked falteringly, as though doubting her own wild hopes.

''Madam,'' said Fafhrd, ''I've known the Gray One for some time. It never does to underestimate his resourcefulness under adversity or coolth in peril.''

11

Tight-packed upright in dirt, as if he had been honored with a Rimish pit burial, the Mouser became aware of a lump in his throat which, as he observed it, slowly grew larger and harder and began to involve or elicit twitching sensations in his cheeks and his mouth's roof, and like painful feelings or impulses toward movement, deep in his chest. A tension grew in that whole area and there began the faintest buzzing in his ears. All these sensations continued to increase without respite.

He recalled that his last breath had been drawn while he still saw the moon.

With a tremendous effort of will he fought down the urge to gulp in a great breath (which could fill his mouth with dust, set him coughing and gasping—not to be thought of!). He began very slowly (almost experimentally, you might say, except it had to be done—and soon!) to inhale, at first through his nostrils but swiftly switching to his barely parted lips, where his tongue could wet them and, moving from side to side, push back intrusive particles of earth, keep them at bay—somewhat like the approved technique for smoking hashish whereby one draws in thin whifflets of air on either side of the pipe to dilute the rich fumes. (Ah, mused the Mouser, the wondrous freedom of the tongue inside the mouth! No matter how the body were confined. Folk appreciated it insufficiently.)

And all the while he was drawing cold sips of precious lifegiving air that had been stored between the particles of solid ground, and while letting no more dirt grains pass his lips than he could easily swallow. Why, in this fashion, he speculated, he might eventually move through the ground, taking in earth at his anterior end, perhaps—who knows? —extracting nutriment from it and then excreting it in a fecal trail.

But then the lump in his throat caught his attention again. He blew out *that* breath (it took an appreciable time, there was resistance) and slowly (remember, always slowly! he told himself) took in a second breath.

He decided after several repetitions of this process that if he worked at it industriously, losing no time but never letting himself be tempted to rush things, he could keep the lump in his throat (and the impulse to gasp) down to a tolerable size.

So for the present, understandably, everything not connected with breathing became of secondary importance to the Mouser—nay, tertiary!

He told himself that if he kept up the process long enough, it would become habitual, and then there would be room in his mind to think of other things, or at least of other aspects of his current predicament.

A question then would be: Would he care to do so when the time came? Would there be profit or comfort in such speculation?

As the Mouser did indeed slowly become able to attend to other matters, he noted a faint reddish glow within his eyelids. A few breaths later he told himself that could not be, it took sunlight to do that and here he had not even moon. (He would have permitted himself a small sob, except under his present circumstances the slightest breathing irregularity was not to be thought of.)

But curiosity, once roused, persisted (". . . even to the grave," he told himself with sententious melodrama), and after a few more breaths he parted his eyelids the narrowest slit, hedged by his lashes.

Nothing attacked him, not the tiniest grain of sand, and there was indeed yellow light.

After a bit he parted his lids still farther, while dutifully keeping up his breathing, of course, and surveyed the little scene.

Judging by the way the view was brightly yellow-rimmed, the illumination appeared to be coming from his own face. He remembered the strange dream or night incident Cif had told him of, in which she'd seen him wearing a phosphorescent half-mask with ovals of blackness where his eyes would be. Perhaps she had indeed foreseen the future, for he now appeared to be wearing just such a mask.

What the light revealed was this: He was facing into a brown wall, so close it was blurred, but not close enough to touch in any way his bared optics.

Yet as he studied it, he seemed increasingly able to see into it, so that about a finger's length beyond the frontal blur, individual grains of earth were sharply defined, as if some occult power of vision were mixed in with the natural sort, the former merging into and extending the latter.

By this means, whatever it might be, he saw a black pebble buried in the earth about six inches away, and beside that a dark green one big as his thumb, and next to *that* the ringed blank reddish face of an earthworm with small central circular mouth working, pointing almost directly at him so that its segments, seen in sharp perspective, nearly merged.

And then for the first time the element of hallucination or pure fantasy entered his vision, for it seemed to him that the worm addressed him in a high piping voice, saying, "O

Mortal Man, what guards you? Why cannot I approach you to gnaw your eyeballs?''

Yet at the same time it so convinced the Mouser that he was beguiled into replying in soft gruff tones, ''Ho, Fellow Prisoner—''

He got no further. His own voice, however diminished, made such a clamor in the confined space, reverberating back and forth within his skull and jaw, like wind chimes in a hurricane, that both his ears felt deep pain and he almost forgot to breathe.

The unexpectedly powerful vibrations raised by his incautious speaking also appeared to have upset the delicate equilibrium with which he hung in the sea of soil around him, for he noted that the two pebbles and the worm had begun to move upward all together, although he felt no corresponding downward pull upon his ankles. Clearly, he had prematurely attempted too much.

He carefully closed his eyes and reconcentrated all his attention on his slowly breathing in and breathing out, resolutely ignoring the deepening of his entombment.

12

Aboveground notable progress had been made in the Mouser search. It had got more organized. Both parties from the barracks had arrived and there was the reassuring presence of young men busily at work, Fafhrd's big, lean ex-berserks, Northerners like him, and the Mouser's reformed thieves, compact and wiry. The two dogcarts that had brought water, food, and lumber had been unloaded and the two-bearhound team of one had been unharnessed and ranged about watchfully. A small hot fire had been built and there were the heavy rich odors of mutton soup warming and gravy brewing. Mother Grum and old Ourph huddled beside the blaze.

Fafhrd's square hole, widened by a foot on each side, had gone deep enough so that the heads of those digging it and feeling through the dirt were below ground level. Fafhrd had given over his job to his trusty lieutenant Skor, a prematurely balding redhead, while Pshawri continued at the same task, assisted now by Mara and Klute. A Northerner stood on the rim and every minute or so drew up a big pail of earth and emptied it to the side in one sweeping throw. The Mouser's other lieutenant, Mikkidu, and another thief had started to put in the first tier of shoring from above, hammering eight-foot planks side by side with wooden mallets. Two leviathan-oil lanterns in the dark side of the hole glowed upward on their three faces. The full moon was three hours higher than when Skama had been honored by the dance across the Great Meadow.

Fafhrd and Cif stood by the fire, sipping hot gahvey with the two oldsters. It was the first rest he'd taken. Behind him were Gale and Fingers, not drawing attention to themselves, partly for fear of being sent back to Salthaven by the next dogcart as May had been, to reassure their families all the girls were safe. Also in the fireside gahveying group were Afreyt, Groniger, and Rill, the last having run to Elvenhold to summon the other two for conference and, as it turned out, argument.

Afreyt said to Fafhrd, without heat, "Dear man, I deeply admire and respect your loyalty to and regard for your old friend that makes you search for him with such stubborn singlemindedness along one trail only, a trail where your greatest success can hardly be more than the digging up of a corpse. But I question your logic. Since there are other trails—and Groniger and I both attest to that—trails promising a more useful sort of success, if any, why not expend at least half our efforts on those? Nay, why not all?"

"That appears to me to be most closely reasoned," Groniger put in, seconding.

"You think I was guided by logic and reason in what I did?" Fafhrd asked with a shade of impatience, even contempt, shaking his hook at them. "*I saw him sink,* I tell you. So did others. Cif *felt* him go straight down."

"I too," from Ourph. "We saw one miracle, why not expect another?"

Afreyt took up, "Yet all of you who saw him sink have admitted, at one time or another since, that he grew insubstantial toward the end. And so did he to Gron and I, I freely admit, in his flight toward Elvenhold. But does not that equality argue for us giving an equal weight to both possibilities?"

Fafhrd replied, a little tiredly. "I'm bothered myself by those impressions of the Mouser fading. In view of them, the idea of also searching for him elsewhere on Rime Isle seems sensible, and when I sent Gib the Mingol back with the second dogcart for more lumber, you heard me tell him to fetch some rag of the Mouser's and the two scent dogs if available."

Cif spoke up. "I keep wondering if there's not some way to use, in hunting Mou, the golden queller Pshawri brought up from the Maelstrom. It's enwedged with the black cinder of god Loki, who I'm convinced is responsible for Mou's present plight. A most treacherous and madly malevolent deity, as I learned in my dealings with him."

"You're right about that last," Mother Grum agreed darkly, but before she could say more, Skor yelled up from the hole, "Captain, I've uncovered something buried seven feet deep you'll want to see. Will send it up."

Fafhrd moved quickly to the rim, took something off the top of the next bucketload drawn up, shook it out and then closely inspected it.

"It's the Mouser's cowl which he wore tonight," he announced to them all triumphantly. "Now tell me he didn't sink straight down into the ground here!"

Cif snatched it from him and confirmed the identification.

Afreyt called "Snowtreader!" and knelt by the shoulder of the white bearhound who came up, working her fingers deep in his great ruff and speaking earnestly in his shaggy ear. He took a thoughtful snuff of the dirt-steeped garment and began to move about questingly, muzzle to the ground. He came to the hole, gazed down into it searchingly for a long moment, his eyes green in the lampglow, then sat down on the rim, lifted his muzzle to the moon and howled long and dolorously like a trumpet summoning mourners to a hero's funeral.

13

It was well that the Gray Mouser had the lifelong habit, whenever he woke from slumber, of assessing his situation as fully as possible before making the least move. After all, there might always be murderous enemies lurking about waiting for him to betray his exact location by an unguarded movement or exclamation, so as to slay him before he had his wits about him.

And it attests to his presence of mind that when he discovered himself to be everywhere confined by grainy dirt and simultaneously recalled the stages by which he had arrived at this dismal predicament, he did not waste energy and invite inquiry by frantic reactions, he simply continued to pursue his thoughts and explore his surroundings, so far as the latter was possible.

To the best of his recollection his second downward slide or glide through the ground had not lasted long, and after coming to rest a second time, he had concentrated so exclusively on the task of breathing a sufficiency of earth-trapped air to stay alive and hold at bay the impulse to gasp that the dark monotony of his occupation had by gradual stages hypnotized him into sleep.

And now, awake again and feeling somewhat refreshed, though perceptibly chilled, he was still breathing regularly, shallowly, slowly—no impulse to pant—with his tongue busy at intervals, keeping his barely parted lips moist and fending off intrusive dirt. Why, this was good! It showed that the whole operation had become sufficiently automatic for him safely to gain the rest he might well need if his incarceration underground proved overlong—which might well be the case, he must admit.

He noticed now that although his arms lay flat against his sides, they had during his second descent—each bent at the elbow and his hands pushed upward by the sandy soil through which he'd descended—crawled up the front of his body toward his waist, so the fingers of his right now rested against the scabbard of his dagger Cat's Claw, a contact he found reassuring. He set himself to working his fingers up the scabbard, pausing to regularize his breathing whenever it became the least bit labored. When his fingers finally reached their goal, he was surprised to discover they touched, not the dagger's crosspiece and grip, but a section of the sharp narrow blade near the tip. The sandy soil encasing him, rubbing upward against his body as he'd descended, had also almost carried the dagger entirely out of its sheath.

He pondered this new circumstance, wondering if he should attempt to return the strayed weapon to its scabbard by drawing it down a little at a time by its blade pinched between his forefinger and thumb, lest some further sliding on his part separate him from it altogether, a prospect that alarmed him. Or should he try to work his hand up farther still and grip its hilt so as to have it ready for action should some unforeseen change in his situation ever permit him to use it? This line of operations appealed to him most, though promising to involve more work.

During the course of this self-debate he thoughtlessly asked himself aloud, "Which or which?" and instantly winced in anticipation of heavy pain. But he had spoken in quite soft tones, and although the words thundered a bit in his ears, there were no other dolorous consequences. He was enheartened to discover that he could enjoy his own conversational companionship underground, provided he spoke not much louder than a whisper, for truth to tell, he was becoming quite lonely. But after trying it out two or three times, he desisted; he found that every time he spoke he felt ridiculously terrified of being overheard and so betraying his presence and being taken at a disadvantage, though what or whom he had to fear deep in the dirty bosom of this scantily populated polar island he could not say. Not carnivorous Kleshite ghouls, surely? But likely the gods, if such rogue beings exist, who are said to hear our faintest spoken words, even our whispers.

After a time he decided to let the problem of Cat's Claw rest a while and once again risk a visual inspection of his surroundings, since the persistent reddish glow within his eyelids told him that he had carried his own peculiar illumination to this deeper spot. He had not done this earlier for two reasons. First, it seemed wise to attend only to one thing at a time besides his breathing; to attempt more would invite exhaustion and a confusion that might well lead to panic and loss of the control that he had with difficulty won. Second, he had so few activities open to him in his constricted circumstance that he would do well to hoard them and dole them out like a miser, lest he fall victim to a boredom that might well become literally maddening, a suicidal tedium.

Taking the same precautions as he had before, he got his eyes open without incident and once again found himself facing a blurred grainy wall, only this time streaked with white and dull blue, as though there were an admixture of chalk and slate in the soil hereabouts. And once again he discovered that the longer he stared at it, to the accompaniment only of his measured silent ex- and inhalations, the deeper he was able to see into it by some power of occult vision.

For a while this time there were no definite objects to be seen, such as the worm and the pebbles, yet there were fugitive glimmerings and tiny marching movements such as the eyes see when there is no light, making it hard to determine whether they were happening inside his eyes or out in the reaches of cold ground.

Eventually, at a distance, he judged, of eight or ten feet out from him, the blue-shadowed white streaks began to organize themselves into a slender female figure, upright as he was and facing him, as pale as death, with eyes and lips serenely shut as though she were asleep. A strange quality in the blue-shadowed whiteness seemed familiar to him and this daunted him, though where and when he had encountered it before he could not tell.

His intimate yet somehow mystic view of this quiescent figure seemed not so much obscured by the three intervening yards of solid dirt as softened by them, as though he were viewing it (her?) through several of the finest imaginable veils, such as might grace some ethereal princess' boudoir rather than these cruel cemetery confines.

At first he thought he was imagining the whole vision and

told himself how apt the human eye is to see definite shapes of things in smoke, expanses of vegetation, old tapestries, simmering stews, slow fires, and similars—and especially apt to interpret pale indistinct shapes as human bodies. But the longer he looked at it, the more distinct it got. Looking away and then back didn't banish it, nor did consciously trying to make it seem something else.

All this while the figure remained in the same attitude with visage serene, never changing as a creation of the imagination might be expected to do, so in the end he decided she must be an actual piece of statuary buried by some strange chance at just this spot, though the style seemed to him not at all Rimish. While her glimmering whiteness still seemed unpleasantly familiar. Where? When? He racked his brains.

Then there came a flurry of those small glimmering marching forms that were so hard to pin down as to location. They resolved themselves into a number of fine-beaded white lines connected to points on the quiescent naked female form—its eyes, ears, nostrils, mouth, and privacies. As he studied them they grew more distinct and he saw that the individual beads were creeping along in single file, toward the figure in about half the lines and away from it in the others. The word "maggots" came into his mind and stayed despite his efforts to banish it. And the finely beaded busy lines became more real, no matter how vehement his self-assertion that they were but strayed figments of his imagination.

But then it occurred to him that if he truly were watching maggots devour dead buried flesh, there would inevitably be diminuations and other changes for the worse in the latter, whereas the slim blue-shadowed she-figure now appeared more attractive, if anything, than when he had first glimpsed her, in particular the small, saucy, unsagging breasts, medallions of supreme artistry, whose large azure nipplets implored kisses. Were the situation otherwise he would surely be feeling desire despite their unromantic and highly constrictive surroundings. He coldly imagined hand-capturing her dainty tits and tormentingly teasing them to their utmost erection, tonguing them avidly—gods! Could nothing break his constant awareness of the dreadful Mouser-shaped *mold* encasing him? (But to not get too far afield, wit-worshipping dolt, he told himself—recall to breathe!) Old legends said Death had a skinny sister denominated Pain, passionately devoted to the loathsome torture that often was Death's prelude.

But she was only a statue, he reminded himself desperately.

Her lips parted and a lissome blue tongue ran round them hungrily.

Her eyes opened and she fixed her red-glinting gaze upon him.

She smiled.

Suddenly he knew where he had seen her opalescently white complexion before. In the Shadowland! Upon the slender face and neck and hands and wrists of Death himself, whom he had twice beheld there. And she resembled Death facially and in her slenderness.

Then she puckered her lips and, through all the dirt that buried them both, he heard the thrilling soft seductive whistle with which a Lankhmar streetgirl invites trade. He felt the hair lift on the back of his neck while an icy chill went through him.

And then, to his extremest horror, this pale ghoul-waif, Sister of Death, seemingly without effort extended both her glimmering narrow hands toward him, blue palms turned invitingly upward and opalescent fingers rippling tremulously, and then gathering those same fingers together cuppingly and kicking back her left and right legs successively, began slowly to swim toward him through the harsh earth everywhere closely encasing them both, as if it offered no more resistance to her blue-shadowed starkly naked form than it did to his occult vision.

Despite all his good resolutions to avoid panicky overexertion while buried, he strained convulsively backward, away from the dirt swimmer, in a spasm like to burst his heart. Then, just as his effort reached an excruciating peak and he abandoned it, he felt emptiness behind him and launched himself into it—with an instant spurt of reverse fear: that he might fall forever into a bottomless pit.

He could have spared himself that last terror. He had barely retreated a half yard, no more than one short step, when he felt himself everywhere backed again from head to heel with cold grainy earth.

But now there was an emptiness in front of him, the space from which he'd just withdrawn his trunk, head, and one leg. And there was time to draw a deep, big, glorious breath—one worth twenty of his cautious air sips—and to retreat the other leg before the forward dirt caught up with him again, brutally slapping his face in its eagerness to mold itself exactly to his central facade, as if matter or its gods and goddesses indeed possessed that abhorrence of vacua which some philosophers attribute to it, or to them.

Neither his startlement at all this totally unexpected occurrence nor his wonderment as to the natural laws or miracles by which it had been effected were great enough, despite the monster breath, to cause him to interrupt his regimen of slow small inhalations through barely parted lips, nor his watchful forward-spying between equally constricted eyelids.

The latter showed his deathly slim pursuer fully a yard closer to him and with her orientation changed almost completely from the vertical to the horizontal by her powerful swimming motions as she chased him head on, so that he found himself staring aghast straight into her voracious red-glinting eyes.

This sight was so she-wolfishly dire to him that it inspired him to another gut-bursting effort to back away, with just at its peak the new hope that the strange miracle he'd just experienced might repeat itself. And rather to his surprise, it did: the dizzying emptiness behind, the half-yard backward lurch, the emptiness before, the glorious deep breath, the stinging impact against his whole front, but most tellingly upon his naked face, of cold grainy earth angrily reestablishing its total hold on him.

This time, assessing the effects of his two short retreats, he saw that he'd lost Cat's Claw, which now lay itself midway between him and his pursuer, its point directed straight at him. Evidently the ground embedding its hilt had torn it away from him at his first backward step, but his finger and thumb on its tip had held on as long as they were able, which had changed the dagger's attitude from vertical to horizontal, while his second backward step had completed the divorcement between him and his weapon. Squinting down with difficulty, he saw the finger and thumb in question beaded with blood where the sharp blade had cut them. Poor digits, wounded in parting, they had done their best!

He wondered if the fell form following hard upon him would knock the abandoned weapon out of her way, for she was headed straight toward it, or perhaps snatch it up to use against him, but he was already into his third soul-wrenching miracle-provoking effort and must concentrate all of his being on that. And when he was congratulating himself on his third half-yard gain (only it seemed more like a yard this time) and giant breath, he saw looking back that his pale pursuer had stroked herself a little higher in the earth-sea so that she overpassed Cat's Claw by a finger's breadth where it lay now midway between the stalactite buds of her downward-jutting small breasts, its keen tip still directed straight at him like a compass needle pointing him out, while her smooth belly traversed the blade.

He noted that Cat's Claw's scabbard had worked loose from his belt and lay in the ground's grip a little way behind him in the same attitude—pointing toward him—as its parent weapon did, now lying beyond his pursuer.

But now he was making his fourth—no, fifth!—bobbing retreat, face pommeled by invisible earth. Damn it! It was all so demeaning—curtseying away from Death's skinny, shameless sister!

The thought occurred to him that her and his means of progression through solid earth were both so strange and yet so grossly different that he might well be in the grip of some powerful hallucination or mighty dream in deathly sleep, rather than that of reality.

Do not believe that! he told himself. Banish the thought! For if you did, you might relax your efforts to breathe, both the tiny air sips and, where circumstances permitted, the deep gulps, for those, he knew at some level far below reason, were vital—nay, fundamental!—to his survival in this dark realm.

And yet as he strongly kept up those breathings small and large, piling repetition upon repetition, and maintained or even seemed to lengthen his lead upon his fell fair follower, (who was now overpassing closely his dagger's scabbard as she had the dagger), the scene surrounding him grew gloomier by slow stages, the mind-light by which he saw it dimmed, his movements manifested a reptilian heaviness along with power, a chthonic scaliness and hairiness, and sleep enshrouded him like blindness, leaving him only an awareness of profound labored progression through grainy blackness.

14

The impression aboveground that the Mouser search had slacked off was misleading. It had simply grown somewhat more routinized and realistic. What it had lost in dash had been more than made up in dogged efficiency. In most of the participants concerned excitement boiled underneath, or at least simmered.

The moon halfway down the western sky was glaringly bright. Her white light shadowed the face and front of another of Fafhrd's men standing with wide-braced feet on the lip of the hole, intermittently busy drawing up and emptying the earth bucket. His sidewise castings now made a wide low mound more than a foot high toward its center. The drawings-up took longer and the glow on his shadowed chest and under face from the lamps inside the shaft at its working foot was much less—both measures of the shaft's increasing depth. In fact, other workers were at the same time lowering down into it planks for a second tier of shorings, the first having been firmly fixed in place by nailed crosspieces, small forged wrought-iron spikes joining the varying lengths of wood so precious on Rime Isle.

The monstrous winterchange of the weather had not moderated, but grown worse, for a strong steady north breeze had set in, redoubling the night's bitter chill. A half tent had been set up, just north of the cookfire and facing it, to give shelter to the latter and radiant heat to the former. Here, among others, Klute and Mara slumbered, quite worn out by their spell of work in the hole, for as Skor had pointed out, "To dig for coal and tubers, even gold and treasure, is one thing; for human flesh you hope alive (somehow!) quite another and most wearying!"

The discovery of the Mouser's cowl seven feet down had led Fafhrd and Cif to take over the digging and sifting work from Skor and the girls in their eagerness to speed the small Gray One's rescue. But after two hour's furious labor they had relinquished their places, this time to Skor again and to Gale, whose girl-size was an especial advantage when the hole was crowded with those putting in the second tier of shorings beneath the first.

After climbing up the shaft by the big pegs set like a ladder in its side, and feeling the north breeze's bite as they emerged into the cold moonshine, Cif and Fafhrd had headed for the cookfire where hot black gahvey and soup were available, whereafter Cif had gone to join the small group conferring just beyond the blaze, while Fafhrd, professing no taste for talk, had moved back under the half tent's shelter and, nursing a steaming black mug laced with brandy, carefully seated himself on the foot of the cot where Klute and Mara slept embracing each other for warmth.

On the far side of the fire they were discussing a matter on which Cif had strong opinions—the proper present use (if any) and ultimate disposal of the trophy Pshawri had brought up from the Maelstrom, the skeletal gold cube enwedged with black iron-tough torch cinder and known as the Whirlpool Queller from the magical use the Gray Mouser had made of it in turning back the Sunwise Sea-Mingol fleet, now almost two years by.

Afreyt believed it should be enshrined in the Moon Temple as a memorial of Rime Isle's most recent victory over her enemies.

With Islish materialism crusty Groniger argued that, freed of its disfiguring cinder—a dubious item which the moon priestesses could have if they wished it—it should be returned to the treasury house to take again its rightful place among the golden Ikons of Reason, as the Sextuple Square or Cube of Square-Dealing.

But Mother Grum averred that the addition of the cinder

had transformed the Cube into a magical weapon of might to be entrusted to the witchy coven she headed, which happened to include several moon priestesses.

Rill seconded her, saying, "I held the cinder when it was yet a torch lit at Loki's fire, and its flame bent sideways, pointing us out the path that led us to the god's new lair in the flame wall at the back of the caverns fronting the root of the volcano Darkfire. Might there not be a like virtue in the cinder to show us the way to Captain Mouser now he is underground?"

Cif broke in eagerly, "Let's dowse for him with it! Suspend the Queller on a cord and move it about the hole and watch what happens. This should tell us if he has deviated from straight-down sinking like the shaft, in which direction he is going. What think you all?"

"I'll tell you this, Lady," Pshawri said rapidly, "when Captain Mouser rebuked me yesternight for meddling with the Maelstrom, I felt the cube vibrate through my pouch against my leg as though there were some occult link between the Queller and the captain, though neither he nor anyone knew then I had recovered it."

The faint tintinnabulation of tiny harness bells shaken briskly drew all Cif's listeners' and finally her own gaze east, away from the moon, to where a bobbing cart lamp told of the imminent arrival of a dogteam from the barracks.

But neither the jingling bells nor the earlier talk penetrated very deeply into the vast melancholy reverie into which Fafhrd had slowly sunk as he nursed his chilling brandied gahvey and rested his aching bones in the half tent's shadows.

It had begun just as he'd gingerly seated himself on the foot of Mara's and Klute's cot with the sudden vivid memory—startling in its power—of another occasion, almost two decades gone, when he'd had to work furiously for seeming hours to rescue the Mouser from death's closest grip and in the end had had to drag the Gray One screaming and kicking from his intended coffin. It had all happened in the sorcery-built magic emporium of those cosmic peddlers of filth, the Devourers, and there had been no rest periods on that occasion either. Fafhrd had first endlessly and most resourcefully to argue with their two cantankerous and elephant-brained

wizardly mentor-masters Sheelba of the Eyeless Face and
Ningauble of the Seven Eyes just to get the all-essential
means and information to achieve the rescue and then battle
interminably and with brilliantly-devised instant stratagems
against a tireless iron statue, a devilish two-handed longsword
of blued steel—not to mention gaudy giant spiders whom his
obscenely ensorcelled comrade saw as beauteous supple girls
in scanty velvet dresses.

But that time the Mouser had been present all the while,
playing the fool, calling out zany comments to the battlers,
and even slain the statue in the end by splitting its massive
head with Fafhrd's ax, thinking the weapon was a jester's
bladder, while he, Fafhrd, had been the one being buried
under the double weight of wizards' words and crushing iron
blows. But this time the Mouser simply vanished without
frills or fanfare, swallowed by earth in fashion most conclu-
sive without warning, without shroud or coffin to shield him
from the ground's cruel cold grip, and without words, foolish
or otherwise, except that piteous, gasped-out "Help me,
Fafhrd," before his mouth was stopped by hungry upward-
gliding clay. And now that he was gone, there was no fighting to be done to get him back, no mighty battling with sword
or words, but only very slow, laborious scraping and digging,
careful, methodical, and which seemed to make sense and
hold out hope only so long as one was doing it. As soon as
you stopped digging, you realized what a last-chance, forlorn-
hope, desperate rescue attempt it really was—to believe a
man could somehow breathe long enough underground, like a
Kleshite ghoul or Eastern Lands fakir, for you to tunnel your
way to him. Pitiful! Why, Fafhrd'd only been able to persuade himself and the others to it because no one had a better
idea—and because they all (some of 'em, anyway) needed
busy-work to keep at bay the sickening sense of loss and of
fear for self lest a like fate befall.

Fafhrd balled his good fist and almost in his gust of frustra-
tion smote the cot beside his thigh, but recalled in time the
sleeping girls. He'd thought the next cot was empty, but now
saw that its dark green blanket hid a single sleeper, whose
slight form and short shock of flame-red hair showed her to
be the self-styled Ilthmar princess and cabingirl Fingers, who'd

been following him around all night gazing at him reproachfully for not somehow saving the Mouser before he sank or
else sinking into the ground beside him like a staunch comrade should. He felt a sudden spurt of sharp anger at the
minx—what cause had she to criticize him so?

Yet it was true, he upbraided himself as another flood of
melancholy memories engulfed him, that he and his gray
comrade had often behaved like death-seekers, as when they'd
sailed in stony-faced silence side by side forever westward in
the Outer Sea, seeking that coast of doom called the Bleak
Shore, or lured by shimmersprites, steered their craft south
into the great Equatorial Current whence no ships return, or
when they'd surmounted Stardock, Nehwon's mightiest peak,
or dared Quarmall's cavern and twice encountered Death
himself in the sunless Shadowland; yet on this last occasion,
when Nehwon had swallowed the Mouser, whatever the ratio-
nale, he had held back.

With a silvery jangle of harness bells the laden dogcart
drew up beyond the fire. As he got down from the driver's
seat, Skullick gave out the news, the words tumbling from his
mouth, that the Great Maelstrom had been observed to be
turning more swiftly, heaving and churning as it swirled
round and round in the cold moonshine. Cif and Pshawri
came to their feet.

The noise broke into Fafhrd's reverie just enough as to
make him aware of what his entranced gaze had been unseeingly
resting on. The girl Fingers had turned over in her sleep so
that her face was visible and one bare arm had emerged to lie
atop the coarse blanket like a pale serpent. Of whom did her
face remind him? he asked himself. He had loved those
features once, he was suddenly certain. What sweet and
yielding female . . . ?

And then as he studied her face more closely, he saw that
her eyes were open and watching him and that her lips were
curved in a sleepy smile. The tip of her tongue came out at a
corner and licked them around. Fafhrd felt his sharp anger
return, if it were just that. The saucy baggage! What call had
she to look at him as though they shared a secret? Why was
she spying on him? What was her game? He flashed that
when she'd first appeared simpering and posing to him and

Gray Mouser in the cellar, they had just been speaking of men snatched under the ground or pursued on high by vengeful earth. Why had that been? What had that synchronicity presaged? Had she aught to do with the Mouser's vanishment downward, this tainted witchchild from the rat city of Ilthmar? He rose up fast and silently, moved as swiftly to her cot and stood bent over her and glaring down, as though to strip her of her secrets by his gaze's force, and with his hand upraised, he knew not to do what, while she smiled up at him with perfect confidence.

"Captain!" Skor's urgent bellow came hollowly out of the hole and boomed around.

Forgetting all else, Fafhrd dodged from under the shelter tent and was the first to reach the mouth of the shaft, over which there was now set a stout man-high ironwood tripod, from which depended a pair of pulleys to halve the effort needed to raise the dirt.

Steadying himself by two of its legs, the Northerner leaned out and looked straight down. The planks of the second tier of shorings were in place, securely braced with crosspieces and tied to the first tier—and the excavating had gone a couple of feet below them. From the pulley by his cheek two lines went down to the second pulley atop the handle of the bucket, which was set half filled 'gainst a side of the shaft. Against two other sides Skor and Gale were pressed back, upturned faces large and small, in shadow, the one framed by scanty red locks, the other by profuse blond tresses. By the fourth side were two leviathan-oil lamps. Their white light fell strongly on the slender object lying flat in the center of the shaft's bottom. Fafhrd would have recognized it anywhere.

"It's Captain Mouser's dirk, Captain," Skor called up, "lying just as we uncovered it."

"I didn't move it the least bit as I brushed and worked the earth away," Gale confirmed in her piping tones.

"That's a wise girl," Fafhrd called down. "Leave it so. And don't move from where you are, either of you. I'm coming down."

Which he accomplished swiftly by way of the ladder of thick pegs jutting from the shoring, going down hand over hook. When he reached the crowded bottom, he knelt at once over Cat's Claw, bending down his head to inspect it closely.

"We didn't find the scabbard anywhere," Gale explained somewhat unnecessarily.

He nodded. "The ground gets chalky here," he observed. "Did either of you find a chunk of the stuff?"

"No," Gale responded quickly, "but I've a lump of yellow umber."

"That'll do fine," he said, holding out his hand. When she'd dug it from her pouch and handed it to him, he sighted carefully along the dagger's blade and rubbed a big gold mark on the foot of the shoring to show which way the weapon pointed.

"That's something we may want to remember," he explained shortly. He lifted the wicked knife from its site, turning it over and reinspecting it from blade tip to pommel, but he could discern no special markings, no message of any sort, on that side either.

"What have you found, Fafhrd?" Cif called down.

"It's Cat's Claw, all right. I'll send it up to you," he called back. He handed the knife to Skor. "I'll take over for a space down here. You get some rest." He accepted from his lieutenant the short-handled square spade that had replaced his ax as chief digging and scraping tool. "You're a good man, Skor." That one nodded and mounted by the pegs.

"I'm coming down, Fafhrd. My turn to help," Afreyt announced from above.

Fafhrd looked at Gale. At close range the golden strands were sweaty and the fair complexion streaked with dirt. Pallor and tired smudges around the blue eyes belied the air of smiling readiness the girl put on. "You need a rest too. And sleep, you hear? But only after you've had a mug of hot soup." He took from her her scoop and handbroom. "You've done well, child."

While she wearily yet reluctantly mounted the pegs, with Afreyt urging her to greater speed from above, Fafhrd drove the spade into the earth near the hole's edge, continuing the excavation straight down.

After Afreyt had climbed into the hole to join Fafhrd in his task, the harlot Rill led the exhausted Gale back to the cookfire beyond the shelter tent. Cif followed them, somewhat like a sleepwalker, staring at the knife she held, which Skor had handed her, and after a bit the others gravitated back too. Standing in the cold to watch folk dig is of no lasting profit.

Rill was pressing Gale to finish the mug of soup she'd poured her.

"Drink it all down while there's some heat in it. That's a good girl. Why, you still feel like ice! You need to be under blankets. And get a sleep, you're groggy. Come on now, no arguments."

And she led her off willingly enough to the shelter tent.

Cif was still staring bemusedly at the Mouser's knife, slowly turning it over and over, so that its bright blade periodically reflected the low firelight.

Old Ourph said ruminatively, "When Khahkht the Conqueror was buried bound and beweaponed alive for treason, but later cleared and dug up, it was found his daggers had worked their way yards from his corpse in opposite directions, so strong and wide were his hatreds."

Pshawri said, "I thought Khahkht was a Rimish ice devil, not a Mingol warchief paramount."

After a while Ourph replied, "Great conquerors live on as their enemies' devils."

"Or their own folk's, sometimes," Groniger put in.

Skullick said, "If dead old Khahkht could make his daggers travel through solid earth, why didn't he have them cut his bonds?"

Rill returned with an armful of girls' clothes which she hung by the fire and then sat down beside Cif, saying, "I stripped her down to the buff and bundled her into a warmed nook beside the drowsy Ilthmar kid, who'd half waked but was bound again for slumberland."

After a courteous pause, Ourph explained, "Khahkht's bonds were chains of adamant."

Groniger said speculatively, "I can see how the Mouser's hood would be stripped away upward as he was dragged down, since it had no ties to his other clothing. And I suppose the up-sliding earth, pressing against the dagger's grip and crosspiece, might effect the same result, though taking longer, as he was dragged still farther down by . . . whatever it was.''

"But wouldn't the knife have been left point down, vertical in the earth, then?" Skullick argued.

Mother Grum interrupted, "Black magic of some breed took him. That's why the knife got left. Iron doesn't obey devil power."

Skullick went on to Groniger, "But the dagger was uncovered lying flat, horizontal. Which would mean by your theory he was being dragged sideways at that point, in the direction Cat's Claw pointed. In which case we're digging the shaft the wrong way, keeping on straight down."

"Gods! I wish we knew exactly what happened to him down there," Pshawri averred, some of his earlier agony coming back into his voice and aspect. "Did he draw Cat's Claw to do battle with the monster dragging him under, free himself of it? Or was he more actively attacked down there and drew the knife in self-defense?"

"How could he do either of those things when closely cased in hard earth?" Groniger objected.

"He'd manage somehow!" Pshawri shot back. "But then how came the dagger to be left behind? He'd never have been parted from Cat's Claw willingly, of that I'm sure."

"Perhaps he lost consciousness then," Rill interposed.

"Or perhaps they were both attacked, the dragger and the dragged, by some third party," Skullick hazarded. "How much do any of us know what may go on down there?"

A look of sheer horror had been growing in Cif's visage as she eyed the knife. She burst out, "Stop breaking our minds and hearts, all of you, with all these guesses!" She took the Mouser's cowl out of her pouch and rapidly wrapped up the dagger in it, folding in the ends. "I cannot think while looking at that thing." She handed the small gray package to Mother Grum. "There, keep it safe and hid," she said, "while we get on to efforts more constructive."

A change came over the small white-clad woman, who'd seemed consumed moments before with nervous grief. She rose lithely from her seat by the fire, saying to Pshawri, "Follow me, Lieutenant. We'll dowse for your captain with his Whirlpool Queller you rescued from the Maelstrom, beginning at the shaft head, and so determine whether and how he's deviated from the straight down in his strange journey through solid earth.'' She wet two fingers in her mouth and held them high a space. ''While we were talking, feeding our woes with horror, the north breeze died—which'll make the dowsing easier for us, its results surer. And you must do the dowsing, Pshawri, because although it galls me somewhat to admit it, you seem the one most sensitive to the Gray Mouser's presence.''

Although looking puzzled and taken aback at first by her words, it was with a seeming sense of relief and a growing eagerness that the skinny ex-thief came to his feet. ''I'm with you, Lady, of course, in any effort to regain the Captain. What do I do?''

As she explained, they started toward the shaft head. The eyes of the others followed them. After a bit Skullick and Rill got up and strolled after and, several moments later, Groniger. But old Ourph and Mother Grum—and Snowtreader and the other cartdog, both of whom had been unharnessed—stayed warm by the fire.

A bucket was coming up from the hole, heaping full. When its earth had been scattered, Pshawri positioned himself by the hole, knees bent and spread a little, head bent forward, looking down earnestly at the black-gold cinder cube suspended on a cubit's length of sailor's twine he'd found in his pouch and held at the top between the thumb and ring finger of his left hand.

Cif stood north of him, spreading her cloak to ward off any remnants of the north breeze, though there seemed no need. The cold air had become quite still.

But although the contraption looked like a pendulum, it did not act like one, neither beginning to swing back and forth in any direction nor yet around in a circle or ellipse.

''And there's no vibration either,'' Pshawri reported in a low voice.

Cif extended a slender forefinger and laid it very lightly and carefully atop the pinching juncture of his finger and thumb. After a space of three heartbeats she nodded in confirmation and said, ''Let's try on the opposite side of the hole.''

"Why do you use the ring finger and left hand?" Rill
asked curiously.

"I don't know," Pshawri said puzzledly. "Maybe because
that finger feels the touchiest of the lot. And left hand seems
right for magic."

At that last word Groniger growled a skeptical "Hmmph!"

Fafhrd and Afreyt seemed to be digging and sifting strenu-
ously yet still carefully at the bottom of the hole, which had
gotten as much as a foot deeper. Cif called down to them an
explanation of what she and Pshawri were doing, ending
with, ". . . and then we'll spiral out from here in wider and
wider circles, dowsing every few feet. When we get a strong
reading—*if* we do—I'll signal you."

Fafhrd waved that he understood and returned to his digging.

The second reading showed the same results. Pshawri and
Cif moved out four yards and began their first methodical
circling of the hole, dowsing every few steps. One by one
their small company of observers returned to the fire, wearied
by sameness. A full bucket came up from the hole.

And after a while, another.

Slowly the white-glowing lantern with which Cif had provided herself grew more distant from the hole. Slowly the pile
of dug earth beside it grew. Fingers and Gale slept in each
other's arms. While the full moon inched down the western
sky.

Time passed.

15

The yellowing moon was no more than two fists above the
western horizon of Rime Isle's central hills when Fafhrd's
probing spade encountered stone. They'd deepened the hole
by about a woman's height below the second tier of shoring.
At first Fafhrd thought the obstruction a small boulder and

tried to dig around it. Afreyt warned him against overspeed but he persisted. The boulder grew larger and larger. Soon the whole bottom of the shaft was a flat floor of solid rock.

He lifted his eyes to Afreyt's. "What's to do now?"

She shook her head.

A spear's cast southeast of the hole the two dowsers began to get results.

The twine-and-cube pendulum suspended from Pshawri's left hand instead of hanging straight down dead, as it had done over a hundred successive times by count, slowly began to swing forth and back, away from the hole and toward it. They both stared down at it wonderingly, suspiciously.

"Are you making it do that, Pshawri?" she whispered.

"I don't think so," he answered doubtfully.

And then the wonder happened. The swings of the cube toward the hole began to get shorter and shorter, and those away longer and longer, until they stopped altogether and the cube hung straining away from the hole, perceptibly out of the vertical.

"How are you doing that, Pshawri?" Her voice was small, respectful.

"I don't know," he replied shakily. "It pulls. And I'm getting a vibration."

She touched his hand with her forefinger, as before. Almost immediately she nodded, looking at him with awe.

"I'll call Afreyt and Fafhrd. Don't you move."

She rummaged a metal whistle from her pouch and blew it. The note was shrill and piercing in the cold still air.

Down in the hole they heard it. "Cif's signal," Afreyt said, but Fafhrd had already chinned himself on the lowest peg and was hauling himself up the rest hand over hook. She hung one of the lanterns on one arm and followed him up, using both hands and feet.

Fafhrd scanned around and saw a small white glow out in the frozen meadow across the hole from where he stood. It moved back and forth to call attention to itself. He looked down the wood-lined shaft and spotted at its foot the yellow ochre mark he'd made to show the direction Cat's Claw had pointed when it was found. It was in line with the distant lamp. He sucked in his breath, took from Afreyt the lit lamp she'd brought up with her, held it aloft, and moved it twice from side to side in answering signal. The one out in the meadow was immediately lowered.

"That tears it," he told Afreyt, lowering the lamp. "The dagger and the dowsing agree. The shaft must now be dug in that direction, footed upon the rock we've just uncovered and lined and roofed with wood to shield it from collapse."

She nodded and said swiftly, "Skullick suggested earlier that was the message the horizontal attitude and pointing of Cat's Claw were intended by the Gray Mouser to convey."

Idlers crowded around them to hear what new was up. The Northerner at the pulley gazed at Fafhrd intently.

He continued raptly, "The side passage should be narrow and low to conserve wood. The shoring planks can be sawed in three to make its walls. We should be able to dig faster sideways, yet great care must still be exercised in breaking earth."

Afreyt broke in, "There'll be a power of digging, nevertheless, just to take the side passage out below the point where Cif and Skullick are now standing."

"That's true," he answered, "and also true that Captain Mouser may have been drawn away we know not how far, judging by the swiftness and ease with which he first sank. He may be anywhere out there. And yet I feel it's vital we continue on digging from that spot, abiding by the one solid clue we have that we know is from *him:* his pointing knife! That's a more material clue than any hints and suggestions to be got from dowsing. No, the digging that we've started must go on, else we lose all drive and organization. That we're not doing it right now carks me. But I myself have grown too frantic for the nonce to do the work properly with all due precautions." He appealed to Afreyt, "You yourself, dear, warned me that I was overspeeding, and I was."

He turned to the stalwart at the pulley and commanded, "Udall, fetch Skor! Wake him if he's asleep. Ask him—with courtesy—to come to me here. Tell him he's needed." Udall went. Fafhrd turned back to Afreyt, explaining, "Skor has the patience for the task that I lack, at least at this moment." His voice changed. "And would you, my dear, not only continue with the sifting for now, but also take on for me the direction of the whole task in my absence? Here, take my signet. Wear it on your fist.'' He held out his right hand to her, fingers spread. She drew the ring from off the little one. ''I want to go apart (I don't think well in company) and brood upon this matter, on ways of recovering the Gray One besides digging and dowsing. I *think* he will return here eventually, exit the underworld same place he entered it—that's why we must keep digging at this spot—yet that's at best the likeliest end. There are a thousand other possibilities to be considered. My mind's afire. The Gray One and I have been in a hundred predicaments and plights as bad as this one.

''Would you do that for me, dear?'' he finished. ''The sifting you can assign to Rill or two of the girls, or even at a pinch to Mother Grum.''

''Leave it all to me, Captain,'' she said, rubbing along his jaw the clenched knuckles of her right hand, which now wore his silver crossed-swords signet upon the middle finger.

Her action was playful, affectionate, but her violet eyes were anxious and her voice sober as death.

Snowtreader had responded as swiftly as Fafhrd to Cif's whistle, bounding out across the frosty meadow. He stopped before Cif, who was still signaling with her high-held lamp. Then his eyes went to bent-over Pshawri and the object hanging oddly from the lieutenant's rock-steady hand. He sniffed at it gingerly and suspiciously, gave a whine of recognition, and hurried on across the meadow a dozen more yards with his nose close to the ground, then paused to look back and bark twice.

Cif lowered her lamp at Fafhrd's answering signal from the shaft head. Pshawri appealed to her, ''Would you mark this spot here, Lady? I think we should follow Snowtreader's lead and hurry on while the scent is hot, dowsing at intervals.''

Using her dagger pommel for a hammer, she drove into the ground over which Pshawri had been hovering one of the small stakes they'd brought and tied to it a short length of gray ribbon from her pouch. She said, ''I think you're right. Though while I was signaling I had the thought that the cinder we're dowsing with is Loki's. It might be guiding us toward him rather than Mouser, and I know from experience what wild goose hunts, what weird will-o'-the-wisp chases that god might lead us on.''

"No, Lady," Pshawri assured her, "it's the Captain's signals I'm getting. I know his vibes. And Snowtreader would never confuse him with that tricksy stranger god. What's more, the dog didn't howl this time, as he did so dolefully when the moon was high, but only whined—a sign he's scenting a live thing, no carrion corpse.''

Cif observed, "You're awfully fond of the Captain, aren't you? I pray Skama you're right. Lead on, then. The others will catch up.''

She was referring to the five dark forms between her and the cookfire and the other lights around the shaft head: Rill, Skullick, Groniger, Ourph, and Mother Grum, all grown curious. Beyond them and the little lights round the shaft head, the setting moon was just touching the horizon, as though going to earth amongst Rime Isle's central hills.

Back at the now-lonely cookfire Fafhrd poured himself a half mug of simmering gahvey, tempered it with brandy, drank half of that off in one big hot swallow, and set himself to think shrewdly and systematically of the Gray Mouser's plight, as he'd told Afreyt he would.

He discovered almost at once that his whirling, plunging thoughts and fancies were not to be tamed that way.

Nor did the rest of the mug's contents, taken at a gulp, enforce tranquillity and logic upon stormy disorder.

He paced around in a circle, breaking off when he found himself beginning to twist, jerk, and stamp in a frenzy of control-seeking.

He shook his fingers in front of his face, as if trying to conjure things from empty air.

In a sudden frantic reversal of attitude he asked himself whether he really wanted to rescue the Mouser at all. Let the Gray One escape by his own devices. He'd managed it often enough in the past, by Kos!

He'd have liked to measure his wilder imaginings against Rill's practicality, Groniger's sturdy reason, Mother Grum's dogmatic witch-reasonings, or Ourph's Mingol fatalism. But they'd all traipsed off after the dowsers. He'd told Afreyt he wanted solitude, but now he asked himself how was a man to think without talking? He felt confused, light-headed, light in other ways, as if a puff of wind might knock him down.

He looked at the things around him: the fire, the soup, the piled lumber, the girls' clothes warming, the shelter tent, its cots.

He didn't need to talk to children, he told himself. Let them sleep. He wished he could.

But his strange nervousness grew. Finally, to discharge it in action, he seized a fresh brandy jug with his right hand, hooked up a lamp with his other upper extremity, set out across the meadow after the dowsers.

He walked unevenly, veering and correcting himself. He wasn't sure he wanted to catch up with the dowsers. But he had to be moving, or else explode.

16

In the cozy nest from which she'd been watching Fafhrd's every action, Fingers roused Gale by yanking the pale tuft of her fine maiden hair. "That hurt, you fiend," the Rimish girl protested, rubbing her eyes. "No one else ever summoned me from slumber so."

"It hurts most where you love most," the cabingirl recited as by rote, continuing in livelier tones, "I knew you'd want to be wide awake, dear demon, to hear the latest news of your hero uncle with the growly name."

"Fafhrd?" Gale was all attention.

"The same. He's just come out of the hole, cavorted around the fire, and now taken a lamp and a jar and gone off after your dark-haired aunt who's dowsing for your other uncle. I think he's fey and wants watching over."

"Where are our clothes?" Gale asked at once, squirming half out of the nest.

"The lady with the scarred hand set them to warm close by the fire before they all went off ahead of Fafhrd. Come on, I'll race you."

"Someone will see us." Gale clapped her slender forearm across her barely budded breasts.

"Not if we rush, Miss Prim and Proper."

The two girls streaked to the fire through the frigid air and, looking around and giggling the while, hurried into their toasty clothes as swiftly as if they'd both been sailors. Then they moved out hand in hand, following Fafhrd's lamp, while the last sliver of full moon hid itself behind Rime Isle's central hills and the sky paled with the first hint of dawn.

17

The Mouser struggled awake from darkest depths. The process seemed to involve toilsome stages of marginal consciousness, but when he finally—and quite suddenly—felt himself fully master of his mind, he found his body sprawled at full length with his bent head pillowed on the crook of his left elbow and the bracing reek of salt sea filling his nostrils.

For a blessed moment he supposed himself to be abed in his trim room in the Salthaven barracks built last year by his men and Fafhrd's, and with the window open to the cool damp morning breeze.

His first attempted movement shattered that illusion. He was in the same dreadful plight he'd been when his awareness had last ebbed away to chthonic darkness while he was most effortfully fleeing Death's skinny sister Pain.

Except his plight had worsened—he'd lost the strange power of movement he'd had then, of laborious crabwise retreat. That seemed to depend, for its generation, upon extremes of terror.

And the sea stink was new. That must be coming from the

grainy earth that gripped him viselike. And that earth was now perceptibly damp. Which must in turn mean that his flight had led him to the Rime Isle coast, to the sea's fringes. Perhaps he was already under the cold, tumultuous, merciless waters of the boundless Outer Sea.

And he was no longer buried upright but lying flat. Truly it was astonishing what a difference that made. Upright, though as closely confined as a statue by its mold, one felt somehow free and on guard. Whereas lying flat, whether supine or prone, was the posture of submission. It made one feel utterly helpless. It was the very worst—

No, he interrupted himself, don't exaggerate. Worse than flat would be buried upside down, heels above head. Best leave off imagining confinements lest he think of one that was still worse.

He set himself to do the same routine things he'd done after his earlier underground lapse of consciousness—regularize and maximize his furtive breathing, assure himself of the continuing glow about his eyes and of his seeming occult power to see, albeit somewhat dimly, for some yards all around him.

The way his head was bent, he found he was looking down his body, along his legs and past his feet. He wished he had a wider range of vision, yet at least there was no blue and chalky female form pursuing him sharklike from that direction.

It was really unnerving, though, how defenseless his flat attitude made him feel, all ready to be trampled, or spat upon, or skewered with pitchfork.

He'd had previous strayings into the realm of Death without his nerve failing, he reminded himself, straining for reassurance and to keep panic at bay. There'd been that time in Lankhmar when he'd entered the magic shop of the Devourers and laid down fearlessly in a black-pillowed coffin and also walked quite eagerly into a mirror that was a vertical pool of liquid mercury held upright by mighty sorceries.

But he'd been drunk and girlstruck then, he reminded himself, though at the time the mercury had felt cool and refreshing (not grainy and suffocating like this stuff!), and he'd afterward nursed the private conviction that he'd been about to discover a secret heroes' heaven high above the one reserved for the gods when Fafhrd had jerked him out of the silver fluid.

No matter. His present friends and lovers, he told himself, must be working like beavers right now to effect his recovery, either by digging (there were enough of them surely) or by working some magic or supernal deal. Perhaps right at this moment dear Cif was manipulating the Golden Ikons of the Isle as she had last year when his mind had been trapped in the brain of a sounding whale.

Or Fafhrd might have figured out some trick to get him back. Though the great oaf had hardly looked capable of such when Mouser had last seen him, goggling down bewilderedly at his disappearing comrade.

Yet how would any of them know where to dig for him, the way he'd moved around? Or be able to dig for him at all, if he were already beneath the Outer Sea?

Which reminded him in turn that according to the most ancient legends, Simorgya had invaded Rime Isle in prehistoric times by way of long long tunnels leading under the wild waves. That was before the more southern isle sank beneath the billows and its cruel inhabitants grew gills and fins.

A fantasy, no doubt, old witches' tales. Yet if such tunnels ever had existed, he was surely in the right place to find them now, Rime Isle's south coast. Or find at least one—surely that was not hoping too much. And so as he industriously sipped air through barely parted lips from the dank earth enfolding him, exhaling in little puffs more forcibly than he inhaled, to drive back intrusive moist granules, he became aware of a pale green undulation parallel to his body some three yards out from him, as though something were moving back and forth out there, up and down a narrow corridor, while it closely regarded him. After a time it resolved itself into the dainty form of the Simorgyan demoness Ississi not more than a quarter—nay, hardly an eighth!—of the way through her girl-fish shape-change: there was the barest hint of a crest along her spine, and the merest suggestion of webs joining the roots of her slender fingers, and only the slightest green tinge to her glorious complexion, she of the large yellow-green eyes and lisping seductive speech, who'd been so amenable to harshest discipline, at least for quite a while.

And she seemed to be wearing a filmy rainbow robe composed of the tatters and rags of the costly, colorful, fine fabric destroyed during his final submarine bout' with her when *Seahawk* had sunk for a space.

For a moment his dissolving skepticism reasserted itself as he asked himself how he could be so certain it was indeed Ississi in this hazy realm where any fish (or girl, for that matter) looked very much like the next (and both like phantoms woven of greenish smoke). But even as he posed that question, the vision became more real, each winsome feature more clearly defined. What's more, he realized he was in no way frightened of her despite the circumstances of their encounter. In fact, as his eyes moved slowly back and forth as they followed her to and froing, he found himself growing drowsy, the regular movement was so restful. He even found himself developing the illusion (surely it must be one?) that his entire body, not just his eyes, was moving slowly forward and back in unison with hers, as if it had unbeknownst to himself escaped into a corridor or tunnel parallel with hers and be afloat in the unresistant air!

Just at that moment he received a shock which caused him sharply to revise any opinion he may have entertained about one young female being very much like the next—or one fish, for that matter. Although he had not seen Ississi's half-smiling lips close up or pucker in any way, he heard a trilling soft seductive whistle.

Looking sharply down along his legs and beyond his feet, he saw the blue-streaked chalky form of Sister Pain advancing toward him in a tigerish rush with talons spread out to either side of her grinning narrow face and eyes aglow with red sadistic fire.

Confirming an earlier intuition of his as well as his guess about the tunnels, without any physical effort on his part, but a tremendous mental one, he began to move away from her at the same speed with which she came horrendously on, so that they both were flashing through the grainy yet utterly unresistant earth at nightmare speed, and Ississi's figure vanished behind them in a trice. . . .

No, not quite. For it seemed to the Mouser that at that point his pursuer paused for an instant while her blue-pied

flesh drank up the other's pale green substance, superadding
Ississi's fishy furies to her own dire hungers before coming
again horrifically on.

He was dearly tempted to glance forward to get some clue
to where they were hastening beneath the Outer Sea, for they
were trending deeper, yet dared not do so for fear that in
trying to dodge some barely glimpsed seeming obstacle, he'd
dash himself into the rocky walls flashing by so close. No,
best trust himself to whatever mighty power gripped him.
However blind, it knew more than he.

There whipped past the dark mouth of an intersecting
tunnel leading southward if he'd kept his bearings, he judged.
To Simorgya? In which case, whither did this branch he was
careening through extend? To No-Ombrulsk? Beyond that,
under land, to the Sea of Monsters? To the dread Shadowland
itself, abode of Death?

What use to speculate when he had yielded up control of
his movements to the whirlwind? Against all reasonable expectations, he found his great speed lulling despite the pearly flash
and fleeting glow of sea fossils. Perhaps at this very moment,
for all he knew, he was breathing softly back in a snug grave
in Rime Isle and dreaming this dream. Even the Great God
Himself must have had moments while creating the universe
or 'verses when He was absolutely certain He was dreaming.
All's well, he mused. He dropped off.

18

Cif insisted on repeating Pshawri's next reading as their
dowsing led them back across the Great Meadow, dangling
the cinder cube from her own left-hand ring finger and thumb,
and when she got the same result as he had, decided they
should alternate taking readings thereafter. He submitted to
this arrangement with proper grace, but couldn't quite conceal

his nervousness whenever the magic pendulum was out of his hands, at such times watching her like a hawk.

"You're jealous of me about the Captain, aren't you?" she rallied the young lieutenant, though not teasingly.

He considered that soberly and answered with equal frankness, "Well, yes, Lady, I am—though in no way challenging your own far greater and different claim on his concern. But I did meet him before you did, when he recruited me in Lankhmar for his band before ever he outfitted *Flotsam* and set sail for Rime Isle."

"You forget," she corrected him gently, "that before your enlistment the Lady Afreyt and I journeyed to Lankhmar to hire him and Fafhrd in the Isle's defense, though on that occasion we were swiftly raped back to this polar clime by Khahkht's icy blast."

"That's true," he allowed. "Nevertheless . . ." He seemed to think better of it.

"Nevertheless what?"

"I was going to say," he told her somewhat haltingly, "that I think he was aware of me before that time. After all, we were both freelance thieves, though he infinitely my superior, and that means a lot in Lankhmar, where the Guild's so strong, and there were other reasons . . . Well, anyway, I knew *his* reputation."

Cif had just completed a reading and clutched the cinder cube in her right hand, not having yet put it in her pouch nor passed it on to him for like securing. She was about to ask Pshawri, "What other reasons?" but instead lost herself in study of his broody features, which were just becoming visible in the gray light without help of the white glow of the lamp, which sat on the ground next where she had dowsed.

Only Astarion, Nehwon's brightest star, was still a pale dot in the dawn-violet heavens, and would soon be gone. Ahead of them but off to their left (for their dowsing was gradually turning them south of the path their party had travelled last evening) a blanket of fog risen from the ground hid all of Salthaven but the highest roofs and the pillars and wind-chime arch of the Moon Temple, tinied by distance. The fog lapped higher round those objects as they watched and, although there was no wind, advanced toward them, whitely distilled from earth. Its far edge brightened where the sun would rise, although a squadron of clouds cruising above had not yet caught its rays.

"It must be cold for the Captain down there below," Pshawri breathed with an involuntary shudder.

"You *are* most deeply concerned about him, aren't you?" Cif observed. "Beyond the ordinary. I've noticed it for the past fortnight. Ever since you received a missive inscribed in violet ink and sealed with green wax, carried on the last trader before *Weasel* in from Lankhmar."

"You have sharp eyes, Lady," he voiced.

"I saw it when Captain Mouser emptied the mail pouch. What is it, Pshawri?"

He shook his head. "With all respect, Lady, it is a matter that concerns solely the Captain and myself—and one other. I cannot speak of it without his leave."

"The Captain knows about it?"

"I do not think so. Yet I can't be sure."

Cif would have continued her queries, although Pshawri's reluctance to answer more fully seemed genuine and deep-rooted—and more than a little mysterious—but at that moment the five from the fire caught up with them and the mood for exchanging confidences was lost. In fact, Cif and Pshawri felt rather on exhibition, for during the next couple of dowsings each of the newcomers had to see for themselves close up the wonder of the heavy cube cinder hanging out of true, straining away from the shaft head definitely though slightly. In the end even skeptical Groniger was convinced.

"I must believe my eyes," he said grudgingly, "though the temptation not to is strong."

"It's harder to believe such things by day," Rill pointed out. "Much easier at night."

Mother Grum nodded. "Witchcraft is so."

The sun had emerged by then, beating a yellow path to them across the top of the fog, which strangely persisted.

And both Cif and Pshawri had to answer questions about the cord's subtle vibrations imperceptible to sight.

"It's just there," she said, "a faint thrilling."

"I can't tell you how I know it's from the Captain," he had to admit. "I just do."

Groniger snorted.

"I wish I could be as sure as Pshawri," Cif told them at that. "For me it doesn't sign his name."

Two more dowsings brought them within sight of Rime Isle's south coast. They prepared to dowse a third time a few paces short of where the meadow grew bare and sloped down rockily and rather sharply for some ten more paces to the narrow beach lapped by the wavelets of the Outer Sea. To the west this small palisade grew gradually steeper and approached the vertical. To the east the stubborn fog reached to within a bowshot of them. Farther off they could spy rising from its whiteness the tops of the masts of the ships riding at anchor in Salthaven's harbor or docked at its wharves.

It was Pshawri's turn to dangle the cube cinder. He seemed somewhat nervous, his movements faster, though steady enough as he locked into position with legs bent, right eye centered over the finger juncture pinching the cord.

Cif and Rill both crouched on their knees close by, so as to observe the pendulum from the side at eye level. They seemed about to make an observation, but Pshawri from his superior vantage point forestalled them.

"The bob no longer pulls southeast," he rapped out in a quick strident voice, "but drags down straight and true."

There were low hisses of indrawn breaths and a "Yes!" from Rill. Cif suggested at once that she repeat his reading, and he gave her the pendulum without demur, though his nervousness seemed to increase. He stationed himself between her and the water. The others completed a ragged circle around her. Rill still crouched close.

After a pause, "Still straight down," Cif said, with another "Yes," from Rill. "And the vibration."

Skullick uncorked with, "If the bob slanting means he's moving in that direction, then straight down says that Captain Mouser is below us but not moving just now."

Cif lifted her eyes toward the speaker. "If it is the Captain."

"But the *how* of all this?" Groniger asked wonderingly, shaking his head.

"Look," Rill said in a strange voice. "The bob is moving again."

They all eyed another wonder. The bob was swinging back

and forth between the direction of the shaft head and the sea, but at least five times as slowly as the period of a pendulum of that length. It crawled its swing.

There was some awe in Skullick's usually irreverent voice. "As if he were pacing back and forth down there. Right now."

"Maybe he's found a sea tunnel," Mother Grum suggested.

"Those fables," Groniger growled.

Without warning the gold-glinting dark-colored bob jumped seaward to taut cord's length from Cif's hand. She gave a quick hiss of pain and it sped on, trailing its cord like a comet's tail and narrowly missing Rill's head.

In a diving catch Pshawri interposed the cupped palm of his right hand, which it smote audibly. He clapped his other hand across it as he himself rolled over and came to his feet with both hands tightly cupped together, as if they caged a small animal or large insect, the cord dangling from between them, and walked back to Cif while the rest watched fascinatedly.

Skullick said, almost religiously, "As if, after pacing, the Captain shot off through solid earth under the sea like a bolt of lightning. If such can be imagined."

Groniger just shook his head, a study in sorely tried skepticism.

Pshawri said to Cif, lifting his elbows, "Lady, would you please unbutton my pouch for me?"

She was studying the red-scored pads of her left ring finger and thumb, where the cord had taken skin as it had jerked away from between them, but she quickly complied with his instructions, being careful not to use these two digits in the process.

He plunged his cupped hands into his pouch and went on saying, "Now tie the cord around the button—no, through the central button hole of the pouch flap. Use a square knot. Although it is not moving now, this thing is best securely confined. I don't trust it anymore, no matter what it's told us."

Cif followed the further instructions without argument, saying, "I thoroughly agree with you, Lieutenant Pshawri. In fact, I don't think the cinder cube has been tracing the

Mouser's movements underground at all, except perhaps at first to start us off.''

The knot was firmly tied. As Pshawri withdrew his hands she closed the flap on the pouch and he buttoned its three buttons.

"Then to what power do you think it's responding?" Rill asked, getting to her feet.

"To Loki's," Cif averred. "I think he wants to lead us on a wild goose chase across the sea. It has all the earmarks of his handiwork: a fascinating lure, strange developments mixed with painful surprises." She popped her injured finger and thumb into her mouth and sucked them.

"It does seem like his tricksy behavior," Rill agreed.

"He's an outlaw god, all right," Mother Grum nodded. "And vengeful. Likely the one who sent Captain Mouser down."

"What's more," mumbled Cif, talking around her fingers, "I think I know the way to scotch his plots and perhaps return the Mouser to us."

"Dowsers ahoy!" a bright new voice called out. They turned and saw Afreyt coming briskly across the Meadow carrying a hamper woven of reeds.

She went on, "There's news from the digging I thought you all should know, but Cif especially. By the way, where's Fafhrd?"

"We haven't seen him, Lady," Pshawri told her.

"Why should he be here?" Groniger asked blankly.

"Why, he left off digging to rest and think alone," Afreyt explained as she reached them and set the hamper on the grass. "But then Udall and another saw him take a jug and lamp and head out after you. They had nothing to do and watched him until he was halfway to you, Udall said."

"We've none of us seen him," Cif assured her.

"But then where are Gale and Fingers?" Afreyt next asked. "Their cot in the shelter tent was empty and their clothes gone that had been warming beside the fire. I thought they must have followed after Fafhrd, like they'd been doing all night."

"We haven't seen pelt or paws of them either," Cif insisted. "But what's this news you promised?"

"But then where in Nehwon . . ." Afreyt began, looking around at the others. They all shook their heads. She told herself, "Leave it," and Cif, "This should please you, I think. We'd driven the sideways corridor about fifteen paces in . . . the digging went faster than straight down—it was a soft sand stretch—and the shoring was easier, despite the added task of roofing . . . when we found this embedded halfway up the face."

And she handed Cif a grit-flecked dirk scabbard.

"Cat's Claw's?"

"The same."

"Right!" Cif said as she examined it eagerly.

"And it was lying horizontal, point end toward us," Afreyt went on, "as if the earth had torn it from his belt as he was being dragged or somehow gotten along, or as though he had left it that way as a clue for us."

"It proves that Captain Mouser's down below, all right," Skullick voiced.

"It does give weight to the two earlier findings of the dirk and cowl," Groniger admitted.

"And so you can understand," Afreyt went on, "why I wanted to tell Fafhrd about it at once. And you, of course, Cif. But what's been happening with the dowsing? What's brought you here to the coast? You surely haven't traced him this far—or have you?"

So Cif told Afreyt how the dowsing had gone and how the bob had tried to escape on the last trial of its powers and was no longer trusted, and also her guess that Loki was behind it all.

Afreyt commented at that, "Fafhrd himself warned me the evidence from dowsing would be uncertain and ambiguous compared with the clues got from actual digging, which he thought should be kept up in any case, to hold open an exit from the underworld for the Gray One at the same point he'd entered it. And you may very well be right about Loki trying to lead us astray. He was a tricksy god, as you know better than I, loving destruction above all else. For that matter, old Odin wasn't reliable either, taking Fafhrd's hand after the loving worship we'd provided him."

Pshawri interposed, "Lady Cif, just before the Lady Afreyt

joined us, you said you'd thought of a way to foil Loki's plots and clear the way for Captain Mouser's return.''

Cif nodded. ''Since the cube cinder is of no use to us as a talisman, I think that one of us should take it and hurl it into the flame pit, the molten lava lake of volcano Darkfire, hopefully returning god Loki to his proper element and perchance assuaging his ire against the Captain.''

''And lose forever one of Rime Isle's ikons, the Gold Cube of Square-Dealing?'' Groniger protested.

''That gold's forever tainted with the stranger god's essence,'' Mother Grum informed him, ''something I cannot exorcise. Cif's rede is good.''

''A golden ikon can be refashioned and resanctified,'' old Ourph pointed out. ''Not so a man.''

''I cannot muster argument against such action, though it seems to me sheerest superstition,'' said Groniger wearily. ''This morn's events have taken me out of my own element of reason.''

''And if it must be done,'' Cif went on, ''you, Pshawri, are the one to attempt it. You raped the cube cinder from the Maelstrom's maw. You should be the one returns it to the fire.''

''If the damned thing will let itself be hurled into the flame pit,'' Skullick burst out, his irreverence at last regenerated. ''You'll hurl it and it'll take flight the gods know where.''

''I'll find a way to constrain it, never fear,'' the young lieutenant assured him, an uncustomary iron in his voice. He turned to Cif. ''From my heart's depths I thank you, Lady, for that task. When I wrested that accursed object from the whirlpool, I do now believe I doomed Captain Mouser to his present plight. It is my dearest desire to wipe out that fault.''

''Now wait a moment, all of you,'' Afreyt cut in. ''I am myself inclined to agree with you about the Queller and Darkfire. It strikes me as the wise thing to do. But this is a step may mean the life or death of Captain Mouser. I do not think that we should take it without the agreement of Captain Fafhrd, his lifelong comrade and forever. I wear his ring, it's true, yet in this matter would not speak for him. So I come back to it: where's Fafhrd?''

''Who are these coming toward us from Salthaven?'' Rill

interrupted in an arresting voice. "If I don't mistake their identities, they may bring news bearing on that question."

The fog blanket to the east was finally breaking up and shredding under the silent bombardment of the sun's bright beams, although the latter were losing a little of their golden strength as the orb mounted and the sky became heavy. Through the white rags and tatters two slight and white-clad figures trudged: who waved their hands and broke into a run upon seeing that they were observed. As they drew closer it was to be seen that the redhead's eyes were large in her small face but the silver-blonde's larger still.

"Aunt Afreyt!" Gale called as soon as they got near. "We've had a great adventure and we've got the most amazing news to tell!"

"Never mind that now," Afreyt answered somewhat shortly. "Tell us, where's Fafhrd?"

"How did you know?" Gale's eyes grew larger still. "Well, I was going to build up to it, but since you ask right off: Uncle Fafhrd has swum up into the sky to board a cloud ship of Arilia or flag a flier from Stardock. I think he's looking for help in finding Uncle Mouser."

"Stop talking nonsense," Cif burst out.

"Fafhrd can't swim through air," Afreyt pointed out.

"Sea tunnels of Simorgya! Cloud ships of Arilia!" Groniger protested. "That's too much nonsense for a cold summer morning."

"But it's what happened," the girl insisted. "Why, Aunt Afreyt, you yourself saw Fafhrd and Mara flying high through air when the invisible princess Hirriwi of Stardock rescued them from Hellfire on her invisible fish of air. Fingers saw more than I did. She'll tell you."

The Ilthmar cabingirl said, "Aboard *Weasel* the sailors all assured me that the strangest sorts of vessels dock at Rime Isle, including the cloud galleons of the Queendom of the Air. And I did see Captain Fafhrd swimming strongly atop the fog toward a cloud that could have been such a vessel."

"Arilia is a fable, child," Groniger assured her gently. "Sailors tell all sorts of lies. Actually Rime Isle's the least fantastic place in all of Nehwon."

"But Uncle Fafhrd did mount up the sky," Gale reaffirmed

stubbornly. "I don't know how. Maybe Princess Hirriwi taught him to fly and he never told us about it. He's awfully modest. But he did it. We both saw him."

"All right, all right," Cif told her. "I think you'd best just tell us the whole story from the beginning."

Afreyt said, "But first you need a cup of wine to calm you down and also warm you. You've been long out on a chilly morning that may go down in legend." She opened her hamper, took out a jug of fortified sweet wine and two small silver mugs, filled them halfway, and made both children drink them down. This led to serving wine to all the others.

Gale said, "Fingers should start it. At the beginning I was asleep."

Fingers told them, "Captain Fafhrd came back from the diggings just after the rest of you all went off. He drank some gahvey and brandy and began to pace up and down, frowning and rubbing his wrist against his forehead as if he were trying to think out some problem. He got very nervous and fey. Finally he took up a jug, hung a lamp on his hook, and went off after you. I waked Gale and told her I thought he needed watching."

"That's right," Gale took over. "So we jumped out of bed and ran to the fire and got dressed."

"That explains it," Afreyt interjected.

"What?" Pshawri asked.

"Why Udall kept watching Fafhrd so long. Go on, dear."

Gale continued, "It was easy to follow Uncle Fafhrd because of his lamp. The darkness was fading anyway, the stars going out. At first we didn't try to catch up with him or let him know we were behind him."

"You were afraid he'd send you back," Cif guessed.

"That's right. At first he seemed to be following you, but where you turned south he kept straight on east. It was getting quite light now, but the sun was still in hiding. Every so often he'd stop and look ahead at the fog and the rooftops and the windchime arch sticking up out of it and lift his head to scan the sky above it—that's when I saw the little fleet of clouds—and raise his hand before his face to invoke the gods and ask their help."

"That was the hand that had the jug in it?" Afreyt asked.

"It must have been," the girl replied, "for I don't recall the lamp going up and down.

"And then Uncle Fafhrd began to run in the strangest slow way, he seemed to float and almost stop between each step. Of course, we started to run too. We were all into the fog by now, which seemed to slow him and support him at the same time, so his steps were longer.

"The fog got over our heads and hid him from us. We got to the Moon Arch and Fingers started to climb it before I could tell her that was frowned on. She got above the fog and called down . . ."

Gale stretched a hand toward Fingers, who continued, "Truly, gentles, I saw Captain Fafhrd swimming strongly through the top of the fog, up its long white slope, while a good distance beyond him, the goal of his mighty self-sailing, there was—I know the eyes can be fooled and my mind was full of the sailors' tales, nevertheless, my word as a novice witch—there was a dense cloud that looked very much like a white ship with a high stern castle. Sunlight flashed from its silver brightwork.

"Then that same sun got into my eyes and I stopped seeing anything clearly. I'd called some of it down to Gale and I climbed down and told her the rest."

Gale took up again. "We ran through Salthaven to the eastern headland. The fog was breaking up and burning off, but we couldn't see anything clearly. When we got there, the Maelstrom was seething and mists rising from it. But overhead it was clear and I could see Uncle Fafhrd, very high now, beside the white cloudship, showing only its keel. There were five gulls around him. Then the mists from below came between us. I thought you should know, Aunt Afreyt. But since it was on the way to the diggings, we decided to tell Aunt Cif first."

Fingers added, "I saw what she saw, gentles. But Captain Fafhrd was very far off then. It could have been a very large marine bird—a sea mandragon escorted by five sea hawks."

The listeners looked at each other.

"This rings true," Afreyt said quite softly. "I feared that Fafhrd was fey when he was last down the shaft."

"You believe what these girls tell us?" Groniger asked only somewhat incredulously.

"To be sure she does," Mother Grum answered.

"But why would he go to air folk," Skullick wanted to know, "to get advice on someone lost underground?"

"You can't guess the designs of a fey one," Rill told him.

"But what of the Gray Mouser now?" Cif addressed Afreyt. "As Fafhrd's spokeswoman, what say you to sending Pshawri to Darkfire?"

"Let him go, of course, and luck with him. Luck and quietus to Loki," that lady responded without hesitation. "Here's provisions for you, Lieutenant." From her hamper she gave him a small loaf and a hard sausage and the near empty sweet wine jug, which would do to carry cool water he'd get at Last Spring on the way.

After a quick glance to assure himself the others were otherwise occupied, Pshawri said to Afreyt in a low voice, "Lady, would you add to your kindnesses one further favor?" and when she nodded, handed her a folded paper indited in violet ink with broken green seals. "Keep this for me. Should I not return (such things happen), give it to Captain Fafhrd, if he's back. Otherwise read it yourself—and show it to Lady Cif at your discretion."

"I'll do that," she said softly, and then resuming her normal voice, called, "Cif dear, you'll take over for Fafhrd and me at the digging. I'll give you Fafhrd's ring."

"Can you doubt it?" Cif replied, turning back from Mother Grum, with whom she'd been conferring.

Afreyt went on, "For it's now my turn to do some thinking about a lost one—and to see that these two outwearied girls do some sound sleeping. I'll take them to your place, Cif, and see to all there. Skama, shield *me* from feyness, except it be *your* inspiration."

So without more ceremony the three parties separated: Pshawri north toward distant, smoke-trailing Darkfire; Cif, Skullick, and Rill back to the diggings; Afreyt, Groniger, and the weary old and young pairs to Salthaven.

Trudging with the last party, and suddenly looking every bit as tired as Afreyt had described her, Fingers recited as by someone already asleep and dreaming,

> *"After the dog has eaten out his heart,*
> *The cat his liver, and his secret parts*
> *Uprooted and devoured by the hog,*
> *He shall sleep sounder then than any log,*
> *A shadow prince enrobed by moonlit fog."*

"Was that your brother, Princess?" Gale asked, wrinkling her nose. "You know the nicest poems, I must say."

After a moment Afreyt inquired thoughtfully, "But what kind of a poem was it, dear Fingers? Where did it come from?"

Still somewhat in a sleepy singsong, the weary child responded, "It is the augmented third stanza of a Quarmallian death spell effective only in its entirety." She shook her head and blinked her eyes and came more awake. "Now how did I know that?" she asked. "My mother was born in Quarmall, that is true, but that was another of the things we weren't supposed to tell most people."

"Yet she taught you this Quarmall death spell," Afreyt stated.

Fingers shook her head decidedly. "My mother never dealt in death spells, nor taught me any. She is a white witch, truly." She looked puzzledly at Gale and then up at Afreyt and asked, "Why does a memory wink off whenever you try to watch it closely? Is it because we cannot live forever?"

19

As consciousness next glimmered, glowed, and then shone noontide bright in the Gray Mouser's skull, he would have been certain he was dreaming, for in his nostrils was the smell of Lankhmar earth, richly redolent of the grainfields, the Great Salt Marsh, the river Hlal, the ashes of innumerable fires, and the decay of myriad entities, a unique melange of

odors, and he was ensconced in one of the secretmost rooms
of all Lankhmar City, one he knew well although he had
visited it only once. How could his underground journeying
possibly have carried him so far, two thousand leagues or
more, one tenth the way at least around all Nehwon world?
—except that he had never in his life had a dream in which
the furniture and actors were so clearly distinct and open to
scrutiny in all their details.

But as we know, it was the Mouser's custom on waking
anywhere not to move more than an eye muscle or make the
least sound, even that of a deeper breath, until he had taken in
and thoroughly mastered the nature of his surroundings and
his own circumstances amongst them.

He was comfortably seated cross-legged about a Lankhmar
cubit (a forearm's length) behind a narrow low table beside
the foot of the wide bed, sheeted in white silk curiously
coarse of weave, in the combined underground bedroom and
boudoir of the rat princess Hisvet, his most tormenting one-
time paramour, daughter of the wealthy grain merchant Hisvin,
in the buried city of Lankhmar Below. He knew it was that
room and no other by its pale violet hangings, silver fittings,
and a half hundred more apposite details, chiefest perhaps
two painted panels in the far wall depicting an unclad maiden
and crocodile erotically intertwined and a youth and leopard-
ess similarly entangled. As had been the case some five years
ago, the room was lit by narrow tanks of glow worms at the
foot of the walls, but now also by silver cages hanging
cornice high and imprisoning flashing firebeetles, glow wasps,
nightbees, and diamondflies big as robins or starlings. While
on the low table before him rested a silver waterclock with
visible pool, upon the center of which a large drop fell every
third breath or dozenth heartbeat, making circular ripples, and
a cut crystal carafe of pale golden wine, reminding him he
was abominably thirsty.

So much for the furniture of his dream, vision, or true
sighting. The actors included slim Hisvet herself wearing a
violet wrap whose color matched the hangings and her lips.
She was seated on the bed's foot, looking as merry and
schoolgirl innocent (and devilishly attractive) as always, her
fine silver-blond hair drawn through a small ring of that metal

behind her head, while standing at dutiful attention close before her were two barefoot maids with hair cropped short and wearing identical closely fitting hip-length black and white tunics. Hisvet was lecturing them, laying out rules of some sort, apparently, and they were listening most earnestly, although they showed it in different ways, the brunette nodding her head, smiling her understandings, and darting her gaze with sharp intelligence, while the blonde maintained a sober and distant, yet wide-eyed expression, as though memorizing Hisvet's every word, inscribing each one in a compartment of her brain reserved for that purpose alone.

But although Hisvet worked her violet lips and the tip of her mottled blue and pink tongue continuously in the movements of speech and lifted an admonitory right forefinger from time to time and once touched it successively on the tips of the outspread fingertips of her supine left hand to emphasize points one, two, three, and four, not a single word could the Gray Mouser hear. Nor did any one of the three ever look once in his direction, even the saucy dark-haired wench whose gaze went everywhere else.

Since both maids in their very short tunics were quite as attractive as their ravishing mistress, their disregard of him began to wound the Mouser's vanity not a little.

Since there seemed nothing for the moment to do but watch them, the Mouser soon developed a hankering to see their naked shapes. So far as the maids were concerned, he might get his wish simply by waiting. Hisvet had a remarkable instinct for such matters and was perfectly willing to let other women entertain for her—distribute her favors, as it were.

But as to her own secret person, it still remained a mystery to the Mouser, whether under the robes, wraps, and armor she affected there was a normal maiden form or a slender rat tail and eight tits, which his imagination pictured as converging pairs of large-nippled and large-aureoled bud-breasts, the third pair to either side of her umbilicus and the fourth close together upon her pubis.

It also was a mystery to him whether the three females and he were all now of rat size or human size—ten inches or five feet high. Certainly he'd had none of the shape-changing elixir that was used in moving between Lankhmar Above and the rat city of Lankhmar Below.

His hankerings continued. Surely he deserved some reward for all the underground perils he'd braved. Women could do men so much good so easily.

There remained the problem of the three women's perfect inaudibility.

Either, he guessed, they were engaged in an elaborate pantomime (plotted by Hisvet to tease him?), or it *was* a dream despite its realism, or else there was some hermetic barrier (most likely magical) between his ears and them.

Supporting this last possibility was the point that while he could see the giant luminescent insects move about in their cages, striking the silver bars with wing and limb while making their bright shinings and flashes, no angry buzzings or sounds of any sort came down from them; while (most telling of all in its way) only silence accompanied the infrequent but regular plashes of the singular crystalline drops into the shimmering pool of the waterclock so close at hand.

One final circumstance suggestive of magic at work and matching the strange quiet of the scene otherwise so real: miraculously suspended in the air above the near edge of the low table, in a vertical attitude with ring-pommeled small silver grip uppermost, was a tapering whip of white snow-serpent hide scarcely a cubit long, so close at hand he could perceive its finely rugose surface, yet spy no thread or other explanation of its quiet suspension.

Well, that was the scene, he told himself. Now to decide on how to enter it, assert himself as one of the actors. He would lean suddenly forward, he told himself, reach out his right hand, seize with his three bottom fingers the neck of the carafe, unstopper it with forefinger and thumb preparatory to putting it to his parched lips, saying meanwhile something to the effect of, "Greetings, dearest delightful demoiselle, do me the kindness of interrupting this charade to give an old friend notice. Don't be alarmed, girls," that last being for the two maids, of course.

No sooner thought than done!

But, from the start, things went most grievously agley. On his first move he felt himself gripped by a general paralysis that struck like lightning. His whole front was bruised, his right hand and arm scraped, from every side dark brown grainy walls rushed in upon him, his ''Greetings'' became on the first syllable a strangled growl that stabbed his ears, pained his whole skull, and changed to a fit of coughing that left him with what seemed a mouthful of raw dirt.

He was *still* in the same horrid buried predicament he'd been in ever since he'd slipped down out of the full-moon ceremony on Gallows Hill into the cold cruel ground that was at once so strangely permeable to his involuntary passage through it and so adamantly resistant to his attempts to escape it. This time he'd been fooled by the perfection of the occult vision, which let him see through solid earth for a distance around him, into thinking he was free, disregarding the evidence of all his other avenues of awareness. Evidently he *had* somehow been brought to Lankhmar's underenvirons, and nothing now remained to do but begin anew the slow game of regularizing his breathing, calming his pounding heart, and freeing his mouth grain by grain of the dirt that had entered it during his spasm, carefully working his tongue to best advantage, in order to assure bare survival. For after the pain in his skull subsided he became aware of a general weakness and a wavering of consciousness that told him he was very near the edge between being and not being and must work most cunningly to draw back from it.

During this endeavor he was assisted by the fact that he never quite altogether lost sight of a larger white and violet visual reality around him. There were patchy flashes and glimpses of it alternating with the grainy dark dirt, and he was also helped by the faint yellow glow continuing to emanate from his upper face.

When the Mouser finally re-won all the territory he'd lost by his incautious sally, he was surprised to see fair Hisvet still going through all the motions of talking, and the winsome maids through those of attending her every word, as animatedly as before. Whatever was she saying?

While carefully maintaining all underground breathing routines, he concentrated his attention on other channels of sensation than the visual, seeking to widen and deepen, and bringing to bear all his inner powers, and after a time his efforts were rewarded.

The next heavy drop fell into the pool of the waterclock with an audible dulcet *plash!* He almost, but not quite, gave a start.

Almost immediately a glow wasp *buzzed* and a diamondfly whirred its transparent wings against the wire-thin pale bars.

Hisvet leaned back on her elbows and said in silver tones, "At ease, girls."

They appeared to relax their attention—a little, at any rate.

She tapped three fingers against the ruby rondure of her lips as she yawned prettily. "My, that was a most lengthy and boring lecture," she commented. "Yet you endured it most commendably, dear Threesie," she addressed the dark-haired maid. "And you too, Foursie," she told the fair-haired one. She picked up from beside her a long emerald-headed pin and flourished it playfully. "There was not once the need for me to make use of *this* upon either of you," she said, laughing, "to recall to attention the willful wandering mind and wake the lazy dreamer."

Both girls shaped their lips to appreciative smiles, while giving the pin most sour looks.

Hisvet handed it to Foursie, who bore it somewhat gingerly across the room to a drawered chest topped with cosmetics and mirrors, and inserted it into a spherical black cushion that held jewel-headed others such, compassing all the hues of the rainbow.

Meanwhile Hisvet addressed Threesie, whose eyes widened as she listened. "During my talk I twice got the distinct impression that we were being spied on by an evil intelligence, one of the criminous sort my father deals with, or one of our own enemies, or a cast-off lover perchance." She searched her gaze around the walls, lingering somewhat over-long, the Mouser felt, in his direction.

"I will meditate on it," she continued. "Dear Threesie, fetch me my silver-inlaid black opal figure of the world of Nehwon which I call the Opener of the Way."

Threesie nodded dutifully and went to the same chest Foursie had just visited, passing her midway.

"Dear Foursie," Hisvet greeted the blonde, "fetch me a

beaker of white wine. My throat has grown quite dry with all that stupid talking.''

Foursie bowed her fair-thatched head and came to the low table set against the wall behind which the Mouser was embedded in earth invisible to him. He studied her appreciatively as she unstoppered the carafe he'd so disastrously snatched at and neatly filled a shining glass so tall and narrow it looked like a measuring tube. Her white uniform tunic was secured down the front with large circular jet buttons.

Returning to her mistress, she went down on her knees without bending her slender body in any other way and proffered the refreshment.

''Taste it first,'' Hisvet instructed.

Getting this instruction, not uncommonly given servants by aristocrats, Foursie threw back her head and poured a short gush of the fluid between her parted lips without touching them to the glass, which she next held out to show its level was perceptibly decreased.

Hisvet accepted it, saying, ''That was well executed, Foursie. Next time don't wait for instruction. And you might lick your lips and smile to show that you enjoyed.''

Foursie bobbed her head.

''Dear demoiselle,'' Threesie called from where she knelt at the chest of drawers, ''I cannot find the Opener.''

''Have you searched carefully for it?'' Hisvet called back, her voice becoming slightly thin. ''It is an oblate sphere big as two thumbs, inset with silver bounding the continents and flat diamonds for the cities and a larger amethyst and turquoise making the death and life poles.''

''Dear demoiselle, I know the Opener,'' Threesie called respectfully.

Hisvet, who was looking at Foursie again, shrugged her shoulders, then set the narrow glass to her lips and downed its contents in three swallows. ''That was refreshing.'' Again the lip pats.

A rutching sound turned her attention back to Threesie. ''No, do not open the other drawers,'' she directed. ''It would not be there. Just search the top one thoroughly and *find it*. Set out the contents one by one on top of the chest if necessary.''

"Yes, demoiselle."

Hisvet caught Foursie's eye again, rolled hers toward busy Threesie, sketched another shrug, and commented confidingly, "This could become a tiresome annoyance, you know, a true weariness. No, girl, don't bob your head. That's all right on Threesie, but it's not your style. Incline it once, demurely."

"Yes, mistress." Her single nod was shy as a virgin princess'.

"How are you doing, Threesie?"

The brunette turned to face them. Her reply was barely loud enough to cross the room. "Demoiselle, I must confess myself defeated."

After a rather long pause, Hisvet said reflectively, "That could be quite bothersome for you, Threesie, you know. As senior maid present, you would be wholly responsible for any deficiencies, disappearances, or thefts. Think about it."

After another pause, she sighed and said, holding out the empty glass, "Foursie, fetch me the springy implement of correction."

The blonde inclined her head, took the glass, and walking somewhat more slowly, returned to the low table, set down the glass, refilled it, and reached across to seize the magically suspended white whip, which she lifted with a little twist and bore off with the glass, thereby solving a minor mystery for the Mouser. The whip had simply been hanging on a hook on the wall. But since the wall had been and was again invisible to him, so was the hook protruding from it.

He felt a stirring of interest in the scene he spied on from his confining point of vantage, and was duly grateful to have his mind taken a little off his own troubles. He knew something of Hisvet's ways and could guess the next developments, or at least speculate rewardingly. Dark-haired Threesie seemed well cast as the villain or culprit of this triangular piece. Leaning back against the chest of drawers and scowling, she looked a bird of ill omen in her uniform black tunic, though the large circular alabaster buttons going down the front added a comic note. Foursie did her kneeling trick a second time. Hisvet accepted the whip and replenished drink, saying graciously, "Thank you, my dear. I feel much better with these both by me. Well, Threesie?"

"I am thinking, demoiselle," that one said, "and it comes to me that when I entered this room Foursie was crouched where I stand now with the drawer open I have just searched thoroughly, and she was rummaging around in it. She pushed it shut at once, but may well have taken somewhat from it, I realize now, and hid about her person."

"Demoiselle, that's not true!" Foursie protested, turning pale. "The drawer was never open, nor I at it."

"She is a vicious little liar, dear mistress," Threesie shot back. "Mark how she blanches!"

"Hush, girls," Hisvet reproved. "I have thought of a simple way to settle this most unseemly dispute. Threesie dear, had Foursie opportunity to hide the Opener elsewhere in the room after she took it, if she did? As I recall, I entered shortly after you did."

"No, mistress, she had not."

"Well, then," Hisvet said, smiling. "Threesie, come here. Foursie dear, strip off your tunic, so she may search you thoroughly."

"Demoiselle!" the blonde uttered reproachfully. "You would not shame me so."

"No shame at all," Hisvet assured her ingenuously, lifting her silver eyebrows. "Why, child, suppose I were entertaining a lover, I might very well—probably would—have you and Threesie disrobe, so as not to embarrass him, or at all events make us both feel conspicuous. Or we might have the whim to ask one of you or both to join in our play under direction. Frix understood these things, as I hope Threesie does. Frix was incomparable. Not even Twosie comes close to matching her. But as you know, Frix managed to work out her term of service, discharge the geas my father set upon her. There's never been another Onesie, and that's why."

Both maids nodded agreement, though somewhat grimly in their two different styles. They'd each heard somewhat too much about the Incomparable Onesie.

The Mouser was beginning to enjoy himself. Why, look, the piece was barely begun and Hisvet had managed to switch around the roles of the two other characters! He wished

Fafhrd were here, he'd enjoy hearing Frix praised so. He'd been quite gone on the princess of Arilia, especially when she'd been Hisvet's imperturbable slave-maid. Though the large loon wouldn't appreciate being entombed, that was certain. Probably too big to survive by scavenging air in any case. Which reminded him, he'd best keep in mind his own breathing. And not lose sight of the ever-present possibility of the intrusion into the scene of some third force from either the under- or overworld. Talk about having to watch two ways!

In response to Hisvet's, "And so, no nonsense, child. Strip, I said!"

Foursie had been arguing, "Have compassion, demoiselle. To disrobe for a lover would be one thing. But to strip to be searched by a fellow servant is simply too humiliating. I couldn't bear it!"

Hisvet sprang up off the bed. "I've quite lost patience with you, you prudish little bitch. Who are you to say what you'll bear—or bare, for that matter? Threesie, grip her arms! If she struggles, pinion them behind her."

The dark maid, who was already back of Foursie, seized and tightly held her elbows down at her sides, meanwhile smiling somewhat evilly at her mistress across the fair maid's shoulder. Hisvet reached out a straight right arm, chucked the girl's chin up until they were looking each other straight in the eye, and then proceeded very deliberately to unbutton the top black button.

Foursie said, with as much dignity as she could muster, "I would have submitted to you, demoiselle, without my arms held."

But Hisvet said only, very deliberately also, "You are a silly schoolgirl, Foursie dear, needing considerable teaching, which you're going to get. You would submit to me? But not to my maid acting on my orders? To begin with, Threesie is not your equal fellow servant. She outranks you and is empowered to correct you in my absence."

As she spoke she went on undoing the buttons, taking her time and digging her knuckles and pressing the large buttons into the girl's flesh edgewise as she did so. At the undoing of the third button the maid's small, firm, pink-nippled breasts popped out. Hisvet continued, "But as it is, you're getting your way, aren't you, Foursie? I am disrobing you and not dear Threesie here, though she is witnessing. In fact, I'm 'maiding' you, how's that for topsy-turvy? You're getting the deluxe treatment, one might say, though I strongly doubt you will get much pleasure from it.''

She finished with the buttons, looked the girl up and down, lightly flicked her breasts with the back of her hand, and said with a cheery laugh, ''There, that wasn't so bad now, was it, dear? Threesie, finish.''

Grinning, the dark maid slid the white tunic down Foursie's arms and off them.

''Why, you are blushing, Foursie,'' Hisvet observed, chuckling. ''On Whore Street that's a specialty, I'm told, and ups the price. Inspect the garment carefully,'' she warned Threesie. ''Feel along each seam and hem. She may have pilfered something smaller than the Opener. And now, dear child, prepare yourself to be searched from head to toe by a maid who is your superior, whilst I direct and witness.'' Taking up the silver-handled whip of white snow-serpent hide from the bed and gesturing with it, she directed Foursie, ''Lift out your arms a little from your sides. There, that's enough. And stand so that your entire anatomy is more accessible. A little wider stance, please. Yes, that will do.''

The Mouser noted that all the maid's body hair had been shaven or plucked. So that practice, favored by witless Glipkerio, the Scarecrow Overlord, was still followed in Lankhmar. A seemly and most attractive one, the Mouser thought.

''There's nothing hidden in the garment, Threesie? You're sure? Well, toss it by the far wall and then you might begin by running your fingers through Foursie's hair. Bend forward, child! Slowly and carefully, Threesie. I know her mop's quite short, but you'd be shocked to learn how much a little hair can sometimes hide. And don't forget the ears. We're looking for tiny things.''

Hisvet yawned and took a long swallow of wine. Foursie glared at her nearer tormentor. There is something peculiarly degrading about being handled by the ears, having them spread and bent this way and that. But Threesie, learning from her mistress, only smiled sweetly back.

"And now the mouth," Hisvet directed. "Open wide, Foursie, as for the barber-surgeon. Feel in each cheek, Threesie. I don't suppose Foursie's been playing the little squirrel, but there's no telling. And now . . . Surely you're not at a loss, Threesie? Perhaps I should have expressed it, search her from top to bottom. You may lubricate your fingers with my pomade. But use it sparingly, its basis is the essential oil with which they anoint the Emperor of the East. Don't agonize so, Foursie! Imagine it's your lover exploring you, dextrously demonstrating his tender regard. Who is your lover, Foursie? You do have one, I trust? Come to recall, I've caught the fair page Hari looking at you in that certain way. I wonder what he'd think if he could see you as you're presently occupied. Droll. I've half a mind to summon him. Well, that's half done. And now, Threesie, her darker avenue of amatory bliss. Bend over, Foursie. Treat her gently, Threesie. Some of these matters appear to be quite new to our little girl, advanced subjects for our student, though I know that's hard to credit. What Foursie, tears? Cheer up, child! You're not proved guilty yet, in fact you're well on the way to being cleared. Life has all sorts of surprises."

The Mouser smiled cynically from his weird invisible prison. Around Hisvet surprises were invariably disastrous, he knew from experience. He was thoroughly enjoying himself, so far as his limited circumstances permitted. He thought of how all of his greatest loves and infatuations had been for short and slim girls like these. Lilyblack came to mind, back when he'd bravoed and racketeered for Pulg and Fafhrd had found god in Issek. Reetha, who'd been Glipkerio's silver-chained maid. Ivivis of Quarmall, supple as a snake. Innocent, tragic Ivrian, his first love, whose princess-dreams he'd fed. Cif, of course. The nightfilly Ivmiss Ovartamortes. That made seven, counting Hisvet. And there was one other, an eighth, whose name and identity evaded him, who was also a maid by profession and particularly delectable because somehow forbidden. Who *had* she been? What *was* her name? If he could recall one more detail he'd remember all. Maddening! Of course, he'd had all manner of larger women, but this elusive memory involved all smaller than himself, his special pantheon of little darlings. You'd think a man in his grave (and that was truly his situation, face it) would be able to concentrate his mind upon one subject, but no, even here there were details to distract you, self-responsibilities that had to be taken care of, as keeping up an even rhythm of shallow breathing, pushing back intrusive dirt off of his lips, keeping constant watch before and behind— It occurred to him that Foursie too must be telling herself that last thing, though much good it would do her—which reminded him to return to the enjoyment of the three-girl comedy which destiny had provided for his secret viewing.

Hisvet was saying, "Now, Foursie, go to the far wall and stand facing it while I hear Threesie's report and confer with her. And stop blubbering, girl! Use your discarded tunic to wipe the tears and snot off your face."

Hisvet led Threesie back to the foot of the bed, set her empty glass on the low table, and said in a voice that Mouser could barely hear, despite the advantages of nearness and occult audition, "I take it, Threesie, you didn't find the Opener or anything else?"

"No, dear demoiselle, I did not," the dark maid replied, and then went on in a voice that was more like a stage whisper, "I'm certain she's swallowed it. I suggest she be given a strong emetic, and if that fails, a powerful cathartic. Or both together, to save time."

Foursie too heard that, the Mouser judged by the way her shoulders drew together as she faced the wall.

Hisvet shook her head and said in the same low tones as before, "No, that won't be necessary, I think, though it could be amusing under other circumstances. Now it suits my design to have her think she's been completely cleared of any suspicion of theft." She faced around and changed to her most ringing silver voice, "Congratulations, Foursie, you'll be glad to hear that your fellow maid has given you a clean bill of health. Isn't that wonderful? And now come here at once. No, don't try to put on your tunic. Leave that soiled rag. You need a lot more practice in serving naked, which you ought to be able to do every bit as efficiently, coolly, and nicely without the reassurance of a frock. And perhaps practice in other activities one generally carries out best in one's skin. Beginning now."

The Lankhmar demoiselle in the violet wrap yawned again and stretched. "That wretched session has quite wearied me. Foursie, you may begin your nude reapprenticeship (that's a joke, girl) by fetching me a fat pillow from the head of the bed."

When Foursie came around with her plump lemon-hued burden, her eyes asking a question, Hisvet indicated with her whip the bottom corner of the bed, and when the fair maid had placed the pillow there, gave her the whip, saying, "Hold this for me," and stretched herself out with her head on the pillow. But after murmuring, "Ah, that's better," and wriggling her toes, she lifted up on an elbow, looked toward Threesie, and pointed with her other hand down at the carpet by the foot of the bed, saying, "Threesie, come here. I want to show you something privately."

When the dark maid came eagerly, all agog for more secrets, Hisvet laid her silver-tressed head back again upon the pillow, whose hue contrasted nicely with her violet wrap, and said, "Lean down, so your head is close to mine. I want this to be quite private. Foursie, stand clear."

But when Threesie stooped down, her lips working with high excitement, Hisvet began at once to criticize. "No, don't bend your knees! I did not bid you crouch over me like an animal. Keep your legs straight."

By bending her waist more, pushing her buttocks back, and also throwing her arms out behind her, the dark maid managed to comply with her instructions without overbalancing. Her and her mistress' faces were upside down to each other.

"But, demoiselle," Threesie pointed out humbly, "when I bend over like this in this short tunic, I expose myself behind. Especially with your rule against undergarments."

Hisvet smiled up at her. "That's very true," she observed, "and I designed them partly with that in mind, so that when told to pick up something from the floor, for instance, a maid would stoop gracefully, as in a curtsey, keeping her head and shoulders erect. It's far more seemly and civilized."

Threesie said uncertainly, "But when you go down like that you have to bend your knees, you squat. You told me not to bend—"

"That's quite a different matter," Hisvet interrupted, impatience gathering in her voice. "I told you to lean down your head."

"But, demoiselle—" Threesie faltered.

Hisvet reached up and caught an earlobe between forefinger and thumb, dug in the nails, twisted sharply and gave a downward tug. Threesie squealed. Hisvet let go and, patting her cheek, told her, "That's all right. I just wanted to rivet your attention and make you stop your silly babble. Now, listen carefully. While you did the body search on Foursie passably well, it became frightfully obvious that you, as well as Foursie, needless to say, were in sore need of instruction in the amatory arts, which it falls on me to give you, since you're my own dear maid and no one else's." And reaching her hand higher, she hooked her fingers around the back of Threesie's neck and pulled her head down briskly but thoughtfully, leaning her own head to the left at the last moment, so that her lips met at an angle those of Threesie, who managed to keep her balance by further and somewhat desperate rearward outthrustings.

The Mouser thought, I knew that this was coming. But one certainly cannot fault the little darlings for their occasional itch for each other, since their taste is so exactly like my own. Strange, come to think of it, that Fafhrd and I have never seemed to experience this like-sex urge. Is it a deficiency in us? I must discuss the question with him some time. And with Cif too, for that matter, ask her if she and Afreyt ever played games . . . no, maybe not ask, I could understand Afreyt lusting for Cif, but not dear Ciffy for that beanpole Venus.

Hisvet shifted her fingers behind Threesie's head to the short hairs there, lifted her head to its original position as briskly as she'd lowered it, and said, "That was passable also. Next time, if such should be, employ your tongue somewhat more freely. Be adventurous, girl."

Wide-eyed Threesie gasped, "Excuse me, demoiselle, but was that kiss, for which I thank you most humbly, the something you said you wished to show me privately?"

"No, it was not," Hisvet informed her, thrusting a hand deep into a side pocket of her wrap. "That is a different matter, rather sadder for you." Pulling Threesie's head down again, this time by the neck of her black tunic, she brought a fist out of the pocket, opened it under Threesie's eyes, displaying on her cupped palm a globular black opal traveled with silver lines and pocked here and there with small, pale, glittering dots. "What do you suppose this is?" she asked.

"It appears to be the Opener of the Way, dear demoiselle." Threesie faltered. "But how—"

"Quite right, girl. I took it earlier from the chest myself and just now remembered. So Foursie could hardly have swallowed it, could she? Or even taken it from the chest, for that matter."

"No, demoiselle," the dark maid agreed reluctantly. "But Foursie's only a servant of the lowest rank, little better than a slave. It was natural to suspect her. Moreover, you yourself must have known—"

"I told you I only now remembered!" Hisvet reminded her in dangerous tones. She raised her voice. "Foursie!"

"Yes, demoiselle?" came the swift reply.

"Threesie is to be punished for bearing false witness against a fellow servant. Since you're the party who would have been injured, I think it's most appropriate that you administer the chastisement. Moreover, you are conveniently at hand and have my whip. Do you know how to use it?"

"I think I do, demoiselle," Foursie answered evenly. "When I was a child down on the farm I used to ride a mule."

"That's nice to know," Hisvet called. "Wait for directions."

As Threesie quite involuntarily started to move away, Hisvet rotated the fist grasping her tunic so that it tightened around Threesie's neck and Hisvet's knuckles dug into the maid's throat.

"Listen," she hissed, "if you so much as move a step or flex your knees during what's coming, I'll have my father put a geas on you. And not a relatively nice and easy one like Frix. She merely had to serve me faithfully and cheerfully as slave until she'd thrice saved my life at risk of her own. Straighten those knees now!"

Threesie complied. She had seen old Hisvin send a berserk cook into mortal convulsions, so he died in his tracks with mouth exuding greenish foam, merely by staring at him fixedly.

Hisvet eased her grip on the top of Threesie's tunic. She scowled in thought. Then her face broke into a smile. She called, "Foursie, here's how. Time your blows to the splashes of the waterclock, one for one, nothing in between—don't let yourself get carried away. Start with the third plash after the next. I'll call the first of those so you get it right."

Hisvet's hand on the neck of the black tunic became busy, undoing the three top big white buttons rapidly.

The waterclock plashed, sounding unnaturally loud. Hisvet called, "Ready!" Tension took hold.

Though pendant, the dark maid's breasts were quite as small and firm as the fair one's, with thicker nipples the rosy hue of fresh scrubbed copper. Hisvet fondled them.

"How many blows, demoiselle?" Threesie asked in a small, fearfully anxious voice. "In all?"

"Hush! I haven't decided yet. You're supposed to be enjoying this. And you really are, I can tell, for your nipples are hardening despite your terrors. And your aureoles are all goose bumps. You should indicate pleasure at my squeezings and finger-dancing across your tits by sighing and moaning."

The waterclock plashed. "One!" Hisvet called, then ominously for Threesie's benefit, "You've started to bend your legs again," and taking the hand away from the maid's bosom, reached out and gave each of her knees a firm shove.

In his retreat the Mouser spared a glance for the ripples spreading and reflecting in the clock's pool. A shiver of genuine fear surprised him at the thought that he seemed to be just too well placed for watching for it all to be a matter of chance. Had Hisvet arranged it so? Did she somehow know that he, or at least some spirit, was watching invisibly? Was it all to get him off guard?

No, he told himself, I'm starting to think too tricky. This was just one of those glorious guilty visions that, it was to be hoped, lightened the last moments of buried men less fortunate or resourceful than he. His eyes feasted on Foursie as the girl positioned herself to the far side of Threesie's quivering rear, measuring distances with her eyes and the white whip, her pink-nippled breasts jouncing a bit as she danced with excitement. She was flushed all over, and not with embarassment, he was sure.

Plash went the waterclock. "Two!" Hisvet called. She shifted her hand to the back of Threesie's neck, pulled down until the maid's blanched tight face was a hand's breadth above her own, said rapidly, "We're doing another kiss. It'll help you bear the pain and I want to feel you getting it, taste your reaction. Keep your knees straight," and she pulled the maid's face down all the way and kissed her fiercely. Her free hand played with Threesie's maiden breasts.

The third *plash* was tailed with a narrow *thwack* and muffled squeal. Threesie bucked. And all for me, the little darlings, Mouser thought. Foursie's blue eyes flashed like a fury's in ecstasy. She was breathing hard. She drew back the white whip to begin another blow, remembered in time to wait.

Hisvet let up Threesie's head to breathe. "Lovely," she told her. "Your scream came down my throat. It tasted like divine spice." Then, "Excellent, Foursie," she called. "Stay on your toes, girl."

Threesie cried, "Hesset help me," invoking the Lankhmar moon goddess. "Make her stop, demoiselle, I'll do anything."

Hisvet said, "Hush, girl. Hesset give you courage," and pulled down her head again, stifling her cries against her waiting lips. Her other hand pressed back on the maid's knees.

The three sounds were much the same. Threesie's buck was more of a caper. The Mouser was surprised by his arousal, felt a flicker of shame, recalled in time to breathe shallowly, et cetera.

The moment Hisvet let up Threesie's head to take a breath, the maid pleaded, "Make her stop, she'll kill me," then couldn't contain indignation. "Demoiselle, you knew she hadn't stolen the jewel. You led me on."

Hisvet's hand, busy with her breasts, seized up flesh and skin midway between them as though her thumb and forefinger knuckle were pinchers, squeezed, twisted, rubbed together, and jerked down all at once. Threesie squealed. "Silence, you stupid slut," her mistress hissed. "You enjoyed making her suffer, now you're paying. You little fool! Don't you realize a maid who falsely betrays her fellow maid would just as readily betray her mistress? I expect real loyalty from my maids. Foursie, lay on hard." And she pulled the maid's face against hers just as the drop *plashed* and the third blow fell. This time when Hisvet released her head, there were no instant words, tears spurted down instead. Hisvet shook them off, dipped her free hand again in her wide pocket.

And this time the Mouser was surprised by his impulse to shut his eyes. But nasty fascination and the urgent messages from his stiffening member were too strong.

Hisvet lectured, "One other thing I expect of my maid: love, when the whim is on me. That's the chief reason she must always keep herself clean and attractive." She mopped Threesie's face with a large kerchief, then held it to her nose. "Blow," she commanded. "And then swallow hard. I don't want you blubbering snot on me."

Threesie obeyed, but then the injustice of it all overwhelmed her. "But it isn't *fair*," she bleated woefully. "It's not fair at *all*."

Those words and tones had a strange and unexpected effect upon the earth-embraced Mouser. They recalled to him the name that had eluded him of the eighth little darling. A score and two or three years slipped away and he was lolling dishabille on the wide couch in the private dining chamber of the Silver Eel tavern in Lankhmar, and Ivlis's maid Freg was pacing back and forth before him in her delicious young slim nakedness, and then she had stopped by him and turned toward him, tears spurting from her eyes, and bleated woefully those identical same trite words.

He knew the circumstances all right, knew them by heart. Barely a fortnight had passed since the fairly satisfactory ending of the affair of Omphal's jewel-crusted skull and other vengeful brown bones from the forgotten burial crypt in the great house of the Thieves Guild. The gems salvaged had been adequate, especially when there was added thereto the person of Ivlis, a lean, shifty, fox-faced glorious redhead. He'd had her the second night after, though that hadn't been easy, and it was more or less understood between Fafhrd and him that Freg was the Northerner's booty. But then the big oaf had delayed making his move, dawdled over nailing down his conquest, seemed hardly grateful at all to the Mouser for having taken on the more difficult seduction, leaving his comrade the juicier, tenderer prey, to be had for no more

exertion than pushing back onto the bed (nine times out of ten
the big man was incomprehensibly slower than he about such
matters), so that after two or three more nights and nothing
more forward, and feeling impatient and feckless and at war
with all Nehwon—and with Fafhrd too, for the nonce—and
opportunity presenting, he'd yielded to temptation and bedded
the silly chit, which hadn't been all that easy either. And then
on their third or fourth assignation she turned stormy and
accused him of getting her drunk and forcing her the first
time and claimed to have been deeply in love with Fafhrd and
he with her, she knew, only they'd been moving slowly so
as to savor fully their romance before declaring and enjoying
it, and the Mouser had cut in with his nasty lust and wily
ways and managed to root a child in her, she was certain of
that, and so spoiled everything. And although he was still
deeply infatuated with Freg, that had angered him and he'd
told the little fool that he always tried out the virtue of girls
who set their cap for Fafhrd and tried to romance him, to see
if they were worthy of him and would stay faithful, and none
of them had passed the test so far, but she'd done worst. And
she had spouted tears and whimpered those nine words
Threesie'd just voiced. And the next day Freg had been gone
from Lankhmar, no one knew where, and Fafhrd had fallen
into a melancholy fit, and Ivlis'd turned nasty, and he'd not
breathed a word then or ever about the part he'd played.

All of which went to show, he told himself, how a suddenly triggered lost memory, like a ghost from the grave,
could be so real as to blot out completely a poignantly
interesting, nastily fascinating present, almost create another
present, as it were, for several heartbeats till it had run its
course inside his eyes.

They were between blows in Hisvet's boudoir. The violet
wrap was undone just far enough to bare her own top pair of
small, palely violet-nippled breasts, and she was holding
down to them the tousled head of the dark maid, who was
tonguing them industriously under instructions. She broke
these off to carol, "To force the unwilling to accept joy is so
rewarding! To cause the recalcitrant to discover pleasure in
pain is even more so!" The fair maid was doing a rapid little
dance in place to contain her pent excitement and rotating the

poised white whip in a little circle in time with her flashing toes. Hisvet called gayly to incite her on, "Remember, Foursie, the slut had her fingers up you prying around, not gently, I'll warrant," and the clock *plashed* and the whip whistled and *thwacked* and Threesie joined in the dance.

When Hisvet let up her head, the dark maid said rapidly, "If you'll have her stop just for a while, demoiselle, I'll lick your ass most lovingly, I promise," and Hisvet replied, "All in good time, girl," and reaching back in an excess of arousal, caught hold with thumb and forefinger knuckle of her by the midst of her maiden mound and gave it the same sort of pincher's tweak as she had the maid's flesh midway between her breasts, where a blue bruise now showed; and the dark maid squealed muffledly.

But then, just as Foursie stayed her dance to strike and the Mouser's erection grew almost unbearably hard, Hisvet cried sharply, "Break off the whipping, Foursie! Don't strike again!" and the maid obeyed with a spasmodic effort, and Hisvet ducked her head and shoulders out from under Threesie's arched front and stared searchingly at the wall by the waterclock just where the whip had hung, her nostrils flaring and with blue-and-pink-mottled tongue showing in her open mouth. She announced raptly and anxious, "I sense the near presence of Death or a close relative, some murderous demon lord or deadly demoness. It must have scented your ecstasy of torment, Threesie, and come hunting."

The Mouser felt they were all staring straight at him, then noted that their gazes went in slightly different directions: Hisvet's intense but cool; Foursie's shocked and terrified as she backed away, dropping the pristine white whip; Threesie's somewhat not yet grasping her good fortune, as she stood in bent position in her sagging and worked-up black tunic stretched back toward her rear, crisscrossed with red welts, and with her knees still straight.

Hisvet continued, "Run, Foursie, and warn my father of this menace. Bid him haste here, bringing his wand and sigils. Nay, do not stay to dress or hunt a towel, as if you were a simpering virgin. Go as you are. And speed! There's *danger* here, you witlet!"

Then, turning her furious attention to Threesie, "Quit standing there so docilely bent over with legs invitingly spread, lamebrain, all ready for the slavering hounds of death to mount you. Spring to and defend *my* rear, mind cripple!"

Just then the Mouser felt what seemed a large centipede crawl across his left thigh, somehow insinuating itself between his flesh and the grainy earth encasing him, and then march down his rigid, like-embedded cock, and settle itself in a ring round his tumescent glans. And there swung in round his head from the other side, moving through the earth effortlessly, a face like a beautiful skull tightly covered by blue-pied, chalky white skin with eyes that were intent red embers, and pressed itself against his own face closely from forehead to chin, so he felt through her blue lips mashing his her individual two ranks of teeth. He realized that the centipede was the bone tips of her skeletal hand (the other pressed the back of his neck at the base of his own skull) and whose bony fingertips now moved slightly upon his stiff member, inducing it to spend one drop, but one drop only, of its load, giving him a sickening, joyless jolt of heavy black pain that left him weak and gasping. But no sooner had that pain begun to fade down when the slim bone fingers moved and the second jolt came equal to the first, and after agonizing pauses the third and fourth.

The stangury! The worst pain that a man can suffer, he'd once heard, when urine must be voided drop by drop—this was the same, except it was his seed.

And it kept on.

His wavering mind confused it with the plashes of the waterclock. But Threesie had suffered only eight or nine stripes at most. How many drops would it take to discharge his heavy load? And render his member flaccid? Two score hundred?

The violet-hung boudoir and Hisvet and her crew were gone. All that remained for vision was the vermilion volume lit by pain's hot ember eyes and his phosphorescent mask, hell in a very small place.

In a voice that was rough, rasping, infinitely dry, sardonic-tender, Death's sister whispered throatily, "My very own dear love. My dearest one."

As his torment continued, his wavering consciousness and

gasping and trembling general weakness warned him the end was near. Despite the continuing jolts of agony, he concentrated regulating his breathing, making it shallow, pushing back with his tongue the grains his gasps had drawn. With the roaring in his ears, it became a surf of boulders he had to keep at bay.

20

Cif was cheered to find things orderly busy at the diggings, the dogcart unloading, some men wolfing midday bread and soup by the fire, while at the shaft head the stubby wide cone of dug dirt had grown visibly higher and the bright growl of a saw spoke of shorings and roofing for the tunnel being readied. Fafhrd's man Fren, on duty at the windlass, told her that Skor, the girl Klute, and Mikkidu were down, the first two working at the face, that last walking dirt between there and the shaft. She commented on a faint stench, coming irregularly.

"I whiffed something myself once or twice already," Fren agreed, making a face. "Like rotten eggs?"

At his offer, she rode the empty bucket down, standing, her small-booted feet fitting with room to spare.

At the shaft the foul odor became stronger. Looking up at Rill and Skullick, she held her nose. They copied her gesture, nodding. As she neared the bottom, Mikkidu came backing out of the tunnel's low entry lugging a full bucket and she stepped out away from him, preparatory to helping switch the hook from the empty bucket to the full one.

But as he swung it around, he pitched over it into her arms. Digging in her heels, she managed to prop the Mouser's small lieutenant, snarling at him, "What's the matter with you, Mik? Are you drunk?"

When he answered her groggily, "No, Lady," his eyes

weaving, she pushed him against the wall, leaving him to recover his wits and balance, and hurried into the tunnel.

Here the stink was intense and she held her breath. A few fast scurrying steps brought her to the end, where the light of a leviathan-oil lamp burning blue and dim showed her Skor on his knees slumped forward against the rough face he'd been scraping, his shoulders slack, while beside him Klute lay prone on the rock floor, evidently having passed out as she'd tried to crawl away.

Cif took her under the armpits and half dragged, half carried her out of the tunnel. Mikkidu was rubbing his forehead. She called, "Skullick!" but he was already climbing down by the pegs. Klute was writhing a little and mewling faintly with her eyes closed. Cif slung her over an arm, stepped into the empty bucket, and signaled Fren to hoist. The pulleys creaked. In passing she told Skullick, "Skor's collapsed at the face. Fumes and foul air, get him out fast."

At the top she passed Klute to Rill and Fren and then stepped out herself. The girl was muttering, "Can't find my scoop." Rill told her, "Wake up, Klute. Try to breathe deeply," and remarked to Cif, "There was such a stench in the cave toward Darkfire."

Cif nodded and turned back to watch Skullick drag Skor out of the tunnel. He called, "He'll come out of it, Lady. His pulse is still there." Mikkidu seemed recovered, for he helped Skullick get a rope around the unconscious man's chest so he could be hoisted up the shaft, and then climbed the pegs alongside to steady the dead-weight burden on its way.

When Fafhrd's lieutenant was stretched out next to the shaft head, Cif took his pulse under the jaw, didn't like its reedy feel, and directed Mikkidu to lift his shoulders and head (by its scanty red hair) while she straddled his lap, clasped him around with both arms, and fed him air from her own lips, alternating with brief tightenings of her hug.

When Skor's pulse seemed stronger, she directed he be carried to the shelter tent and delegated Rill to keep close watch and continue her nursing as needed. Then she quizzed Mikkidu sharply.

"You were going into and out of the tunnel, you must have noticed the fumes."

"I did, Lady," he replied, "and warned Skor. But he made light of them, being so concentrated on speeding the digging."

"Well, he was right about that, though imprudent," she said with weight. "The digging must continue at the face if we're to have a chance of saving the Captain. Fresh air must be conveyed there in good supply. And speedily."

"Aye, Lady," Mikkidu agreed dubiously, "but how?"

"I have had opportunity to think that matter through," she told him. "Mik, last autumn you were with the captains on their great snow-serpent hunt in the Death Lands that lie midway betwixt the volcanoes Darkfire and Hellglow?"

"Who of us wasn't, Lady?" that one replied. "Aye, and busy for a fussy fortnight afterward flaying and curing the uncut hides."

"As I recall," she went on, "there were some forty perfect hides got in all."

"Two score and seven to be precise, Lady. All laid up at the barracks with camphor and cloves against the next trading voyage by one of the captains. They'd bring a fortune in Lankhmar."

"As I too thought." She nodded. "The dogcart is still here. I've a mind to send you back in it to fetch out those same hides. All of them."

He stared at her puzzledly.

"Are you aware," she asked him, "that each of those hides constitutes a wrist-wide, sound leather tube nine or ten cubits long? Three or four yards?"

"Yes, Lady," he began, his brow still clouded, "but—"

"Come on, I'll go with you," she said with a merry grin, standing up from where they'd been sitting beside the fire. "For you'll need someone to attend to the hides while you're busy seeing to the unshipping of the great bellows at the smith-forge preparatory to its conveyance here."

"Lady," Mikkidu said, his face lightening up, "I do believe I get a glimmering of your intention."

"And so do I!" was voiced admiringly by Skullick, who'd been listening in.

"Good!" Cif told the latter. "Then you can take charge here whilst I'm away."

And she dragged Fafhrd's ring off her thumb and gave it to Skullick.

21

Pshawri broke a pane of ice to free the waters of Last Spring for easy imbibing.

When he had lapped his fill he backed away, dancing his thanks in a solemn little jig such as no one had ever seen him foot. He was a secretive young man.

He ended his jig with a slow rotation widdershins, scanning his still, chill, hazy-white surroundings from right to left. Darkfire's smoke plume was a smudge in the northern milk-sky. His gaze lingered studiously on the southwest and south, as though he expected pursuers there, and from the height to which he roved it, either flying ones or else very big and tall indeed.

He was at the boundary between the Moor and barren Lava Lands, though a dusting of snow hid the blackness of the latter, blurring the distinction.

He undid one button of his pouch hanging against his belly in front and carefully wormed out the bottle Afreyt had given him, mindful of the pouch's precious contents, and drank off half the remnant of fortified sweet wine, toasting the smoke plume. Then he bore the bottle back to the spring, submerged it until it was almost full, recorked it and returned it to his pouch. After rebuttoning the latter, he felt it over with a gesture curiously reminiscent of a pregnant woman feeling for movement.

He sketched a second jig that included a stamping defiance toward the south-southwest, then turned and loped away north.

22

Toward evening the girl Fingers woke refreshed in the bed at Cif's house she'd occupied night before last. She slid herself from under the blanket without waking Gale, slipped into one of the two robes of toweling lying across the foot, belted it, and wandered down to the large kitchen, where Afreyt, similarly clad, stood beside a narrow door of gray driftwood with a row of pegs and two small windows of horn in the wall alongside it. The pegs were empty save for two, whence hung a worn robe larger than her own and an iron-studded belt bearing sheathed dirk and smallaxe, with boots set below.

"I bathe in steam," the tall lady said. "Will you join me?"

"Gratefully, Lady," the girl replied. "You heap me with kindnesses I can never repay."

"My privilege," Afreyt replied. "In return you might tell me of Ilthmar and Tovilyis, where I've never been." Her violet eyes twinkled. "And scrub my back." She hung her robe, Fingers copying her, on an empty peg and led the way into a narrow chamber consisting of four wide driftwood steps and dimly lit by four small windows, and shut the door behind them. Beside it were a long-handled dipper and two buckets, the farther one filled with water, the near with round stones glowing dark red toward their center and toasting Fingers' calves and knees as she passed close to them. Afreyt poured two-and-a-half dippers of water into the hot rocks. There was an explosive sizzling and clouds of steam enveloped them. Afreyt seated herself on the third step, Fingers following suit, and noting or divining the girl's looks of surprise and mild alarm at the increase in the moist heat, remarked, "It teases the heart a little, does it not? Do not fear to inhale deeply. Move down a step if it's uncomfortable," she advised.

"It does indeed, Lady," Fingers agreed, but held her level.

"Now tell me of foul filthy Ilthmar and its nasty rat god," Afreyt suggested. "In what figure is he shown or depicted?"

"In that of a man, Lady, with a rat's head and long tail. On ritual occasions his human priests wear a rat mask, carry a long snaky whip resembling a giant rat's tail, and go naked or robed according to the nature of the rite."

"How is the relationship between humanity and the ratty kind rationalized?" Afreyt inquired.

"In olden times, when rats had their cities aboveground, they warred with and enslaved a race of giants. Ourselves, Lady, humankind. Then in the course of numerous revolts and repressions, the rats transferred their cities underground for privacy and to give them peace and quiet to perfect their culture, but maintaining secret dominion over their servant-slaves." The girl's voice was thoughtful. Her left hand played with a ridgy white seashell embedded in the gray plank in which their sweat dripped. Beside it was a boreworm hole, into which she ran her little finger back and forth. It fitted nicely. She continued, "There's a dark magic known only to the doubly initiated (which mother and I were not) whereby rats and their allies may switch size back and forth between rat and human. The rats' prophets and chiefest allies amongst humankind are numbered among their saints, of whom the recentest to be canonized are St. Hisvin of Lankhmar and his daughter, St. Hisvet, Lankhmar Below being the chiefest city of the rats, although, unlike Ilthmar, the worship of the rat god is forbidden in Lankhmar Above."

Afreyt handed Fingers a stiff-bristled brush and presented her back, on which the girl, kneeling, got to work industriously. The tall woman asked, "Have you seen representations in Ilthmar of this female saint?"

"Aye, Lady, there's a carving at her small shrine in the Rat's dockside temple. (Rats were also the first mariners, teaching man the art.) She is depicted nude with her hair in one braid long as her slender self and with eight dainty rat dugs; two centered in small high breasts, the next pair low on her rib cage, two flanking her cord scar, and two close to either side her maiden mound above the leg crease."

"My, such a multiplicity of charms! One wonders whether to envy or despise." Afreyt chuckled.

"Her cult's a very popular one, Lady," the girl replied somewhat defensively as she scrubbed away. "She commands demons, it is believed, and has enjoyed the services of Queen Frixifrax of Arilia."

Afreyt laughed. "Truth to tell, child, I would have been inclined to rate your whole rat tale nonsense, like half the stories fed us Rime Islers dwelling on the edge of things to awe and befool us, did it not fit so well with what Fafhrd has told me about his and Captain Mouser's greatest adventure (though there were more than one of those, to hear them talk) during the last days of Overlord Glipkerio's reign, when there was an incursion or eruption of armed rats into Lankhmar City, along with many other weird events, and involving the unscrupulous grain merchant Hisvin and his scandalous daughter Hisvet, both the rats' allies and bearing the same names as the two saints in your own strange tale."

"I am grateful your Ladyship believes at least partly in my truthful account," Fingers replied a little huffily. "I may be overcredulous, Lady, but never a liar."

Afreyt turned around smiling. "Don't be so formal and serious," she chided merrily. "Give me the brush and turn your back."

The girl complied, facing the two high horn windows to the outside, which were now whitening with the rising moon a day past full. Afreyt scraped the brush across a lump of green soap and set to work, saying, "During the twists and turns of that famous rat-man fracas in Lankhmar (it happed at least ten years ago—you'd have been still an infant at Tovilyis), the Gray Mouser had to pretend a great love for this Hisvet chit (so Fafhrd tells me), pursuing her through a series of magical size changes from Lankhmar Above down to Lankhmar Below and then back again. His true love then was a royal kitchen slave named Reetha, at least she was the one he ended up with. At that time Fafhrd's consort was the Ghoulish warrior-maid Kreeshkra—a walking skeleton because Ghouls' flesh's invisible, their bones on view. Truly there are times when I don't know if I can believe half of the things Fafhrd says, while the Mouser's always a great liar—he boasts of it."

"I was told Ghouls ate people," Fingers observed, bracing

her back against Afreyt's brisk scrubbing. "And much later I heard about the latter-day rat war in Lankhmar. Friska told me about it in Ilthmar, after we'd moved there from Tovilyis, when she was warning me against believing everything the rat priests told us."

"Friska?" Afreyt questioned, pausing in her scrubbing.

"My mother's name when she was a slave in Quarmall before she escaped to Tovilyis, where I was born. She hasn't always used it afterward and I don't think I've mentioned it until now."

"I see," Afreyt said absently, as though lost in sudden thought.

"You've stopped doing my back," the girl observed.

"Because it's done," the other said. "It's pink all over. Tell me, child, did your mother Friska escape from Quarmall all by herself?"

"No, Lady, she had her friend Ivivis with her, whom I grew to calling aunt in Tovilyis," Fingers explained, turning back so she faced the narrow gray door again, its outlines visible once more through the thinning steam. "They were smuggled out of Quarmall by their lovers, two mercenary warriors quitting the service of Quarmal and his two sons. The cavern world of Quarmall's no easy place to escape from, Lady, deep, secret, and mysterious. Fugitives are recaptured or die strangely. In the ports that rim the Inner Sea—Lankhmar, Ilthmar, Kvarch Nar, Ool Hrusp—it's deemed as fabulous a place as this Rime Isle."

"What happened to the two mercenaries who were your mother's and aunt's lovers and worked their escape?" Afreyt inquired.

"Ivivis quarreled with hers, and upon reaching Tovilyis, enlisted in the Guild of Free Women. My mother was nearing her time (*my* time, it was) and elected to stay with her friend. Her lover (my father) left her money and swore to return some day, but of course never did."

There was a flurry of knocking and the narrow gray door opened and closed, admitting Gale, who peered around eagerly through the thinning steam.

"Has Uncle Fafhrd flown back down from the sky?" she

demanded. "Why didn't you wake me? Those are his things outside, Aunty Afreyt!"

"Not yet," that lady told her, "but there have been messages of sorts from him, or so it seems. After you two were sleeping, May brought me Fafhrd's belt, which she'd found hanging on a berry bush as though fallen from the sky. Her words, though she'd not heard your tale. I sent her and others hunting and went out myself, and there were soon discovered his two boots (one on a roof) and dirk and smallaxe, which had split the council hall's weathercock."

"He cast them down to lighten ship when he got above the fog." Gale rushed to conclusions.

"That's the best guess I've heard," Afreyt said, reaching the dipper to Gale, handle first. "Renew the steam," she directed. "One cup."

The girl obeyed. There was a gentler sizzling, and warm steam came billowing up around them again.

"Maybe he's waiting for tonight's fog," the girl suggested. "I'm much more worried about Uncle Mouser."

"The digging goes on and another clue's been unearthed—a sharpened iron *tik* (Lankhmar's least coin) such as the Gray One habitually carries on his person. So Cif told me when she was here early afternoon to bathe and change, while you two were still asleep. There'd been some difficulty about the air, but your aunt took care of it."

"They'll find him," Gale assured her.

"I share both your hopes for both the Captains," Fingers put in, returning somewhat to formality.

"Fafhrd will be all right," Gale asserted confidently. "You see, I think he needs the fog to buoy him up, at least until he gets started stroking well, and the fog will be back before dawn. He'll swim down then."

"Gale thinks her uncle can do anything," Afreyt explained, scrubbing her vigorously. "He's her hero."

"He certainly is," the girl maintained aggressively. "And because he's my uncle, there can't be anything between us to spoil it when I'm fully grown up."

"Truly a hero has many lady loves: whores, innocents, princesses," Fingers observed in tones that were both earnest and worldly wise. "That's one of the first things my mother told me."

"Friska?" Afreyt checked.

"Friska," Fingers confirmed, and then bethought herself of a compliment that would sustain the worldly mood which she enjoyed. "I must say, Lady, that I greatly admire the coolness and lack of jealousy with which you regard your lover's previous attachments. For Captain Fafhrd is surely a hero—I suspected as much when he began so swiftly and resolutely to dig for his friend and set the rest of us all helping. I became completely certain when he took off so blithely into the sky on his friend's service."

"I don't know about all that," Afreyt replied, eyeing Fingers somewhat dubiously, "especially my coolness toward love rivals of whatever age or condition. Though it's true Fafhrd's had an awful many sweethearts, to hear him talk (the Mouser the same), and not only from those classes you mention, but really weird ones like the Ghouless Kreeshkra and that wholly invisible snowmount Princess Hirriwi and (for Mouse) that eight-tit slinky Hisvet—everything from demonesses to mermaids and shimmersprites." Warming to it, she continued, "But I think Cif and I are a match for them, at least in quality if not numbers. We've bedded gods ourselves—or at least arranged for their bedding," she added correctively and a bit guiltily, remembering.

Listening to this recital, Gale seemed to get a bit uneasy, certainly wide-eyed. Fingers put an arm around her shoulders, saying, "So you see, little one, it *is* better to have one's hero a friend and uncle only, is it not?"

Afreyt couldn't resist saying, "Aren't you overdoing the wise old aunt a bit?" Then, recalling Fingers' circumstances, she dropped her smile, adding, "But I was forgetting . . . you know what."

Fingers nodded gravely and fetched a sigh that she thought suitable for A Cabingirl Against Her Will. Then she gave a squeal. Gale had yanked her hair.

"I don't know about Uncle Fafhrd," the Rimish girl told her, making a face, "but I certainly want you as a friend and not an auntie!"

"And now it's time we stopped talking heroes and she-devils and got back to worrying about two real men,'' Afreyt picked that moment to announce. "Come on, I'll rinse you.''

And taking up the water container, she poured a gush each on the blond and reddish heads, then emptied it over her own head.

23

Returning back to that same eventful day's darksome beginning, we find Fafhrd trudging frantically east by leviathan light from the lamp he carried and with a feather-footedness and hectic lightheadedness that puzzled and alarmed him, across the frosty Great Meadow toward fog-blanketed Salthaven and the horizon beyond, paling with the imminent dawn. His anxiety for the Mouser in desperate plight, his selfish urge to shuck off that bondage, and his wishful hope for a miracle solution to this problem . . . these three feelings balled up unendurably within him, so that he lifted the brown brandy jug in his right hand to his teeth and fixed them around the protruding cork, biting into it, and drew the jug from off it, spat the cork aside, and downed two swallows that were like lightning brands straight down his throat.

Then yielding to an unanticipated yet imperative impulse, born perhaps of the two blazing swigs, he scanned the sky ahead above the fog.

And, lo, the miracle! For a wide stream of brightness, travelling up the pale sky from the impending sun, called his attention to a small fleet of on-cruising clouds. And as he inspected those five pearl-gray white-edged shapes with a sharp clear vision that was like youth returned, he discerned that the midmost was shaped like a large slender pinnace with towering stern-castle driven by a single translucent sail that bellied smoothly toward him, by all signs a demigalleon of the cloud queendom of Arilia, fable no longer.

And as if there had resounded in his ear a single chime, infinitely stirring and sweet, of the silver bell with which they'd sound the watches upon such a vessel, the knowledge came to him—a message and more—that his old comrade-mistress Frix was aboard her, captaining her crew. And the confident determination was born on him to join her there. And his concern for the Mouser and what Afreyt and his men expected of him dropped away, and he no longer worried about the girls Fingers and Gale following him, and his footsteps grew carefree and light as those of his youth on a Cold Corner hunting morn. He took a measured sup of brandy and skipped ahead.

The women whom Fafhrd loved seriously (and he rarely loved otherwise) seemed to him when he thought about it to split into the two classes of comrade-mistresses and beloved girls. The former were fearless, wise, mysterious, and sometimes cruel; the latter were timorous, adoring, cute, and mostly faithful—sometimes to the point of making too much of it. Both were—apparently had to be, alas—young and beautiful, or at least appear so. The comrade-mistresses were best at that last, on the whole.

Oddly, the beloved girls were more apt to have been actual comrades, sharing day-to-day haps, mishaps, and boredoms, than the others. What made the others seem more like comrades, then? When he asked himself that, which he did seldom, he was apt to decide it was because they were more realistic and logical, thought more like men, or at least like himself. Which was a desirable thing, except when they carried their realism and logic to the point where it became unpleasantly painful to him. Which accounted for their cruel streak, to be sure.

And then the comrade-mistresses more often than not had a supernatural or at least preternatural aura about them. They partook of the demonic and divine.

Fafhrd's first beloved girl had been his childhood sweetheart Mara, whom he'd got pregnant, only to run away with his first comrade-mistress, the wandering actress and failed thief Vlana, one of the unsupernatural ones, her only glamors those of stage and crime.

Other super- and preternatural females had included the

Ghoulish she-soldier Kreeshkra, a transparent-fleshed beautiful walking skeleton, and the wholly invisible (save when she tinted her skin or resorted to like stratagem such as wetting herself before being pelted by a lover with rose petals) Princess Hirriwi of Stardock.

Sample beloved girls were Luzy of Lankhmar, the fair swindler Nemia of the Dusk (not all of this class, too, were law-abiding), and faint-hearted and bouncing Friska, whom he'd rescued from the cruelties of Quarmall—not altogether willingly. On learning his wild plan she'd told him, "Take me back to the torture chamber."

But of all his lady lovers, first in his heart was Hisvet's onetime slave-maid and guardian, the tall, dark-haired, and altogether delicious Frix, now again Queen Frixifrax of Arilia, although she was almost, but not quite, *too* tall and slender. (Just as he knew that Hisvet herself, though heartless and mostly cruel, was somehow the Mouser's inmost favorite.)

Above all else, Frix's love was ever tactful, and even in scenes of extremest ecstasy and peril she had an utterly fearless and completely dispassionate overview of life, as if she saw it all as a grand melodrama, even to the point of coolly calling out stage directions to the participants of an orgy or melee whilst chaos whirled about them.

Of course this train of reasoning left out Afreyt, surely the best of comrade-mistresses as well as his current one, a better archer than himself, loving and wise, an altogether admirable woman—and able to get along with Mouser too.

But Afreyt, though greatly gifted, was wholly human, while the demonic and divine Frix fairly glimmered with supernatural highlights. As at this very moment, when after another and larger swig of brandy on the fly, a short but steady sighting far ahead miraculously showed her standing at the bow of her cloud-pinnace like a figurehead carved of pale ivory as she cheered and welcomed him on. This wondrous apparition of her touched off a memory flash of an assignation with her in a mountaintop castle where they'd ingeniously spied together on two of her waiting ladies tall and mantis-slender as herself while they were mutually solacing each other, and later joined them in their gentle sport.

That ivory prow-vision, together with attendant memories,

made him feel light as air and added yards to his stride, so that his next two skimming skips carried him knee-deep and waist-deep into the fog bank, while the third never ended. He drained the brandy jug of its last skimpy swallow, cast it and the lamp behind him to either side, and then swam forward up the face of the deepening fog bank, employing a powerful breaststroke while flattening his legs like a fish's tail.

Exultation suffused him as he felt himself mounting the side of a long stationary swell in an ocean of foam, but his strong sweeping strokes soon carried him above the fog. He resolutely forebore to look down, keeping his gaze upon the wondrously prowed white pinnace, concentrating all his attention and energies on flight. He felt his deltoid and pectoral muscles swell and lengthen and his arms flatten into wings. The rhythm of flight took over.

He noted that, though still mounting, he was veering to the left because of the lesser purchase his hook got on the air than the palm-paddle of his good right hand, but instead of trying to correct he kept on undauntedly, confident the motion would bring him around in a great circle in sight of his goal again and closer to it.

And so it did. He continued to mount in great spirals. He noted that along the way five snowy sea gulls had appeared and were soaring up circularly too, evenly spaced around him like the points of a pentacle. It gave him a warm feeling to be so escorted.

He was well into his fifth spiral and nearing his goal, momentarily waiting for the cloud-ship to swing into his view from the left behind him, the sun's rays baking through his clothes becoming almost uncomfortable. He was selecting just the right words with which to greet his aerial paramour when he flew into shadow and something hard yet resilient struck the back of his head a shrewd blow, so that black spots and flashing diamond points danced in his eyes and all his senses wavered.

His first reaction to this unexpected assault was to look up behind him.

A dark pearl-gray wind-weathered, smoothly rounded leviathan-long shape hovered above him just out of reach—as he discovered when he grasped at it with hand and hook, his second reaction. It seemed to be drifting sideways slowly. He'd bumped into the hull of the cloud-ship he'd been seeking and then rebounded from it somewhat.

His third reaction, as the pain in his skull lessened and his vision cleared somewhat, was a mistake. He looked down.

The whole southwest corner of Rime Isle lay below him, uncomfortably small and far down: Salthaven town and harbor with its tiny red roofs and wisp-pennoned toothpick masts thrusting through its thinning coverlet of fog, the rocky coast leading off west, the narrow lofty headland to the east, and north of that the Great Maelstrom spinning furiously, an infinitely menacing foamy pinwheel.

The sight froze Fafhrd's privates. His reaction was anything but beat his wings (arms, rather), flutter his legs-tail, resuming flying, and so land lightly on the cloud-craft's deck and sketch a bow to Frix. The blow had halted all those avian rhythms as if they'd never possessed him; it had nauseated him, switched him from glorious drunkenness to near puking hangover in a trice. Instead of master of the air, he felt as if he were flimsily glued to it up here, pasted to this height by some fragile magic, so that the least wrong move, or wrong thought even, might break the flimsy bond and pitch him down, down, down!

His sailor's instinct was to lighten ship. It was the last resort when your vessel was sinking, and so presumably the wisest course when falling was the danger. With infinite caution and deliberation he began a series of slow contortions calculated to bring his manual extremities of hand and hook into successive contact with his feet, waist, neck, and so forth, so as to rid himself of all abandonable weight whatever *without* at the same time making some uncalculated movement that would cause him to come unstuck from the sky wherein he was so precariously poised.

This course of action had the added advantage of concentrating all his attention on his body and the space immediately around it, so he was not tempted to look down again and suffer the full pangs of vertigo.

He did note, as he gently cast aside his right and left boot, ax and dirk, their sheaths, finally his pouch and iron-studd d belt, that they floated off slowly to about the distance of a man's length, then dropped away as if jerked down, seeming almost to vanish instantly—suggesting some magical sphere or spell of safety about him.

He didn't trust it.

So long as he confined himself to discarding such relatively ponderous and rigid items, his convoy of gulls continued to circle him evenly, but when he continued on to divest himself of all his garments (for this seemed certainly no time for half measures) they broke formation and (either attracted by the flimsy and flappable nature of his discards, or else outraged at the shameless impropriety of his action) made fierce darts and dives at and upon each piece of clothing to the accompaniment of raucous barking squawks and bore them off triumphantly in their sharp talons as if reasserting the honor of their squadron.

Fafhrd paid very little attention to these captious avian antics, concentrated as he was upon making not the least incautious or marginally violent movement.

Eventually he had divested himself of his very last implement and garment save for one.

It shows how much he had come to think of his hook together with the cork-and-leather cuff carrying it as his true left hand that he did not jettison them with the rest of the abandonable material.

But it was not until he'd stripped himself stark naked (save for hook) that he bethought himself of a final way to "lighten ship." He was admiring the bright golden gleam of the powerful stream of urine arching above him and then down over his head out of his vision's range (it had first hit him in the eye but he corrected); it was not until then that he realized that in the course of his emergency undressing he had passed out of the shadow of the cloud-craft's hull and was bathed in full hot sunlight (which had, coincidentally, counterbalanced nicely any chill he might otherwise have felt at abandoning his last scrap of clothing in the sharp air of early morning).

But where had the Arilian cloud-vessel got to? He looked about and finally saw its narrow deck its own ship's length *beneath* him—a score of yards at least. Meanwhile, he himself was slowly but steadily mounting to portside of its rather ghostly or at least somewhat translucent mast top and upper rigging, whereon were perched the five raptorial gulls, busily shredding with claws and beaks the clothing they'd appropriated from him and, looking more now like cormorants than gulls, staring at him from time to time disgustedly.

And now a wholly different, in fact opposite fear took sudden hold of Fafhrd—that he might continue to rise inexorably until all below became too tiny to be seen and he was lost in space, or until he reached the forever frost-capped height of mountaintops and perished of cold—especially when chilly night came on (how stupid he'd been to discard *all* his clothes—he'd been in a dismal panic that was sure!)—or got himself devoured by the airy monsters that inhabited such altitudes such as the invisible giant fliers he'd first encountered on Stardock, or even reach the mysterious stars (if he lasted that long before dying of thirst and hunger) and be dazzled to death by them or suffer whatever other fate the Bright Ones kept in store for impudent venturers such as he must appear to them.

Unless, of course, he had the good fortune to encounter the moon first or the secret (invisible?) Queendom of Arilia, if that were anything more than a great fleet of cloud-ships.

This thought reminded him that there was such a ship close at hand, of which he'd had great hopes and expectations before the brandy had died in him.

After a moment's gloomy apprehension that it had heartlessly sailed off or perhaps vanished entire (its upper works at least had looked so very ghostly), he was relieved to see it still floated below him, though some thirty feet farther down than at last glimpse—there was at least that distance between him and the masthead with its quincunx of cormorantishly-behaving sea gulls, who still shredded his garments vindictively, although their shrill squawkings had subsided.

He searched the vessel with his eyes for Frix, but the tall, supernally attractive beauty was nowhere to be seen, not in the bow impersonating a figurehead, or anywhere else—if she ever had been present, he added wryly, to anything but his overeager and overbrandied imagination.

He did spot, however, a sixth figure in the rigging, besides the birds, a trim young woman halfway up it on the other side of the rigging, faced away from him and leaning back against the ratlines with arms outspread as if to expose herself to sun's rays. She wore an abbreviated white lace chemise, was barefoot, and carried a small curved silver trumpet slung round her neck. She was also too short for Frix and a blonde to boot, instead of raven-tressed.

Fafhrd called down "Ahoy!" not softly, but not unnecessarily loudly either, for although his new fear of rising indefinitely preoccupied his thoughts, he still entertained the conviction that any violent movement or speech would be unwise. Just rising a few yards did not convince him that he could not fall, especially when he surveyed the emptiness below.

The lazing maiden did not look up or give the least other indication that she had heard him.

"Ahoy!" Fafhrd repeated, quite a bit more loudly, but again with no discernable reaction from her, unless her yawn now was intended as that.

"Ahoy!" Fafhrd bellowed, forgetting his worries about the possible dire effects of loud noises.

Rather slowly, then, she turned her head and lifted her face toward him. But nothing more.

"Cloud girl," Fafhrd called down in friendly tones but a shade peremptorily, "summon your mistress on deck. I'm an old friend."

She went on staring at him. Nothing more, except perhaps to lift her brows superciliously.

Fafhrd called sharply, "I'm Captain Fafhrd, out of *Seahawk*," naming his ship riding at anchor in Rime harbor. "And as you can plainly see, I'm in distress. Inform *your* captain of these circumstances. And be assured she knows me well."

After staring at him a while more, the cloud girl nodded moodily and descended to the deck hand over hand, taking her time, and after another look up at him, strolled toward the sterncastle.

Fafhrd was annoyed. "Oh, hurry up, girl," he called, "and if it's formalities you want, tell the Queen of Arilia that an old friend respectfully craves instant audience."

She paused in the door of the sterncastle to look up at him once more and inquire in a shrill pert voice, "Was that the

respect led you to piss on our ship?'' before she flipped up
the tail of her chemise and vanished inside.

Fafhrd made dignified growling noises in his throat, though
there were none to hear them but the gulls, and was emboldened to try to swim down to the cloud-ship's mast top,
getting himself positioned with head turned down toward it,
body upside down, though it took an intense effort of will to
make himself use full power in what persisted in seeming an
attempt to come unstuck from the heights and launch a disastrous fall. He kept himself aimed at the rigging so he'd
intercept it if the worst occurred.

He was breathing heavily and had fought his way down, he
judged, about a quarter of the distance when the saucy cloud
girl reemerged, followed (at last!) by Frix, garbed like a
dashing captain of Amazon marines in tropical dress uniform
of silver-trimmed white lace which strikingly set off her
slender form, dark hair, and coppery complexion wonderfully, white deerskin hip boots, a wide-brimmed hat of like
material, with ostrich plumes and a silver-studded belt of
snow-serpent hide from which depended a long slim saber
with silver fittings.

She glanced up at shaggy-headed, hairy, naked Fafhrd
laboring down toward her with prodigious effort and spoke a
word to the cloud maiden clad in her scanty lace, who lifted
her silver trumpet to her lips and blew a sweet and stirring
call.

Whereupon there came trooping from the sterncastle six tall
willowy women akin to Frix in figure and dress-uniformed
like to the soldiers in such a captain's company, except that
from their unstudded belts there hung, not swords, but in each
instance three objects which Fafhrd first identified as a cased
small-dirk, a tiny sporran, and a small cylindrical canteen,
while upon their neatly short-cropped heads were uniform
caps of colors peach, lime, lemon, vermilion, lavender, and
robin's egg, counting from first to last as they lined up. They
were followed by a smaller she, who might have been the pert
trumpeter's twin, except the silver instrument she carried was
a crossbow from which depended a coil of thin silver line.
Frix spoke to her, pointing upward. She dropped to a bare

knee, and bending her back acutely and letting the coil fall to the deck beside her, aimed her piece at Fafhrd.

Fortunately for his composure, he divined her intent and dear Frix's purpose just as she let fly.

Her flashing missile mounted swiftly and surely. The line it carried aloft uncoiled from the deck with rippling smoothness and nary a tangle. The blunt silver quarrel reached the apex of its flight a foot from Fafhrd's face. His right hand closed upon it confidently, as if he were capturing a stingless glow wasp. The six tall and almost spidery-slender mariners took up the other end of the silvery line and began to haul. Fafhrd felt the line tighten without parting and himself drawn down perceptibly as they hauled, and at that very instant he began to experience a sweet relief such as is felt only by one who knows himself to be secure in the true hands of love.

His breathing evened out, his relaxing muscles seemed all to lengthen individually, he felt himself become as willowy (in a wholly male wise, he assured himself) as the six delightful creatures drawing him down against his natural (unnatural, rather!) buoyancy. After a final flutter or two of his lower limbs and sweep of his hook-terminated free arm, he resigned to them that small and almost frolicksome labor. He might even have closed his eyes, it felt so restful, except he was beginning to enjoy so thoroughly using them to inspect his destination. The cloud pinnace was such a handsome vessel, and the longer he gazed at its rigging and sails the realer they got.

From time to time as he let himself be played in, like a willingly caught fish of air, came nagging remembrances of his friends on Rime Isle below, and the Mouser still deeper down, and of their likely worries over him, and their own more troublesome plights. But he wasn't gone for long, not really gone, just receiving sorely needed refreshment aloft, he told himself more than once.

Finding himself now level with the mainmast top, he gave some thought to how he appeared to his rescuers. He decided against transferring to the rigging—no one seemed to expect him to and he might well seem ridiculous, as in trying to decide whether to go down the rigging head first or feet. So he merely avoided becoming entangled in it. There wasn't much he could do about nakedness except let himself be drawn in behind the handheld quarrel with grace and easy dignity, no contortions, his legs together like a fish's tail. He sketched a wave or two with his hook to the glowering cormorants (no, gulls!) as he passed them by.

When his descent had begun, his rescuers had been no more than six tallish very slender like-clad females hauling in unison upon the line with easy gracefulness, but now he began to perceive their individualities. The first on the line, she of the peach cap, was a rangy blonde structured like a coursing leopard (Nehwon's swiftest four-foot beast) from the desert steppes of Evamarensee, with small breasts like firmly-bedded half pomegranates, while through the white tropic lace of her uniform showed a rosy orange hue, indicating she wore an under-chemise of like tint to her cap. Withal she was of haughty mien, with jutting brow, icy-blue eyes, and hollowed cheeks, a mole on the left one near the nostril. By Kos, it was Floy! During his last rendezvous but one with Frix and her ladies in a star-grazing Arilian pleasure palace upon a sky-scraping peak in the moon-raking mountain range which rims the northern shore of Nehwon's southern continent, facing the planet-ringing equatorial ocean, he had on a wager let himself be bound naked so securely he could move not a finger and then watched Frix and Floy erotically delight to culminating first themselves with themselves alone and then, exercising infinite slow inventiveness, each other whilst alternately Floy recited "The Rapes of St. Hisvet and Skeldir" and Frix gave a dry clinical account of her and Floy's every least action and the response thereto—until he came, which he'd bet he'd not.

But now his steady descent turned Fafhrd's attention to the approaching deck. Reaching down his left arm, he hooked a ratline, and drawing himself down strongly with both arms, he jackknifed his body without bending his knees and landed solidly on the soles of both feet at once.

Then, maintaining the downward pull with hook alone, he straightened himself erect, facing the grinning crossbow girl. She was of the small wiry acrobatic sort the Mouser favored, fair complected, and the lace of her chemise showed through no extraneous color. He nodded his approval and handed her upon his palm the silver quarrel by which he'd been drawn in.

She took it without demur or change of grin and gave him, as if in return, a gold bracelet of doughnut shape large enough to fit his thick wrist. It was of the solid soft metal, he judged—massy enough by itself to balance his weird buoyancy.

"Thank you, archer," he said. She nodded and began to coil the line that the marines with caps of varying hue (should he think of them as Frix's color guard?) had let drop.

His recognition of Floy having intensified his general awareness and brought pertinent memories close to hand, Fafhrd was able to greet the next two lady marines—the ones with pale green and yellow caps and lace-revealed underthings—with an easy, "Greetings, dear Bree, sweet Elowee."

But although both smiled guardedly, neither ventured so much as a word in reply. Bree shook her head slightly but sharply, frowning, while demure Elowee rolled her eyes back toward the end of the line, where Frix stood, and worked her features as though to say, "She's in one of her moods. Be careful."

Fafhrd recalled how he'd first met those two without their knowledge while he and Frix, wine cups in hand, were on a secret spying expedition to reawaken their venereal appetites. Entering a dark apartment, the Queen of the Air had led him to where black cushions closely circled a window in the floor that let upon a closet below, brightly lit by ranks of candles. Through painted gauze they'd observed these long-legged coltish creatures erotically ministering to each other. Bree enthusiastic and masterful, sometimes giving explicit directions, Elowee coy, protesting, and somewhat overheated (those candles!), even indignant. The infatuated pair had knelt closely side by side, kissing, fondling each other's small breasts, teasing the nipples big, and oft and anon a hand would drop down for a more thrilling and intrusive caress. After a while Frix had begun to whisper in Fafhrd's ear how the kneeling lovers might vary their touches were he the partner. He'd warned her the unconscious actors might overhear, but she'd assured him their ears had been well rubbed with a salve that reduced audition. Much later he'd discovered that things had not been as secret, or the actors as unknowing, as they'd seemed.

("That little hole was hot as hell," Bree confided at a subsequent orgy, "but Frix insisted on them so you'd have no trouble seeing us clearly through the painted gauze. She's a fiend for detail. Oh, the things we've endured to tickle your lust and satisfy an artsy mistress—and Elowee got splashed with hot wax. It's a wonder we didn't burn down the pleasure palace.")

But now Bree's and Elowee's hidden warnings about Frix had caused Fafhrd to give thought to his own appearance and to the impression he was creating. He decided a bit more dignity and restraint were called for. He straightened himself further, slowed his stride, and let the golden torus dangle down from his hand with seeming carelessness, yet positioned so that it served somewhat as a golden fig leaf.

Yet he was hard put to maintain his unnatural gravity and not burst into laughter when he saw that the last three color-marines were his oldest erotic pals among Frix's ladies: the boisterous redhead Chimo, wicked-eyed and black-haired Nixi, and the saintly-appearing Bibi, who was forever finding new ways to play the simpleton and innocent.

There sprang up in his mind the memory of an idyllic Arilian vacation afternoon when he lay supine with his head pillowed upon Chimo's inner thigh where she sat spread-legged while Nixi knelt beyond her knee on his side and Bibi crouched high in the equilateral triangle made by his own spread legs. And ever and anon he'd roll his head to the near side and implant a long slow nibbling kiss along the length of Chimo's carmine nether lips and then roll his head the other way to suck and tongue the faintly rugose nipples of Nixi's small upstanding breasts, now pendant, while Chimo caressed them with her right hand. Bibi busied herself variously with his own erotic gear (whilst Chimo worked on hers—employment for the left hand) until waves of pleasure rolled in over him and time came almost to a stop.

And now, by all signs there was shaping up, he told himself, the possibility of another such great moment of supernal ecstasy indefinitely prolonged, or of an even greater one, did he not blow it by some unintended rejection or piece of boorish behavior.

Yes, indeed, he assured himself rapidly, things did seem to be working around to a grand payoff in the great game of trading heroic feats for intimate maidenly favors that all heroes lived or at least hoped by, no matter how disordered and irregular the bookkeeping.

And now, having greeted and inspected, as it were, the six slender marines of Frix's color guard, he found himself facing the dashing captain herself, attended by her trim trumpeter, standing before the inviting hatchway of the aftercastle from which there poured warm, sweetly perfumed air. During the short tour he'd recovered a sense of his proper weight and thirst and appetites, only slightly troubled by an awareness of hairy and unwashed uncouthness.

Frix lifted a lace-gauntleted hand. "Greetings, old friend," she spoke. "Welcome aboard *Soft Airs.*"

"My thanks, dear lady," he replied according to form, "for greatly needed and desired hospitality."

"Then you shall accompany us below, where are greater amenities," she responded. "My ladies will busy themselves refreshing and arraying you, whilst you regale us, if you will, with an account of your recentest adventures, feats, and forays."

Fafhrd inclined his head. It occurred to him that this was the largest company of ladies with whom he'd ever been entertained by Frix. Had he really become a seven-maiden hero? Or, counting the two girls, a nine?

Smiling graciously, Frix turned to lead the way. The pert girl grimaced comically.

Fafhrd followed, thinking that the resources of a pleasure pinnace might well exceed those of a palace.

As the long-legged ladies trooped up around him familiarly, he noted that the objects depending from their white belts were actually a shaving mug, a large shaving brush (the sporran), and a razor.

24

When Fingers and Gale came hurrying downstairs from dressing, they found Afreyt deep in the perusal (or reperusal) of a creased and somewhat sullied paper with broken green seal writ in violet ink.

Gale cried out reproachfully, "Aunty Afreyt! You're reading the letter Pshawri gave you for safekeeping!"

Afreyt looked up. "You have sharp eyes," she remarked. "Know child, it is the right—nay, duty!—of any grown-up (especially a woman) to read any document entrusted to them, so they may give testimony to its contents should it be stolen or taken forcibly from them before they are able to return or deliver it." She folded and thrust it down her bosom. Gale eyed her dubiously, Fingers without expression. Afreyt arose. "And now on with your cloaks and winter gear," she directed. "There's work for us at the diggings, I've no doubt."

A flurry of wind stung their faces with ice needles as they entered the night pale with the chill glow of the barely gibbous moon and a faint deep melancholy note resounded from the wind chimes the other side of Salthaven. Afreyt set a fast pace for the barracks. No others were abroad. At irregular intervals the wind chimes repeated their profound reverberation, like a god muttering in his sleep.

At the barracks were lights and labor and a loaded dogcart ready to leave. Afreyt commandeered it for herself and the girls, pulling rank on Mannimark, which drew from Gale a look of further disillusion with "grown-ups" as she clambered reluctantly aboard. Fingers took it more naturally, copying the older woman's queenly mien and manner.

"Any message for the diggings?" that one asked the mustached man as she took the long whip from its socket. "I'll make your excuses, Sergeant. I'm sure the other cart will be back for you soon."

"No mind, Lady," he answered. "We'll walk."

"Very well, Sergeant." And with a whip crack and jingle of bells the cart was off, making a sharp turn that headed them into the cutting wind and away from the risen low-moon. The girls ducked their faces into their hoods but Afreyt lifted hers high. The occasional boom of the chimes grew less faint as they approached the Moon Temple, and then there was added to it a still deeper clanking as a heavier beam was struck and boomed its note.

"The north blast quickens," she commented. "It will be bitter crossing the Meadow."

Soon the fire facing the shelter tent became their beacon and promise of warmth. Afreyt signaled their approach with a flurry of whip cracks.

"Where's Lady Cif?" she asked the knot of soup drinkers.

"At the face, Lady," Skullick replied.

"Unload," she directed, and springing down, followed by the girls, made for the pit, whence rose a short pale column of white light.

Beside it the pile of dug dirt was higher and wider and Fren walked a strange short sentry-go, stepping on the forward edge of the big forge-bellows next the pit edge, mounting its slant in three short steps (which made it sink), giving its top handle an upward yank after stepping off it (which helped an interior spring expand it again), drawing in air, and so back to the pit edge and repeat the mini march.

Peering down the shaft from the opposite edge of the hole, the three females saw how the first furry snow-white serpent's hide emerged from the bellows' front and curved downward, its crested head clamping its jaws on the tail of the second, and so on downward until the fifth entered the cross corridor at the shaft's bottom, where two leviathan lamps provided illumination.

They could see the furry tube slacken and swell as each successive giant's breath of fresh air travelled down.

Afreyt explained to the girls, "Each tail tip is clipped off short and thrust inside the jaws of the preceding snow serpent, a clear glue making the juncture airtight. Spirits of wine dissolve this, so the hides may be parted, cleaned, and restored (the tail tips are kept) to something like their original value afterward. Else all would be monstrously unthrifty."

And with a sign to the windlass man and a "You next" to the girls, she stepped into the empty pail and travelled down beside the slowly pulsating, furry white tube, stepped out at the bottom and waited until it returned with Fingers and Gale.

The horizontal passage was a dimly lit, stone-floored, narrow, unlofty rectangle, so that Afreyt must stoop as she led the way, although the girls were able to walk upright as they followed.

"I expected it to be warmer underground," Gale observed.

"The dragon's breath we're blowing down is chill," the older woman reminded her. "Look, there's a fortune in wood around us," she told the girls.

"A hero's life is worth any expenditure," Fingers assured her somewhat loftily.

"So it behooves those who may have to ransom or rescue them to lay up cash," Afreyt responded. "Luckily the lumber's all salvageable, like the hides."

Just ahead appeared to be solid rock, and seemingly from it, but actually from around it, there materialized a short man carrying a full pail before him and another behind. It was the Mouser's other lieutenant, Mikkidu. They managed to squeeze past him and then along a short section of corridor where the left wall was stone, the right wood, until it had jogged past the obstruction into bright light, which showed their journey's end eight yards ahead.

From the ceiling's last short crossboard hung a large leviathan lamp, while beneath the as yet unroofed yard of tunnel, Cif knelt away from them and worked at the naked face with wooden trowel and gloved left hand, scraping and brushing away the stuff that was of a consistency between flaky sandstone and packed sand. While supported by an upslanted peg in the right-hand wall, the last snow-serpent puffed chill gusts that stirred the falling dust and fine debris.

So great was the small woman's concentration on her exacting task that she was unaware of their presence until Afreyt touched her shoulder.

She turned on them a blank stare, swiftly rising to her feet. Then her eyes wavered and she lurched forward into her friend's arms.

"You're out on your feet," Afreyt protested. "You should

have been relieved at the face hours ago! Here, take a swallow of this,'' she added, withdrawing a silver flask from her
pouch and uncorking it with her teeth while continuing to
support Cif with her other arm.

The outwearied woman grasped it and gulped the watered
brandy greedily.

"Have you had any rest at all since coming out this noon?"
Afreyt demanded.

"I lay in the tent awhile, but it made me nervous."

"So you're coming up at once with me. There's a new
matter we must discuss alone. Gale! Take over here at the
face. Fingers can help you—it's a sort of work her deft hands
should be good at."

"Oh good!" said Gale.

Fingers: "You honor me."

Cif made no demur, accepting support but asking, "What
new matter?"

"All in good time."

Just past the jog they encountered Mikkidu returning with
empty pails. Afreyt addressed him, "I'm taking the lady Cif
home for long-needed rest. You're in charge now. Gale and
our new friend Fingers are working the face. See that they
aren't kept at it too long and are both sent to Cif's house by
midnight."

When he shot Cif a look of inquiry, she nodded and then
remembered to give him Fafhrd's ring.

Aboveground the dogcart had been unloaded and Skullick
was greeting Mannimark and Faf's berserk Gort as they came
loping in.

Afreyt poured Cif a mouthful of hot soup and directed,
"Hitch up fresh dogs. I'm driving the lady Cif home. She
needs rest badly. No other load. Here Mikkidu has the ring."

"Mara and May were due to go this trip," Skullick pointed
out. The blond girls waved from where they huddled in the
shelter tent.

"I'll take them, of course," Afreyt said. "Girls, climb
aboard! And take a blanket with you. And another for Lady
Cif."

Returning to Salthaven, they all had the wind at their
backs, which was some improvement. None was inclined to

talk. Midway Cif asked suspiciously, "Was there poppy dust in the watered brandy you fed me? It has a sickly, bitter aftertaste."

"Only enough to induce tranquillity and encourage sleep, but not enforce it."

Afreyt drove straight to Cif's and had the girls return the cart to the barracks before wending to their own homes. She warmed a solid meal while Cif got comfortable, saw it consumed, then poured them both brandy and handed Cif the letter Pshawri had entrusted to her, saying, "I've read it, of course. Matter of import for you, certainly."

Cif studied the broken green and the violet-inked address as she unfolded it. "This sheet was in the Captain's last mail bag from Lankhmar," she averred, "before he distributed the letters to his men."

Then she was silent while she read to herself the following:

Dear Son Pshawri,

I hope this finds you alive and continuing to prosper on your northern adventure in service of that notable rogue the Gray Mouser.

I am to tell you he has more reason to make you his lieutenant than even he weens.

When you were young I pointed him out to you among other noteworthy Lankhmarts. But I did not see fit to tell you (or him) that he was your father. Such tactics seldom work out to my knowledge and experience, and I would scorn to curry favor in such a way.

It happened in my salad days, before I became a professional woman, and while I was body maid to the dancer Ivrian and we were all caught up in a supernal intrigue involving the Thieves Guild, some of its jeweled relics, and the Mouser's uncouth barbarian comrade Fafhrd.

They vied with each other to seduce me. Fafhrd loved me the more, but the Mouser was tricksier and measured his drinks more carefully—and mine. The best of what I know of the uses of evil and falsity was taught me by that devil.

But now you find yourself by chance in service of the

very same man, you may find the knowledge of advantage to you. Use it as you see fit. Luckily the relationship is supported by evidence. Triads of equidistant
moles run in his family.

Thanks for the silver ring and seven rilks.

Prosper,
your loving mother Freg

Cif lifted her eyes to Afreyt's. "That letter rings true to
me," she said, nodding soberly.

"You think so too?" the other replied.

"By Skama's scales, what else! It is man's nature to plant
his seed where'er the soil looks good."

"A hero's doubly so . . ." Afreyt chimed, "whence else
his deeds of daring?"

Cif mused, "When we told Mou and Faf of our courting of
the stranger gods Odin and Loki in Rime Isle's service and
even setting sexual lures and ties for them, I recall they hinted
of their own conquests among female divinities—the viewless
Stardock princesses, some nixies of the sea, the rat queen
Hisvet, and some princess of the air who served her as a
maid."

Afreyt pointed out, "This woman claiming Pshawri as her
son would seem to have no noble blood at all, let alone
divine. How would you feel should he claim son-right of
Captain Mouser?"

Cif looked up sharply. "Pshawri has served Mou faithfully
and may do more than that in this now quest! I favor Pshawri's
claim. The resemblances between them run deep—Mou bears
upon his hip a triad of dark moles."

"Another question," Afreyt went on. "Has your Gray
lover ever professed to you any out-of-way sexual tastes?"

"Has your red-haired barbarian?" Cif countered.

"I don't know if you could rightly call it out-of-way," the
other said with a wry laugh, "but once when we were playing
somewhat listlessly abed, he suggested inviting Rill to join
us. I told him I'd strangle him first and indeed tried to. In the
excitement of the delirium this led to, the original proposal
was forgotten at the time and just how playful or serious it
had been at the time of it being made."

Cif laughed, then grew thoughtful in turn. "I once recall the Mouser pestering me as to whether I'd ever felt an attraction to the same sex as my own. At the time I put him in his place, of course, telling I had no truck with any such filthy practices, but since I have wondered once or twice about his curiosity."

Afreyt looked at her quizzically. "Oh," she said, "so you didn't tell him about our . . ." She left her words hanging.

"But we were barely more than girls when that happened," Cif protested.

"True indeed," Afreyt said. "Barely fourteen, as I recall. But you are drowsing off, I plainly see. And so, to tell the truth, am I."

25

Next time the Gray Mouser came first to consciousness, he had forgotten not only who but what he was.

He wondered why a darkness-dwelling creature that was no more than a limp fleshy pocket not moist enough for its own comfort and occupied by two hard, smooth, pointy semicircular ridges that fit together neatly and by a sort of blind sessile snail busy exploring itself and its container endlessly and scavenging life-giving air from the dry grainy outside, should be equipped with a mighty mind capable of mastering whole worlds of life and experience.

The sentient pocket with in-dwelling restless mollusk knew of its mind's might from the variety and rapid sequence of its inscrutable mysterious thoughts and memories which threatened momently to burst into clarity and stain the omnipresent dark with flaring colors. It knew its dry, grainy, closely packed immediate surroundings by a dull yellow glow so dim as hardly to deserve the name of light at all. It was a sort of dim seeing locked in solidity.

Without preamble or warning there blazed up for this buried mind the moving picture of a brilliantly lamp-lit room,
lined with a great map of Nehwon-world and shelves of
ancient books, wherein a venerable, kingly, seated biped
beast silently discoursed to a considerably smaller version of
itself standing attentively before it.

Memory told the sentient pocket that the beast was man,
and then in a flash of insight it realized that behind the
handsome full red mobile lips known as mouth lay such a
moist pocket as itself with pale pointy smooth ridges called
teeth and an indwelling anchor named tongue, and that as a
consequence of all this there must be attached to it a body
such as that of the beast under view and itself be man also,
however cabined and confined in grainy earth.

Instantly his mind began to get a host of little messages
from this attached body, which turned out to be in fetal
position with both hands tenderly cupping its genitals, rag-
limp after their torture by stangury-style orgasm in the skeletal embrace of blue-pied Sister Pain.

Memory of that terrible triggering made him wonder for a
moment if he were not simply gazing into another room in the
apartments of Hisvet in Lankhmar Below, perhaps that of her
sorcerer-father Hisvin, with Foursie due to burst in naked the
next moment chattering out her demon alarm—and the dread
blue lady once again centipede-walk her bone hand round his
waist from behind as he lay trapped and confined by dirt.

But, no! The very earth that clasped him so intimately had
changed profoundly in texture and in reek. The rocks from
which nature had ground it had been igneous and metamor-
phic rather than sedimentary, he could tell. The moisture in it
was not Salt Marsh and Hlal-mouth brackish, but had the icy
bite of the mineralized streams rivuleting from the mountains
of Hunger, a thousand Lankhmar leagues to the south of that
metropolis. The commingled effluvia were not those of poly-
glot Lankhmar but of some more intense and secret commu-
nity with a pervading mushroom odor. Toadstool wine!

A second contemplation of the new buried room and its
occupants made much clear. However had he for a moment
confused schoolmasterish, peevish Hisvin with this imperious
figure discoursing to the crafty-looking lad who stood before

him—the beaky nose, the wattled cheeks, the proud hawklike visage, but above all the ruby-red eyeballs with white irises and glittering jet pupils—those last alone should have told him (but for lingerings of his torture-wrought amnesia) that this could be none other than Quarmal, Lord of Quarmall, on numerous counts his and friend Fafhrd's dearest enemy.

As soon as this realization struck him he noted other clues to the scene's identity and locale, such as a curtain of dangling cords bellowing inward at the room's far end, and behind that, dimly glimpsed, a thick-thighed, short-armed human monster walking without moving forward—one of the almost mindless slaves specially bred to work the treadmills that spun the great wooden fans that sucked down air into the many ramp-joined levels of the buried city and its low-ceilinged mushroom fields.

Unquestionably he was half again as far from Rime Isle as he'd been when overtaken by Sister Pain while spying on Hisvet's remedy for boredom on tedious afternoons in Lankhmar Below, the distance demi-doubled—a prodigious feat of subterranean transversing, one must admit. Unless, of course, both experiences were incidents in a lengthy nightmare dreamed while shallowly buried on Gallows Hill—which more and more seemed the explanation of choice for all this underground hugger-mugger, provided he were eventually rescued from it, to be sure.

Coming out of this reverie, the Mouser checked that his shallow breathing of earth-trapped air was still unlabored and then scanned anew the long room lined with books and charts and philosophic instruments. How characteristic of most of his life, he told himself, was his present situation! To be on the outside in drenching rain or blasting snow or (like now) worse and looking in at a cozy abode of culture, comfort, companionship, and couth—what man wouldn't turn to thieving and burglary when faced at every turn with such a fate?

But back to the business at hand, he told himself, resuming his scanning of the spacious room with its two-and-one-half occupants (the half being for the monstrous treadslave, laboring behind the wavy curtain of cords at the far end).

The soundlessly lecturing Lord Quarmal perched on a high stool beside a narrow table, and the attentive lad (whose

dutiful answers or replies were likewise inaudible) were like a
study in old and young skinniness . . . and wariness, to judge
by their expressions. He also noted a family resemblance in
their features, although the lad's eyes had no sign of the old
man's ruby-red balls and white irises, while the latter's long-
hair tufts between his shriveled ears and bald pate had no
greenish cast such as that shown by the other's short-cropped
locks.

What were they being cagey about? he asked himself.
Damn it, why was this talk blocked off? Recalling he'd had
the same trouble hearing Hisvet and Company at first, he
focused his attention (or, rather, the occult auditory) in one
effort to make it come through to him as clearly as the visual
did.

Failing to achieve any results, he decided shortly he must
be pressing. He relaxed his concentration and let his mind
drift. A gesture of Quarmal with the long thin stiff wand or
rod he carried turned his attention to the big Nehwon map,
the handsome craft of which tempted the Mouser to scan it
almost idly for a while. The colors were mostly naturalistic,
with blues representing seas and lakes, yellow for deserts, white
for snow and ice, and so forth. Close to the west edge,
near the dark blue of the Outer Sea, Quarmall stood out in
royal purple as clearly as if there'd been a sign reading "You
are here."

Just north of it were several small white ovals—the peaks
of the Mountains of Hunger. Then a great space of pale
brown with the blue thread of the Hlal winding through
it—the grainfields. Then Hlal mouth with the city of Lankhmar
on its east bank, and above those the paler blue expanse of
the Inner Sea.

Next above that, the dark green Land of the Eight Cities
ending in the white-topped wall of the Trollstep Mountains
and, everywhere north of that, the white of the Cold Waste.
And, off in the Outer Sea deep blue of the top-west corner,
something he'd never seen on a map before, Rime Isle. It
looked very small. The Mouser shivered to see depicted the
distance between his home port and Quarmall. This had all
better be a nightmare dream, he told himself.

His gaze next traveling east beyond the Cold Waste, it

came to the Sea of Monsters and, beyond that, another shiversome first in his experience of charts: an elliptical black blotch with a glowing sapphire blue spot at its center that had to be the Shadowland, Abode of Death. Why, in the Empire of the East it meant execution by torture for a cartographer to limn that land.

Scattered across the map, but mostly near cities, were enigmatic glowing small purple dots, along with a lesser number of gleaming red ones, as though it had been generously arrayed with amethyst-headed pins, sparsely with ruby ones. What might they signify? The Mouser frowningly noted that one of the reds marked Rime Isle at its Salthaven corner.

At this point the Gray One became aware he had been hearing for some time a faint but steady whispering roar, like that of an array of monster seashells, and realized that it was the hollow noise of the treadslave-driven fans that kept Quarmall from suffocating. It was more than ten years since he'd been employed here bodyguarding Prince Gwaay and heard that sound, but once one heard it, one didn't forget.

Then he began to get strange hissing modulations of the soft roar corresponding with the more vigorous shapings of old Quarmal's lips. They were like the sinister whispers of vindictive ghosts. The Mouser felt a thrill of accomplishment when he provisionally identified the language as High Quarmallese and a surge of triumph when he caught the first indisputable phrase in that sibilant tongue, "treasure caravans of Kush," while Quarmal ticked off with his long rod on the map that jungle kingdom far south of the buried city he himself ruled. Next thing the Mouser knew, he was hearing the entire dialogue with perfect clarity and comprehension. It seemed like a miracle, a wondrous witchcraft, despite his high opinions of his own linguistic skills.

QUARMAL: While it is true, dearest Igwarl, son of my loins and heir of my caverns, that the taking of revenge on injurers and traducers of Quarmall is the chiefest duty of a Lord of Quarmall, it must never be achieved at risk of breaching Quarmall's secrecy. That is why the purple points on the map representing our spies and hidden allies are many more than the crimson ones, marking our assassins.

IGWARL: So the brave wielders of the knife, revered parent,

must always be outnumbered by the softspeakers and double-dealers?

QUARMAL: Not many of my assassins employ the knife. Some steal away priceless life by poisons sweet as sleep or lulling deathspells fair as a dream of love.

IGWARL: Why must things never be done forthrightly, as in war!

QUARMAL: Ah, the impetuosity of youth. Quarmall tried war and lost, now works a surer way. Let me pose you a question. Whom may a Prince of Quarmall trust in furthering his designs?

IGWARL: You, sire. Not my mother. A brother, never! But he may trust his playmate concubines, if they be sisters and he has had the training and command of them.

From his close-buried coign of vantage the Mouser saw the in-blown cords part as a naked girl entered the long chamber past the toiling treadslave. She was of Igwarl's age, looked his wiry double, had the same greenish-blond hair close-cropped, and bore before her like a sword at thrust a slender two-edged knife as she advanced inexorably upon the unperceiving boy. She moved rhythmically yet with a limp, favoring her left foot. The expression on her face was that of a sleepwalker—blank, serene.

QUARMAL: What of a sister? Issa, say. She's to be trusted?

IGWARL: Better than lesser playmate concubine—since she has been like trained even more carefully.

QUARMAL: I am glad to hear so. Look behind you.

Igwarl turned. And froze.

Quarmal let him come to full realization of his plight. The old man's eyes were as intent as those of a leopard. He held the rod ready in his right hand. He shook his left hand free from its sleeve and poised it at head level a foot from his face.

The girl reached striking distance.

Swift as a snake, Igwarl drew a dagger from his belt.

His aged parent rapped his knuckles with the rod and the weapon clattered on the rock floor.

This second betrayal rendered Igwarl moveless.

Quarmal snapped the fingers of his left hand thrice with measured rapidity, slipping his spatulate middle finger off his thumb and bringing it down precisely upon the crevice between his ring finger and his thumb's root with a crack loud as that of a carter's whip. And again. And yet again.

At the first crack the girl halted her forward movement with her knife a handsbreadth short of Igwarl's belly and her eyes widened.

At the second crack realization grew in them of the enormity of the deed she had attempted. She paled.

At the third crack their pupils rolled upward and they fluttered shut as self-horrified unconsciousness enwrapped her. The knife slipped from her fingers and dashed on the rock floor. She swayed forward. Quarmal's rod darted past the bemused boy's shoulder and its brass ferrule took her a handsbreadth below a point midway between the nipplets of her budding breasts. She winced shut-eyed and went a shade paler.

"Catch Issa ere she falls," Quarmal directed his son. To his credit Igwarl managed to comply swiftly enough, supporting her supine slim form with one arm beneath her shoulders, the other under her thighs.

"Dispose her here," said Quarmal, indicating the narrow table.

Igwarl did that too. The ability to act in crisis with a certain precision and a minimum of fuss seemed to run in the family, it occurred to the Mouser.

QUARMAL: You were not expecting an instructive demonstration. (Quarmal pointed this out matter-of-factly, almost casually.) Ensconced in our cavern world, you were not on guard against assault. A sister, no matter how well trained, is not to be fully trusted if there are those can undercut your training. To teach you a lesson I entranced Issa to attack you without her conscious knowledge, then countermanded her before the end.

IGWARL: Your sinister fingers' treble snap? (Old Quarmal nodded.) What if the countermand had failed to work?

QUARMAL: You saw the celerity and sureness with which I used this rod, both to stay Issa's fall and prevent you from shortening your lesson and wasting one of Quarmall's more promising female servants.

IGWARL: But what if the rod had failed also?

QUARMAL: Why, there are always more where you came from, youngster. Do you suppose a father who for Quarmall's good would let your gifted elder brothers kill each other, would spare you in like circumstance? Besides, my demonstration was designed to teach you not to trust me overmuch.

IGWARL: You have proven your point, devious parent.

QUARMAL: (lifting Issa's left foot to display angry red circles upon heel and toe) And why this damage and disfigurement to Quarmall's precious property?

IGWARL: (sulkily) It was needful to correct. Those are not regions normally seen, contributing to beauty.

QUARMAL: A limp's a beauty mark? There was the instep to be considered, not to mention the armpits.

IGWARL: I bow to your superior wisdom, sire. Impart to me the skill of enchantment.

QUARMAL: All in good time, my son. I must reassure Issa.

The old man tweaked her left breast sharply, bringing her awake with a gasp. But when he would have spoken to her, his red eyes lifted away and went distant. His right hand fixed on Igwarl's shoulder and bore down. The boy grimaced with the pain.

"A hostile force is in the rocks surrounding us," the old man hissed. "It came on whilst I was rapt instructing you."

His two children, looking up, quaked at what they saw in his ruby orbs.

In his grainy retreat the Mouser was aware of the intrusion. The pressure of the earth around him on his body increased, reached a breath-stopping maximum, then slackened off till he felt almost free to shoot off at the speed of light and reach the ends of Nehwon in a trice, then began to tighten up again. It happened over and over in a vast chthonian pulse, as though a giant were pacing overhead.

In his spell-casting map room and library, red-orbed old Quarmall found words. "It's my old enemy of twelve years back, Gwaay's champion, that cutpurse of empires and spoiler of dominions, the Gray Mouser. He's somehow learned of my plot against his pal and (mayhap with aid from his wizards Sheelba and Ningauble) come to spy upon me. Loose the boreworms and poison moles against him! The rock-tunneling spiders and the acid slugs that eat through stone!"

These dire threats, clearly heard by the Mouser and half believed, were too much. When the next surge of tremendous pressure came together with the dizzy pulse of freedom, he blacked out.

26

Since Pshawri's self-rule was to do the necessary with least effort, he laid no plans, looking to find inspiration and allies in the developing situation. So when he surmounted Darkfire's crater rim and felt the full force of the north blast, having climbed her by her moonlit east face, he anticipated nothing.

The first thing his eyes lit on was a black rock the size and shape of a narrow man-skull. He reached forward crouching and budged it. Instead of being foamed or clear wave volcanic rock, it was something far heavier, leadstone at least—which explained its being free yet staying where it was in the gale.

Bracing himself, he scanned around the cloud-streaked night, again sensing menace to the southwest—something on tall invisible legs or shouldering down out of the sullied moonshine.

He advanced three paces and peered down into the volcano's narrow-throated fire pit.

The tiny rose-red lake of molten lava flooring it looked very far down and startlingly still, yet on his windchilled cheeks and chin he felt the prick of its radiant heat.

His hands shot toward the pouch between his legs so he might take from it the strange talisman of the foreign god who was his captain-father's foe and hurl it down before hostile night could gather its powers.

But the next instant, as if it had read his mind, the small massy Whirlpool Queller came alive and dashed back and forth, this way and that, seeking escape, outdinting the pouch confining it, drubbing him about the thighs and genitals, inflicting jolts of sickening pain.

His actions shaped themselves without pause to this supernatural flurry. His horny hands closed on the dodging Queller in its bag. He turned around, lunged to the leadstone skull-rock, and pressed tightly against it the encindered and empouched (and certainly ensorcelled!) gold talisman. It shook strongly. He was glad it had no teeth. He felt night's awfulest powers looming over him.

He did not look up. Keeping the vibrating Queller confined against the leadstone with left hand and knee, he used his right to draw his dirk and cut the straps by which his pouch hung from his belt. Then, holding his dirk in his teeth by its cork-covered grip, he used the coil of thin climbing line hanging at his side to bind together firmly the skull-rock and the tight-woven wool pouch along with its frantic contents— with many a thoughtful look and hardest knots.

While concentrating on this job with blind automatism, steadily resisting the urge to look over his shoulder, his mind roved. He recalled what his co-mate Mikkidu had told him about how Captain Mouser had had them double the lashing of the deck cargo of *Seahawk* so that the galley retained its integrity and buoyancy when foundered by leviathan dive beside it, and how he'd lectured them on a man's need to bind securely all his possessions to be sure of them, and how he was guessed to have treated the same a beauteous slim she-demon who had sought to enthrall him and secure the ship.

Next came the memory of a tranquil twilight hour when the day's work ashore was done and Captain Mouser, wine cup in hand and in a rare mood of philosophizing familiarity, confided, "I distrust all serious thought, reasoned analysis, and such. When faced with difficulties, it is my practice to dive but once, deeply, into the pool of the problem, with supreme confidence in my ability to pluck up the answer."

That had been before Freg's letter had transformed his captain and mentor into his hero and sire—and set him seeking special ways to prove himself. And in so seeking he'd loosed, poor fool, his father's fellest foe.

Where was his father now?

And could he now recoup?

His task was done, the last loop drawn tight, the last knot tied, bag firmly lashed to stone. Again, without one instant's hesitation, he tightly gripped the weighty package in both hands, turned, took two steps into the icy gale and toward the pit, lifted it to its apex, and then very suddenly (and with the feeling that if he took one moment more, something very big above him would snatch it from him) hurled it straight down at the rosy-red target.

He ended in a low crouch on the rim, which he immediately gripped, shooting his legs back so that he lay flat—prone with his face thrust over, peering down. And it was well that he effected this additional descent for he was smitten by a chill gust from above which else had knocked him after his projectile—and crosswise brushed by a huge wing which would have done the same had he been inches higher.

He kept his eye upon the black grain of the plummeting skull-rock package. From it two tiny, whitely incandescent eyes glared up at him. One of them winked. He saw the grain enter the molten pool, from which a single like-sized red drop rebounded, whereupon the whole small lake 'gan to seethe and shake and churn and coruscate, its level crawling upward, as if a dam had burst. The speed of this ascent of the lava pool 'gan to increase as he watched. The crawl became a scramble, then a rush. And what did this portend? Had he saved the Gray Mouser? Or doomed him?—if there were connection between man and talisman.

A blast of hot air traveling ahead of the upgushing lava near seared his slitted eyes. Without pause, groping thought gave way to arrow-swift action. Escape was the one word or he'd not live to think. Pushing himself to his feet and twisting around, he began a skipping moonlit descent of the black cone he'd but now laboriously climbed. Perilous to the point of madness and beyond, yet utterly necessary were he to live to tell.

His eyes were fully occupied spotting the landing points of the successive leaps toward which he steered his feet. The moonlight turned bright pink. There was a giant hissing. He smelled sulfur and brimstone. There was a mighty roar, as if a cosmic lion had coughed, and a hot gust clapped his back heartily, turning three of his leaps into one, speeding his flight. Red missiles flashed past him and burst on impact to either side his course ahead of him like angry stars. The steep slope gentled. His leaps became a lope. The leonine coughing reechoed like thunder rolling away. The pink moonshine paled and darkened.

At last he risked a backward look, expecting scenes of destruction, but there was only a great wall of sooty darkness that reeked of acid smoke and billowed overhead to besprinkle Skama with black.

He shrugged. For good or ill, his work was done and he was headed south on the front of a second monstrous weather change.

27

Fingers knew she was dreaming because there was a rainbow in the cave. But that was all right because the six colors were more like those of pastel chalk than light and there was a blackboard at which she was being taught to pleasure Ilthmar sailormen by her mother and an old old man, both wearing long black robes and hoods which hid their upper faces.

For teaching, her mother bore her witch's wand and the old man a long silver spoon with which he managed the cleverest demonstrations.

But then, perhaps to illustrate some virtue—persistence?—he began to tap the bowl of his spoon on the hollow top of the desk at which they all three sat. He beat softly with a slow funeral rhythm that fascinated her until that doleful sound was all that was left in the world.

She woke to hear water a-drip, in the same slow beat as the dream-spoon, upon the thin horn pane of a slanting roof window close overhead.

She realized she had grown warm and thrown back her

blanket, and as she listened to the drip she thought, *The frosty spell has broken. It's the thaw.*

From the pillow beside her, Gale, who'd also thrown back her bedclothes, murmured ungently in exactly the same rhythm as the water drops: *"Faf-hrd, Faf-hrd, Un-cle Fafhrd."*

Which told Fingers that the drops were a message from the engaging red-haired captain, boding his return. And she told herself that she had a closer relationship to him than Gale's or even Afreyt's and must bestir herself and venture out and assure his safe return.

This decision once made, she wormed her way off the bed—it seemed important to make no stir—and drew on her short robe and soft fur boots.

After a moment's study and thought, she dropped the thin sheet back across Gale's frowsy supine sprawl and stole from the room.

Passing the bedroom where Cif and Afreyt lodged, she heard sounds of someone rising and turned down the stairs, tiptoeing next the wall to avoid the treads creaking.

Arriving in the banked warmth of the dark kitchen, she smelled gahveys heating and heard footsteps above and behind her. Without haste she made her way to the door of the bath and concealed herself behind Fafhrd's robe of coarse toweling hanging beside it in such a way as to be able to observe without herself being seen, she trusted.

It was Cif descended the stairs, dressed for the day's work. The short woman threw wide the outer door and the sounds of the thaw came in and the low white beams of the setting moon. Standing in them, she set to her lips a thin whistle and blew—without audible results, but Fingers judged a signal had been sent.

Then Cif went to the banked fire, poured herself a mug of gahvey and took it back to the doorway where she sipped and waited. For a while she gazed straight at Fingers. But if Cif saw the girl, the woman made no sign.

With a jingle of bells but no other sound, a dogcart and pair drew up beyond her—without driver, so far as Fingers could see.

Cif walked out to it, stepped aboard, took the whip from its vertical socket and, sitting very erect, cracked it once high in the air.

Fingers came out from behind Fafhrd's robe and hurried to the door in time to see Cif and her small vehicle moving west beneath the barely diminished descending disk of Satyrs Moon as the two big dogs bore them off toward the spot where they sought Captain Mouser. For a long moment Fingers enjoyed the feeling of being a member of this household of silently occupied witchwomen.

But then the drip of the thaw reminded her of her own quest. She fetched Fafhrd's robe from its peg, and hanging it over her left arm and leaving the house door open behind her, as Cif had, Fingers circled the dwelling and headed out across the open field toward the sea, treading the steaming grass and feeling the caress of the soft south wind that set its seal on the great change of weather.

The moon was directly behind her now. She walked straight up the long shadow of herself it cast, which stretched to the low moondial. Overhead the brighter stars could be discerned, though dimmed by their moon mistress. To the southeast a cloud bank was rising to cover them.

As Fingers watched, a slender single cloud separated itself from the bank and headed toward her. It came coasting down out of the night sky, moving a little faster than the balmy breeze which drove on its fellows and lightly stroked her. The last of the moonlight shone brightly on its swan-rounded prow and sleek straight sides—for it truly did look more like a delicate ship of the air than any proper cloud of aqueous vapor should, so that a spiderwebbing shiver of wonder and gossamer fear went along Fingers' rosy flesh beneath her belted robe and she crouched a little and went more softly.

She was nearing the moondial now, passing it just to the south. Where its curving gnomon did not shadow it, its moon-pale round crawled with Rimic runes and half-familiar figures.

Beyond the dial, a bare spearcast distant, the eerie ship-cloud came coasting down, moving in a direction opposite to the girl, and settled to a stop.

At the same instant, almost as if it were part of the same movement, Fingers spread Fafhrd's robe across the wet grass ahead of her and gently stretched herself out upon it so that the moondial's low curb was sufficient to conceal her. She held still, intently studying the strange cloud's pale hull.

The last bright splinter of Satyrs Moon vanished behind Rime Isle's central peaks. At the opposite end of the sky the dawn glow grew.

From a direction midway between out of the cloud ship there came the doleful music of a flute and small drum sounding a funeral march.

Simultaneously and silently there thrust down out of the heart of the cloud and touched down a third of the distance between it and Fingers a light gangplank which appeared broad enough for two to go abreast.

Then down this travelway as the dawn lightened and the music swelled there came slowly and solemnly a small procession headed by two slim girls in garments of close-fitting black, like pages, and bearing the flute and small drum from which the sad notes came.

Following these there came two by two and footing with a grave dignity six slender women in the black hoods and form-fitting robes of the nuns of Lankhmar whose plackets showed the pastel tints of underthings of violet, blue, green, yellow, orange, and red.

Upon their shoulders they bore with ease and great solicitude a black draped, wide-shouldered, slender-hipped tall male form.

Following these there strolled a final slim, tall, black-clad female figure in brimless conical hat and veils of a priestess of the Gods of Lankhmar. She bore a long wand tipped with a tiny, glowing pentagram, with which she sketched an endless row of hieroglyphs upon the twilit air.

Fingers, watching the strange funeral from her hidden point of vantage, could not name their language.

As the procession debouched upon the meadow, it swung west. When the turn had been fully completed, the figure of the priestess lifted her wand in a gesture of command, bringing the dim star to a stop. Instantly the girl-pages stopped their playing, the nuns their dancing forward march, and Fingers felt herself seized by a paralysis that rendered her incapable of speech and froze her every muscle save those controlling the direction in which she looked.

In a concerted movement the nuns lifted the corpse they carried on high, brought it down to the grass with an uncomfortable swiftness, and then twitched aloft the empty shroud.

The point where they had deposited the corpse was just out of Fingers' range of vision, but there was nothing the girl could do about that except grow cold and shiver.

Nor did it help when the priestess lowered her wand.

One by one the nuns knelt with hands out of view and performed a not overlong manipulation, then each dipped her head briefly out of sight and finally all rose together.

One by one the six nuns did this thing.

The priestess touched the last nun's shoulder with her wand to attract her attention and handed her a white silken ribbon. The latter knelt, and when she rose no longer had the ribbon in her hand.

With more speed than solemnity, the priestess once again raised her star-tipped wand, the page-girls struck up a jolly quick-step, the nuns briskly folded the shroud they'd borne so solemnly, the whole procession about-faced and quick-marched back aboard the cloud ship no less swiftly than it takes to write it down, and the crew set sail.

And still Fingers could not move one.

In the interval the sky had brightened markedly, sunrise was close at hand, and as the cloud-ship sailed away west at a surprisingly fast rate, it and its crew, momentarily less substantial, were suddenly on the verge of fading out, while the music gave way to a ripple of affectionate laughter.

Fingers felt all constraints lift from her muscles. She darted forward, and the next moment, it seemed, was looking down into the very shallow depression wherein the dancing nuns had laid their mortal burden.

There on a bed of new-sprung milky mushrooms stretched out serenely the tall, handsome, faintly smiling form of the man she knew as Captain Fafhrd and toward whom she felt such a puzzling mixture of feelings. He was doubly naked because recently close-shaven everywhere, save for eyebrows and lashes, and those trimmed short, and quite unclad except for ribbons of the six spectral colors and white tied in big bows around his limp genital member.

"Keepsakes of his six lady loves who were his pallbearers, or dancers, and from their mistress or chieftainess," the girl pronounced wisely.

And noting the organ's extreme flaccidity and the depth of satisfaction in his smile, she added with professional approval, "And loved most thoroughly."

At first she felt a strong pang of grief, thinking him dead, but a closer look showed his chest to be gently rising and falling, and also brought her within range of his warm exhalation.

She prodded him gently in the chest over his breastbone, saying "Wake up, Captain Fafhrd."

The warmth of his skin surprised her, though not enough to make her think of fever.

The smoothness of his skin truly startled her. It was shaved more closely than she'd thought possible, with sharpest eastern steel. Bending down just as the new risen sun sent out a wave of brightness, she could see only the faintest copper-pink flecks as of fresh-scoured metal. Yesterday she'd noticed gray and white hairs among the red. He'd merited Gale's "Uncle" fully. But now—the effect was of rejuvenation, the skin looked babyish, fair as hers was. He continued to smile in his sleep.

Fingers gripped him firmly by the shoulders and shook him.

"Wake up, Captain Fafhrd," she cried. "Arise and shine!" Then, in an impish mood, irked by his smile, which now began to seem merely foolish and stupid, "Cabingirl Fingers reporting for duty."

She knew that was wrong as soon as she heard herself utter it when in response to her shaking he reared up into a sitting position, though without opening his eyes or changing expression. Suddenly these things became frightening.

To give herself time to think about the situation and consider what to do next, Fingers returned to fetch his robe from where she'd left it spread out on the wet grass back at the moondial. She doubted he'd want to be seen naked, and certainly not wearing his ladies' colors. Yet the sun was up and at any moment Gale, Afreyt, or some visitor might appear.

"For although your ladies playing nuns had every right to mark you as their lover—seeing you'd been most free (I think) with all of them, that does not mean I have to go along with their naughty joke, though I do think it funny," the girl said as she came hurrying with his robe, speaking aloud because she thought he really did still sleep and wanted in any case to check upon this fact.

In the interval she had jumped to the rather romantic conclusion that Fafhrd was in the situation of the Handsome Tranced One, a male equivalent of Sleeping Beauty in Lankhmar legend—a youth with a sleep spell on him that can be lifted only by his true love's kiss.

Which at once suggested to Fingers that she convey the sleeping (and strangely transformed, even frightening) hero to the Lady Afreyt for the reviving kiss.

After all, they had been introduced to her as lovers (and proper gentlefolk) except for Fafhrd's straying with the naughty nuns, which was the sort of straying to be expected of men, according to her mother's teaching. Moreover he'd been under all the strain of directing the search for his comrade Captain who'd slipped underground.

Surely to bring Fafhrd and Afreyt back together would be a most proper return for all the courtesies they'd shown her, beginning with her rescue from *Weasel*.

Back at the mushroom bed Fafhrd had made no further progress toward awakening. So she draped the sun-warmed robe around him, gently urging him by words and assisting movements to don it.

"Arise, Captain Fafhrd," she suggested, "and I will help you into your robe and then to some shadowed and comfortable spot where you may have your full sleep out."

When with some repetitions of this routine and patter she'd got him up (safely asleep on his feet, as it were) with his robe belted about him so his colorful honors were completely concealed—and a long look around showed they were still unobserved—she breathed a sigh of relief and set about to lead him back to Cif's house using the same methods.

But they'd got no farther than the moondial when it occurred to Fingers to ask herself, Where's everyone?

It was a question easier to ask than answer.

You'd think after the second great weather change, every last soul would be out to see, soaking in the heat and talking about the wonder.

Yet wherever you looked there wasn't a person to be seen or heard. It was eerie.

All yesterday the digging for Captain Mouser had kept up a steady traffic between the diggings, the barracks, and Cif's place. Today no trace of that since Cif's departure by moonlight hours ago.

It was as if Fafhrd's sleep spell were on everyone in Salthaven save herself. Maybe it was.

And the somnambulistic spell on Fafhrd was a lot stronger than she'd judged at first. Here, he and she were halfway back to Cif's and it showed no signs of falling off.

She began to doubt the power of Afreyt's kiss to dispel it. Perhaps it would be better if he had his full sleep out, as she'd been suggesting to him in her patter.

And what if Afreyt didn't go for her idea of the Handsome Tranced One and the revivifying kiss? Or tried it and it didn't? And then they both tried to wake Fafhrd and couldn't? And Lady Afreyt blamed her for that?

Suddenly she lost all faith in the ideas that had seemed so brilliant to her moments before. Getting Fafhrd back to full sleep again (as she had been promising him over and over in her patter) as soon as they'd reached a suitable place for that seemed the thing to do. She recalled an infallible sleep spell her mother had taught her. The sooner she recited it to Fafhrd, the better. Fully asleep again, he'd no longer be her responsibility.

Perhaps it would work on her too—and perhaps that was just what she needed to straighten her out—a good sleep.

The idea of falling asleep with Captain Fafhrd seemed vastly attractive.

They'd just got back to Cif's without encountering anyone. She was relieved to find the door ajar. She thought she'd closed it.

Stopping her soft talk to Fafhrd, but keeping up a pressure

on his arm, she worked the thick door open and guided him inside. The house was silent, she was pleased to find, and that Captain Fafhrd, being barefoot, made no more noise than she.

Then, as they were halfway across the kitchen, nearer the cellar stairs than those to the second floor (or the sauna door), she heard footsteps overhead in Cif's bedroom. Afreyt's, she thought.

She decided at once on flight and chose the cellar because it was nearest and also the place where she had first met Fafhrd. She stuck with her choice because the Northerner responded instantly to her silent guidance, as if it would have been his choice too.

And then they were down in the cellar and the die was cast—simply a matter of whether the firm, decisive footsteps of Afreyt followed him down into the cellar or did not. Fingers had led him out of the space at the foot of the stairs visible from the kitchen and sat him down on the bench facing the large square of unpaved loamy earth, illuminated, she now saw, by one of the long-lasting cool leviathan-oil lamps. But she dared not turn that off now, no matter how unsuitable for sleeping, for if Afreyt saw the light dim in the cellar, she'd surely come down to investigate.

The footsteps finished the upper stairs, came five paces across the kitchen, and then stopped dead. Had she noticed the light on in the cellar and would she come down to turn it off?

But moments gave way to seconds and seconds to minutes, or at least lengthened unendurably, and still there'd been no sound. It was as if Afreyt had died up there or just evaporated. Until Fingers, to stop herself growing tired or numb and getting a crick in her neck or shoulder and making a violent involuntary move, edged forward step by silent step and seated herself on the bench beside the northern Captain, facing away from the unpaved square of earth.

She felt herself growing more and more tired, forgot about Afreyt hearing, and hastened to recite the sleep spell softly so that she and Captain Fafhrd would receive the full benefit of it.

Meanwhile something very interesting and quite unsuspected by Fingers had actually been happening to Afreyt.

She had wakened alone just before dawn and heard the thaw, opened the window overlooking the headland and moondial just in time to observe the wondrous sailing of the Arilian moon pinnace with Fafhrd's mistress and her naughty train, and heard the last notes of the quick march give way to the ripple of derisive laughter.

Thereafter, Afreyt had watched from the distance the tricksy and ambitious cabingirl Fingers seemingly rouse, then robe her magically rejuvenated father (for the woman had noted many other resemblances between parent and offspring besides hair color), and then work their way at leisure back to Cif's place, getting their two stories straight, thought Afreyt, but above all murmuring of their great incestuous love (for after all, what else did they really have to talk about?), and while Fafhrd's lady was thus reacting to their manifold treacheries, she furiously laced on her shoes and belted her robe and hurried downstairs to confront the miscreants.

When she found them gone, Afreyt made the deduction Fingers had anticipated about the cellar light. She thought for a moment, then to surprise them, knelt and silently undid the shoes she had so furiously laced, stepped out of them and tiptoed downstairs without a sound.

But when she stepped out suddenly into full view she found them both faced away from her on the bench, gazing at the unpaved square of earth, Fafhrd resting his head against Fingers' chest, "lying in her lap," as it's expressed, just as the girl started to recite in a small bell-like voice what she thought was her mother's sleep spell but was in truth, as she had inadvertently revealed to Gale and Afreyt the second morning of the cold by reciting its last five individually harmless lines, the direst of Quarmallian death spells taught her under hypnosis by the infinitely vengeful and devious Lord Quarmal of Quarmall.

> *"Call for the robin red breast and the wren*
> *Since o'er shady groves they hover*
> *And with leaves and flowers do cover*
> *The friendless bodies of unburied men.*

> *Call unto his funeral dole*
> *The ant, the field mouse, and the mole*
> *To rear him hillocks that shall keep him warm*
> *And safe from any savage hurt or harm . . ."**

As Afreyt heard Fingers recite the first of those eight lines, she saw emerge vertically upward from the soft earth of the left forefront of the unpaved square a small serpent's head or tentacle tip, followed almost at once close to either side by a second and third at the same even rate, then a short fourth in line at the same short distance to the left, and lastly a thick fifth erecting alone two inches in front of the rest, and then she saw that the four serpents' heads or tentacles were joined at their bases to a palm, and taken with the thick separate member, constituted the fingers and thumb of a buried hand digging itself upward and bursting from the ground, while down off it the revealing earth sifted and tumbled.

As Afreyt, all a-shiver at this prodigy, listened to the recitation of the innocuous-seeming second and third lines and realized that the situation must be different, with Fafhrd playing a more passive role than she'd suspected, a second and larger emergence started, that of a head behind and to the right of the hand and with its hairy earth-mired crown beginning at the level of the palm.

The forward-facing brow, as it emerged at the same even rate as had the hand, showed more bright yellow in its illumination than white leviathan light would account for, which reminded Afreyt of Cif's dream of the Mouser wearing a glowing yellow mask and was Afreyt's first clue to the identity of the underground traveler. By now it was apparent that the escaping hand was attached to and directed by the rising head, and Afreyt, shaking with terror at the unnatural sight, at least need not fear the dartings, scuttlings, and

---

*The White Devil by John Webster, Act V, Scene 4. Sometimes called Cornelia's dirge, this ends in the play:

> "To rear him hillocks, that shall keep him warm
> And (when gay tombs are robbed) sustain no harm,
> But keep the wolf far thence, that's foe to men,
> For with his nails he'll dig him up again."

gropings of a hostile, detached, and independently roving hand.

As she heard the child's clear little voice recite the somewhat sinister fourth line of the Quarmallian death spell, which Afreyt already suspected to be something of the sort (which Fingers did not as yet), the eyes beneath the rising brow came into view and opened wide.

Afreyt at once recognized the gray eyes of the Mouser, saw that they were fixed upon Fafhrd and full of fear for him and that it was the very fear of death. At that moment she would have given a great deal to know whether Fafhrd's own eyes were open or closed, if the Mouser had made his deduction from the expression in them or from his comrade's extreme pallor or other physical symptom. She did not think (at least as yet) of getting up and looking for herself—her awe of what was happening, rather than her fear (though that was great) kept her frozen.

As a matter of fact his eyes were closed with the spell's workings, which operated by degrees, line by line, from sleep to death.

Fingers, reciting the death spell Quarmal had taught her hypnotically after her kidnapping and which she now thought of as a sleep spell of her mother's (as he'd told her 'twas) saw the same figure emerging from the earth that Afreyt did, but it did not catch her interest. She hoped it would not interfere with her recital of the spell and its working on Fafhrd and herself. Perhaps it was the beginning of a dream they'd share.

The Mouser had last lost consciousness underground spying on old Quarmal's buried map room and chamber of necromancy while asking himself questions about Rime Isle.

He came to awareness now with head, shoulders, and one arm emerged into a familiar cellar on the latter island and with the answers to his questions in plain view: Fafhrd dying in the arms and against the breasts of his daughter by (the Quarmallian) slave girl Friska, and the child's unwitting recitation of the death spell.

Who else could be the assassin indicated by the lone red dot on Quarmal's world map? And so what Mouser must do at once to save his dearest friend from life's worst ill—even before Mou inhaled the unrationed breaths he longed to, stretched the cramped muscles, or tasted the wine for which his dry throat cried—was to countermand that death spell by snapping his fingers thrice, as he'd just now seen Quarmal do to stay the instructional assassination of his son Igwarl by the latter's sister Issa.

And, if Mou knew anything about the rules of magic and the ways of Quarmal, those snaps must be perfectly executed, delivered without delay, and loud as thundercracks—or else he could go whistle for Faf's life forevermore.

And so it happened that as Afreyt listened to Fingers recite the idyllic fifth, sixth, seventh, and eighth lines of the spell (but getting closer to the nasty ones she'd "spelled" to them in her fatigue the second morning of the cold), the Rime Isle woman was puzzled and nonplussed to see the earth-traveler—just as there rose into view Mouser's mouth set in a narrow slit for air scavenging—wave his limply held free hand vigorously, as if it were a dusting rag from which he shook the dirt, and then carefully settle the pad at end of his middle finger against the ball of his thumb above ring and little finger bent back against the palm, and against which the poised and powerfully tensed middle finger now flashed down.

It was, quite simply, the loudest fingersnap she'd ever heard. So might a most impatient god summon a reprehensibly straying angel.

And as if that prodigious snap were not enough to prove whatever point was being contested, it was followed with preternatural swiftness by not one, but two repetitions of the same sound, each one a little louder than the previous one, which as any knowledgeable gambler knows, is not a bet to be backed, an achievement to set a wager on.

The Mouser's fingerbolts had their desired effect on the others in the cellar, including their sender.

They brought Afreyt to her feet. Fingers was silenced, Quarmal's death spell canceled. The bell tones ceased to sound, the cabingirl fell backward. Fafhrd collapsed, sank sidewise against her.

This should have made it easier for Afreyt to see the Mouser, but it didn't. The effort he'd put into his fingerbolts had taken it out of him. As if time had been turned back to that night of full Satyrs Moon on Gallows Hill, his outline grew fainter, the steady leviathan light flickered, his emergence slowed and stopped, without reaching his waist, and he began to slip backward into the earth.

His eyes fixed on Afreyt's most dolefully. His lips opened and a low moaning came out, such as a ghost utters at cockcrow, infinitely sad.

Afreyt plunged to her knees before the unpaved square. Her grasping digging hands encountered only loose dirt. She clambered to her feet and turned back to the fallen figures.

The man with the child's skin and the child lay as if dead. But a closer inspection showed them to be but sleeping.

28

Cif scraped the wooden scoop four times across the earthen tunnel face before her, detaching small chunks and granules of loosened sand, which pattered down on and around her boots.

The leviathan-oil lamp behind her cast her head's shadow on the fresh area of tunnel face thus uncovered and the newly attached snow-serpent hide (which was the twenty-third in from the shaft) puffed warm air upon it from outside, where Satyrs Moon was two hours set and the bright sun almost as long arisen.

She had been working at the tunnel face all of that time, advancing it at least two feet (and making room for another length of the flexible snowy piping, which had just now been attached).

With her free hand she felt, deep in her pouch, the reassuring touch of the brazen loop, wide enough to be a ring for two fingers, with which Mikkidu had greeted her this morn, telling her that it had been recovered during the digging last night and was (as she well knew) an item the Captain was seldom parted from.

She judged she had another hour of face work in her before she lost her freshness and must give place to Rill, who now assisted her and only had been below for half an hour.

But now 'twas time for one of the quarter-hourly checks she made.

"Cover the lamp," she called back to Rill.

The lady with the crippled left hand pulled up around the coolly burning lamp a thick black sack and drew it together at the top.

The tunnel grew black as pitch.

Cif stared ahead and this time seemed to see, floating at eye level, a phosphorescent yellow mask such as she'd seen the Mouser wearing in the dream she'd had the first night of the cold. It was dim but truly seemed there.

Letting fall the scoop and withdrawing her left hand from her pouch, she dug her gloved fingers into the sandy face where the mask was drifting. It stayed there, did not fade out or waver, but grew brighter. The featureless black ovals that were its eyes seemed to stare back at her commandingly.

"Uncover the lamp," she managed to enunciate.

Rill obeyed, not trusting herself to ask questions. Almost with a rush the white light flooded back, revealing Cif staring fiercely at the tunnel face. Rill could no longer contain herself.

"You think . . . ?" she managed to ask in a voice fraught with awe.

"We'll soon know," the other replied, drawing back her clawed right hand and driving it into the loosened sand of the tunnel face at the level of her chin, twisting it this way and that, back and forth, feeling around before withdrawing it. (Small chunks and grains showered around.) She repeated this action twice, but on the second occasion paused with her hand still dug in.

Her gloved fingers had encountered and were now uncovering two hard, serrated, semicircular ridges with a half-inch gap between them.

Wetting her lips with her tongue and guiding them with her gloved hands held close beside her cheeks, she pressed them against the dry and gritty pair of lips that closely framed the serrated ridges that opposed and almost touched her own teeth.

Puffing a breath of air ahead of it, she ran her tongue's wet tip around the inside of the dry lips hers pressed, repeated that tender action and then inhaled.

Her nostrils and foremouth filled with the exciting acrid reek of the Gray Mouser, familiar to her from a long season's lovemaking.

It made her tremble and shake to realize this was so, that she held between her hands his precious face returned from the grave.

She exhaled to one side that wonder breath, drew in a fresh one from the serpent's mouth, again clamped her lips down upon his still-dry ones and gently blew that breath deep into him, praying it retained its healing serpent's character.

"Dearest, beloved," she heard him croak.

She realized she was staring deep into his eyes, but was so close the two appeared as one.

"Owl eyes," she replied foolishly, recalling their lovers' name for that two-equals-one phenomenon.

Then recollecting more of her situation, she said, "Dear Rill, our captain's back. He's in my arms and I am feeding him air. Do you work in your hands from behind me and dig and brush the earth away from's body and speed his freeing from its dreadful grip."

"I will be very grateful, Rill, I assure you," the Mouser broke in sotto voce, croaking rather less than he had on "dearest."

The witch-whore complied, gingerly at first, then with larger strokes as she realized the amount of earth there was to be moved. She found the scoop Cif had dropped and used it to increase the scope of first her right hand, then her crippled left, where the advantage it provided was greater.

Meanwhile Cif continued to brush dirt from his cheeks as she alternately kissed him and fed him air, working her hands nearer to the back of his head and a full embrace, with each stroke freeing more of the margins of his eye sockets and ears.

The Mouser said, "I'll keep my eyes closed, Cif, save when you tell me I may open them," and was emboldened to ask, "And would you be a bit more generous with your perfumed saliva, dear? That is, if you've to spare. I've been without refreshment all of two days (or is it three, perchance?) save for such moisture as I've sucked from stones. Or begged from passing worms.''

"I have," Rill mentioned ingenuously. "I happen to have been chewing mint the past half hour. The smallest leaves.''

"You *are* a witch, dear Rill," Cif commented cattily.

Fafhrd's lieutenant Skor chose that moment to appear behind Rill, filling the tunnel with his stooped tall form and reporting past her to Cif as commander of the diggings, "The Captain's returned from wherever he was yesterday and last night, milady. I gather strange things have been happening, some in the sky. He just arrived by dogcart with the Lady Afreyt and with them the child Gale and the Ilthmar cabingirl.''

At that point he got a good look at what was going on in the tunnel, recognized the Mouser's face and became speechless. (Later he tried to describe what he saw to Skullick and Pshawri. "She was kissing him out of the sandstone, I tell you, kissing and caressing, working a mighty magic whether she knew it or not. While her sister witch worked a like sorcery upon his bottom half, his nether limbs and members. Our captains are fortunate to enjoy the favor of such women of power.'')

Cif turned her head back toward him and straightened up, bringing the Mouser with her out of the tunnel face and shedding sandy debris.

"Things have been happening here too, as you can see," she said briskly. "Now harken, Skor. Return aloft and tell the Lady Afreyt and Captain Fafhrd I wish to speak with them down here. But do *not* tell them (or *anyone* up there) of Captain Mouser's passing strange return, else everyone will be crowding down to view and celebrate the wonder.''

"That's true enough," the tall man with thinning hair agreed, doing his best to sound rational.

"Do as she tells you, Skor," the Mouser put in. "There's wisdom in her rede.''

"Don't *you* return down here, of course," Cif continued. "Take charge up there, maintain order, and keep the dragon breathing." She nodded toward the pulsing white snow-serpent piping. "Here, take the ring of command off my top middle fingers and wear it on your thumb." She held out the hand on which was Fafhrd's ring. He obeyed. She had an after-thought. "Send the two girls down also, Fingers and Gale. Else they'll make mischief while your hands are full."

"Harkening in obedience," Skor responded, bowing to Cif as he turned around and made off speedily.

"That last thought of yours was inspired, my dear," the Mouser said breezily, turning from Rill to Cif. "Mischief? Yes, indeed!—for it turns out that the Ilthmar cabingirl Fingers is the assassin sent to wipe out her father Fafhrd by reciting an outlandish death spell—sent out by our old enemy Quarmal, Lord of Quarmall, as I learned when I breakfasted there al fresco this morn's morn on cave dew, boreworm bread, and toadstool wine—and spied on Quarmal in his most secret lair."

"Fingers Fafhrd's get?" Rill remarked. "I suspected it from the red hair. And there's a definite facial resemblance. And something about her cool manner . . ."

The Mouser nodded emphatically. "Though, to be fair to Fingers, I don't think she knew what she was doing—old Quarmal had her most securely hypnotized. Fortunately I learned at the same time how to scotch his spells ('twas as easy as snap your fingers, and as hard) by observing him foil at the last moment his son Igwarl's murder by *his* sister Issa, which he had masterminded for purposes of instruction. (He makes a positive religion of treachery and mistrust, the old man does.) If I hadn't studied his finger-snapping trick and been able to repeat it perfectly, Fafhrd would be dead as mutton by his daughter's unknowing agency. Whereas, if we can trust Skor, he's as fit as a fiddle."

"My, my," observed Cif, "we *have* managed to keep busy underground, haven't we?"

"You *do* know more about the worser side of human nature than any man I know. Or woman for that matter," Rill chimed in.

The Mouser shrugged apologetically. The comic gesture caused him to really look at himself and his garments for the first time since coming out of the wall.

His reaction caused Cif and Rill to do the same thing.

His gray jerkin, which had been stout, thick cloth when last observed by any of them, had somehow grown fine as gossa-

mer and quite translucent, while his exposed skin looked as if
it had been pumiced.

As if on his journey underground he had endured for hours
a blasting sandstorm, suffering such wear and tear as might
be accounted for by a trip to Quarmall. The *strangeness* of it
all gripped their minds.

At that long moment Fafhrd appeared in the tunnel, followed closely by Fingers and Afreyt, with a wide-eyed Gale
bringing up the rear. He was wearing a winter jacket with
attached hood fallen away behind, revealing his close-shaven
pate.

"I *knew* you had been found," he said excitedly. "I read it
in Skor's face when he returned with Cif's summons. Though
he's fooled the rest, I think. Make no mistake, it was a good
idea to keep it a secret for a bit. There are things to be said
before we face a celebration. It appears that I owe you my
life, old friend—and my child her memory as well. Look
here, you rogue, however did you learn old Quarmal's finger-
snapping dodge?"

"Why, by traveling underground to his buried city, of
course, and spying on him," the Mouser replied airily. "And
studying his maps," he added. "Either I did that in the body
or else my ka did in horn-gate dreams. If his boreworms got
to me, and I believe they did, it argues for the former."

"Oh well," Fafhrd said philosophically, "boreworms don't
kill, only excruciate."

"And then only if you're awake while they're entering
you," Fingers piped up consolingly. "But truly, Uncle Mouser,
I'm grateful to you beyond words for saving my father's life
and me from parricide and madness."

"Tut, tut, child! No need for melodrama. I believe you,"
the Mouser said, "and entreat your pardon for my earlier
doubts. You are the daughter of your mother Friska, truly,
who resisted all my efforts to seduce her, which were neither
few nor unskillful, to my recollection."

"I believe you," Fingers assured him. "As she's oft told
me, your seduction attempts were responsible for her friend
(and your lover, Uncle Mouser) Ivivis quitting the escape
party at Tovilyis and persuading my mother to quit with her
and have me there."

"I truly planned to get gold and return to Tovilyis and rejoin her," Fafhrd apologized. "But something always intervened, generally the absence of gold."

"Friska never blamed you," Fingers assured him. "She always came to your defense when Aunt Ivivis made you the target of one of her tirades. Aunty would say, 'He should have stayed with you and let the little jackanapes go on alone,' and Mother would answer, 'That would have been too much to hope for. Remember, they're lifelong comrades.' "

"Friska was always most forgiving," Fafhrd averred. "Just as Fingers is to you, Mouser," he added, shaking his middle digit under the Gray One's nose. "Do you realize that that terrible treble fingersnap that saved my life almost slew Fingers at the same time? Stretching her senseless and unconscious across the bench where we'd sat watching you emerge from earth like a pale vengeful mole—I was knocked out myself as well, stretched out across my daughter on the bench. As Afreyt here can attest, who was a full quarter hour eliciting from either of us the least sign of life."

"That's most true, masters," the tall blonde averred, her violet eyes flashing. "I breathed for Fafhrd fully that long before his wits returned. Meanwhile Gale, who'd awakened and come downstairs fortuitously, performed a like service for Fingers."

"Yes, I did that," the child confirmed, "and when you came to, you beast, you bit my nose, like an ungrateful and confused kitten."

"You should have spanked me," the girl from Ilthmar told her piously.

"I'll remember that at the first opportunity," Gale threatened darkly.

"For that matter, I lost consciousness myself completely at the climax," the Mouser asserted, getting back into the game. "So much depended on getting those fingersnaps of old Quarmal just right, each one a little louder than the last. It literally took everything out of me, so that my task accomplished, I sank back into the earth like a dying ghost, to be transported here by whatever potent agency has guided my long journey, and await dear Cif's revivifying kiss."

And he slowly shook his head from side to side, raising his

brows and parting his hands a little in a gesture of uncomprehending wonder.

Relaxing then a little from this posture (one got the impression everyone in the tunnel let out a small sigh), he turned with a sweet and gracious smile to Fafhrd and inquired, "But now tell me, old friend, how came you to be parted from your hair? And so very thoroughly, judging from the portions of you I'm able to see. In my underground travels I've lost some skin (and body hair presumably) from friction with sand, gravel, clay, and rock. My garments certainly have suffered a diminishment, as is plain to see. But you, my friend, have not that excuse."

"Let me answer that," Afreyt demanded with such resolution that no one, even Fafhrd, seemed inclined to contest her claim. She took a deep breath and addressed, chiefly to the Gray Mouser (though all heard, for she spoke very clearly) the following remarkable extended statement.

"Dear Captain Mouser, when you first slipped down into the earth early upon the night of Satyrs full and the second of the coming of the cold, it was Captain Fafhrd who set us digging after you here on Goddess Hill. Not all of us agreed with his idea, but when the digging turned up evidence of your passage (your hood, your dagger Cat's Claw, et cetera) we were logically compelled to change our minds. The work begun then has now culminated in the rescue of Captain Mouser by the ladies Cif and Rill after today's miraculous survival underground. All honor to Captain Fafhrd for laying the foundations of this wonderful achievement!"

Gale started to applaud, but none of the others took it up, and when Fingers shook her head at the other girls, she broke off.

Afreyt resumed her extended statement, ignoring the interruption.

"It was at this point, I think, that it began to become apparent, dimly at first, that a supernatural power, or powers, were taking a hand in the developing events.

"In the matter of Captain Mouser, it was the dowsing for him by the Lady Cif and his lieutenant Pshawri which seemed to indicate the Mouser was moving underground at unlikely speeds over incredible distances far beyond the limits of these diggings, even extending out under the Outer Sea.

"Besides that, there's an altogether amazing action that occurred this morning in the cellar of the Lady Cif's house and which Fingers and I both witnessed: the Mouser's saving of Fafhrd from a horrid outlandish death spell by employment of information he could hardly have obtained anywhere in Nehwon nearer than buried Quarmall." And she gazed fiercely, almost accusingly, at the Mouser.

Gale parted her hands to start another round of applause, but then made a face at Fingers and forebore.

The Mouser endured the steely stare a moment more, then said apologetically, "I'm sorry, Lady Afreyt. I can't fully satisfy your curiosity as to how far I went or all I did below ground. Mostly I recall sucking pebbles to quench my thirst and breathing most shallowly to make best use of the air I scavenged (often having to make do with mephitic gases), and meditating on my sins and those of others (very interesting, some of those). Otherwise I seem to have slept a lot (doubtless a good thing since it reduced my consumption of air) and dreamed some remarkable dreams. So please, Lady Afreyt, continue with your fascinating hypothetical reconstruction of what's happened to us the last two mysterious days—always remembering to end with an explanation of how Fafhrd came to lose his hair. Which was, I believe, the question you set out to answer in the first place."

"That's true," she said. "Well, Captain Mouser, just as a supernatural element entered your movements underground, enabling you to move to far places at fantastic speeds and causing you considerable wear and tear—" She eyed his translucent jerkin. "—a like element began to influence Fafhrd, though functioning in the opposite direction, not below ground, but above.

"Late on the night of Satyrs full he got drunk and set out for Salthaven next morning under the influence. For this part of the story we have the evidence of the children Gale and Fingers, who followed him. They saw him set to swimming through the fog and then mount up into the sky in widening spirals.

"Somewhere aloft above Salthaven he disrobed (to lighten

ship, he tells me) and dropped his boots, belt, pouch, bracelet, and other gear, which fell on roofs and treetops, whence they were brought to me yesterday, forming a set of objects not unlike the items Captain Mouser left behind him as he traveled through the earth.

"For the rest of my narrative I must depend chiefly on the testimony of its principal actor, given to me earlier today after he recovered from Captain Mouser's spell-breaking.

"To summarize, a short time after lightening ship, Captain Fafhrd was picked up by a cloud-pinnace captained by Queen Frix of Arilia, his one-time paramour, and crewed by a company of her notorious ladies. Being still somewhat under the influence, he was easily enticed into an orgy, during the course of which he was completely shaven, upon the pretext of increasing his pleasure."

"Half the civilized races of Nehwon believe that firmly and act accordingly," Fingers commented. "They regard all hair as a disfigurement, eyelashes being the one exception."

"Don't come the old hooker on me! Or presume to instruct us in the sexual fashions of so-called civilized races, you cabingirl princess!" Afreyt told her tartly, violet eyes flashing. "So far I've been inclined to forgive you all the evil you've innocently been mixed up with, but it wouldn't take much to make me change my mind and give you that shrewd spanking you have been asking for!"

The girl drooped her eyes, gave her lips a reproving tap with her fingertips, covered her mouth with a palm and dropped a submissive curtsey. Gale poked her surreptitiously a little above the hips, where the side is soft.

"But is this true, old friend?" the Mouser asked Fafhrd concernedly. "Pardon me, Lady Afreyt, but I'm somewhat shocked."

"I am content with Afreyt's statement of my case," Fafhrd said stolidly, "and grateful to her for saving me embarrassment."

"Well, then," the Mouser said, "since we're talking so freely, resolve us: does shaving augment carnal delight? In your case, at any rate?"

"That's not a suitable question for public discussion," Fafhrd responded somewhat primly. "Ask me in private and I may give you an answer."

Afreyt looked at the Mouser sweetly and gave a little nod before continuing her statement.

"At some point during the night's licentious doings aboard the aerial whorehouse of Queen Frix, Fafhrd succumbed, but whether from an excess of carnal delight, or of brandy and poppy and other narcotic drugs that may have been administered to him, we have no way of knowing.

"Just before dawn the abominable cloud-pinnace landed on Rime Isle on the headland between Salthaven and the Maelstrom and Fafhrd was given a mock funeral which was secretly observed by his long-lost daughter Fingers."

The girl, her eyes still downcast, nodded twice, rapidly.

"With derisive ceremony and soft music," Afreyt went on, "Fafhrd was laid to rest—abandoned—on a bed of new-sprung mushrooms wet with dew, naked in the dawn's chill save for some ribbons the color of the underclothes of Frix's whores tied in unsightly mockery around his limp member, his flaccid Wand of Eros."

"Lovers' Mementos," Fingers explained, "a custom observed in—" she began, then broke off. "Oh pardon me, Lady Afreyt, I didn't mean to speak, I got carried away. . . ."

"I am glad to hear you say so," that one observed neutrally. "*When* the sinister funmakers had departed, Fingers' first action was to enrobe her father decently, then guide him still in a stupor to Cif's abode and make her hypnotically-enforced attempt upon his life, which was providentially foiled by Captain Mouser's most timely emergence, as I'm sure you've all heard by now."

"Yes indeed, we've had quite enough of that," the Gray One said modestly. Then, bowing low, "Thank you, Lady Afreyt, for answering my questions as fully as was possible for you, I'm sure." Then turning to Fafhrd, "And now, old friend, could you not be induced to add a few words of your own, sort of wrap the whole matter up, as it were?"

Setting his hands on his hips, Fafhrd replied, "Listen, little man, we've had enough of this nonsense. I recall something you said last winter at the dinner we had for you at the Sea Wrack to celebrate your successful trading voyage to No-Ombrulsk. Cif was teasing you about your erotic involvement

(bondage and discipline, et cetera) with the Simorgyan sea
demoness Ississi, who almost scuppered you and *Seahawk*.

"You replied to her teasing—manfully, it seemed to me
(you blushed)—that you had attempted something somewhat
beyond your powers.

"Well, so had I, I confess most emphatically, in this
business of Frix and her ladies! I met total defeat in a war of
pleasure! So let's have no more of it! For today, at least! I'm
sorry, Afreyt, but that had to be said."

"I think so too," she told him. "Let's all cool down."

"Before some fresh surprises refire our interest," Rill put
in, who was standing close behind the Mouser in the somewhat crowded section of tunnel.

Her words were prophetic, for just then Pshawri, coming
from the shaft, edged his way into the press. He was still
stripped for running, wearing only loincloth, belt, and pouch,
carrying over one arm a robe he'd been handed above but not
yet donned. When he saw the Mouser, the young lieutenant's
weary face lit up wonderfully, but it was Cif to whom he first
spoke.

"Lady," he said, bowing, "at midnight, following your
instructions, I threw into Darkfire's lava pool the talismanic
Whirlpool Queller I'd won from the Maelstrom and with
which we'd dowsed for Captain Mouser. There was an eruption from which I barely escaped, racing the ensuing weather
change south and losing badly. When I crossed the headland I
noted Maelstrom had calmed once more."

"That's wondrous news, brave lieutenant," Cif replied in a
ringing voice. Then turning to the Mouser, who was frowning, she dipped rapidly into her pouch. "Before you say
anything, Captain, here's something you should read."

The Mouser spread the worn violet-inked sheet, but had not
got very far before he motioned Fafhrd to come view Freg's
letter with him. So they read it side by side and line by line.

When they got to the bit about the Mouser's tricksiness,
Fafhrd muttered, "I always suspected you got at her, you
dog," and he replied, "Cheer up, at least she recognizes your
moral superiority."

"Is that my uncouthness or my love?" the big man grumbled.

And when they got to the "triads of moles," Rill, who'd

been sneaking glances, could not resist touching with three fingers the three shoulder moles that showed clearly by leviathan light through the worn-to-gossamer fabric of the Mouser's jerkin. When he glared at her, she laughed and said, "Look at mates to these on Pshawri's side. We're packed too close here to hide anything."

Afreyt lifted the robe from Pshawri's arm and held it for him, saying, "You have my thanks too, Lieutenant." He thanked her back and let her help him don it.

The reading done, the Mouser gazed quizzically at Pshawri a long moment.

"Still want to work for me, son, now I'm your father? I suppose I could pay you off in some way, if that's your choice."

"Most certainly, sire," the young man responded. The Mouser spread his arms and they embraced, quite formally to start with.

"Come," said Cif, moving past them, "it's time we told the others the good news."

They followed her, the Mouser admiring her dragon's breath system of ventilation and going on to praise the bucket lift in the shaft.

Halfway along this route, at the floor of the shaft, Mikkidu appeared, bearing one of the Mouser's gray house robes. The Mouser donned it and thanked him, then stepped in the bucket and was drawn up.

Fafhrd emerged from the tunnel followed by Afreyt and the rest. He drew his hood over his shaven pate, then mounted the shaft swiftly by the ladder of pegs.

As the Mouser swung off at the top, his loosely assembled men gave a cheer. Fafhrd's joined in, redoubling their shouts as their captain came into view and stood beside the Mouser. As the cheering ebbed, they were able to exchange a few words in private as the late summer midday sun shone down from low in the south.

MOUSER (indicating the shallow mound of dug earth near where they stood): Mikkidu tells me there's talk of renaming Goddess Hill (formerly Gallows Hill), Mount Mouser.

FAFHRD (a shade resentfully): That's losing no time.

MOUSER: Should I suggest Mount Faf-Mou?

FAFHRD: Forget it. I must say, you're looking remarkably fit after your incredibly long sojourn buried.

MOUSER: I don't feel that way. I died down there so many times, I doubt I'll ever trust life again.

FAFHRD: For every time you died, you were reborn. Contrariwise, I think you have become Death's dearest friend.

MOUSER: That's a most dubious distinction. I'm tired of killing.

FAFHRD: Agreed. Fingers is a joy. She came along barely in time to rescue me from boredom.

MOUSER: I'm doubly fortunate—to have been able to instruct my son before I knew he was one.

FAFHRD: I think we can expect more of these strays.

MOUSER: Perish the thought!

29

That day the chief topic of gossip in Godsland was the mysterious vanishment of the troublesome stranger divinity Loki. One of the few deities to know the true explanation was the spider-god Mog.

On a whim Death had sought Mog out to inform him of the continued survival of his chief worshipper, the Gray Mouser, who'd been under Loki's curse, and to boast a bit of the trickery by which he'd managed this, for even Death is vain.

"Actually," Death confided, "the one to consign Loki firmly to the lava lake was none other than the Gray Mouser's son, who promises also to become a very useful character to me."

"I've good news too of my man Fafhrd, my lapsed Lankhmar acolyte," limp-wristed Issek, who'd been listening along with Kos, Fafhrd's barbarian father-god, interrupted impudently. "He's had himself shaved entire—in my honor, I presume, as once befell him in Lankhmar."

"Faugh on such effeminate practices," Kos pronounced.

"Wherever has Death got to?" Issek asked, looking about.

Mog answered, pointing, "I fancy he caught sign of his sister Pain approaching and slipped back to the Shadowland. He's much ashamed of the way she parades about naked, preening herself upon her conquests and inflictions."

And this may very well have been the case, for Death is never cruel or uncouth.

30

A fortnight later Captain Mouser's and Fafhrd's officers threw them a barracks party, without asking permission, on the strength of one of them now being a blood relative and close member of the inner family.

Haste was needful because next morning Sergeant Skullick was sailing on a fast Sarheemar smuggler bound for Ilthmar, on a mission for Fafhrd to Fingers' mother Friska after first determining if she were still a free agent and not a brain-washed tool of old Quarmal once more.

"Fingers' memories have grown uncertain again," the Captain informed his humorous sergeant. "Besides, from now on we must keep a watchful eye on that cunningest wizard. He's sure to be seeking revenge, ever since Captain Mouser so cleverly foiled his try on my own life."

Also aboard the early-sailing smuggler *Ghost* would be Snee, the most knowledgeable of the Mouser's thieves turned sailor, to bear a message from Pshawri to his mother Freg in Lankhmar and gather information of interest on the Thieves Guild, the Overlord's court, and the Grain Merchant's Cartel, which meant chiefly Hisvin and his daughter Hisvet.

A third passenger aboard *Ghost* would be Rill, dispatched by Cif and Afreyt to contact witch covens in Ilthmar, Lankhmar, and (if possible) Tovilyis to get news of Friska and Freg.

"It behooves us," Cif told her friend, "to keep our own tabs on our husbands' previous bedmates."

Afreyt emphatically agreed.

Fafhrd commented, "I confess I find it strange and somewhat distasteful to be forever sending other men on adventures, rather than setting forth on them myself." He looked quite youthful in his cap of pale red hair and with pinkish down covering his arms.

"I think my journeying tired me more than yours did you," the Mouser replied. "Moreover, I look forward to the days, which surely must come, when Arilia falls on hard times and is forced to hire out its airships with their efficient female crews. Their greater speed should make it possible to run things from a home base while still managing an interesting field assignment from time to time."

"You see how their minds work?" Afreyt commented to Cif sotto voce.

THE END

CLASSIC SCIENCE FICTION AND FANTASY

__DUNE Frank Herbert 0-441-17266-0/$4.95
The bestselling novel of an awesome world where gods and adventurers clash, mile-long sandworms rule the desert, and the ancient dream of immortality comes true.

__STRANGER IN A STRANGE LAND Robert A. Heinlein
0-441-79034-8/$4.95
From the *New York Times* bestselling author—the science fiction masterpiece of a man from Mars who teaches humankind the art of grokking, watersharing and love.

__THE ONCE AND FUTURE KING T.H. White
0-441-62740-4/$5.50
The world's greatest fantasy classic! A magical epic of King Arthur in Camelot, romance, wizardry and war. By the author of *The Book of Merlyn*.

__THE LEFT HAND OF DARKNESS Ursula K. LeGuin
0-441-47812-3/$3.95
Winner of the Hugo and Nebula awards for best science fiction novel of the year. "SF masterpiece!"—*Newsweek* "A Jewel of a story."—Frank Herbert

__MAN IN A HIGH CASTLE Philip K. Dick 0-441-51809-5/$3.95
"Philip K. Dick's best novel, a masterfully detailed alternate world peopled by superbly realized characters."
—Harry Harrison

For Visa and MasterCard orders call: 1-800-631-8571

FOR MAIL ORDERS: CHECK BOOK(S). FILL OUT COUPON. SEND TO:

BERKLEY PUBLISHING GROUP
390 Murray Hill Pkwy., Dept. B
East Rutherford, NJ 07073

NAME_____

ADDRESS_____

CITY_____

STATE_____ ZIP_____

PLEASE ALLOW 6 WEEKS FOR DELIVERY.
PRICES ARE SUBJECT TO CHANGE WITHOUT NOTICE.

POSTAGE AND HANDLING:
$1.00 for one book, 25¢ for each additional. Do not exceed $3.50.

BOOK TOTAL $ ____

POSTAGE & HANDLING $ ____

APPLICABLE SALES TAX $ ____
(CA, NJ, NY, PA)

TOTAL AMOUNT DUE $ ____

PAYABLE IN US FUNDS.
(No cash orders accepted.)

279